Clouds, Birds, Frogs and Me

**VANGUARD PAPERBACK**

© Copyright 2025
**Aristophanes, Son of Philip**

The right of Aristophanes, Son of Philip to be identified as author of
this work has been asserted by him in accordance with the
Copyright, Designs and Patents Act 1988.

A CIP catalogue record for this title is
available from the British Library.

ISBN 978 1 83794 211 4

*Vanguard Press is an imprint of*
*Pegasus Elliot Mackenzie Publishers Ltd.*
www.pegasuspublishers.com

First Published in 2025

**Vanguard Press**
**Sheraton House  Castle Park**
**Cambridge  England**

Printed & Bound in Great Britain

Aristophanes, Son of Philip

---

Clouds, Birds, Frogs and Me

Vanguard Press

# Table of Contents

# MAPS

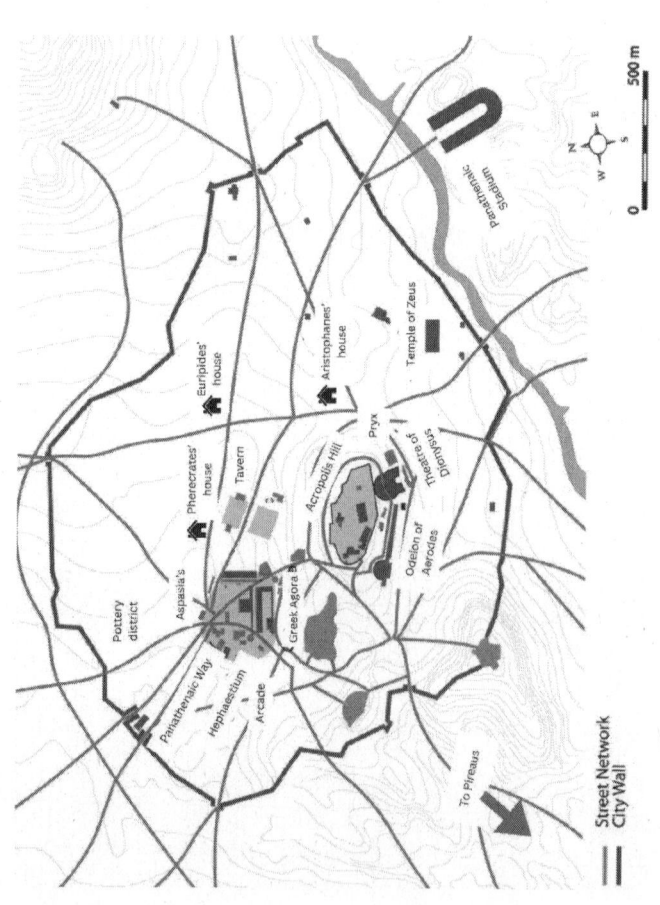

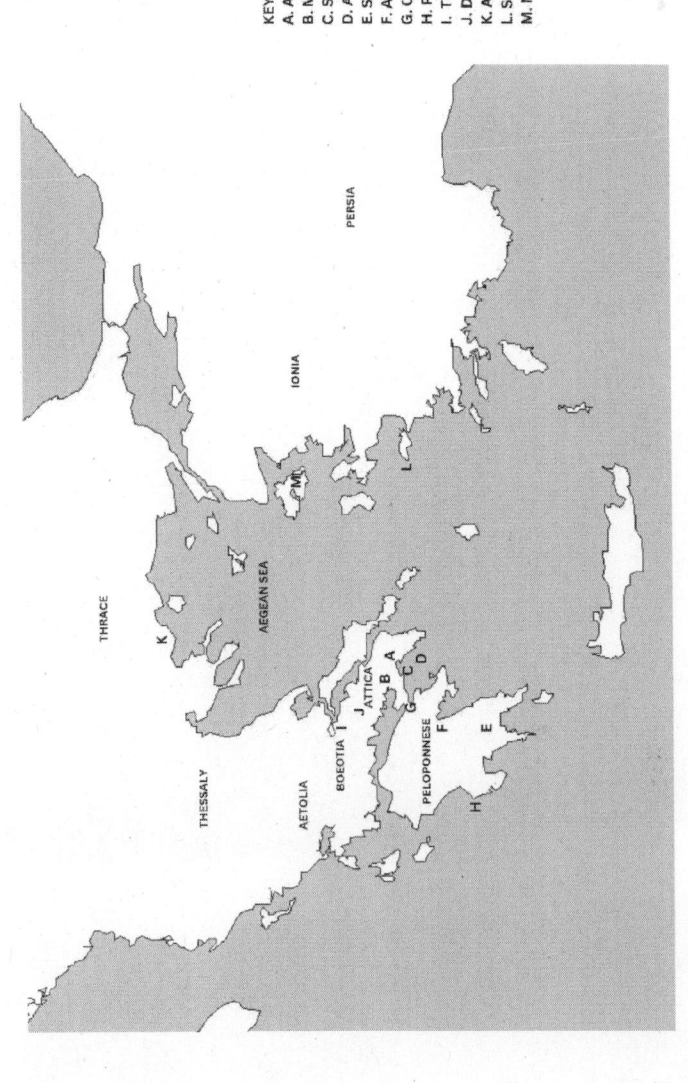

KEY
A. Athens
B. Megara
C. Salamis
D. Aegina
E. Sparta
F. Argos
G. Corinth
H. Pylos
I. Thebes
J. Delium
K. Amphipolis
L. Samos
M. Mytilene

# GETTING THERE

# 1

I can't remember if it was before or after he buggered me that Sophocles told me I'd never make a real playwright. I wasn't too keen on the encounter because Pherecrates had promised he'd take me to Aspasia's after the prize-giving, but you don't often get the personal attention of a brilliant tragedian like Sophocles, so I went along with it. After all, he had just won the tragedy competition with his *Electra*. "You are too superficial", he said, as he pulled his tunic up (or possibly down, I can't remember). "Life isn't really that funny and not everyone deserves to be laughed at. I hope you grow up to learn the dramatic value of grief and sympathy, and the poetic values of metre and cadence, but I don't expect you will." We were celebrating my first play as well as his victory. Amazingly, I had got the famous Callistratus to produce it at the Lenaea festival, and even more amazingly for a nineteen-year-old, I won the second prize for comedy. Better still, I beat Bloody Eupolis.

What was it someone said at the baths the other night? "The unexamined life is not worth living." I think he's wrong, mind – I've had a great life without examining anything very much, my own life or others, but it might be interesting to see what this examining does for you. In this my story I will try to explore the things that drove me to do the things I did. Sophocles' cutting remark led to the achievement that gave me the most satisfaction in my whole life, even though I had to keep it so secret that no one would have believed me when I could finally tell them. I will also try to make sense of what other people were up to. I never thought about that much before. If you show someone being an idiot, it's comedy. If you try to explain why they are being an idiot, it's tragedy.

And of course, my story bumps into lots of other peoples' stories too. Most of my life was lived during the war against Sparta. That was all pretty miserable – and then we lost! We had some great leaders like Pericles and Nicias and Demosthenes, and some awful ones like Cleon and Hyperbolus and Cleisthenes. There were weirdos like Socrates and Alcibiades. Wonderful women like Aspasia and Cunna and, of course, Praxagora. Talented writers like Sophocles, Euripides and, some say, Thucydides. With just twenty-five thousand or so citizens and things like festivals, military service, the Assembly and jury duty, you get to know a lot of them somehow. I am sure young Plato will go far. That's why I've trusted him with this book and hope he doesn't do something silly like object to the bit about Socrates at the famous symposium and destroy it. I don't think he will. A lot of people say Plato's a prude, but I know better.

Some people complain that I made fun of dead people. I don't see the problem. We remember great men after they have died. Why should fools and crooks have the privilege of being forgotten? Many of them will come back to be made fun of again in these pages. And I expect I'll be made fun of in my turn.

People have always asked me my political views. Perhaps the fact that they have to shows that I don't really have any. Of course I always did my homework and attended debates and trials. I tried to be even-handed and make fun of people of all classes and persuasions and only attacked someone seriously if there was an angle the audience was likely to find comical. Cleon had to threaten to sue me before I really chopped him up – and the judges loved it. In general I preferred the more dignified politicians from the old families to the new demagogues, but I was always happy to ridicule both. But I suppose there are some things I believe in: I love Athens, I prefer peace to war, I don't like politicians lying and I only like practical jokes when they are funny. Alcibiades' never were.

To be a comic poet you have to be everyone, and that's who I am. Aristophanes.

# 2

Aspasia's house was the longest in the street, about one hundred paces across the front. Little windows high on the walls provided ventilation with complete privacy. They were dark except for an occasional flicker of lamplight. The only door was on the left. Entering through a thick curtain, Pherecrates and I found ourselves in a large open space. To our right, all was dark. In front of us, lamps revealed half-a-dozen large couches, richly upholstered in deep purple, three of which were occupied by men and one by a woman. Two of the men were leaning forward in animated conversation, while the other appeared half asleep.

Everyone knew of Aspasia. She came from the other side of the Aegean and had been the great Pericles' partner for years. When Pericles died, she moved in with his old friend Lysicles, confirming a rumour that had been around for a long time, but he died too, just a few weeks later. She was renowned for her intelligence as well as her beauty and her establishment was as famous for the conversations she hosted as for the escorts it housed. People say she could influence Socrates and helped Pericles write the public funeral oration that restored our spirits in the early days of the war. She was still amazingly beautiful in her long blue and saffron robe and heavy gold jewellery and looked far too young to have had the career she had.

Of the men, I recognised the sophist Cratylus from his deformed left arm, and the old man who was lying back on his couch looked familiar, though I couldn't place him. The third was a stranger, and a large one, wearing gaudy Persian slippers and a golden band on his head whose lustre was rather outshone by the grease in his straggly locks. Wherever he was from, he had obviously come through Asia. Aspasia smiled at Pherecrates and gave him a little wave, indicating we should sit and join the group. I have to say it was the weirdest conversation I had witnessed up to then.

Cratylus was speaking to the stranger: "But, Gorgias, if this Democritus fellow thinks everything is composed of tiny identical particles, how does he explain that some things are wet, some are dry, some are ethereal and so on?"

"I asked him that, but I couldn't quite understand his answer."

"Did you ask if these identical particles took different forms according to their relation to the four elements of earth, air, fire and water?"

"Yes."

"And if he thought there might only be two elements instead of four, with the whole earth kept in place by the sky like a baking lid?" Yes, I'm sure he said baking lid.

"Yes."

"I suppose his theory is compatible with Anaximenes' idea that everything is formed from condensation of gas." Aspasia had joined in, tossing her long dark hair like a little girl, but speaking like a serious scientist. "Or even with Diogenes' view that thought is air and moisture impedes it."

"He didn't mention either of them."

"I expect he quoted Anaxagoras then: 'Each one is most manifestly those things of which there are the most in it.'" Hard to argue with that really, I thought. I looked at Pherecrates to see what he was making of it all, but his face gave nothing away.

"No, he didn't mention him either."

"What did he say, then?"

Gorgias shifted his considerable weight awkwardly. "He laughed at me and said I'd missed the point."

"Well, you had of course." The man I thought I recognised had finally spoken. He was much older than the others and even more serious looking. "How can you try to understand the physical world without relating it to man, the measure of all things?"

"But what is man himself made of? Surely that is what we're trying to get at."

"That is a meaningless question."

I wondered who this old guy was, speaking so confidently on a subject he probably knew as little about as I did. I soon found out.

Gorgias had obviously been expecting a bit of support from the group and was offended by the putdown. "You're the one who's missing the point, Protagoras. You should stick to your rhetoric teaching and not try to understand the world. Reality isn't very relevant to your work. In fact, you seem to find it an obstacle." Of course. This was the famous sophist Protagoras all the rich families were sending their sons to so they could learn to become persuasive speakers, no matter how weak the argument they had to make. He must have been doing a good job because people were already starting to complain about the Assembly being misled by this new generation of Protagoras-trained orators.

He now bared his perfect set of teeth, which remained largely clenched as he said, "I don't know what they told you in Sicily or Asia, Gorgias, but if you'd been in Athens more than a few days, you'd know that I don't just teach rhetoric but logic too and, whichever side of the argument you choose to take, you can't make a speech logical without understanding the reality – the physical reality and the human one, the profane and the divine, the sun and the moon, the oceans and the mountains, the animal and the mineral, the birds and the fishes…"

He would have gone on thinking up vaguely compatible or contrasting pairs, but Cratylus was feeling left out of things and decided to go on the attack himself. "You're both missing the point. Does universal instability mean nothing to you? Flux, flux, flux." I'm pretty sure he said 'flux.'

Aspasia didn't like the turn this was taking. She stood up, robe swirling round her ankles and jewellery clanking on her neck and arms. The gold and gems caught the lamplight and proved rather more illuminating than the conversation so far. "Now, boys." (*Boys*!). "Let's show each other a little more respect, shall we?" She sounded just like I expect my mother must have sounded. "We're all smart and our differences of opinion should be a cause for celebration. Imagine how boring these conversations would be if we all thought the same. Cratylus, I never tire of hearing you explain how static science can't deal with the unstable state of the world, so we'll talk about that later. Meanwhile let's hear our honoured visitor Gorgias' own opinions and stop worrying about atomism until we find someone who can explain it all to us." She signalled to a slave who had been tending one of the lamps to bring wine for Pherecrates and me and to fill up the others' cups. A shocked female cry came from the darkness at the other end of the hall. It sounded like "Never."

I had been completely lost by the previous conversation, but Gorgias' next sally was simpler to follow – and rather memorable. He patted his headband as if for reassurance, crossed his legs the better to display one of his slippers, and in a voice as reasonable as the words were daft, announced: "Well, of course, nothing exists."

There was a guffaw from Protagoras.

"If it did, we couldn't know about it," continued Gorgias, evidently feeling he was starting to make an impression. He was met by another guffaw.

"If we knew about it, we couldn't describe it." A weaker guffaw this time.

"If we did describe it, we wouldn't be understood." Protagoras had given up and was supine again.

Just then, as if to prove to us all that some things did actually exist and could be known and described, we heard a scream from the darkness, followed by running footsteps. A red-faced Ariphrades was making for the door as fast as he could, pursued by a furious woman and a hail of crockery and small coins she was throwing at him. I was surprised to see Ariphrades there anyway. His brother the musician was rumoured to be a virgin at nineteen!

"Excuse me a moment," murmured Aspasia. "Pherecrates, I think it's time you took Aristophanes in. He looks tired already. Cunna and Salabaccho are in tonight and not busy, so you can take your pick." She winked at Pherecrates and then raised her voice, "Now Pellene, come here." Calm but firm, just like my mother would have been.

She led the furious woman to another part of the house. We heard sobbing and then a high-pitched shout, "All right, I'll go somewhere else where that doesn't happen."

Our wines arrived, the best stuff just in from Chios of course, and we took the cups with us as Pherecrates led me through the darkness to a semi-lit waiting room where Cunna and Salabaccho were to come and introduce themselves. I assumed we'd take one each, and, as the person who was introducing me, he'd get first pick, so I was surprised when, after both girls had given us a polite hello and a provocative smile, he asked me which I'd prefer. I don't know if this happens to all young men on their first time in a place like that, but I felt so awkward and self-conscious I couldn't have made a rational choice between a lump of gold and a donkey turd, so I just pointed to the one nearest me, who turned out to be Cunna. I looked to see

Pherecrates going off with Salabaccho, but he wasn't. She shrugged and left the room and he told me, "I'll wait for you here."

# 3

Pherecrates was a strange fellow, but also one of the kindest I have ever known. I think I owe him and Euripides everything. He was unusual looking for a local, with fair hair like Menelaus and Achilles, which always goes down well with the ladies, though it didn't stop Menelaus' wife running away with the dark-haired Paris and starting a bloody war. Actually I don't think the Trojan War was nearly as bloody as the ones we have nowadays. Homer probably exaggerated the numbers. The main difference is that they had heroes and we don't any longer. And they were closer to the gods. We seem to be thrashing around between our traditional gods, new ones from Asia and natural phenomena, which those philosophers seem to think explain everything. I know for a fact they don't.

Excuse me. I still worry about where the city is heading sometimes. Back to Pherecrates. Despite his fair hair, his regulation good looks were offset somewhat by a lazy eye and the reluctance of his facial muscles to participate in whatever excitement he might be feeling. You could only tell he was moved when his right eyebrow twitched, and that didn't happen often. He never said very much unless he knew you well and it was hard to tell what he was thinking. He suffered from regular bouts of a mysterious sickness he refused to discuss.

Our relationship was a strange one too. It's customary for young men to have older men as lovers and mentors, but being short, skinny and prematurely bald I'd only had a few very unattractive propositions from smelly, incontinent veterans. I met Pherecrates when he came to talk about drama to our class at school, which he'd been a member of himself ten years earlier. Two of us were so interested in what he told us about the challenges of writing plays, using his latest comedy as an example, that we kept him talking for ages after the rest of the boys went home and he invited us to come to a day at the next Dionysia with him. We'd met a few times since then and talked about the plays he was working on, but he never seemed to want to touch me.

Agathon and I met him outside the entrance and he took us into the area reserved for playwrights and their friends. His own play *The Good Guys* had been shown the previous evening and his seat allocation for it had been taken by people who had helped with the production, so we were sorry to miss that but excited to see anything. We were lucky. The tragic trilogy that day was by Sophocles and the comedy by the great Magnes, the last one he ever wrote.

Agathon and I were wrestling partners at school, so we'd shared a few orgasms, but we weren't really friends. In fact, I don't think he actually had any friends, though we did have a common enemy in Bloody Eupolis. Agathon lived in a world of his own imagination, which seemed vivid enough as he was always banging on about nymphs and satyrs and demigoddesses running around in woods or bathing in streams. His delicate female features were invariably complemented by new pieces of expensive jewellery from his most recent lover. He was known to be not very discriminating, as long as the men were rich.

We were early so we had time to absorb the feel of the place. The theatre was full, as it always was since Pericles had arranged a payment to allow everyone to attend; two obols a day wasn't really enough to live off, but just enough to encourage people to go and hope to make up the shortfall another day. Even though it was under repair in parts and was to continue so for most of the war, the theatre still held seventeen thousand spectators, almost three times as many as the Assembly. Wooden benches filled the hundred-metre space between the stone wall that rounded it on three sides and the circular area in front of the stage where the chorus performed around a low altar. Behind that dance floor, the stage was slightly raised, about four metres deep and stretching about sixteen metres in each direction. At the back a painted screen ran the length of the stage and ramps on each side led down to the dance floor. In the centre stood a canvas-fronted building with doors on the ground level and windows on the one above. More windows and booths were cut in the screen cloth. Over the roof of the building, where gods usually appear, there loomed a large wooden beam.

I had started dreaming of how I would make this amazing place my life when the eponymous archon who was in charge of the festival stepped forward from his seat in the centre of the front row and, moving to the little altar in the centre of the dance floor, prayed loudly to Dionysus, god of the festival, and sacrificed a lamb. The meat, together with some more that had just been killed, was distributed to the poorer citizens who identified themselves by choosing to sit at the back. For many of them, these lambs or the bull that was sacrificed on the first day of the festival was the only meat they'd get all year. Once the ceremony was over, the meat distributed and the dance floor mopped, we were underway.

Sophocles' trilogy was wonderful. Of course, we'd read and enacted *Ajax* and *Antigone* at school, but that was nothing like being in an audience of seventeen thousand, all shaken to the core as the actors boomed out Sophocles' magic words. I can't remember much about the first play, but the second was *Oedipus the King*, probably his best ever. When the king pulled his eyes out, thirty-four thousand other eyes dissolved too. The satyr play that followed the tragedies was as irrelevant and predictable as they always are, but it fulfilled its purpose of breaking the spell of the tragedies before the comedy came on. A lot of people seemed happy to miss it altogether and went to get refreshments from the vendors outside. I watched them for a while and when I turned back, I noticed Agathon was crying. Crying at a satyr play! It might not have been particularly funny, but it certainly wasn't sad. Pherecrates asked him what the matter was, but he wouldn't answer. I whispered to Pherecrates that it was probably because he felt his woodland fantasy beings were misrepresented. I think Agathon heard me, because he cried a bit louder.

Magnes' comedy was *The Lute*. I loved the way it unfolded – the clever scene-setting, the dramatic entry of the chorus, the address to the audience and so on. Looking back, it wasn't all that funny either – just escapist rubbish about musical instruments going on strike – but the poetry was strikingly elegant and the dances original. Afterwards, when Pherecrates asked us what we thought we'd like to be, we both said tragic poets.

He turned to Agathon. "Good choice," he said. "You have a sensitive nature, you're easily moved, you love myths and you choose your words well. The competition is tough though; Sophocles dominates and dozens are trying to match him. Euripides is running him close at the moment and we haven't seen the best of him yet. If you are going to succeed, you'll have to develop your own distinctive style – grandeur like Aeschylus, pathos like Sophocles or female psychology like Euripides. What do you think yours will be?"

"I'm not sure. Perhaps something around writing especially lovely verse that will bring out the tragedy and elevate the tone. I thought Sophocles missed a chance there. You'd think someone who has just poked his eyes out would have a bit more to say about all the beautiful things he won't be seeing – the birds, the butterflies, the mountain streams, the forest glades and the soft clouds in a deep blue sky." How Agathon reconciled these ethereal visions with the vigorous reality of man-on-man action I'll never know.

Pherecrates' right eyebrow twitched at the precocious criticism, but he remained calm and encouraging and kept a straight face. "Not a bad aim. If you work at it and cultivate your natural talents, there's no reason you shouldn't succeed with a novel style of verse." Agathon gave a little simpering giggle and made to kiss Pherecrates goodbye; he avoided it tactfully and sent Agathon on his way before leading me down to the chorus' dancing circle in front of the stage.

A red cloth phallus that had detached itself from a costume lay on one side and a couple of giant cooking pots near it, all that was left of Magnes' play. The stage was empty except for a couple of slaves manoeuvring long tables for the cast's post-performance dinner. The real celebrations would come the next day after the final judging. "I'll show you the backstage area if you like," he offered. Of course I said yes.

We mounted a ramp and made our way through the door in the stage building into a large hall at the back which ran the length of the stage. It was fascinating to see so many tricks of the trade. There were rolling platforms to bring characters on through booths cut in the screen, to convey an interior setting. The beam I had seen from my bench was attached to a massive crane that could pick up characters from the stage or deposit gods there. It looked a bit rickety to me but apparently it was a long time since there'd been a fatal accident. Flimsy outsize musical instruments lay piled in one corner, more props from the comedy. There was a little room at the back for the actors to change in and tents to the sides to accommodate the chorus. At the end of the hall to our right was Dionysus' shrine, from which a man with a huge chest and belly was walking towards us.

"Hello, Pherecrates," he whispered.

"Hello, Bronchus. Great job tonight. This is Aristophanes. He wants to write plays."

"Comedy, I hope. Write one for me!" The great belly shook in silent laughter as he turned away.

"Was that really the great Bronchus?" I asked. "And why was he whispering?"

"All actors have their little foibles. Bronchus' great talent is in projecting his voice so that whatever he says, even the fastest rhythms, can be heard very clearly. He thinks whispering when he's not on stage will keep his voice box safe. Rhombus is a bit similar, but he specialises in tone variation and tends to sing a lot. Archinous is more of a slapstick performer, so he does a lot of strength exercises."

"How do you decide which actor to pick for a particular play?"

"Oh, you don't pick your actors, at least not the two leads. They are allocated by the archon when he selects the plays to be performed. You have to adapt your material to suit the actors you're given."

I could have spent forever poking around, asking questions and imagining myself there as a well-known tragedian, receiving the grateful thanks of the performers for the magnificent lines I had given them, but after a little while Pherecrates turned to me and said, "I hope you didn't mean that."

"You mean about becoming a tragic poet?" I asked.

"What did you think of the comedy?"

"Well, it was very well put together and the dances were wonderful. It wasn't a great plot though, and in the middle when the chorus leader addressed the audience, he didn't seem to have much to say."

"What do you think he should have said?"

"He could have said something about the war or about politicians who are up to no good – at least made some points that might be useful guidance to the city."

"Would you do that?"

"Yes," I said, having no idea of the unpleasantness that would bring down on me over the next few years.

"Then why on earth would you want to be a tragedian? It would be a complete waste. Comedies are much more challenging. In tragedies, you can assume your audience knows the story and you can use high-flown language, which is surprisingly easy to write. In comedies you have to make up your own plot and connect it to an audience that has no idea what's coming. And you have to make them laugh, tell them a few home truths and send them home happy, maybe a little wiser. And the stagecraft requires far more skill. The chorus is twice as big, the dancing is fast and lively, you have characters popping in and out of two or three doors instead of one, any use of stage machinery must be innovative, not just lowering gods at the end of the play, and the actors invariably have to play several different roles. You've got a wicked sense of humour and you've just told me you can do a better job than Magnes. Surely that would appeal to you more than telling yet another version of Heracles' labours or Oedipus' misery?"

That was the longest speech I ever heard from Pherecrates and more than I was really ready to cope with at that time. I hadn't given a lot of thought to how I would earn a living. My father was what they call comfortably-off but there wasn't much left over to support me. We had no craft workshops at home, so I hadn't learned pottery or metalwork or carpentry. But I didn't want to be a part-time craftsman anyway. I wanted to have a positive impact on Athens somehow, which meant a public role. I'd thought about being a politician, but you needed money for that. It was possible to do well as a playwright with your share of prizes and payments from sponsors, but you had to be very talented and lucky. I could see the appeal of comedy. Magnes' play had given me a few ideas now about how a comic poet could do the public some good by inventing plots that had some relevance to their daily concerns and by using the opportunity to address the audience directly to warn them about things that weren't being properly dealt with. I could be the voice of the quiet people, standing up for them against incompetence and corruption among our political leaders. But I still really wanted to write tragedies and see and hear the audience weep at my verse. What power!

"Well?" asked Pherecrates.

"Perhaps I could try writing comedies and when I've got more practice at composition, move across to tragedy. I might even be able to make it more dramatic by using some of the stagecraft from comedy."

"Good luck. No one has made that transition successfully, but maybe you'll be the first." Now there was a challenge, one Sophocles was to throw down again a couple of years later.

We said goodbye, with no kissing attempts on either side. Come to think of it, I'd never seen Pherecrates in physical contact with anyone. I had begun to suspect he was asexual. If so he was definitely living in the wrong city.

# 4

Cunna was wearing a long white robe, a golden necklace in delicate filigree, much lighter and prettier than Aspasia's, and a pair of fashionable hooped silver earrings which reflected a reddish gleam in her dark brown hair. More jewellery was scattered on a table where a small dressing box probably contained more still. Her couch was one of those luxury ones made by the Demosthenes family business, soft, colourful, well-upholstered and wide enough for two people to lie side by side, though that wasn't its principal function. I asked her what all the fuss had been about.

"He likes the taste of piggy," she explained, "but Pellene thinks that's disgusting."

"Piggy?" I asked.

She gave a wry smile at my naiveté and demonstrated her meaning by pulling her robe up a little. "Ah, we're off," I thought. But we weren't.

She wanted to talk. I was surprised as I thought we'd done the talking already with Aspasia and the mad philosophers, but apparently conversation is an important part of an escort's work too. She asks me for my background, obviously not wanting to mess around with riffraff. I tell her I'm a citizen of the tribe Pandionis and my suburb is Cydathene. My father Philip is a landowner on the island of Aegina, living with one of his slave girls. He had moved there after the island had revolted and the so-called Thirty Years' Peace (which actually lasted fourteen years) supposedly gave Aegina independence. My mother died in childbirth with my still born brother, Ararus. I live in the family house in Athens with a slave Ismenias, who suffers from hiccups, and his wife Nerita. My father sends them housekeeping money and me pocket money.

"Do you miss your mum?"

"No, I can't remember her." That was not quite true. A life without a mother is even emptier if you can't remember her looks or sound or smell until something brings it back to you and things often did.

"Who's your favourite goddess?"

"Artemis."

"Why?"

"Well, she's the ultimate paradox: virgin and goddess of childbirth; hunter and protector of wild animals. Whatever you want she can fix it."

"Do you pray to her?"

"Yes, quite a lot."

She said I was the first comic poet she'd had, though Euripides had visited recently and introduced Agathon. The evening hadn't been a success; Euripides seemed to have a problem with the whole business and she thought it had been an experiment to see if either of them enjoyed being with a woman. She had concluded that they didn't.

She had never seen a play – "Festivals are a busy time for us girls" – though she had heard people talking about them, so she had some ideas about drama. I told her how comedy is different from tragedy, and much harder to write, just as Pherecrates had once told me. I explained the six-part structure of a comedy: the 'Set Up', in which the basic fantasy is explained; the 'Entry of the Chorus'; the 'Contest', or debate, between the main characters; the 'Address' in which the chorus leader harangues the audience on the topics of the day, hurls scurrilous criticism at prominent citizens and praises the poet; a series of 'Farcical Scenes'; and a final 'Celebration', invariably in the form of a banquet or a wedding.

She asked me if all comedies were like that and I told her they were, although the Lenaea tonight wasn't quite as prestigious as the Dionysia which would take place in three months' time in the spring. Some of the competitors were novices like me, others people who had failed at the Dionysia. It went for three days, compared with the Dionysia's six and just involved two tragedies and a satyr play by each of two playwrights, followed by five comedies. The Dionysia had fifteen tragedies, five satyr plays and five comedies and there could be over a thousand dancers involved.

I started to describe the different metres required for different parts of the play, but she didn't seem very interested so I explained how comedy allows you to put things on stage you just couldn't get away with normally.

"For instance?"

"Well, because it's a festival, there are no holds barred. The gods are mocked, religious rituals are sent up, politicians are ridiculed, men become women and women men, there are plenty of lavatory jokes and sexual humour, and it generally ends with garlands, wine and dirty dancing."

I was going on to explain how this differed from tragedy, but she said she could guess. So, I told her the real reason I was trying to make a go of comedy before turning my hand to tragedy: to make the audience think about real problems in the city and to make them laugh at their own mistakes. No one expected a comic poet to actually solve the problems or suggest how things might really be fixed. He could come up with some fantastically improbable means of escaping the problems that might have no connection with reality, but the key was to get the audience to recognise that something should be done. You have your average bloke, generally a bit of a rogue, a cheeky chappie with attitude, who is confronted with an intractable problem facing the common people and comes up with an ingenious solution. He towers over life and will do anything to bring it under control and invariably succeeds with some combination of guile, magic and brute force. It is the city's mirror to nature and, unlike many aspects of daily life, it includes the marginalised, like farmers from remote parts of Attica and impoverished old soldiers.

"Stereotypes help." I told her. "You have the sympathetic types – the hero and his supporters, the downtrodden and neglected who really deserve better. And you have unsympathetic representatives of various unattractive behaviours, especially the newfangled ones like sophistry and ostentatious expenditure. Demagogues are a great target; people like to laugh at them, though they still go and accept their advice in the Assembly and in the law courts."

She asked me how one became a comic playwright and I told her it was actually a lot harder than I'd hoped. You had to be lucky; in my case the luck was the friendship of Pherecrates. At his recommendation, I had been taken on at the age of seventeen by a producer called Callistratus, as part of his writing team to support the comic poet Cratinus. As you only had a few months' notice between seeing if your idea for a play was selected for production and actually having to produce it, there was an awful lot to do to get all the words, music and action sorted out as well as rehearsing the actors and chorus, who only had one chance to get it right. As a result, some poets inserted the same choral songs in more than one play and they contracted out some of the stock scenes to apprentices like me. In my first internship, I got the Celebration at the end, which was quite easy – a simple metre for the dirty kordax dance, lots of jokes about drinking and a couple of naked flute girls. It had gone well and Callistratus approved.

Perhaps it was the mention of the flute girls that made Cunna remember that I wasn't only there as her drama instructor. "OK, piggy time," she said with a little laugh. I said I'd make a joke of that in a play one day. But I didn't think about the stage for a little while after that, though I do remember we laughed a lot. I knew I was being naïve thinking that my first high-class escort was special and we would always mean a lot to each other but I couldn't help it.

When it was time to go, Cunna took me back to where Pherecrates was sitting. His eyes were closed but he started up as soon as we entered the room. "Sorry you had to wait so long," I said.

"Not a problem; I had plenty to think about."

"Er, how much…?"

Pherecrates grabbed my arm, gave a throaty laugh and with a nervous glance at Cunna to see if she had heard, said, "Come on Aristophanes, we've got lots to discuss."

We said our goodbyes and once we were outside the building, I asked him what that was about. "She's an escort, not a whore," he explained. "She doesn't sell her services, she expects 'gifts' at the client's discretion."

"How do I know what to give her?"

"Oh, don't worry about that. I've looked after her. One day I'll explain to you how the business works." So I'd put my foot in it already – and I realised I'd been so busy describing my job that I hadn't asked her anything about herself. I wondered if I'd be allowed back.

We had only gone a few paces when the great Sophocles emerged from a tavern where he had obviously been carrying on the party with his colleagues from the festival. The son of a prosperous arms dealer, he had been able to devote himself entirely to writing from an early age; in fact, his first victory over Aeschylus was more than twenty years before I was born. He still looked good, something I hadn't really noticed on our earlier encounter that evening; you could see why as a boy he had been chosen to lead the thanksgiving after we defeated the Persians at Salamis. He was a

28

respected general as well as being so famous for his plays that they say many foreign rulers invited him to attend their courts, but he never went.

He ignored me, not appearing to remember me at all, but seemed to look on Pherecrates as almost an equal, despite the age difference of thirty or forty years – a remarkable compliment from the famous man. They discussed the day's dramas, Sophocles displaying extraordinary modesty when Pherecrates tried to compliment him on his work. "I'm still learning," he said. "I hope I'm getting better."

"This is Aristophanes. He had a great success tonight, coming second in the comedy competition with his first play but he thinks he wants to write tragedies."

"I know. He'll learn." He patted me on the head. He did remember me after all. Of course it had only been a few hours.

We went our separate ways and when I got home I found I was locked out.

# 5

Ismenias had barricaded the door. Through a gap by the hinge I could see he had piled up the couches and tables from the uninhabited women's room. It wasn't the first time it had happened and I knew from experience that he was good at jamming them together at angles so that it would take three or four of us to shift the door. None of the neighbouring houses showed any light so that was out of the question. I cursed Ismenias loudly and hoped he heard me, but I knew he would pretend not to.

Most people get to choose their slaves, but I certainly didn't. When my father moved to Aegina he took three slaves with him, including his long-term squeeze, and left two old grumpy ones to look after me. Ismenias seemed to think he was responsible for my behaviour, so while he always claimed he was barricading the door as usual for security and thought I had already come home, I have no doubt he was trying to punish me for enjoying myself. That night he knew perfectly well I was going to be late at the festival. Nerita had made me a new cloak specially. And anyway, if he was trying to protect my morals, he would have done better to barricade me in.

I didn't want to sleep out and I wasn't that tired anyway, so I walked the streets for a while. The plague was almost over, so there weren't any corpses in the streets as there would have been a couple of years earlier. The taverns were empty and most had extinguished their lamps. Near some of them a drunk or two had passed out. Here and there people were bedded down on mattresses in front of private houses, presumably some of the farmers who came into the city every summer while the Spartans destroyed their land. They would normally be back home now, but these ones must have had their farms wrecked so badly and so often they couldn't be bothered to go back and repair things. The temples and their precincts were filled with them too. No one seemed to be moving through the streets except me. Even the crooks must have been tucked up in bed.

After an hour or so of walking in large, aimless circles, I found myself near Pherecrates' house. I noticed a light was on, so I thought I'd ask if I could sleep on a couch there.

"I don't mean to disturb you, but I've been locked out again."

"You aren't disturbing me. I had a lot of ideas for my next play while I was waiting for you at Aspasia's and I've been trying to get them down."

"Carry on; I'll just go to sleep."

"No, wait a bit. I'm almost done."

I was pretty tired by now after a very full day and quite a long walk, but he obviously wasn't and he was my host and mentor, so I couldn't just lie down and curl up as I would have liked. I waited.

After a few minutes, he put down his pen. I examined his face to see if he was happy with what he'd written, but I learned nothing. He swung round towards me on his couch and began a conversation I wasn't really in the mood for, though I know his motives were kind. "I think I'd better explain how the escort business works so you don't embarrass yourself and anyone else in future." There was some irony in someone who wasn't interested in sex starting a conversation about it in the small hours of the morning with someone who had had quite enough of it for a while, but I thought it would be rude to stop him.

"Now, I assume you were introduced to sex by one of your slave women, but you've probably been to a brothel too." I didn't enlighten him, being too busy trying not to think about being introduced to sex by Nerita. It would have put me off for life.

"Brothels are generally run by women, often by people who were once whores themselves. They are also called workshops and the ladies, working girls, partly because of the wool spinning they do to earn money when they are vertical. They have been seen as a vital part of the city since the first one was set up by the great lawgiver Solon two hundred years ago. You don't get much conversation from the girls, but they can sing a bit and that's often how they introduce themselves in a group for the client's selection. They are also hired out to parties, where they are expected to entertain the guests with a flute as well as in their professional way."

"Where do they come from?"

"They are generally slaves or foreigners, but there are some wives or widows of poor citizens who need the money but don't have the education they'd need to be an escort. Most whores work in brothels but some try their luck on the streets or at the baths, usually under the protection of a pimp. That's where male whores work too. They all tend to do very well at festival times and when they follow the army. The slaves get to keep some of their earnings and can generally afford to buy their freedom after a few years. The key thing is that it's a straightforward, unashamed, financial transaction, with the price agreed and paid upfront. They keep very good records because the taxman audits them regularly and has ways of checking up."

"You're joking! How?"

"Well, tax collectors are pretty sharp. They'll have paid a lot of money to be able to collect the tax and so they are keen to make sure they collect more than they bid. They might tip clients to check whether their visits were recorded, they might send friends for the same purpose or they might just watch outside for a while. As a result, most of the working girls are pretty honest in their records, though no doubt there are times when they offer the taxman payment in kind."

It occurred to me that being a taxman might be quite a good job, then I realised it needed capital.

Pherecrates continued: "Now escorts are quite different. They are generally slaves too but might be citizens' family or well-bred permanent residents and they are invariably smartly dressed, well-educated, talented and able to talk intelligently on most subjects. The financial transaction is never referred to. They select their 'friends', typically based on the value of the 'gifts' they receive, but the whole game is about playing hard to get and needing to be chatted up and seduced with lavish presents. Some are internationally famous and have statues erected to them. They are all financially independent and generally operate alone. Aspasia's salon is an exception. She didn't want to relinquish her role in the intellectual life of the city after Pericles and Lysicles died and thought the best way to attract the kind of people she wanted was to give people like Salabaccho and Cunna a room whenever they want one. As you saw tonight, it's working."

"But how do you know what to pay an escort?"

"Well, you have to spend much more than you would on a whore. As you know, you can have a quickie with a whore for one obol." Great Artemis! I'd paid four and it wasn't very good. "For a session with an escort you would present her with a gift worth at least a dozen times as much, perhaps hundreds of times." I did a quick calculation – a dozen obols makes two drachmae, more than two days' pay for a typical worker. I wondered if I'd ever be able to see Cunna again. "Of course, you can pay much more. With whores, price can depend on position – horseback is the most expensive – but with escorts it's their status that fetches the big money. A citizen mother and daughter together cost a fortune."

"You made the booking this evening. How did you arrange it?"

"Oh, the usual way. I sent Cunna a piece of jewellery and a note saying what great things I'd heard about her and that I wanted to introduce you."

"How did you know Cunna was going to be there and that I would choose her?"

"Aspasia had told me earlier – and in fact Cunna chose you, remember? No, you probably don't. You looked a bit confused. Salabaccho had an appointment with Gorgias and was just there as a formality. Anyway, a note and a gift is always the way to try to get an appointment, even if you know the girl well. And remember, she still won't necessarily agree to see you."

"In that case, do you get your gift back?"

"Not unless you've really upset her."

That was a lot to think about. It's extraordinary how much this great city revolves around sex. Still, I suppose a lot of life is about reproduction in some form. I slept very well.

# 6

I'd told Cunna my first apprenticeship with Callistratus was a great success. I didn't tell her how I nearly blew it. Athens was going through an especially tough time; Sparta had started her annual invasions of Attica and Pericles had persuaded the farmers to abandon the countryside. He gave his own estate to the city in case his old friend the Spartan general spared it, which would have made him look bad. As a result, the city was vastly overcrowded every summer; people who had no city house, or no relatives with a large one, were living on the streets or in temples. Once sacred pieces of land now had buildings on them.

It was made worse by the plague which had just arrived from Egypt. It was a horrid disease: violent headaches, inflamed eyes, and internal haemorrhages were followed by sneezing and coughing fits, diarrhoea, vomiting, and ulcers and pustules all over the body. Worst of all, they say, was the continual feeling of being burnt, so that touching anything, even wearing clothes, was unbearable, accompanied by an unquenchable thirst. Most people lasted about eight days. Any who survived longer usually only suffered more before they too succumbed. The few who recovered had often lost their memory.

When the disease first hit, the city couldn't cope with the dead. Bodies lay in piles around hovels or on the streets. There were no proper funerals and people just threw their own dead on others' pyres. Inevitably there was an increase in lawlessness and a surge in spending on luxuries.

That was the state of things a couple of weeks before the Lenaea, though the overcrowding wasn't so bad because it was winter and most of the farmers were back in the countryside. The team of four that Callistratus had got together to support Cratinus' comedy *Wealth Gods* was down to two as a result of the plague. The other was Bloody Eupolis, a couple of years older than me and tall, good looking, witty, well-spoken, charming, immaculately dressed… in other words, nauseating. Most annoying was the fact that he had his own play on in competition with Cratinus', but Callistratus had begged him to help out in the crisis and he was cocky enough to think he could do both. Of course, he was just trying to increase his chances of success and although he had plenty of money of his own, it is always wise for a playwright to keep in with regular producers.

Financing an evening of plays was seen as a public service on the part of wealthy men and some of the more cultured ones preferred producing plays to funding a trireme or an expedition. The funder had overall responsibility for all the productions and had the title 'chorus leader', but the actual role of leading the chorus on stage was often delegated, as no one could really take it on for three or four different plays in one evening. Quite often the author would do it, in addition to a lot of the directing and rehearsing tasks, and sometimes a professional actor was engaged.

I found Callistratus good to learn from, though rather intimidating at first. He wasn't much taller than me but had the eyebrows of a giant. They weren't enough to hide his bulbous eyes, the ensemble set off by a large hooked nose and a protuberant chin which I kept wanting to bend upwards to see if it would meet his nose. He had a booming voice and often took the part of chorus leader in the comedies he produced, though seldom in the tragedies, and was as good as any professional. People said that with a face like that he didn't need a mask, but they only said it behind his back, as his temper was as well-known as his features were striking.

The shortage of staff and the fact that Cratinus was usually drunk meant that Bloody Eupolis and I had to do much more than apprentices would normally do. I even had to draft a chorus and the special dance that goes with it. It was the entry song, pretty standard stuff about gods and nature, but it took ages and of course it was heavily edited by Cratinus before being used in the play. It gave me a feel for how to set words and music together and how to fit words and rhythm to a dance for twenty-four men. The ending scene was all mine though.

On the day of our second rehearsal, Ismenias answered the door and it was a messenger from Callistratus: "Theatre being used for state funeral. Meet at Temple of Olympian Zeus two hours before midday. Don't be late." I'd been up all night working on the Entry Chorus, trying to find a suitable segue into the Contest, and it still wasn't quite right, but it would have to do.

35

I ran most of the way towards the temple, which was just the other side of the theatre where they were carrying out the final ceremonies for those killed in the war. The bodies had been laid out in a tent three days earlier for their relatives to bring offerings. For the procession, each corpse was placed in a huge cypress coffin along with other fallen members of their tribe and put on a cart drawn by oxen. One empty coffin, alone on a cart, commemorated those whose bodies had not been recovered. That day it seemed that everyone who had survived the plague had joined the procession. The theatre was full and I had to push and shove to try to get past the crowd who couldn't get in but wanted to hear the Oration. I didn't have time for that, so I kept trying to get through, much to the annoyance of all the people wanting to hear what Pericles had to say. He was the natural choice, having been elected general a record thirteen times. He had faced a couple of indecency charges, one for hitting on the wife of one of his offsiders and the other for luring women with gifts of peacocks that he had been given on an embassy to Persia, but no one thought much the worse of him for that and he was the nearest thing we had to a hero. The last couple of years hadn't been easy for him. He had lost quite a lot of popularity by abandoning the countryside to the Spartans, but it was probably the sensible thing to do even though the overcrowding made the plague worse.

His powerful voice could be heard clearly outside the theatre and with my way being now completely blocked, I had no choice but to listen: "Let us praise our grandfathers whose valour made our country free and independent. Let us praise our fathers who built our empire. Let us praise those still with us who have added to our empire and helped secure our future..."

This was good stuff! I had to hear a bit more. "Our laws offer equal justice to all. Our public offices are open to all. We look after the injured and disabled. In our private lives we are tolerant of each other and don't meddle, but we hold our legal system as sacred and we shun lawlessness wherever we may find it..."

He was coming to a close and one or two people had started to drift away but I was transfixed and wouldn't have missed another word for the world, especially the grand peroration. I can still remember bits of it today: "Fix your eyes on the greatness of Athens and fall in love with her... The brave have the whole world as their memorial. Their memory lives and grows in men's hearts… The only thing that will not age is the sense of honour… Life's finest possession is not money but respect."

I was late now and ran the last couple of hundred yards to the theatre. We were only allowed three full scale rehearsals and this was the second and we were going to go through the whole play from start to finish. The Entry Chorus I had drafted was supposed to be near the beginning and Cratinus hadn't worked on it yet, so they had had to skip it. Callistratus and Cratinus were furious. Cratinus had an attack of hiccups and Callistratus' eyebrows seemed to be trying to move themselves to the back of his neck. They told me that if they weren't so short-staffed they'd have kicked me off the team there and then.

In the end we were unplaced. So, I am glad to say, was Bloody Eupolis' *Helots*. It hadn't helped our play that Callistratus as chorus leader couldn't manage the rhythms and some of the rapid alliterations in the Entry Chorus. Of course, he blamed me, but Cratinus kindly pointed out that he'd rewritten most of the stuff, so it was his work that Callistratus was criticising. This led to a furious row between the two of them and they never worked together again, but at least Callistratus saw me as blameless. We were to work together a lot. The following year he had me on his team again, though I didn't especially want to work for Bloody Eupolis who was the playwright. I worked hard though and although the play was unplaced again, Callistratus was sufficiently impressed with my contribution to say he'd be happy to produce a comedy for me next year if I could come up with a good enough plot, which was a big vote of confidence. I started to rack my brains for a plot that would make the audience think a great new talent had arrived.

I saw Pericles in action once more and again he made a great speech, defending his policy of quitting the countryside when the Spartans invaded. He told us it was only the horrors of the plague that had made us want to change the policy, and it was still a good one because we needed to keep our resources to defend our empire and prevent revolts among our tribute-paying allies. These had started occurring rather frequently. They hated us, and with good reason. Most of the money they paid for us to protect them went on new temples and public buildings. One line in this last speech of Pericles that stood out for me was: "Hatred does not last long, but the brilliance of the present is the glory of the future, forever stored in man's memory." He may have incurred the allies' hatred, but his building program was designed to make the city immortal and I expect it has.

Sadly, political hatred lasted long enough for the frightful demagogue Cleon to have Pericles charged with corruption. No one can remember why. He was removed from office and fined. Soon afterwards he lost his sister and both his legitimate sons to the plague and they say not even Aspasia's companionship could stop him weeping for days. He died himself soon after, perhaps from sadness as much as the disease. Just before his death, the Assembly allowed a change in Pericles' own citizenship law that made his bastard son with Aspasia, Pericles the Younger, a citizen and legitimate heir, which would have pleased him at the last.

## 7

I developed an original idea for a plot, an attack on the new sophistry to be called *The Banqueters*. I thought the teachers of twisted logic and rhetoric were becoming a serious problem for the city and for our democracy and needed to be made fun of. I discussed the concept with Pherecrates and together we approached Callistratus who agreed to produce it.

To be one of the five comedies picked for the Lenaea was the greatest thrill of my life to that point. The selection system was complex and very competitive. For the Lenaea in January and the Dionysia in April, producers had to submit an outline of their plays, together with a few songs or scenes they planned to include, to the relevant archon the previous summer. This gave the teams for the Dionysia more time to prepare as they were expected to meet a higher standard. In making their selections, the archons tended to favour established producers over new ones, so for a newcomer like me the only way to get selected was through an experienced producer like Callistratus. The producer was expected to fund the whole exercise, tragedies, satyr play and comedy, so he had to be rich and to feel pressured to be seen to be spending generously for the city. He had to pay the actors, house and feed the choruses for the entire duration of rehearsals, and buy the costumes, props, set pieces and anything else needed for the show. The costs of one day's theatre would amount to several years' pay for a skilled craftsman and although the prizes for success were quite generous, the producer was expected to share it among the performers, the writers and the support teams, taking nothing himself except the respect of fellow citizens and a permanent record of his name on a memorial stone if he won at the Dionysia.

One of the challenges was not being able to pick your own principals. The archon assigned each play two lead actors and the producer had to recruit the rest of the cast (usually one or two more actors), the chorus and the musicians. In our case the chorus leader was not going to be a problem because Callistratus liked to take that role himself and he was generally pretty good, but unfortunately we were assigned Archinous as our lead actor. He specialised in slapstick but lacked the depth of lungs required to make himself heard clearly enough throughout a long fast speech or while performing a vigorous dance. I had been hoping to get Bronchus or Rhombus and being assigned Archinous meant I had to put in more ribald scenes near the end, go easy on powerful declamatory passages and be careful not to give him too many kicks and twirls while speaking or singing.

The play was about two sons reaching manhood and a father introducing them to his club, an essential part of the process of growing up as fellow members always help each other out when they can. One son had had the usual education in athletics, music, poetry, wrestling and so on, while the other had been educated by the sophists in the techniques of persuasion and false reasoning (the team soon started referring to the play as *The Good and the Buggered*). The father gives a banquet for club members and the evening is ruined by squabbling between the two young men. They agree to change places and a number of scenes follow showing how neither can cope with the other's lifestyle. In the end the chorus of club members decide not to admit the Buggered Boy, condemning him to social isolation and obscurity. I felt it was an important warning to Athens that if you educate people to deceive and mislead, you won't get them to reform – and you probably won't want them around.

For the first time I was now responsible for the whole play. I would delegate some of the simpler parts to apprentices in the usual way but I knew, based on my own experience, I'd have to do a lot of rewriting. Now the work began. I put a lot of time into the Contest – essentially between the old ideas and the new ones – illustrating them with absurd pseudo-philosophical statements by the Buggered Boy, such as the best education being what sons teach their fathers, or that nothing is stable, therefore the laws are unstable, therefore there's no need to obey them. In fact, I probably put too much time into it and not enough into the real challenge of getting all my thoughts into the appropriate metres. The rhythm of the Set Up with its iambic trimeters (ti-tum-ti-tum times three) was easy and the spoken parts of the Chorus' Entry and the Contest were just the usual anapaests (ti-ti-tum) and trochees (tum-ti-tum-ti). The farcical slapstick after the boys swap places was easy to write once I'd conceived the scenes, so I delegated them to the interns. That left me clear to work on developing some original songs and dances and the Address, which was not only the chance to get any serious messages across, but by far the most complex to write.

The Address has to be composed in multiple parts in several different rhythms. You start with some free lyrics or songs before moving into the main Address which is in anapaests. That's where the chorus leader praises the poet (I enjoyed writing that bit the first time) and gives serious advice to the audience, though the advice has to be wittily expressed. The Choke comes next, in which the chorus leader has to deliver at least fifty syllables all in one breath and loud enough for every word to be heard at the back. That is in double-speed anapaests. It was not Archinous' strong point, so I had to choose words with consonants that were easy to make out, mainly 's' and 'ch'. That is followed by the sung Ode in free meter and the Flow in trochees, and then the corresponding Antode and Counterflow. Once you'd worked out what you wanted the Address to say, you had to find the words to say it in all those different metres. You never wanted to compromise the message to fit the form but sometimes you had to play around with the order of topics.

It was the first time I'd been involved in every aspect of the play and there was a massive amount to do. Fortunately Callistratus kept it all together with a bit of help from his friend Philonides, an unsuccessful comic poet whose unquenchable enthusiasm for the theatre made him want to get involved in any way he could. His own entry for the Lenaea had just failed to get selected. My task was not only to write, or at least edit, every word and make up all the stage directions and dance moves; I also had to lead all the rehearsals for the actors, chorus and musicians. I specified the props I needed – quite simple, mainly tables and couches – and when we discussed the costumes there didn't seem a requirement for anything special as the play was supposed to represent everyday life. The chorus wore the usual bodysuit under a tunic and cloak, with a pocket inside the cloak in which was stitched one end of a large red cloth phallus to be brought out and waved around at appropriate moments in the choral songs. To make the chorus look like a typical collection of clubmen we used six different mask shades across the twenty-four chorus members. The actors' costumes were standard, except that the beard attached to the Buggered Boy's mask was slightly shorter than the norm, and the hair much longer to show his aspiration to be one of the clever young aristocrats about town.

We nearly had a disaster at the final rehearsal. From the start Archinous had been muttering about the fact there was no scene with the crane. He said he never worked without one. I resisted at first as it made no sense in the plot, but he kept on about it until Callistratus tapped me on the shoulder and said we'd better put in something for him. We racked our brains for a couple of days and the best we could come up with was to change the scene near the end where the Buggered Boy is sacrificing to his new gods of natural phenomena and the clouds punish him for putting them above the traditional gods by sending down a massive downpour, so he goes dripping off the stage. Quite funny and not hard to represent the downpour with the conventional gestures and music, so I used the idea in a later play as well. Archinous as the Good Boy is off the stage at the time, so it was an opportunity to put him on the crane. We decided to have him descend as Dionysus, god of the festival, and carry the Buggered Boy away to be punished. Not as funny, higher risk, requiring a very quick mask change for Archinous back into the Good Boy after the Dionysus scene, and the Buggered Boy had to be written out of the final Celebration, so we lost some of my best lines. Still, we decided to go with it.

On the last day of rehearsal Archinous turned up a little the worse for wear, though it wasn't yet midday – a typical problem for actors who generally earn their living between festivals by giving private performances where the hosts tend to be overgenerous with the wine. He stumbled through his speeches, forgetting some lines, and took a tumble three times, once when he wasn't even dancing. We'd given him lots of water and I had been expecting him to start to sober up as the rehearsal progressed. When he didn't, I became suspicious and went behind the screen cloth. There just inside the door onto the stage was a large, half-empty wineskin. I hid it, but I should really have stopped the crane scene. Archinous was in no state to manage equipment of any sort.

In the event he failed to latch his harness properly and lost his balance just as the beam swung him out over the stage. His life was probably saved by the fact that he'd managed to get his foot tangled in the harness that should have been round his shoulders. As a result, he was left swinging upside-down about six feet off the ground with his tunic and cloak round his ears. Despite his danger we all found it hard not to laugh, not least the Buggered Boy, who I gathered had personal reasons not to like Archinous, though his laughter stopped abruptly when the vomiting started immediately overhead. At that point we thought we'd better rescue Archinous, so six of the chorus held a large cloak under where he was swinging in case his leg slipped out of the trap, while the crane operator brought him slowly back up. That was pretty much the end of the rehearsal, with the Buggered Boy written out at this point and Archinous also out of service. I just had to hope it would be all right on the night.

Worried that it might not be, I asked Callistratus how we could make sure Archinous didn't put in the same or a worse performance at the festival.

"Oh, that's OK," he reassured me. "Twenty-four hours before the event he'll come to stay at my house and the slaves will watch him every moment to see he gets no wine or beer."

"But won't he object to that?"

"Of course not. He's used to it. Most actors are."

It was so exciting to be part of the Lenaea. The procession was not as big as the one for the Dionysia, but it still must have been over a thousand people in all, most of them dancers. I was really proud to be part of it and wished my parents had been there to see it. Even my father might have been proud. I know my mother would have been.

And in my first chance at such an important event we came second! I couldn't believe it when the judges read out my play and my name along with Callistratus. Or that I was actually walking up the ramp to the stage to take my place in the line of tragic and comic poets whose works had been honoured. That is how I came to be standing next to Sophocles.

# 8

The day after the celebrations for the *The Banqueters* and Sophocles and Cunna and everything, I was making my way back home from Pherecrates' house, plotting how to deal with Ismenias, and just as I was passing the flower market I was grabbed from behind and forced to kneel with my nose on the ground.

"Smooth as an eel, eh?" said a gravelly voice in my ear. "An eel with curly hair, huh?"

From that I could tell it was friends of the aristocratic tearaway Alcibiades whom I'd described in those words in the play. This was soon confirmed by the high-pitched giggle of Alcibiades' friend, one of his many lovers of both sexes, the pampered Callias. I had no respect for Callias. He came from a long line of shits and hadn't improved the family reputation. They say that at the Battle of Marathon his unkempt grandfather confronted a Persian who thought he was a king because of his long hair and prostrated himself and showed him a lot of gold he had buried in a well before the battle. Callias senior took the gold and killed the Persian. His descendant had spent the fortune he inherited almost as soon as he got it on sycophants and loose women and now lived off his rich friends. I was more ambivalent about Alcibiades, otherwise I'd have been much ruder. In some ways you couldn't help admiring him. A lot of people resented his lavish lifestyle, wild ways and lack of concern for what other people thought of him. On the other hand, he was courageous, high-spirited and generous to a fault. He was also as highly born on his mother's side as anyone in the city which one would think should count for something.

Had I been older and wiser in the knowledge of what can happen to playwrights, I would have avoided the flower stalls because that's where the spoiled rich generally hung out. There were four of them besides Callias, all young and fit though more inclined to luxury than fisticuffs, so there was nothing for it but to listen to the insults while my nose was being rubbed in the dirt.

When I got home, Ismenias was out, presumably not keen on the usual showdown. I cleaned myself up and went out again. The Assembly was meeting and I thought I'd try and see what was going on, as it only met once a month, except in emergencies and this was an important one. There was no pay for attendance in those days, and sometimes slaves were employed to drive citizens into the meeting, using a rope covered with wet red paint, so everyone knew who had been uncooperative and trying to avoid their civic duty, but this was a special meeting and I knew it would be full. I was going to be too late to get a seat, but still had enough excited energy from the last twenty-four hours to be able to face the prospect of standing.

The meeting had been called by the Council of Five Hundred to make an important and delicate decision. Our so-called ally, the city of Mytilene, had taken over all of the island of Lesbos and had been turning it against us, and Sparta had extended her usual summer invasion of Attica to distract us while she sent forty ships to support the Mytileneans. Fortunately, the Spartan ships took too long to get there and by the time they arrived, we had put down the revolt; the city and most of the island had been under the control of our troops since the autumn. The question now was how to punish the Mytileneans. If we couldn't discourage independent allies from fomenting revolts and inviting Sparta to cross the Aegean to support them, we'd be finished.

By the time I arrived, Nicias had spoken in favour of doubling Mytilene's taxes and executing the ringleaders. This wasn't enough for Cleon though. Red in the face and shouting his message to the world, he insisted on an exemplary punishment to make sure no allies would be tempted to do the same again. Unattractive as he was physically and morally, he somehow always managed to carry the Assembly and when he had finished a show of hands revealed overwhelming support for his motion to put all Mytilenean men to death and to enslave all the women and children. A trireme was despatched that afternoon to carry out the order.

I wandered around the Agora for a while, musing about Cleon and how he managed to wield so much influence. He had started with plenty of money, his father having owned a tannery in the district of Cydathon which was the only place you were allowed tanneries, so he had almost a

45

monopoly in the business. He had risen to fame as an opponent of Pericles and a war hawk and he somehow had the strange power of being able to convince an audience even when he was clearly lying. He was widely suspected of having enriched himself further whenever he was chosen to lead an embassy and, as today's debate had shown, he was callous and vindictive. I thought he might make a good target.

Before heading home, I stopped at my favourite pub, hoping to catch up with my old friend Lysander who normally drank there too, and see what he thought of it all. He wasn't there but the place was crowded and noisy and the voices were angry. They had been discussing the resolution of the Assembly and a number of people were arguing that it should be overturned. Others said that the punishment was fully justified and it was too late now anyway, as the boat with the order had already sailed. I sipped my wine quietly and listened, hoping as always to hear something funny or stupid to put on stage. A young studious-looking chap came and sat next to me.

Eventually it was agreed that half-a-dozen of them would present a petition to the Council which was sitting that afternoon that the Assembly be reconvened. It was too late to get the Assembly itself together before the next morning, which would almost certainly mean the original resolution would be carried out, but it was felt that the people should be given a chance to rethink the cruel decision and reverse it if they wished.

The delegation left and the studious chap turned to me and said: "You're the guy who came second yesterday in the comedy, aren't you?" I admitted I was. "I'm going to be a comic poet." Oh, yeah? "I've been studying technique." Oh, dear. "I've figured out how you reinforced the metaphysical dichotomy first revealed in the Contest by the clever juxtaposition of meters in the Ode and Flow of the Address. Am I right?"

I had no idea what he was talking about but didn't want to appear ignorant. "Clever of you to spot that," I cried, clapping him on the shoulder.

"I'll try and work that into the play I'm working on. I'd like to show it to you sometime. Oh, by the way, I thought the use of the crane at the end was brilliant."

As I made my way home, I thought how much nicer it was when the audience didn't talk back.

I had a lot on my mind, not least Mytilene, so I didn't feel like confronting Ismenias right away and told him we'd talk in the morning. In the event I overslept and had to run up the hill to see if the Assembly had been reconvened, so the difficult conversation was postponed again.

When I got to the Pnyx, the Assembly was under way and Cleon was on his feet again, vigorously defending yesterday's vote. Red in the face and shouting again, he was criticising the Assembly itself for treating debates as a spectacle rather than an attempt to come to the best answer. "You go to the debates as you'd go to a wrestling match, you believe any rumour, you judge proposals by the wit of their advocates and not on their merits, you believe their accounts of past events against the evidence of your own eyes, you accept any argument, however absurd and if you aren't speaking yourselves you try to show how smart you are by anticipating the speaker's remarks before he has finished making them."

What a hypocrite! If anyone was responsible for the poor quality of public debate it was Cleon and his fellow demagogues. It got worse as he, a rich man himself who had almost certainly made himself richer at public expense, attacked his opponents for getting paid for their advocacy by people who wanted them to represent a particular point of view.

Diodotus pushed back. He was tall and lean, a quiet, modest man with kind eyes, rumoured to have the happiest home life in Athens. His father Eucrates was my father's best friend. Calmly and without insulting anyone, he pointed out that it was wrong to judge the worth of a proposal by whether the speaker was paid; it meant good ideas were often rejected for the wrong reasons and however good an idea was, speakers would be suspected of base motives and have to lie and exaggerate to get their point across. He said yesterday's decision was a dangerous one for the city. It would alienate more allies and more of them would stop paying the tribute we now needed more than ever. This time the show of hands was decisively in favour of reversing yesterday's decision, though the ship sent off to implement it was already the best part of a day into its journey. Lesbos was about four hundred kilometres away and, unless the first boat was going exceptionally fast, it would take a good two days. The second boat would have to try to do it in one.

It was now time for the leaders of each of the ten tribes to nominate seventeen rowers for the journey. While they were getting ready, I wandered over to where I'd seen Pherecrates standing to ask him what he thought of Cleon.

"What you see is what you get," he offered, expressionless as always.

"Well, what I see is simply awful. He's not doing the city any good and I can't understand why anyone would follow him."

"He pretty much explained it himself, saying how gullible the Assembly was and that it was more interested in clever speeches than in identifying the best policies."

"I've a good mind to get stuck into him in my next play."

"Be very careful."

The tribal chiefs came forward to read their lists of names. They always kept a list of who was next to be called up based on fitness, military experience, how recently they had served and, in the case of the kinder-hearted chiefs, personal circumstances such as a recent bereavement or a wife about to give birth. Now each in turn introduced his list in the usual manner by saying how proud his tribe was to serve the city in this way and mentioning a few recent campaigns in which members had distinguished themselves. The head of my tribe, Pandionis, added a sort of apology to his introduction, saying that, while he was delighted to be able to nominate several fine sturdy fellows, his tribesmen had suffered a lot in recent campaigns and from the plague which had come back again, and not all of his list would have been their first choice in other circumstances.

When he got to about number twelve or thirteen, I noticed a few people's eyes starting to roll; the chief was alternating people who were clearly a little too old with those who were probably a little too young. The seventeenth name he read out was Aristophanes.

The good news was that I didn't need to buy armour as I would for a military campaign, and we'd be paid four obols a day – not much but double the usual rate. The bad news was that I didn't even have time to go home. All one hundred and seventy of us were lined up and made to run the five miles down to the Peiraeus, where a messenger had already gone to have a boat prepared. I wasn't the last to arrive, which didn't bode well.

# 9

When some bright spark a few generations ago decided a ship would go faster with three banks of oars rather than two, the challenge was how to achieve that while allowing each oar enough sweep without getting in each other's way. The first attempt was the obvious one of having three decks, but this made the ship very unstable and likely to capsize in rough weather; it also required such long oars on the top deck that few could manage them. Eventually they hit on the plan of two decks and an outrigger on each side at the level of the top deck so that the top deck's oars swept between the ship and the outrigger and the outrigger's were further out. This made for three groups of rowers. I was allocated to the smelly, sweaty, stifling lower deck.

We had hardly got to our places when the captain gave the order to cast off and his number two told us to start rowing and not expect to stop for twenty-four hours. In front of me and diagonally across my chest was a substantial tree trunk which must have been my oar. I tugged at it and nothing happened. I tugged again with the same result. I stood up and leaned my whole weight on it. I was swinging there with both feet off the ground and it was just starting to move when a massive body knocked me down. It belonged to the rower in front of me (towards the stern of the ship) who had just completed his stroke. I sat there bemused for a while and tried again. Same result. As I was wondering how I could contribute to this team effort, the massive rower turned to me and said, "Look, you're in my way. I can't pull back properly when you're there and your oar is dragging in the water. Move aside and give me that."

With that he swung round, straddled his bench and took my oar in one hand. Swinging from side to side for each stroke, he managed to keep time with both oars. His face was red and angry looking, like a grotesque version of Cleon, but showed no sign of physical strain. I thought I might as well do what he said and get out of the way. I got up and started heading for the gangway to ask the number two if there was anything else I could do when the man on the bench opposite said, "Hey, aren't you the playwright fellow, Aristobolus or whatever?" I admitted I was at least the whatever. "Why don't you sing us a song to keep us happy and in time?"

So, I did. There hadn't been time to bring the usual piper on board to give the time to the rowers and I had worked out by now that they needed a simple two-beat rhythm which meant I could only use trochees (tum-ti) or iambs (ti-tum), which rather limited me at first. I used up all the relevant passages from the *The Banqueters* and moved onto incomplete drafts I had made of other songs and passages I could remember from my apprenticeship. Somehow I was able to keep going for over an hour before repeats. Well before the first hour was up, some rowers on the top deck near the gangway had heard me and the number two asked me to move to the top of the gangway so all three sets of rowers could hear me.

Twenty-four hours' continuous rowing is huge. There was no stopping for refreshments and the captain, the number two and I handed out bread and wine every few hours while the men kept rowing. Some of them were strong enough to continue rowing with one hand, while others we had to hand-feed. There were only two instances of choking and both recovered quickly. While my voice was recovering between performances, I helped manage the sleeping shifts. One in every five rowers was allowed two hours off and we would then wake them and the next lot would take their turn.

We just made it! And only just. The decree had been read out when our captain arrived in Mytilene's town square with the order countermanding it. The massacre was prevented, though we did destroy the walls and took over their navy. We found out later that one thousand Mytileneans resident in Athens had been put to death – presumably more vindictiveness by Cleon.

I sought out Massive Rower and took him to the nearest tavern to buy him a drink. Our troops had taken over the pubs, so the wine was free and they were all overcrowded. By the time I got back from the bar to where he was sitting, he was fast asleep, and I'm told he stayed there without moving for twelve hours. He had quite a thirst but seldom the funds to go on a bender, so for the next three days, whenever he woke up, he drank himself to sleep again – a hero of the old school! Whenever I ran into him, I couldn't help studying his face closely. If I ever dared put Cleon on stage as a character, rather than just have other characters insulting him, I knew how I'd decorate the mask.

I was proud of our success in my first campaign and felt I had contributed a little to it, though not in the conventional way. The voyage home, of course, was much more relaxed. We took nearly three days over it. Massive Rower was in no state to cope with two oars and could barely manage one, but it didn't matter as there was no hurry. I was asked to sing again and this time it was less important to give the rowers their time, so I had more scope and was more inventive. I tried out more new chorus songs and demonstrated some novel dance steps I had come up with, though it was hard on a ship and I kept overbalancing. I also floated a few insults about Cleon, which got a lot of laughs. I took that as guidance from Artemis that I should go after him in my next play.

I had been thinking about Cunna a lot while we were away and planned to visit her as soon as we got back. When I got home to change and clean up, Ismenias gave me a nasty grin and handed me a message from my father:

*My old slaves need replacing. Lampito has died and Sosias is too old to be any use. Obviously, by half Heracles, I can't look after myself any more. (Any more!) Send me Ismenias and Nerita. Here's some money to buy a couple of new ones.*

You can imagine how pleased I was to be getting rid of Ismenias and Nerita and to be able to replace them with slaves I could choose myself. And the money looked adequate to get a couple of quite good ones. I was just congratulating myself on this happy homecoming when I noticed a scrawl on the back of the message:

*By the way, I have decided that without Ismenias to keep an eye on you, it would be best if you got married now. One of my neighbours here has suggested his daughter. I haven't met her, but she sounds suitable enough. She will be arriving in Athens in ten days' time. I am busy here and will not be able to attend. Nor will her parents, as they seldom visit the city. Eucrates will be willing to stand in my place for the ceremony. Her name, I believe, is Praxagora. I hope she's all right.*

# 10

That night with Cunna we just talked for ages by the light of the new moon which shone through her high window. She made me tell her all about the rowing and pretended that it must have been my singing that got us there in time. I got her to tell me a bit about herself for a change. She came from a good family and had had an expensive education, but left her home in Asia Minor because of an abusive husband. She fled to Athens to her cousin Aspasia, who had taken her in and set her up to make a living. She had a daughter, five years old, whom she hoped would follow in her footsteps, as she thought the escort business offered the most satisfying and rewarding career for non-citizens. It also provided independence. "No need to risk marriage," she laughed.

I didn't find this as funny as I might have a couple of hours earlier before I got my father's message. We talked about that for a while. She said she hoped I'd keep coming to see her; after all most of her friends were married men. We talked about the slaves I was going to buy and how pleased I'd be to see the back of Ismenias. Dawn was breaking when we fell asleep in each other's arms.

When we awoke, I set off for the slave market. I stopped at the pub to see if Lysander was there and could come and help me with my purchases but again, I couldn't find him. Pherecrates would have been supportive, but I felt he'd helped me out enough and I didn't want him getting fed up with looking after me. I decided I'd have to manage by myself.

Passing the pottery district near the cemetery I started to wonder about life as a craftsman. Most of the tradesmen in that area were full-time potters, except in the middle of winter when the clay wouldn't dry properly, though some had farms they attended to at harvest time. A pretty dull life, I thought. I'd seen neighbours making simple plates and bowls in their home workshops to save money or sell to friends, but this was quite a different business. The potters here were experts in making complicated vase shapes and some of the workshops had highly skilled painters as well. They had full-time furnace managers and clay preparers and wheel turners, so some operations had six or seven people.

A voice greeted me from one of the workshops. "Hey, aren't you Aristophanes?"

"Yes."

"So am I!" A long thin shape uncoiled from the chair where he had been sitting painting a vase. "My name is Aristophanes too. I've been hearing our name a lot recently, but not because of my painting. Nice that we are both creative artists."

"Lovely," I said, though I'd never really thought of poetry and painting as being related.

He showed me what he was working on, a picture of Hephaestus giving Achilles the brightly decorated shield he had made for him, and some of his completed commissioned work that was waiting for the customers to collect. Though I didn't know much about pottery I did notice he had a very distinctive style: he drew lines round each of the figures to make them stand out more clearly against the background. I wondered if that was something I could adapt for my work. What was the dramatic equivalent of outlining your characters with a paint brush?

I was still musing on this when I arrived at the slave market. There were a lot of slaves standing on tables and carts, and, as always, more females than males, but not that many customers. The war and the plague had reduced the average lifespan of citizens closer to that of slaves, so demand wasn't growing in the way it usually did. The importers stood by their wares to make sure they were looking at their best, not slouching or showing the holes in their tunics. I had plenty to choose from, though I hadn't given much thought to how to make my selection except that I wanted a couple as different from Ismenias and Nerita as possible.

Before I could start my inspection a lot of shouting broke out at one of the tables nearby. It was the Fatties playing up as usual. For some reason Glaucetes, Morychus and Teleas weren't ashamed of their weight. In fact, they revelled in it and enjoyed making silly jokes about it. From what I could hear of the row, it seemed they had been pinching the thighs of some of the slaves, pretending they were going to eat them. One slave, knowing nothing about Athens but probably coming from a place where such things were not unknown, had taken it seriously and kicked Teleas in his huge belly. As a slave he could have been subject to the death penalty for assaulting a citizen, but the Fatties weren't vindictive, just childish. After telling the importer they'd see him in court, a bluff whose effect they spoiled by giggling, they made their way out of the market. That is one more thing I love about this city: it's full of absurd people. Great to live among and better still for a comic poet.

My selection task suddenly seemed to be made easier, at least in reducing the field by one. As I was passing one of the tables a burly slave with a huge head, his face almost completely hidden by eyebrows and beard, oddly short skinny legs and a label giving his name as Xanthias, called out to me, "Bugger me, you arsehole!" I moved quickly on.

The females ranged from about twelve years old upwards, all with short hair to differentiate them from the wives and daughters of citizens. There must have been thirty or forty of them, all decked out to look their best. I was despairing of where to start when I noticed a rather attractive one had a sign round her neck with the name Artemis. This was obviously a message to me personally. Just imagine having a slave with the name of your favourite goddess! I could order her around instead of just praying. Praxagora would be impressed to find she had a slave with such a distinctive name. She could teach our children all the stories about her namesake. And of course, I could…

My thoughts were interrupted by her owner asking if I wanted her or not. She was well within my budget and I had no idea how to choose from among the rest, so I said yes. "In that case you'd better take her husband as well. He's just over there. Hoy! Peisias! Customer for Xanthias."

Peisias came over. "No, I'm definitely not a customer for Xanthias," I said and explained what had happened.

Peisias laughed and said, "I did tell him not to say anything, but he speaks no Greek and probably didn't understand me."

"What do you mean he speaks no Greek?" I exclaimed. "His Greek was perfectly clear to me, I'm sorry to say."

"It seems some smart guy on the ship he came on told him 'Bugger me, you arsehole' was a polite form of greeting. He was only trying to impress you." Artemis' vendor roared with laughter and Peisias stopped to join him before continuing, "And his name isn't really Xanthias. His real name has six or seven syllables and a couple of sounds we Greeks don't make, so I thought I'd call him something easier. A lot of slaves are called Xanthias." Both importers seemed to find this even funnier. I thought it rather embarrassing and just wanted to get the whole thing over and done with, so the possible disadvantages of having a slave who spoke no Greek didn't occur to me. I left with the two of them and a surprising amount of change.

Xanthias was silent on the way back, which, given his conversational range in Greek, was a good thing. Artemis chatted away in their native language, pointing things out to him and occasionally turning to me and asking what particular buildings were and whether they were new. Her Greek was fluent and unaccented. I began to wonder whether they really were married or if it was just something the importers had cooked up to get rid of the one they called Xanthias. I never found out. And I no longer felt sure that Artemis was the woman's real name. All in all, it hadn't been a great morning's shopping.

When we got home, we were greeted by a shower of small sharp pebbles. Ismenias and Nerita were throwing things at us. On closer inspection, it turned out the missiles were sweets and nuts and this was a traditional slave-welcoming ceremony. I took the opportunity to rebuke Ismenias for starting a home ceremony without a prayer to Hestia and led one myself, just to set a good example to the newcomers, though who knows what gods they prayed to. I had hardly finished when Ismenias was back throwing more hard objects at Xanthias and wouldn't stop until he had run out of ammunition. Xanthias remained still and silent, but his eyes twinkled through the forest that constituted his face, which I took as a good sign.

It was less comforting to think that before long there'd be another ceremony in the house.

# 11

Thanks to Callistratus again, my next play, *The Babylonians*, had been accepted for the Dionysia (the Dionysia! Only my second play!). When I arrived home from rehearsals a few days later, Praxagora was there. I was relieved to find her very attractive, though we did make an odd couple. She was a lot taller than me, as was only to be expected. She had very long black hair, which sort of compensated for my baldness. Every now and then her dark eyes would flash as if with a dangerous inner fire; I learned to look at her mouth when this happened to see if it betokened anger or mischief. She was wearing little in the way of jewellery, though I soon discovered she had plenty and her favourite hobby was buying more. Her voice was a little shrill, but I got used to that quite quickly. We were both twenty, which meant I was about five years too young to get married and she was about five years too old. I have never understood that convention, by the way. It's why there are so many widows in Athens. Lysander once calculated that if it wasn't for all the deaths in childbirth the city would consist almost entirely of widows. It is only the rich ones that get married again because their relatives want to keep the estate in the family, so they marry a brother-in-law or cousin or uncle; the others have to resort to selling vegetables or worse. Praxagora had had a rather better education than most women of her class but, having lived all her life on Aegina, seemed rather naïve. I soon learned she had a sharp native intelligence and a fierce determination to have her own way. Besides the obvious disadvantages for me personally, this did mean I could be confident about letting her manage our household, our slaves and our finances. And of course, she could weave and spin, though she wouldn't have dreamed of selling her output. Overall, I thought I'd done rather well in my father's selection, but frankly I would have preferred to wait a few years.

We'd arranged to get married that day because she was coming to live with me immediately. It was a rather unusual ceremony, as weddings are supposed to be family affairs and neither of us had any family in Athens. I invited Lysander and Pherecrates for moral support and Eucrates was there as my father had arranged. I hadn't met him before. He was a minor politician whose family made ropes for the navy. You could tell it was a successful business because he could have been one of the Fatties but he was much older and he didn't have much more hair than I did. Praxagora didn't seem to mind that the only other female there was Artemis. She told me she had had the hen party back in Aegina – a dull, traditional bit of women's business getting the bride ready, ending with a feast at her father's house. She had made the traditional offerings to the female gods, Athena, Artemis and Aphrodite, and presented them with her childhood girdle, and she showed me the small patch on the side of her head where her hair had been cut short in the ceremony.

Wedding rituals are all about transferring the bride to her new home, but as Praxagora was already there, we had to fudge that a bit, Eucrates taking her outside and bringing her back in a few minutes later. We started with the usual prayer to Hestia and the premarital sacrifice of a lamb. Fortunately, my father had sent Eucrates money to pay for it; I couldn't normally afford meat. Human Artemis then took Praxagora for her bath while we men stood around feeling a little foolish, and Xanthias got on with preparing the meal. I had got Artemis to disabuse of him of the notion that 'Bugger me, you arsehole' was a good conversational gambit but he had remained silent ever since, communicating only with an occasional twinkle in his eye showing through his facial hair. I still had no idea whether he understood anything said to him in Greek, and had got into the habit of giving all my instructions through Artemis.

"Interesting name, Praxagora," said Lysander, trying to make conversation. He'd been my closest friend since our schooldays though we didn't seem to have much in common. He was tall and athletic and loved sport and had no time for literature. What we did share overcame all those differences: a sense of humour and an irrepressible delight in causing mischief.

"Yes, I wonder which she'll turn out to be." This was Pherecrates, boldly doing his bit.

"What do you mean 'which'?" I asked.

"Well," explained Pherecrates. "The name obviously stands for activity in the marketplace, so which is it to be, public affairs or shopping?" I was to find out soon enough.

"Clitagora is similar. Could stand for anything and I've heard she does. In fact, they say you can sometimes…" Fortunately the bride and attendant came back before Lysander went further. A wedding didn't seem a great time to be discussing whores, and I wasn't sure how Eucrates would react. He wasn't nearly as easy-going as his son Diodotus who had saved the Mytileneans.

I have to say Praxagora looked stunning in her long saffron robe, drooping golden earrings, a huge gold necklace and the most delicate beaded slippers you've ever seen. Most beautiful of all were her flashing eyes which shone through her veil and outsparkled her jewellery. Her appearance was greeted by a dirty chuckle from Lysander, a raised eyebrow from Pherecrates, a twinkle from Xanthias and a coughing fit from Eucrates. I suddenly felt proud of her.

She and I made our offerings and we sat down to the dinner of lamb and cakes. Eucrates insisted that the men and women sit at separate tables in accordance with tradition, which left Praxagora on her own to be served by Artemis while Xanthias served the three men. It all seemed a bit silly, so once everything was in place on the tables, I insisted Xanthias and Artemis sit down to eat with us. Lysander thought that was a great joke, but Pherecrates didn't even raise an eyebrow. I thought Eucrates was going to object, but he must have chosen not to make the day even more peculiar by having a row with the groom. I decided I would use his irritating combination of primness and girth in future plays.

Towards the end of the meal, prompted by Eucrates, Artemis completely removed Praxagora's veil, symbolically the most important part of the ceremony. We were both crowned with garlands and sprinkled with perfumes. I wished my mother had been alive; she would have been there, I'm sure. Lysander led the aphrodisiac hymns, which he seemed to know rather too well. Pherecrates and Eucrates joined in and, rather to my surprise, so did Xanthias, tunefully and with a pretty accurate pronunciation of words he was probably hearing for the first time. By the second or third choruses of each hymn he was leading us.

Now it was sweet throwing time again. Xanthias had distinct memories of this from his own entry to the house and his greeting from Ismenias. He picked up a large handful of sweets, gave me a fierce look and drew back his arm as if about to hurl them at me with all his force. Seeing my concern (I was cowering under a table), he gave a throaty chuckle and lobbed the sweets gently at my feet. That was the last bit of the ceremony before Artemis, still playing the part of Praxagora's mother, went to light the torch in the bedroom and returned to lead her off to bed.

When we got to the bedroom, Praxagora's thoughts immediately turned to sex, though not in the way I might have hoped. "You are not to sleep with that Artemis," she told me. I didn't think this was a good time to explain that the idea of sleeping with someone called Artemis was the reason I'd selected her, or that the one time I'd started to attempt it, she had such bad breath I had put it off for another day. I started to say, "Nor you with Xanthias," but thought better of it. Nevertheless, she got my gist and seemed deeply offended. "I've heard about you comic poets and what you write. You think all women are interested in is drinking and sex." This was fair comment. It's hard to make women on stage funny otherwise, though I did try a few years later.

"And you must stay away from whores. You know Alcibiades' wife divorced him for that." This wasn't quite true. Her attempt at divorce had backfired and anyway it had been escorts, not whores. Anyone in Athens would have known that, but again I didn't think I would help matters by putting her straight.

Her final shot was: "Go to the baths and have men if you just want a change sometime. I wouldn't be jealous. But if I find you going after other women there'll be trouble. Now do we understand each other?"

Whether it was the peculiar excitement of the day or the effect of this anti-erotic lecture I don't know, but we didn't have sex that night. Still, I soon learned that Praxagora had quite an appetite and was suspiciously accomplished for a young virgin from an island. I didn't visit Cunna for a few weeks.

# 12

The rehearsals for *The Babylonians* had gone off well. The plague had died down, most of the leading actors were still around and though the choruses had a lot of newcomers they were young and keen, so they not only learned quickly but added some clever ideas of their own.

The play was based on the story of how the new god Dionysus arrives in Thrace and King Lycurgus tries to suppress his worship, a theme recently used by Aeschylus in a tragedy and similar to one that I would use again myself when Euripides died. The chorus of Babylonian mill slaves represented our tribute-paying allies, showing the rotten way they were treated by Athenian politicians and how poorly they were represented by their own ambassadors. It gave me an opportunity to make fun of Cleon and his associates, the selfish allied leaders, and the gullibility of the Athenian Assembly. I also chucked in some quite specific accusations of taking bribes.

The Dionysia festival was very special. It went on for six days with processions, sacrifices and choral performances. On the first day, crowns of laurel were presented to the city's benefactors and there was a parade in full armour of boys whose fathers had been killed in the war, followed by the ritual presentation of their annual tribute by representatives of our allies. On each of the last five days there was a tragic trilogy and a satyr play followed by a comedy. Someone told me there were one thousand one hundred and sixty-five dancers involved in the choruses, all of them exempt from military service. I was glad I only had to direct twenty-four.

My play was on the fifth day of the festival, the fourth day of drama. It's hard to know whether it's better to be first or last in order to make the maximum impression on the judges, but you can be pretty sure there is nothing special about going fourth. The judging system is clever and complicated so as to avoid bribery and malpractice. Each of Athens' ten tribes sends in as many nominations for judges as they want which are then sifted and shuffled and put in ten sealed jars. The archon in charge selects one name from each jar and these ten are called forward to the front row and made to swear they will vote for the best plays and performers. At the end of the contest, each judge writes a list, giving his order of merit for the tragedies and for the comedies and puts it in another jar. The archon chooses five of the ten jars at random, and adds up their votes to come up with a winner, a second and a third for both tragedy and comedy.

I sensed it was going well from the audience's reaction. The slave chorus excelled in dancing as if they were working in a mill and my description of grasping public officials 'gaping like mussels on a barbecue' raised a good laugh. The next twenty-four hours passed slowly as I waited for the final plays and the judging, and when the time came, the judges seemed to be taking an awfully long time to go through their process, but eventually the order of merit was read out and I had won! I leaped up, sat down, sprang up again, turned in all directions and blushed like mad as I was summoned to the stage. The prize money went to the producer, but the convention was to share it around and the standard share for a winning author was quite substantial, at any rate enough to give me a little pocket money independent of my allowance and Praxagora's own money.

Sophocles wasn't there this time; I think he'd been too busy with wartime public duties to come up with a new trilogy. I did meet Euripides at the banquet afterwards and we chatted for a long time. He was physically unimpressive, not very tall, quite shabbily dressed even at the festival, and distinguished by a shaggy and permanently arched left eyebrow and sagging lips. I knew a bit about him, as did everyone else in Athens, as he was in the prime of his career. He'd been selected for the Dionysia a dozen times already and had won the tragedy competition twice in the last four years. His family were hereditary priests of Apollo Zosterius but had fallen on hard times and when she was widowed his mother ended up having to make a living as a greengrocer. He himself was quite an all-rounder. As a boy he had been selected as a dancer and torch bearer in major ceremonies and been a successful athlete; when he developed arthritis, he took up painting, as well as writing some of the most original tragedies Athens had ever seen. With his income from the two occupations, he had bought himself a large seaside estate on a small island off Salamis, two hours sailing from Athens, where it was thought he did much of his writing.

61

His most famous play to that point had been *Medea* but the *Andromache* he had written for this Dionysia was almost as good and had won him first prize, so we were the stars of the evening. He was kind enough to say my play was the funniest he'd seen in a long time. I told him I hoped to be able to write tragedies too and he was much more encouraging than Sophocles.

"It's become easier now to imagine someone doing both. If you go back to when I started in the business, it would have been impossible. Tragedies were all about two-dimensional characters saying conventional things in bombastic verse and comedies were still close to the old erotic village dances and chants. Now, thanks to the new generation of comic poets like you and Pherecrates and Eupolis, comedy is much closer to real life and tragedies are becoming more realistic too."

I wished he hadn't mentioned Bloody Eupolis and prompted him to say more about how tragedy was moving.

"Well, some of us are trying to get away from stylised interactions between humans and gods and home in on what the characters must actually have been thinking and feeling in the tragic situations in which they find themselves. We try to present real people, real motives and real misery. And we are beginning to acknowledge that women have feelings and motives and tragedy too, and aren't just props in the struggle between men and fate."

When he said, 'Some of us', I knew he really meant himself. Very few tragedians at that time shared his taste for realism and a lot of people thought it was inappropriate. It was generally felt this fear of the new had reduced his success rate, so this was a special triumph for him, though he was too modest about it for anyone to guess. We talked for a long time and arranged to meet again to share thoughts about our respective genres. I was feeling pretty smug as I left the theatre; not only had I won but I'd made a new friend and supporter out of one of the cleverest men in Athens.

Just when I thought things couldn't get much better, they suddenly got a lot worse. At the gate a figure moved out of the shadows. It looked a little familiar and it was. This was the first time I'd seen my father for about six years. He looked rather out of place in his rustic coat, and was obviously frustrated at having to wait till I left the banquet, but I was delighted he'd come and was a witness to my triumph. I felt I must have made him really proud.

"Well, this is a surprise, Father," I said. "What are you doing here? And why didn't you tell me you were coming?"

"It was a last-minute decision. Eucrates told me you had a play in the festival and asked me over. I haven't heard very good things about the way you conducted your wedding, by the way. Slaves eating with the bride and groom! By half Heracles, what next? Men and women at the same wedding tables? I've stayed with him the last three nights and I'm going home tomorrow. Of course, I'd like a word with you first." I thought he was about to congratulate me. His next words were, "Don't expect me to come and watch your nonsense again."

"Nonsense, Father! The judges didn't think so."

"Huh! I don't know what kind of people are judges nowadays but they should be ashamed of themselves. So should the whole city for tolerating this filthy trash."

"Filthy trash!"

"Filthy trash. Full of smut, innuendo, toilet humour, mockery of religion and a ridiculous plot. I'll bet you've upset Cleon and that won't do you any good. It's about time you got yourself a proper source of income, by half Heracles! I'm not going to support you any longer and Praxagora will manage her own dowry. She will make sure you and the slaves are fed and clothed but her father and I have agreed that if you want any spending money, you'll have to earn it yourself."

"But, Father, remember Solon's law, that if a son isn't taught a trade by his father, he is not obliged to care for his father in his old age. You haven't taught me one."

"The last thing I want is to have you caring for me in my old age, you dribbling moron. And anyway I'd be perfectly happy to teach you farming if you could just tear yourself away from this cesspool that Athens seems to have become."

He was pretty angry now and it was a relief to see Callistratus hurrying towards us. At least it was a relief till he opened his mouth. "Aristophanes, Aristophanes," he panted, eyebrows working overtime. "Oh, excuse me sir, I must tell Aristophanes Cleon is going to denounce me at the next Assembly. Be there. Please!"

My father said, "Bah!" which I think was short for 'Well, what did you expect, you idiot?' and we didn't even say goodbye. My self-satisfaction had turned to self-pity in record time. As I walked home to see if at least Praxagora would give me some praise and comfort I wondered what I could do to earn an income. I had no intention of giving up writing as my father expected me to, but while my share of the prizes might be good like that night, it was sporadic and of course there were going to be failures. Options were limited: no citizen would take paid employment with another for more than a day or two, say at harvest time; permanent public employment was mainly confined to slaves; army pay was small and irregular; and I had no skills other than writing. A lot of people got extra income by making things at home. The women in pretty much every household made clothes for themselves and the men, so if there was a high enough ratio of women to men, they might have a surplus to sell. We didn't. Lots made pottery for themselves and their neighbours. Some had simple metal-bashing operations. But of course any such business was under the control of the mistress of the house, who often did much of the work as well, and I wasn't sure if that really counted as the independent income my father expected. Nor had Praxagora suggested that she had any real interest in making things, even clothes, though that was all right if she was always willing to buy clothes for the household. I thought I'd better spend some time exploring possibilities, though I was not optimistic.

# 13

The praise and loving sympathy I had hoped for from Praxagora when I got home were not forthcoming. It seems my father had visited her during the day and they had agreed that I should be kept on a pretty tight rein and made to do something useful, which apparently didn't include writing comic poetry. Her only response to my win was to say that she hoped I made the most of it because I'd be too busy to do it again. I pressed her on what I was to be busy doing, but she seemed to have as little idea as I did. She didn't really care she said, and then asked me if my success had brought any prize money to contribute to the household. I argued that if the whole plan was for me to start getting an independent income, there wasn't much sense in me putting anything I earned straight back into housekeeping, but she said a prize wasn't really earnings and certainly wasn't reliable. Eventually she allowed me to keep half. It was just as well, as I'd spent the last of my father's final allowance.

We spent that night in separate beds, and in the morning, I started to look for income-earning ideas. I went straight to the Agora and spent hours wandering around, looking at all the different crafts represented in the stalls and wondering if I could be good at any of them.

Clothes and food seemed to occupy most of the market area, though there were plenty of specialist resellers of a wide variety of other things. Most of the clothes on sale were simple tunics and cloaks, but at two or three stalls, importers were selling fine robes and gowns from the East and their displays were as bright as the peacocks' tail feathers on a stall nearby. I didn't spend long looking at the clothes because that was Praxagora's responsibility. Whether we made a surplus to sell was entirely up to her and wouldn't get me an independent income. Weaving and spinning were largely women's work, and fulling and dyeing were dirty and required more strength and a less sensitive nose than I had.

There were some more masculine trades with their products on show. A row of stalls offered chopping-blocks, brooms, rulers, door bars, walking sticks, simple stools and chests and more. They all looked quite simple to make and I thought carpentry was something I could learn. I was a little less keen when I heard the prices being asked. It struck me that by the time you'd invested in tools, bought the wood, worked it and taken it down to the market, there wouldn't be a lot to show for your effort. I got into conversation with a man who was running a stall with a wide variety of wooden items for sale, and expressed my surprise at his low prices. "You're surprised!" he chuckled. "You should see the looks on the faces of the people who make this stuff when I tell them what I'll give them for it. They seem to expect that a couple of hours hacking away with a saw or chisel will make them as rich as Croesus. They don't realise just how many people are making the same objects with the same ideas. I have to keep my prices low to be able to sell anything at all, and of course I have to make it worth my time, so there's not much left for the makers."

"But surely some people can make a good living in woodwork? The Demosthenes family for instance seem to have done very well."

"Oh, that's different. They make luxury couches. You won't find any of that stuff round here. It's all very high quality and done on commission. They can charge a fortune because of their reputation. Not like this garbage." He kicked a wheelbarrow.

So, not clothes or carpentry then.

The next row of stalls sold metalwork. Some catered principally for the kitchen with sieves, skewers, meat hooks, tripods, trays and pans, others for farmers with pitchforks, shovels, crow bars, ploughs and bits for horses. The prices seemed a bit better than for woodwork, and none of the items seemed to display delicate craftsmanship, so presumably one could learn to make them quite quickly. On the other hand, you'd need to invest in more equipment and I imagined bashing hot metal with a heavy hammer might be a little taxing for someone my size. And Praxagora did not seem the sort of woman who would welcome a large furnace in the house.

The jewellery stalls came next, but I thought I'd leave that till later. I felt I was getting behind with my presents to Cunna and I planned to come back after lunch and get something to give her that evening. I had told Praxagora that I was going to a symposium at Lysander's that night and not to expect me home early, if at all. Lysander's symposiums were famous for the amount of wine consumed and the number of flute girls attending, but he wasn't giving one that night.

I moved to the pottery area, which had more stalls than either of the last two; making a little pottery for sale seemed to be a favoured occupation for a huge number of households. Some stalls were selling their own products while some were reselling the products of several potters. It was mainly household items, basic plates and mugs and bowls, with the occasional piece of glazed ware or a badly painted vase. The good painted vases were bought on commission and only appeared in the market second-hand. Even those weren't the best, which got better prices exported to Italy.

As I was standing at one of the stalls, the man next to me pulled a one obol piece out of his mouth – a lot of people used their mouth as a purse – and walked off with twenty-five small, glazed bowls! This, I thought, was worse than carpentry, which I confirmed with the stallholder. He was a reseller and had the same story to tell as the one I had just heard about woodwork. I asked specifically about lamps, because there was a stall nearby specialising in them at what seemed to be much better prices and he laughed. "I wouldn't get involved in that if I were you. That stall belongs to the family of Hyperbolus the politician. Their reputation for lamps goes back years and if anyone tries to compete with them, they just cut price until the new guys give up. They can afford to."

It was time to eat and the smell of baking bread drew me to the food area, conscious that all I'd achieved in the morning was to rule out the most common ways of getting a little income.

One of the things we discussed in drama class at school was why comedy often represented sellers and seldom makers, and the food area of the market provided an obvious reason. The cries of the vendors as they tried to draw attention to their wares were deafening and some of the insults they threw at each other were quite clever. In moments of high excitement, they were also prone to throw real things. The women bakers and the fruit and vegetable sellers were the loudest and funniest and it was strange to think Euripides' mother was once among them. The poultry stalls with eggs, live chickens and small game birds were almost as noisy as the vegetable sellers. Other meat was only sold here at festival times. Boeotian eels were in short supply at that time of year and the prices were too steep for me; the day was hot, so the remaining fish did not look very inviting. On days like that you really have to buy fresh fish down at the docks. I bought some hot bread and a leg of partridge from the bird stalls, and spent a little time trying to choose between the dozens of different types of vegetables, fruit and herbs on offer. The stalls were a kaleidoscope of colours, reds, oranges, purples and every shade of green. They offered a huge range of produce: cucumbers, onions, cress, radishes, celery, beans, beets, leeks, sprouts, olives, figs, gourds, apples, pomegranates, sage-apples, acorns and nuts. The herb stalls sold garlic, cloves, chervil, oregano, saffron, mustard, coriander, thyme, silphium, lavender and a whole lot of things I couldn't identify. I eventually settled for a stick of celery and some dried figs, washing the whole thing down with some very ordinary wine that claimed to be from Mende, but almost certainly wasn't.

In the afternoon I went from the manufactured goods to the services area. First to the sorceresses, some selling potions and magical cosmetics and medicines, all of which required special ingredients, growing conditions and mixing to be any good, and appropriate incantations to make them effective; others just selling prophecies and advice with no products to go with them. Their harsh tones and cackles in rough Asian languages rivalled the food area at times, though some were sitting quietly in front of tents in which they could prophesy and advise less publicly. I could have spent the afternoon watching their mixing rituals and listening to the chanting, but this seemed an even less suitable trade for me than the ones I'd seen in the morning, so I pressed on.

There were three or four huts selling shoes. Now there was a possibility. Basic shoes weren't all that complicated to make. You just cut the base round the shape of the customer's foot and then added one thong across the front of the foot and another that ran between the toes and tied round the ankle. Most of the shoemakers were slaves and they tended to work alone, even those with the same owner. I was just wondering why they all had their huts close together but still operated independently when I caught sight of Socrates and I knew the answer. Cobbling was a clean and physically undemanding occupation and people frequented the shops for conversation while watching their own and others' sandals and boots get made. That was probably why Socrates was going into Simon's hut. I could see the attraction of a nice quiet way to spend the day in interesting conversation, but wasn't sure if you could attract a regular client base if you only worked part-time as I intended to. I also wasn't sure I'd enjoy listening to someone like Socrates or the other sophists all day. I had found at Aspasia's that a little speculation about what the world is made of goes a long way.

I had a look at some of the other leather goods on offer in the area, whips, reins, dog-leads, wine skins, knapsacks, farming caps and so on, and thought most of that would require even less skill than shoemaking. On the other hand, I had learned in the morning that that probably meant less income too.

Next to the shoe huts were the barbers, similarly full of conversation but with larger and noisier groups. Now this really appealed. With the right blades and a bit of practice I could certainly learn to cut hair and trim beards and this was the sort of conversation I could enjoy. In fact, it would give me so much material for my writing, I could afford to work longer at it if I had to, though I still didn't plan to be full time. Of course there was one rather important drawback. Personal services like this were only ever provided by slaves. A citizen grooming, massaging or otherwise manhandling another citizen was very much frowned upon – except of course in the way of sex, and then the financial exchange had to be obscured. Still, it didn't mean I couldn't be the first to break that particular convention. I didn't mind competing with slaves because the amount their owners expected them to bring in for a day's work was more than I needed for spending money and I thought I might do rather well: the only barbershop run by a citizen and a slightly famous and very witty one at that! New jokes, puns and hilarious conversation guaranteed! Tragic parodies twice a month! Perhaps it would be such a draw that I could charge higher prices and only operate two or three times a week. My father would hate it, but there didn't seem any point trying to please him anyway.

I had half convinced myself that becoming a barber was not only feasible but a rather brilliant idea when I found myself back at the jewellery stalls. I thought I'd pretty much explored all possibilities and I'd already spent as much time in the market as I normally would in a year, so I decided to get Cunna's present. There was so much to choose from: rings, pins, brooches, crowns, necklaces, pendants, and a whole lot of items I couldn't name. Some of it was brilliantly fashioned; there were faience headbands, there were brightly coloured gems set on beaded silver wires, there was a large gold tiara with a huge amethyst set in the middle, all way beyond my price range, and even more beyond my capability of ever making them myself and not getting ripped off by a supplier. I spent most of what was left of my share of the winnings on a silver hairband for Cunna and headed off to Aspasia's, though it was way earlier than the time she was expecting me.

# 14

In the event, I was far too early and Aspasia told me Cunna wouldn't be free for a couple of hours. There was a serious looking man sitting writing at a table and she introduced us.

"This is Thucydides," she said. "He owns a gold mine and has distinguished himself as a general, but the thing you have in common is writing. He is trying to put together the whole story of this war. Thucydides, this is Aristophanes. He's our most promising new comic poet. Now, people come here for conversation, so you must tear yourself away from your writing for a while, Thucydides, and talk. Tell Aristophanes what led to this war. And you'll have to excuse me; I have a friend of my own I promised to entertain." Well, fair enough. She was still very attractive and probably a bit lonely after losing Pericles and Lysicles three years earlier.

"Well, if I must go through it with you," Thucydides began when she was out of the room, "the proximate causes were to do with the ultimate indefensibility of the Megarian Decree and the unfortunate but predictable troubles in Corfu, but really you can trace it all back to some fundamental principles that underpin the workings of mankind and his response to social, ecological and political imperatives."

"Principles?" I asked. I could probably have picked any of the other multisyllabic words he had used and it wouldn't have affected the conversation.

"Yes, the fundamental and undying principles of human organisation and social evolution. First, you have migration patterns, which are dictated by relative soil conditions and climate. People leave the barren for the fertile. They always have and they always will. Second, there is competition for control of the seas; naval power is vital for acquisition of colonies, for defending them and the homeland, and for securing the indubitable benefits of trade. For good or bad, we are condemned by our ecology to rely on control of the sea for almost all our grain and timber. Other states depend on other imports. Troy would have fallen in one year instead of ten if the Greeks hadn't had to spend so much time getting provisions, or perhaps if they had anticipated the challenges and managed them better. And, of course, the state makes a lot of money out of harbour taxes, so we need a port that offers security in order to maximise socially and economically beneficial traffic."

I wasn't going to argue so I thought I'd get him to focus on what actually mattered to most of us. "But why is it all blowing up now?"

"We are historically primed for a great and lengthy war. The tyrants who ruled Athens a hundred or so years ago were focussed on local issues. They also had a lot to fear from making the wrong decisions, so they ensured they were well advised and didn't get into situations which might strengthen internal opposition, which applies to most wars. Nowadays we have lost the art of policy consistency. When we don't like an idea, we are quick to find its faults, but when we do want something to happen, we don't plan for it but content ourselves with hoping it will work out." He spat out the last few words.

Of course much of this went over my head at the time, though it made sense a few years later when I read the whole of his book. In any event neither of us were keen to continue the conversation and it was a relief when he said, "If you'll excuse me, I was just in the middle of a very tricky passage. I'd just like to revise a speech I've been working on." I didn't mind and Aspasia clearly wasn't coming back, so I said fine, but the thought of spending the next two hours watching him chew his pen and write didn't appeal, so I asked if I could read some of the writing scattered across the table he was working at. He grunted and pushed a roll of papyrus towards me.

It turned out to be one of the things he had referred to as a proximate cause of the war, the debate at Athens between the Corinthians and their allies from Corfu who had revolted from them. Both cities were trying to get Athens onside by speaking at the Assembly. Corinth mainly relied on the point that encouraging revolts sets a terrible precedent and that Athens would suffer from it more than any other city, while the men from Corfu appealed directly to Athens' short-term self-interest. It was fascinating stuff and each party made its points in a lengthy speech, but I didn't think long speeches were the best way to present it. It would have been much better as a Contest – the sort of line-by-line point scoring that I had been producing for my plays. I asked one of Aspasia's slaves for pen and papyrus and came up with this:

Corinth: You should never encourage defections.
Corfu: We've always loved Athens at heart.
Corinth: We offered them free, fair elections.
Corfu: That wasn't much good for a start.
Corinth: We showed them our strength, just a sample.
Corfu: That didn't impress us at all.
Corinth: You'd be setting an awful example.
Corfu: You'd be causing dear Athens to fall.
Corinth: They've never been very supportive.
Corfu: You really should listen to me,
Corinth: Our attempts to make peace were abortive.
Corfu: Our navy controls the West Sea.

I thought this was pretty good and captured the spirit of the original while making it much more fun to read. I made a little note at the end, "choral dance of Athenian Assembly", where the chorus could comment on the quality of the arguments and take sides. I thought that with such a good set-up Thucydides could write that bit himself and I proudly took the piece over to where he was writing.

"What is it now?" he grumbled.

"I've had an idea how you could make the debate much livelier. Look!" I shoved my scrap of papyrus under his nose. He glanced at the format and scowled. He read a couple of lines and glowered.

"It's not about being lively," he growled. "It's about the unending and delicate balance between war and peace, between life and death, between loyalty and treachery, between ideals and pragmatism. The argument isn't a snappy exchange of views in doggerel, it's a well-thought-out battle of ideas and a search for the eternal verities behind temporal conflicts. Most of all it's about truth and falsehood, though you comic poets wouldn't understand the difference with your crazy fantasies and attacks on our leaders. I just hope you don't do us too much damage with your fabrications at such a critical time. In the meanwhile, some of us are trying to record the truth."

He was spitting again and would have gone on but just then Salabaccho came in and gave him a broad smile and an inviting sort of wiggle. To my surprise, he didn't wave her away while he finished whatever he was working on, but, hurling my scrap towards the fire, picked up his rolls of papyrus and his pen and followed her meekly out of the room. I was just retrieving my own scrap of papyrus, sure I could use some of those great lines in future plays, when Cunna came in to fetch me. "Sorry to be so long," she said. "Anyway, I'm very clean now." That was her way of telling me her previous friend had been Ariphrades.

We had a long chat before celebrating my win in the way she knew best. I told her about my father cutting me off and we discussed how I might make a living. I explained my idea of becoming a barber and she couldn't stop laughing. Her suggestion that I become a male escort made a funny sort of sense, because it would be part-time and required few skills other than conversation, which I was good at, and passivity, which I thought I could manage. A lot of male escorts did very well. On the other hand, it didn't really appeal and I think she was just being kind because I didn't think many clients would come up with generous gifts for a little bald fellow when there were much more handsome specimens available.

The more immediate problem was how I was going to afford to keep coming to see Cunna. Fortunately, she anticipated me there. "Look, I really enjoy your visits but until you get yourself sorted out financially, I understand you won't be able to keep giving me lovely presents like this gorgeous silver hairband. So, here's the deal: you can come anytime you like, but if there's a clash, my other friends will take priority, and we'll only make love when I decide we will." Such a sweet woman!

When I awoke, I remembered it was the day set for Cleon's denunciation of Callistratus in the Assembly.

# 15

From Aspasia's I went straight home to tell Praxagora about Lysander's symposium and my research at the market. I felt a little relieved to discover she wasn't there. Neither was Xanthias. Human Artemis was doing some dusting and when she saw me she said, "You cannot step into the same river twice." Perplexed but not wanting to argue, I set off for the Assembly. Even though it was Callistratus who was being denounced, I had to be there because everyone knew who was responsible for the plot and the words that had caused offence.

I saw Lysander heading for the Assembly too, and ran to catch up with him. I'd need moral support and I also needed him to get his story straight about the previous night. While we were waiting for proceedings to begin, I told him about my father cutting me off and my limited inspiration from spending a day in the market. Like Cunna, he thought the idea of me as a barber was hilarious, but in his unquenchably optimistic way, told me I'd be sure to find a solution. He said he'd take me down to the docks at the Peiraeus when the Assembly was over. He thought there might be something more suitable there.

First up after the prayers and sacrifice, was Cleisthenes, asking to be made an ambassador. He had been sitting with a group of his unpleasant friends and it was Aristodemus the Arsehole, who rose to introduce him and tell a few lies in his favour. Passive homosexuals like Cleisthenes and his friends are called arseholes for two reasons: first, they are dirty and smelly and second, that is the most active part of their bodies. Aristodemus was such an extreme example that Magnes used his name for the body part in his plays. Cleisthenes' staggering unpopularity led the Assembly to vote in his favour just to get rid of him. He and his group squealed with delight and with good reason. Ambassadors got paid three times as much as other state officials, lived in luxury on the public purse and had almost infinite scope for accepting bribes.

After Cleisthenes' little triumph, a few informers and sycophants came forward with improbable accusations against people they had a grudge against or who had refused to give in to blackmail, but the Assembly moved quickly through them and we came to the big one of the day, Cleon denouncing Callistratus.

As recognised defender of the city, an unofficial but powerful role secured by fawning on the people, lying about his achievements and paying for public events with money he had acquired improperly, Cleon had a big say on the Assembly's agenda, irrespective of what had been sent down from the Council. His PA Phanus had planned the whole performance. Cleon's chum Theorus spoke first, complaining that the play had let the city down in the eyes of our allies. Showing them as ill-treated slaves could only cause trouble and encourage revolts. Hyperbolus added some insults he must have picked up in the street. Cleon then got up himself and questioned my mother's nationality and thus my right to have my plays produced at all. I noticed how the real reason for Cleon's tantrum, the fact that I had suggested that he personally was crooked, wasn't mentioned. It was a clever attempt to make a private resentment a public cause. Sadly, the Assembly went along with it. Instead of throwing the motion out as they should have, they all looked to me to see how I'd explain myself. I decided to play for laughs and quoted Homer that no one really knows who their mother is. It went down well, but I wasn't the one being charged. The vote went narrowly against Callistratus, though it was just a denunciation with no penalties attached. Nevertheless, I was relieved that at the final banquet he'd agreed to produce my next play at the Lenaea and wondered just how restrained I'd have to be not to get him into trouble again.

I was feeling a bit battered as we started the longish walk down to the port, despite Lysander's stream of jokes and saucy banter with the passers-by. I made a mental note to get him to tell me the jokes again, when I could concentrate. Some of them might come in useful.

A short distance before we arrived at the Peiraeus, we passed a huge factory. It was the biggest workshop I'd ever seen, about the size of a large temple. Just as we arrived an oversized cart drew up, pulled by six oxen and filled with large timber discs. A young man appeared at the door of the workshop. "Hi there, Lysias," said Lysander. "This is Aristophanes, the famous playwright." I blushed, but that was all right because neither of them noticed. "Great! Catch you later, Aristomenes," was all Lysias seemed to have time to say before waving his arms to steer the delivery cart into the factory. I asked Lysander who that was and what the workshop made. He told me it made shields and Lysias was the elder of two sons of the famous craftsman Cephalus, who had been invited over from Sicily by Pericles to set up here. He was doing extremely well out of the war and was reputed to employ over a hundred slaves on the work. We peered in and I could see about a dozen teams of them walking round huge lathes to hollow out the shields, while others prepared the timber discs or fitted handles and straps or beat the bronze that fitted on the front. If I could own a business like that all my problems would be solved, but of course it would require a lot of capital to buy the slaves and the lathes.

More to make conversation than because it was a sensible topic, I asked Lysander if he thought it was altogether fair that foreigners like Cephalus and his sons could come here and make a fortune while citizens like me couldn't find a way of making even a basic income. "There's nothing to stop you," he replied. "Anyone can set up in any business – as long as it's not a slavish one like being a barber." He giggled annoyingly. "In fact these resident aliens contribute a lot to the city. They do most of the importing and exporting, quite a lot of the retail trade and they are over-represented in several manufacturing businesses like this one. That's why they are generally treated with more respect than non-resident barbarians and Egyptians, and allowed to come to various public events and festivals, though of course they can't vote or stand for public office. Some say the city's economy would collapse without them."

By this time we had arrived at the Peiraeus. The thing that always strikes you when you get there is the clever layout. Hippodamus built a grid system with all the streets intersecting at right angles, completely unlike anything in the city at the top of the hill, or as far as I know any other city, so it's really easy to find your way around.

It was busy down at the docks. Lots of triremes were being repaired and a few new ones were being built. Teams of carpenters were working on the hulls, workshops on the quayside were making canvas and ropes and teams of slaves were hauling wooden components to the ships that were close to being ready to sail, some of them on carts that had come all the way from workshops in the city. The quayside was buzzing with voices in a hundred different accents and a dozen languages. Merchants had come to meet their ships and grill the captains on the success of the voyage, the condition of the cargo and any liabilities incurred on the way. Those owners of transport vessels who were just investors and leased out their ships had come to check that their property had arrived intact. A general was inspecting some refitted triremes, looking to make sure nothing important would give way if there was fighting on the decks. In a noisy corner, importers were negotiating the sale of perfumes, ointments, rare dyes, top quality wines, fine wool and a range of other luxury items with resellers who would take them up to the market in the city.

Lysander wasn't very interested in all that activity. He directed our steps to a long row of tables. "These are the money changers and lenders," he said. "You might find this interesting."

The main activity of the slaves working the banking tables seemed to be weighing. There were a lot of foreigners in town for the Dionysia and the start of the trading season. They brought coins of all types from all over the place which had to be assayed and weighed carefully before exchanging them for our beloved drachmas and obols with Athene on one side and an owl on the other. Burly slaves stood around the tables and occasionally a merchant would approach one of them and the banker would produce a bit of papyrus and, after a bit of discussion and writing, the merchant would hand over a bundle for safekeeping. Interesting, I thought, but not very relevant to my problems. If I was going to break into a career that conventionally belonged to slaves, I'd much rather be a barber.

I was musing on this while Lysander chatted with one of the banking slaves when I was tapped on the shoulder. I spun round to see a well-padded farmer carrying a smallish knapsack and a very large oar. "Excuse me, mate," he said. "Any idea when the fleet sails for the Aetolia campaign?" I couldn't enlighten him, not being aware there was an Aetolia campaign.

"I wish they'd bloody hurry up. I can't go back to my farm till the fucking Spartans piss off and I can't take another day in the city with my wife's family. I guess I'll just fart around here until some nancy boy makes up his pathetic apology for a mind." He turned his back and I watched him go, thinking what an impressive character he was. Salt of the earth farming guy, no time for the ways of the city, will take the initiative to try to get ahead. I decided not to tell him that buying his own oar was a waste, though

I knew he'd soon find out. Each trireme was fitted with two hundred oars, one hundred and seventy for the rowers and thirty spare. But I also knew he'd take that in his stride, bounce back and find other improbable short-cuts to getting what he wanted. He'd make an excellent comic hero.

I turned back to Lysander, who was deep in conversation at one of the tables. "Any news?" he was asking.

"We know they've collected the cargo and were ready to sail back a few days ago, so they should be here tomorrow or soon after."

"And the cargo was all right?"

"Excellent, I understand."

"And the weather good?"

"Seems pretty settled."

"So we should be looking forward to a good return."

"Yes, you'll get your fifty percent profit."

I had no idea what this was about, but fifty percent profit sounded interesting, so I asked Lysander to explain.

"Well, the merchants who import products and sell them here often can't afford to buy and run their own ships and, even if they could afford one of their own, one bad storm and they'd be completely wiped out. So they get other people to finance the voyage and pay them a very handsome return when the cargo arrives."

"And if it doesn't arrive?"

"You win some, you lose some," Lysander shrugged. "The reason returns are so good is that every now and again you lose all your money. Smart investors like me like to have a little invested in three or four ship voyages. That way, if one goes down, you make enough from the rest to cover your losses."

This sounded a rather undemanding way to earn money so I thought I might give it a go, perhaps putting a little of the money I had left into three or four ships as Lysander advised. "How do you set about it?"

"Oh, that's simple. You decide how much you want to invest and then you talk to those people over there," waving at where the merchants were congregating, "and work out which deal sounds most attractive in terms of profit and risk. Some of the merchants only take large amounts and like to have just one or two investors backing any voyage; others syndicate the finance between lots of small investors. You could get in on a reasonable voyage for two hundred drachmae if you wanted to."

As this was a lot more money than I had left, I nodded wisely and made a mental note to remember to come back here next time I had some winnings. We were just turning to go, when Xanthias came hurtling towards us. His Greek had not improved much from the state of complete ignorance he was in when he arrived, but he had obviously been coached in the three words he kept repeating at random: "Call-up. Tomorrow. Aetolia. Tomorrow. Call-up. Aetolia. Aetolia."

# 16

Athens seemed to be putting quite a lot of troops in the field that summer, but my tribe must have been suffering badly for me to be nominated so soon after the Mytilene campaign. This time it wasn't just a question of showing up and being given an oar. I was to go as a hoplite, which meant I had to buy a full set of armour, as I discovered when Xanthias pressed a list and some money into my hand. Praxagora had written: 'Shield, helmet, leather corselet, spear, short sword, neck guards, greaves.' I had a spear and shield from my military training a few years earlier, and I toyed with the idea of using them and telling Praxagora I had bought new ones so I could keep more of the eighty drachmae she had sent me, but I remembered the trouble I had had lifting the shield and really didn't want to have to lug the great round bronze-covered lump of wood on a long land campaign. I conveyed this to Lysander and we stopped at the shield factory on the way back.

"Sorry, can't help you," was Lysias reply to my enquiry. "All our shields are the same size. Of course they are heavy. They are meant to save your life. You wouldn't want something flimsy, would you? Oh, wait a minute; my brother was organising some children's shields for the war orphan parade. I'll see if there are any spare."

He went back into the factory and, after a bit of shouting, re-emerged with a shield that was too small even for me. The disc would look ridiculous piled up near other ones. I weighed this up against the thought of carrying a normal shield all over Greece and, comforting myself with the thought that even if more of my body would be exposed than I would like, the actual area exposed would make a smaller target than it did for most people, I bought it. I started rolling it up the hill towards the city, but Xanthias, clearly unimpressed, picked it up as if it was made of feathers and walked along, swinging it merrily on one arm.

With a bit of help from Lysander it was easy to find suppliers of the rest of the bronze and leather pieces near the marketplace, and a couple of hours after Xanthias had found me we were home again with all the equipment and nineteen drachmae in change. I offered Praxagora eleven, thinking at least I could put aside a little spending money for my return. She inspected the armour carefully and said, "I think you must have miscalculated. You have another eight drachmae somewhere." She seemed neither surprised nor offended and the farewell kiss she gave me was truly affectionate. "Take good care of yourself. Be honourable and brave, but not foolish. And if you conquer any cities, treat the women with respect. When you get back, we'll have a long chat about everything." I took that as a threat.

This time the rowing was done by the lighter armed troops, spearmen, archers and so on, and as a hoplite with full armour I wasn't expected to contribute. My offer to keep time with some songs was cheerfully accepted by General Demosthenes whose trireme I was on. He said we might as well use a professional and told the official piper to stand down. He asked me to make it as loud as I could so the other ships could hear. I couldn't keep that up for long, but, at least for the benefit of those nearby, I ran through my repertoire of old favourites and some of the new material I had been putting together for *The Acharnians* and *Fast Food Cooks* which I had been working on. When we put ashore on the first evening, Demosthenes asked all the ship captains to send their pipers to learn new tunes from me and I spent two hours teaching them a few basic songs that were easy to remember and perform.

We cruised round the Peloponnese for a couple of weeks before landing to attack a place I'd never heard of called Leucas, which was on a peninsula. We were joined by various allies from the area and there were so many of us the Leucadians just sat there while we destroyed their crops and orchards and built a wall to cut their city off from the land behind it. I saw no action at all. I wasn't sure whether to be disappointed or relieved.

Our troops then met up with the main army under Nicias and we attacked Tanagra, again with speedy success and not much fighting. There didn't seem much agreement about what we were going to do next, though the original plan we'd been called up for, to attack Aetolia, hadn't been abandoned and our local allies the Messenians were quite insistent we went ahead. In the end it was agreed that Nicias would take his troops back to Athens while the rest of us would stay and fight under Demosthenes.

The evening before Nicias' troops were due to leave, one of his hoplites came round our camp calling my name. When I identified myself, he told me he had a message for me from Pherecrates. I stuck my hand out for it, but it seemed he was scared of losing it, so he had left it in his camp. We were under strict instructions to have our belongings with us at all times to be ready for sudden action, so I picked up my armour and rucksack and followed him over to where Nicias' men were based.

My greeting was rough but friendly. "So Demosthenes is trying to get rid of you then."

"Yes, he thought I should take over you lot from Nicias. Teach you a few things."

"Sorry mate, we only fight under people with hair."

"You should join the Spartans then. They're much hairier."

"You're that bloody poet, aren't you? I recognise your sense of humour."

Smiles and murmurs of "oh, yes" ran round the group of men and I felt confident enough to squat down beside them and see what Pherecrates had to say. His message was full of affectionate kindness and good news:

*'My dearest funny old man. I hope this finds you not only alive and uninjured but in the sort of high spirits which can keep up the morale of your fellows. If not, I trust this message will restore them. First, the Cleon fiasco is over. He has decided not to bring a personal suit against you or Callistratus. I suspect this is because he thought he might lose, but you need to take this little episode as a serious warning. Callistratus still mutters about how he gave you too much scope for mischief. He is still going to produce* The Acharnians *for you. Congratulations, by the way. It got up for the Lenaea. And in case you haven't heard,* Fast Food Cooks *was accepted for the Dionysia. Callistratus wasn't going to risk you twice in one year, so he has got Antimachus to take it on. You'll have a busy time when you get back. Stay brave and safe, Ph.'*

He was right about lifting my spirits. Having two plays accepted for production in the same year was very special, especially for a relative newcomer, and having Cleon off our backs was a relief. There were just two things bothering me. When I had offered both plays to Callistratus we agreed that *The Acharnians*, set in contemporary Athens and with a strong

83

message in favour of peace, was right for the Dionysia. *Fast Food Cooks* was just escapist nonsense, in which a group of street food cooks hear the underworld is a great place to be, but when they get there, they are disappointed with the food; that would be fine for the Lenaea. I wondered why he'd changed his mind and guessed he had decided not to risk me at the Dionysia again but still wanted to produce the better play himself. The second worry was Antimachus; he always took a lot of persuading that it was his turn to spend some of his wealth for the city. Funding an evening of plays was one of the cheaper options and he had chosen it under similar pressure before. While anxious to ensure he got the credit for the exercise, he tended to cut corners in the production and didn't share the winnings as much as protocol and kindness dictated. Still, at least I had a producer and it was good of Callistratus to find me one when he could have just walked away.

I was sitting occupied with these thoughts and reading the message again when everyone around me stood up and picked up their baggage and equipment. I did the same and was heading back to rejoin Demosthenes' army when a loud voice shouted, "Hey, you there! Little bald guy! Get over there with the hoplites and move!"

My attempt to explain that I was in the other army had not progressed beyond "But, sir…" when it was met with "Any talking and I'll have you flogged." I chose to keep quiet.

It seemed Nicias had decided to move out at night to minimise the chances of the enemy attacking his troops on their way to the ships that were to take them back to Athens. The ploy worked and we got to the coast safely after a couple of days' march. People laughed at my little shield but right then I wouldn't have changed it for the world. On the voyage home I decided it would be better not to draw attention to myself by singing as the men would be bound to remember that I hadn't sailed out with them, so I sat and brooded about Cleon and about trying to develop some sort of relationship with Praxagora. Cleon deserved a play to himself and I thought I'd do that next, though I knew I might struggle to find a producer. I had less idea what to do about my wife. I was prepared to try to find income, and though I was not prepared to give up Cunna or writing, I'd be very discreet about Cunna. I wouldn't be able to conceal writing, which not only required a quiet place to create but also involved dozens of engagements for proposals, script conferences, prop purchasing, rehearsals and so on which I'd never be able to explain away. Mainly I wanted a settled, affectionate home life without constant competition for supremacy, so I thought I'd give way on everything else.

When we got back to the Peiraeus and were walking up to the city, we heard what had happened to the troops that had stayed behind with Demosthenes. About a dozen local tribes and villages had come to help the Aetolians and had placed themselves on the hills around Demosthenes' army, making unpredictable raids on the camp and setting up ambushes to cut them off whenever any of them tried to move. About a third of the men I had left behind in camp when I went to get Pherecrates' message would not be coming home. Demosthenes himself was too scared to come back to Athens, fearing punishment for his failure, but quickly redeemed himself with a couple of more successful campaigns. Even though I hadn't intended to leave, I had a strong sense of guilt that I had in effect run away. Then it occurred to me that dear old Artemis must have been looking after me and she might be preserving me for something special. I resolved to work extra hard at the political and moral lessons in my plays to justify her confidence. *The Acharnians* would be my first demonstration.

When I finally got home, having trudged up the hill in my heavy armour and gone out of my way to avoid the social offence of appearing armed in the marketplace, I found Human Artemis asleep on a couch. She told me Praxagora was out. I called for Xanthias. He was out too.

# 17

I lay down on my couch for a couple of hours, tired out after the campaign, the voyage and the hike home. I couldn't sleep and decided I might as well head down to the theatre to see if I could find Antimachus and work out who was going to do what to get *Fast Food Cooks* ready for the Dionysia. Praxagora and Xanthias still weren't back.

Antimachus told me I'd done my bit and could leave the rest to him, which made me very suspicious he was going to do it on the cheap – probably just three actors, two of them amateurs, few props, weak costumes and not much scenery. In fact he'd probably suspend his actors on the crane to avoid the cost of an upper storey. But I couldn't do anything about that for the present and it meant I could really concentrate on *The Acharnians*. I'd try to get back some control of *Fast Food Cooks* after the Lenaea.

On the way back near the Agora I saw Xanthias in the distance with a woman in a veil that covered most of her face. They seemed to be heading in my direction, so I ran to catch up, but Xanthias turned round and saw me and said something to the woman who hurried off. Xanthias charged up to greet me with his usual enthusiasm and we made our way home, Xanthias stopping to admire something every now and then as if he was in no hurry to get there. Praxagora was home when we arrived.

I had forgotten just how gorgeous she was. Her lovely dark eyes sparkled as she hugged and kissed me and told me how worried she'd been while I was away. She asked me to tell her all about the campaign and I told her about most of it, but left out Artemis' brilliant decision to have me sent home early. I asked her what she'd been up to and told her what Pherecrates had said about her name meaning either shopping or public affairs. I added that she didn't seem very interested in public affairs, so I had thought of calling her The Shopper – purely in the way of affection of course.

"Well, you can if you like," she smiled, "but actually I don't spend a lot of time shopping. I've been listening to the philosophers."

"Is that what you were doing this morning when I got back?"

"Yes. I was looking for a change. I am a bit bored of Gorgias and Protagoras, and Socrates only talks to men." Who could blame him? His wife Xanthippe had a reputation as the shrillest old crone in Athens and they say he took up public philosophy just to get out of the house. "Artemis found out that today Cratylus was speaking about instability, so I went along. It was really interesting. You should come and listen to him sometime. You know Heraclitus said that you can't step in the same river twice?"

"Of course." I was bluffing.

"Cratylus goes further. He says you can't even step in it once. Even once! How about that? It all makes sense when you think about it."

Not to me it didn't, and I rather doubted if it made sense to her, but her eyes were still sparkling and at least I knew where Human Artemis had got her little saying from. I thought I'd better show I could be sympathetic but masterly. "You are welcome to listen to as many philosophers as you like," I told her, as firmly as I could, "but do remember a lot of them are charlatans just looking for sponsorship, and I don't think that would be a good use of your dowry. And you mustn't go out without an escort."

"Oh, I always take Xanthias. He's lovely. I've been teaching him Greek. No success at speaking yet, I'm afraid, but you'd be surprised how much he seems to understand. Now, my dear, it's time to discuss how we are going to manage our little household." I was not convinced by the 'we' but it was nice of her to take me into her confidence. "I've decided you can continue writing on two conditions. First, you still try to find other sources of income, and second, if you have no wins in any period of two years, you give up. You've already made a mark with your first two plays and not many people can say that. There's no point embarrassing yourself if you can't stay at that level. There might be other things you could be good at."

"That sounds fair," I said. "If I can't keep winning, I wouldn't want to keep composing. I'll become a barber or something."

She shuddered slightly but continued, "Now, as for finance, we've agreed that I'll pay for everything for the household, and if you want any spending money you have to earn it yourself. Well, you are off to a good start; you must have saved about twenty-seven drachmae from your army pay. That should keep you going for a while." In fact I had saved exactly twenty-seven drachmae. "I will, of course, consider any future requests for spending money, but you will have to account for them. Now to important business. Now that you are home and shouldn't be called up again for a while, and now we've settled the financial arrangements, we must start planning for a family. I want at least five children. Three boys, two girls."

"I shall do my best to contribute."

Our relationship seemed to have taken an important turn for the better.

A couple of days later, I was at home working on *The Acharnians* when I remembered I'd promised Cunna I'd put a piggy joke in my next play. I wasn't quite sure how widespread the use of the term was and sat staring at nothing for a while, wondering whether I should take the risk with it. Xanthias saw my lost look and enquired vigorously with his shoulders and hands what the problem was. I saw no chance of making him understand but amused myself by pointing to my papyrus, my private parts and those of Human Artemis who happened to come by. He gave a broad grin and ran out of the room.

I was still writing an hour or so later when Xanthias ran back in, the grin on his face even broader than when he left. "Pork sword!" he cried, roaring with laughter. "Barbecue spit!" These were the first recognisable words I'd heard from him since he accosted me in the slave market, other than the ones he had been taught about my call-up. I was beginning to guess what he was on about and "Ship's mast!" and "Persian sausage!" confirmed those suspicions. I thought it was a brave attempt, but he seemed to have missed the whole point – my gesture towards Human Artemis. I need not have worried. His next words were "Treasure chest! Garden! Shaving place! Piggy! Little box! Cooking pot! Sausage bracelet!" Piggy was all I needed to hear, but I found it hard to get back to work for wondering how Xanthias had got his information and hoping it didn't rebound on me in some way.

I worked really hard on *The Acharnians*, knowing I would have to make it a success if I was to be able to produce plays in my own name, and that the attack on Cleon I had in mind would not find another producer to take it on. Callistratus had already rejected my first draft because it had three relatively inoffensive references to Cleon in it. He had treated me well so I didn't want to upset him and I decided to give the lines directly to Philonides, who was now leading the chorus, after the rehearsals were over, without putting them in the copy of the script that Callistratus had, hoping he wouldn't notice on the night. He had brought in Philonides to co-produce, probably wanting to share the blame around if things got nasty again, but he explained it more positively: "Look, this is going to be huge," demonstrating 'huge' with his eyebrows. "We're going to have five actors, three doors and a couple of quick mask changes. We've got Bronchus as the lead and Archinous will play the soldier and Euripides. The props and costumes will be the best and most original this stage has ever seen, and you are going to devise your most dramatic songs and dances yet. Of course we need extra help with the production. You'll like Philonides. He might even produce for you in future."

His enthusiasm redoubled mine. With nothing to do for *Fast Food Cooks* for the time being, I lived, slept and breathed *The Acharnians* for the next four months.

## 18

As *The Acharnians* was one of my cleverest plots, I'll explain it in detail. Those who know the play as well as it deserves to be known can skip this chapter. Those who know Greek comedy but have either overlooked or forgotten this masterpiece will enjoy being reminded of it. If there are any who know nothing about Greek comedy, they had better pay attention.

My hero, Dicaeopolis, was the farmer I had met at the Peiraeus the day of my call-up, a salt-of-the earth type of the old and rather rough school, who gets so fed up with the failure of politicians to put an end to a war they should never have started that he makes his own private peace with Sparta. Bronchus was brilliant in the first scene, waiting impatiently for the Assembly to start and declaiming in a voice that could have been heard at Marathon, "I sigh, I yawn, I stretch, I fart, I fiddle, I scribble, I scratch, I do sums."

Various ridiculous speakers come forward to address the Assembly, including Amphitheus, a private peace-making entrepreneur, whose offer to make peace is rebutted when he asks to have his expenses covered; some ambassadors who have embezzled a vast amount of public funds; and a Persian dignitary accompanied by a couple of eunuchs who turn out to be two well-known effeminate Athenians in disguise. After the Assembly is over, Dicaeopolis engages Amphitheus to make a private peace.

The chorus is a mob of aged farmers and charcoal burners from Acharnae, tough veterans of past wars who hate the Spartans for destroying their farms and who also hate anyone who talks peace. Most of all they hate being forced to live in the city. They chase Amphitheus, but can't stop him returning with Dicaeopolis' peace. Dicaeopolis enters with his wife, daughter and two slaves carrying a large phallus for a private celebration of the Rural Dionysia, beginning with a small parade outside his own house, prayers to Dionysus and a song to the phallus about the joys of sexual opportunism. They are attacked by the chorus. Parodying Euripides'

*Telephus* in which the hero takes a child hostage in order to be allowed to speak in favour of peace, Dicaeopolis grabs a basket of Acharnian charcoal, their main source of revenue, and demands the old men leave him alone. They agree that if he will only spare the charcoal, they will allow him to make a speech advocating peace.

Needing help with the speech, Dicaeopolis goes to Euripides' house, where a slave explains that physically the tragedian is at home composing tragedies but mentally he is out collecting 'versicles.' After the slave has come up with a few more excuses, Euripides has himself wheeled out on a couch. Dicaeopolis asks him for some rags like those worn by tragic heroes so that he can make a powerful, impassioned speech to the chorus. Euripides sorts through a selection of rags worn by his heroes and they settle on Telephus' clothes. Dicaeopolis adds a beanie, a cane, a bottle and a sponge, the better to fool the chorus, and of course his final request is for the vegetables and chervil that Euripides' mother used to sell.

All set up for a tragic speech, Dicaeopolis gives his reasons for opposing the war: he says it wasn't the Spartans' fault; the real reason was that some drunken Athenian hooligans kidnapped a whore from Megara on the instructions of Alcibiades and the Megarians took two of Aspasia's escorts in revenge. So, the great Pericles thundered his decree banning the Megarians from our markets. The Spartans asked us to rescind it and relieve the Megarians, but we wouldn't, so there was war. (This wasn't quite how Thucydides liked to explain it, but it was much more interesting. He'll never make it as a popular writer).

For the Contest, I introduced a professional soldier called Lamachus who terrifies Dicaeopolis with his martial dress. Dicaeopolis persuades Lamachus to give him his shield and a plume and uses the latter to make himself vomit into the former. He complains about elected generals doing nothing for their pay, while people like the Acharnians fight but never get to be elected to anything. Lamachus can't put up much of an argument, the rest of the chorus is won over and Dicaeopolis announces that he will set up a market with all the luxuries of peace and open to everyone except Lamachus. He and Lamachus retire to their separate houses.

I was ambitious with the Address: I started with the usual anapaests (ti-ti-tum) but used cretics in the ode and the antode (tum-ti-tum) to give a more emphatic feeling than the more typical Aeolic metres (tum-ti-ti-tum-ti-tum). Later on I was to come up with my own variation on the Aeolic which was better still and it was named for me: (tum-ti-ti-tum-ti-tum-tum). Callistratus' fear of Cleon meant Philonides had taken over as chorus leader and he starts by lavishing exaggerated praise upon the playwright of the *The Babylonians* for warning the people about being deceived by flatterers. I made it quite clear we were not criticising the city itself for its gullibility but the "wicked little men" who were misleading them. People are coming from far and wide to see his plays, Philonides sang, and he'll always give you the best advice, unlike some people we could mention (he did actually mention Cleon in the performance, though not in Callistratus' copy of the script). He goes on to lament the ill treatment that old men like the chorus suffer at the hands of slick lawyers, suggesting that in future old men should prosecute old men and young ones the young. This powerful, though irrelevant, argument brings over the rest of the chorus.

The Farcical Scenes start with Dicaeopolis setting up his private market. Various minor characters come and go and I got in my 'piggy' joke when a starving Megarian trades his famished daughters, disguised as piglets, for the garlic and salt in which Megara had abounded in pre-war days but now lacked. The daughters were virtually non-speaking parts, though they grunted a bit and wiggled suggestively a lot. They were played by young boys with a snout on their masks and their 'piggies' painted on their leotards, which were displayed at all the right moments to get the most out of the pun. The farmer promises they'll grow pubic hair like their mother and says they should be sacrificed to Aphrodite, most apt for piggies.

Dicaeopolis refuses to share his peace with people who have done nothing to work for it. An informer or sycophant, distinguished by having no phallus on his costume, tries to confiscate the piglets and is driven off by Dicaeopolis. "You need a wick to be an informer," he tells him. Dercetes, the well-known war-hawk, has had his pair of oxen rustled, and begs for a slice of the peace but is turned away. The hero does agree to trade with a Boeotian, securing one of their famous eels in exchange for another Athenian informer, but when a slave brings orders for thrushes and an eel from Lamachus, Dicaeopolis refuses to deal with him and sets his household to work preparing a massive feast. (About here I got in a dig at Antimachus for his meanness last time he produced a play, hoping that would encourage a bit more generosity at this year's Dionysia. It didn't work.)

A best man and a bridesmaid come and offer Dicaeopolis some meat if the groom can have a bit of the peace so as to enjoy his new wife. When Dicaeopolis refuses, the bridesmaid whispers the bride's very personal reason for keeping a particular part of her husband at home, so he gives them some of his peace and pretends to pour something out from the rolled-up treaty for the bride to rub on the relevant part of her husband.

Other visitors come and go before two heralds arrive, one calling Lamachus to war in the snow, the other calling Dicaeopolis and a couple of flute girls who are now fluttering around him to a dinner party with the Priest of Dionysus. Lamachus returns from the war and there is a quick-fire exchange on their respective situations. Here's a sample:

Lamachus: "Oh! Ah! Support my injured leg, please! Ah! Ow! Hold it tenderly, my friends!"

Dicaeopolis: "Oh, my little lovelies, grab on to this, both of you!"

Lamachus: "That blow with the stone made me dizzy; my sight grows dim. I must lie down. I can do nothing in this darkness."

Dicaeopolis: "I want to lie down too; I can hardly contain myself and there are lots of things I can do in the darkness."

Lamachus: "Take me to surgeon, Pittalus."

Dicaeopolis: "Take me to the festival judges. Where is the king of the feast? Hoy, that's my wineskin!"

The finale is the usual feast. Dicaeopolis clamours cheerfully for the wine skin he has won in a drinking competition, while Lamachus is carried off. The chorus hail Dicaeopolis.

Pretty good, you must admit.

# 19

The audience thought it was pretty good too, and, more important, so did the judges. The biggest laughs were at the Euripides scenes, which Archinous played brilliantly, and at the piggy jokes and the Dance of the Little Piggies. Bronchus' Dicaeopolis won the acting prize. He was great but I hoped the judges were also rewarding the character, so typical of the best of our stock. The audience was strangely quiet during the Address and murmured a lot when it finished, but one or two cheers and no boos seemed a good sign and it was.

When the judges read out the winners and I made my way to the stage with Philonides, I shot Callistratus a glance of triumph, expecting to see a smile or wave in return. I had never seen him look so cross or his eyebrows so eloquent. As we made our way to the celebratory banquet he hissed, "Different script for Philonides, eh? You thought I wouldn't notice, did you? Well, that's it as far as I'm concerned. If I can't trust you not to invite trouble, you can find someone else to produce your damn plays." I was planning to do that anyway after *Fast Food Cooks*, but it was a sad break in what had been a very productive relationship.

I would have liked to talk to Pherecrates about it, but he was overseas on an embassy. He had heard about the play though, and sent me a message of congratulations which concluded with the words:

*I presume you took my advice not to attack Cleon. It's just not worth the risk.*

More upsetting was a note from Cunna the day after the festival:

*Aspasia is very displeased about your explanation of the start of the war. Why on earth did you do that? I'll let you know when it's safe to come back, but it won't be soon, I fear. Big cuddles, C*

I consoled myself with the thought that at least my writing was going well: two firsts and a second with my first three plays. I was developing my own style, somewhere between the vulgarity of Cratinus, whom I otherwise admired very much, and the slicker verse of Bloody Eupolis. I was more confident in scripting choral dances and more willing to experiment with them, which I had learned came more easily when I was a bit tipsy. My Addresses were starting to have the impact on political sentiment I had aimed for when I took up writing. In short, I had started to assume my early successes were bound to continue.

They didn't. The production of *Fast Food Cooks* at the Dionysia was a fiasco. I had tried hard to intervene, but Antimachus paid no attention to my suggestions and told the cast and chorus not to listen to me either. The shortage of actors meant a lot of awkward delays while they changed masks and when the lead was supposed to be upstairs looking down at Hades, he had such trouble balancing on the crane for the lack of an upper storey that he forgot his lines. My only consolation was that Bloody Eupolis was unplaced.

Antimachus offered me a share of the third prize which was so small I turned it down rather than have to explain it to Praxagora, and of course he was too mean to produce a banquet. On the way home I stopped at the pub for company and a badly needed drink. It was almost empty of course; it was late and people had already been celebrating for six days. The small studious man was in his usual corner and leapt up when he saw me.

"A privilege to see you here again, Aristophanes! Why aren't you celebrating? I thought *Fast Food Cooks* was brilliant. It deserved to win. My name is Criticus by the way." Shame you weren't on the judging panel, I thought, but I didn't feel like explaining about Antimachus.

"We'll have our final dinner another night. Thorus hurt himself on the crane," I lied.

"Anyway, congratulations. The way the Celebration at the end echoed the paradigmatic themes of the Contest, providing a sort of nuanced metrical architecture that neatly framed, or should I say counterpointed, the more intense tones of the Address, was just brilliant. How did you think of it?"

"Oh, it just sort of came to me, you know."

"And the prosody of those mysterious long aeolics in the Antode created exactly the right psycho-emotional setting for the conceptualisation of Hades-based cuisine."

"I was wondering if you'd pick that up."

"You've been listening to Thrasymachus, haven't you? Come on now, I know."

"Well, sometimes." I was wondering who this Thrasymachus was, presumably some species of philosopher.

"I could tell. You deploy your metaphors in exactly the way he teaches young politicians to. It's ironic that you use them to make fun of politicians."

"Indeed."

"I loved that line about the underworld being better because that's where the most loaded end of the scales always heads for."

At least he had noticed I was a comic poet. I had finished my wine by now and was turning to get another when I saw the publican coming towards us. He walked straight past to a dark corner, where he whispered to someone I had not noticed before, who got up and followed him back to the bar. The man was short and hunched and his clothes were old and shabby. I caught a glimpse of his face as he passed and the sagging lips and permanently arched left eyebrow told me it was Euripides. I had been meaning to talk to him since *The Acharnians* to make sure he wasn't too upset by the way he'd been portrayed and I jumped up as he passed, but he avoided my eyes, quickened his step and disappeared through a door behind the bar. As I was already standing and wasn't keen to hear more of Criticus' comments, I said goodbye.

"Goodbye, Aristophanes, and thank you. It's always great to hear what you have to say. I learn so much. By the way, I've finished the eighth draft of my own play. Do you think eight drafts is enough?" I knew he was going to ask me to read it.

"Up to you. I always believe in fifteen, unless it's really complex. Sorry, must get home now. Promised the wife, you know."

A few days later I saw Euripides in the street and he seemed even keener to talk to me than I was to him. It was around midday, so we got ourselves honey cakes and some wine and sat on a bench in a secluded corner of the marketplace.

"I'm sorry," we both began at once.

"You go." We both laughed.

"No, you." We were forming a wonderful impromptu chorus but he nodded to me, so I told him I hoped he wasn't offended by the port in *The Acharnians*. He wasn't. He said he loved it and said I could pu on stage as often as I liked, though he'd rather I didn't mention his mc I agreed and didn't mention her again for years.

"So what were you saying sorry to me about?" I asked.

"I know you recognised me in the pub the other night and I preter not to see you, so I thought I should explain." He hesitated for what see ages before resuming in a nervous tone I hadn't heard from him bef "I've always had a difficult time with women. It's not something I find e to talk about. Choerine, that's my second wife you know, is being unfaitl just like Melito was before I gave her away to the actor I should never h introduced her to. I never get any attention at home, which is a probl because I seem to have an unusually strong sex drive. I can't bear doin; with boys and men and I thought I'd be all right with escorts, but I tri once and it was a disaster."

I realised I had already heard the other side of this story from Cunr "What went wrong?" I asked innocently.

"She was too smart. In my plays I have tried to understand things fro a woman's point of view, their emotions, their passions, their motivation their extraordinary intuitive intelligence, and when I met a woman just lik one of my heroines, I couldn't bear the thought of just using her for sex."

"You don't have to think of it like that," I told him, speaking from m; great depth of experience. "You can just develop a proper friendship witl lots of mutual respect and everything and the sex just fits in."

"I can't. I've thought about it a lot and I just couldn't bring myself to try again. That's why you saw me going behind the bar with the landlord. Sordid I know, but it works for me."

I had been wondering what he was on about but then I remembered Pherecrates' lecture. The cheapest whores attached themselves to bars and landlords were their pimps. "Think nothing of it," I said. "We all have our little weaknesses and if furtive sex is all you have to be ashamed of, you'll find you have a few co-conspirators in this great city of ours."

"Thanks for your understanding, but I'd rather it didn't go any further. As you saw, I don't like to be recognised. Now let's talk about drama."

We talked till the sun went down. He told me about the way he was trying to reconceive formulaic heroes and heroines as real flesh and blood people with normal human frailties and fears, acting in circumstances the audience could relate to; about how he wanted to give a voice to the underrepresented members of society, especially women; about the devastating power of violent passions and the tension between the rational and irrational; about the human cost of war, so trivialised by previous poets and tragedians. He went on to talk about some of his technical innovations, the long soliloquies which worked brilliantly on papyrus but not always so well on stage, the reasons he liked to resolve plots with gods descending on the crane, and why he sometimes gave the chorus lyrics with little or no connection to the plot.

"But that's what I do," I exclaimed. "The Address is an opportunity to impart important messages. To hell with the plot when you have a chance to do that."

"Exactly. I told you comedy and tragedy are coming closer together. Now what are you up to?"

"Well, I'm sticking with comedy for the time being, but I'd still really like to write a tragedy one day."

"You could work on one of mine if you think that would be a good experience, you know, like the apprentices most comic writers use."

"I'd love that. What are you working on?"

"It's called *Hecuba* and it's about the wife of King Priam of Troy and her grief over the death of her daughter Polyxena after the war, and the revenge she takes for the murder of her youngest son."

"Sounds a bit like the *Oresteia*, only that happened back in Greece and the mother was avenging her daughter."

"Yes, it's strangely parallel to events occurring on the other side of the Aegean at the same time, but it will be quite different in style from Aeschylus, as you'll see. I focus less on the influence of the Gods and fate and more on what Hecuba must have thought and felt. I've almost finished the first draft. We'll go through it together when I have. So, what are you working on?"

I told him about my plan to produce a play in my own name if I could find the money, and how it would have to be in my own name as I didn't want to get another producer into trouble. I gave him a quick outline of the plot: a citizen called Demos has two faithful slaves, and has just bought another who is referred to as the Paphlagonian but is obviously Cleon. The Cleon character is a wheedling, flattering con-artist who has Demos completely under his thumb – a political allegory so obvious no one could miss it. A sausage seller turns up who proves to be an even greater rogue than the Paphlagonian and the two compete for Demos' favour with lies, promises, flattery and absurd oracles. The sausage seller eventually wins but, in a sudden change of character I didn't bother explaining, turns out to be quite sensible and explains to Demos where he went wrong. The play ends with the usual feasting and celebrations, mainly at Cleon's expense.

Euripides loved it. I told him Pherecrates had been warning me not to go too hard at Cleon because he might ask for a serious penalty next time, or even try to have me ostracised, but I didn't see any point in having a large audience and not using the opportunity to draw attention to serious problems the city needed to think about. He agreed and thought the risk was small as long as I did the job well. If the audience liked what I did, Cleon wouldn't risk attacking me. As we said our goodbyes, he asked me if I really didn't have a backer, and when I confirmed that, he said he would fund it for me. "I've done pretty well out of my plays and my painting; I'm certainly not going to be spending money on my wife and, as you saw the other night, my tastes are not expensive. I can't think of a better use of my money than sticking it to Cleon. And you can still produce it in your own name unless you want me to share the risk. And of course, I'll look after the tragic plays myself."

# 20

My record to date combined with Euripides' reputation meant *The Knights* was always likely to be selected for the Lenaea, though the archon did ask one or two questions about whether I was experienced enough to take overall responsibility for the comedy production. Fortunately, I wasn't called up that summer, so I was able to give it my best attention, while also working on *Farmers* for the next Dionysia.

It happened to be a very active year for my target. Cleon had just lost us the support of several allies by doubling the protection money they paid us, most of which still went on great big public buildings as it had in Pericles' time, rather than the navy it was supposed to be paying for, and he now carried on his hawkish attitude to the war. He had blocked every peace initiative since the war began.

After a successful and very bloody victory in the west, Demosthenes had stranded a Spartan force on an island opposite the city of Pylos and they were suing for peace. Lysander and I went to the debate in the Assembly. A messenger described how the Athenian besiegers were suffering in the long campaign and would not be able to last out much longer, and several speakers argued that this was a good opportunity to make peace on advantageous terms. This was not good enough for Cleon who was determined to keep the war going as it helped him avoid scrutiny for his misuse of public funds. He claimed our troops were doing just fine. To try to settle this, the Assembly appointed him and Theogenes to lead a reconnaissance mission, but he argued that it was unnecessary; they should just send Nicias with reinforcements.

I liked Nicias. He was enormously rich – he owned about one thousand slaves he contracted out to work in the silver mines for people who had bought mining leases – but he was honest and always seemed to be doing the best for Athens rather than for himself. They said he was more scared of the Athenians than of the enemy after lying informers drove his brother into voluntary exile. Since Pericles died, he and Demosthenes were the only leaders we could trust. Certainly, they were the only ones interested in peace.

Nicias was not keen to be responsible for continuing the war when there was a chance of an honourable peace, so he called Cleon's bluff by offering him the generalship. Of course, Cleon tried to back out, knowing that the situation was much bleaker than he was claiming, but the Assembly wouldn't let him. Red faced and furious he blustered that he would capture the island in twenty days and stormed out of the Assembly.

While we were waiting for Cleon to get his comeuppance, two other ghastly demagogues, Hyperbolus and Cleonymus, took the opportunity to increase their public profile. Hyperbolus' father was rumoured to have been a freed slave, but he had set up a very profitable lamp business, so his son had nothing to do but cause trouble in the Assembly. Agathon told me he got all his populist ideas from sitting in the baths and pretending not to listen. Agathon should know; he's a world expert on the baths. Cleonymus was just as bad. As if we deserved furher punishment, Cleisthenes was back from his embassy on which he had further enriched himself and he was flabbier and more effeminate than ever. I was sorely tempted to set them up alongside Cleon in *The Knights* but it would have taken a lot of rewriting and would have been contrary to my arrangement with Euripides. And frightful as those two might be, Cleon was in a class of his own.

To the horror of all right-thinking people, Cleon had an incredible stroke of luck at Pylos. Demosthenes' problem had been that while it was easy to maintain a blockade, it was impossible to land his troops to finish the job off. The island had no natural harbours and thick vegetation ran down to the sea on all sides, which made it easy for the Spartans to defend. Just before Cleon arrived, a great fire cleared much of the vegetation on one side of the island, making landing much easier. Cleon had done what he promised and won the victory within twenty days. He brought back two hundred and ninety-two hostages and was showered with public honours, including free meals at the town hall and front row seats at the Lenaea and Dionysia. Of course, this made me more determined than ever to bring him down. The glory should really have gone to Demosthenes, who set it all up, or to Nicias who could have been the victor himself, so I decided to represent them in *The Knights* as the fine, loyal slaves displaced in Demos' favour by the Paphlagonian. Pretty good political allegory, I think you'll agree. Only those near the stage would be able to recognise their features on a mask, so to make it clear who they were I gave them each some memorable lines from their recent speeches.

I was more anxious for *The Knights* to succeed than I had been about any of my previous plays. The service to the city I was doing by exposing Cleon was reason enough, but the fact that it was my first play in my own name and the point Euripides had made about safety lying in the audience's reception made me work even harder. Callias had attacked Cleon the previous year in *Men at Leisure*, but it had been so feeble Cleon didn't mind; in fact, he seemed to think it made him more popular. I put in some very pointed remarks about Pylos and Cleon's luck in the way it turned out, and sharpened my witticisms about his fear of making peace and using the war to enrich himself and hide his embezzlements. I managed to get in a good few tragic parodies and some suitably impenetrable prophecies. My tragic writing skills were developing all the time and I fully expected to be able to prove Sophocles wrong. As an innovation I split the Address in two, with some of the Farcical Scenes coming between. In the first I asked for indulgence for my boldness in putting the play on in my own name and followed it with a prayer to Poseidon god of horses; in the second I mocked a few people who deserved it, including Hyperbolus and Cleonymus and Ariphrades with his taste for piggy.

When rehearsals began, I had to work even harder. It was a good tight plot and only required a small cast, but I had to play the Paphlagonian myself as no actor was willing to do it. The lead actor became the chorus leader (rather a waste of Rhombus' talents), the second played Demos and we had to organise a few mask changes purely in order to give the other actor we'd been assigned enough to do before he appeared as the sausage seller. I struggled at first with my part though of course I knew it so well. The bright red mask modelled on Massive Rower would make it obvious whom I was representing, but I couldn't imitate his voice which was booming and aggressive; mine was more of a high-pitched squeak. In the event I decided a squeaking Cleon was funny anyway, so I just spoke naturally (well, naturally for me).

The chorus presented another challenge. They represented spoiled young tearaways of the Alcibiades type and at the Entry twelve of them rode in on the backs of the other twelve who were wearing horse masks and did a little galloping sort of dance. We selected twelve large and twelve small dancers and for the rest of the play when they were all on their feet, we had to do some clever choreography to stop them looking ridiculous as a group. I told them they needed to practice their entry and dance moves as much as they could, but I didn't want to give the show away, so I asked them to do it in pairs at home. In the event it worked out fine; they had become so practised at the two-tier dancing that not even a minor earthquake during our final rehearsal upset them. Euripides was there and he enjoyed the run through so much he told me it didn't matter if *The Knights* won or lost, it would still have the impact I had been hoping for.

Perhaps the most pleasing thing about the lead up to the performance was the attitude of the whole team, actors, chorus, apprentices and stagehands. None of them liked Cleon and we were all fully committed to making our attack on him a success.

## 21

It worked out as well as I could have hoped. *The Knights* won the Lenaea, my second in a row! The parts that seemed to go down best were the Dance of the Gape-Arsed Politicians and the Parable of Pylos, in which Demosthenes makes a cake, the Paphlagonian cooks it – and the sausage-seller sells it! The brief jokes about Hyperbolus and Cleonymus got good laughs and I also put in a piece about Aspasia, Cleon claiming that he was now the leading man after Lysicles, Cunna and Salabaccho; in other words, you had to be one of Aspasia's people to succeed the great Pericles. I thought it was quite complimentary and hoped it wouldn't delay my return to favour. It was a good night in other ways too. Euripides won the tragedy with *Hecuba* which I had helped him with, and Bronchus, my Dicaeopolis from last year, won the acting prize again, this time for his part in Cratinus' *Satyrs* which came second. Pleasingly, Bloody Eupolis was third with a silly effort called *Nanny Goats* and the awful Ariphrades was unplaced.

I had promised Euripides that I'd give a symposium if *The Knights* won, so a couple of days after the festival, I gave Xanthias two drachmae from the winnings I'd retained and told him to run down to the Peiraeus and buy any salted fish he could find and, on his way back through the market place, whatever there was in the way of leftover vegetables at the Residue Stall. He should spend the change on wine and if there wasn't enough, we'd have recourse to Praxagora's bin. The food wouldn't be very good, but that wasn't the point of a symposium, which was all about wine and conversation. Two hours later, scarcely time for a fast runner to get to the Peiraeus and back, he staggered in with a large joint of pork, a huge range of vegetables and enough wine for twenty. There was no point asking him how he did it and I didn't really want to know.

I had agreed the guest list with Euripides and we invited Pherecrates, Lysander and Philonides to make five. Euripides had a special request: "Do you mind if we don't have flute girls? I'm afraid I might do something we'd all regret." I didn't mind at all as I was sure Praxagora wouldn't have allowed them in the house, and I told him quite truly that I'd been planning to close the event with the vulgar kordax dance rather than flute girls anyway.

I can't remember very much about the night, which suggests it must have gone well. Everyone was most impressed with the food, though they wondered why Xanthias gave me a huge wink with every dish he brought out. Lysander came up with a string of jokes about baldness, an affliction Philonides shared with me. Of course, we discussed drama; Euripides was much more sympathetic to the idea of a convergence between tragedy and comedy than Pherecrates and Philonides were, and Lysander entertained us with an impromptu presentation of a play which veered rapidly between the two modes. His juxtapositions were highly amusing and he had stumbled on a truth that I was increasingly taking advantage of myself: that high-flown tragic dialogue can make an absurd comic scene even more absurd.

I awoke to the glare of the sun coming through the window and a similar glare from Praxagora coming through the door. She noticed a couple of wine stains and sniffed around a bit in an unsuccessful hunt for traces of cheap perfume before asking how I was. I was wondering whether to tell her about my head when everything suddenly went dark. "I think I've gone blind", I said. "Don't be silly. If you listened to the philosophers, you would have known there was a partial eclipse of the sun coming. Anyway, you don't look in too bad shape, all things considered." She was wrong, but kind.

Just then Human Artemis came in, obviously expecting to see me on the wrong end of a row. "You cannot step into the same river twice," she told me firmly, as though she had just caught me trying to. "Never mind that. Come along now or we'll be late for Prodicus' exploration of the concepts of courage and rashness. Xanthias, you meet us there when you've tidied this room." With that Praxagora led her out of the house.

I had recovered enough to decide I needed some fresh air and had gone about a hundred metres when I was accosted by Cleon's friend Theorus and four or five thugs. "The denunciation wasn't enough for you?" he asked. "You needed to make a whole evening of fun out of the Defender of our city, did you? You really want to get yourself into trouble, don't you?" He had clearly been put up to this by Cleon, but I think he was also taking it out on me for sending him up in *The Acharnians*.

He had obviously spent too much time with sophists, and I thought he would have gone on asking me rhetorical questions forever but he suddenly changed tack without abandoning his inquisitorial approach. "Do you want to get your arm broken?" he asked, signalling to one of the thugs to grasp it. "Or would you like to promise you'll not go on damaging the city with slanderous attacks on our great leader?"

I knew the answer to that one. "I promise never to damage the city," I replied. Before he could get to the obvious follow-up question, Xanthias emerged from my house, caught sight of us and ran up, emitting the most fearsome growls and baring his large white teeth through the forest of facial hair. Forgetting their numerical superiority, Theorus and his thugs chose to leave in a hurry. So first Alcibiades sends his bullies and now Cleon. I was obviously having an impact! But I vowed to take Xanthias with me in future when I went out shortly after a production.

Two messages marked the aftermath of *The Knights*, one good, one bad. The good one said:

*Aspasia thought that was hilarious. Ready when you are. More cuddles. C.'*

The other:

*'I was thinking of reinstating your allowance and had written to Praxagora to see if she approved. Now, by half Heracles, I hear you are persisting in your mischievous, unpatriotic frivolities. You cannot expect me to encourage them by funding you in any way. For Poseidon's sake, get a job! Incidentally, Athens will be receiving a whole load of the people who lived here in Aegina before we kicked them out and sent them to Thyrea which we have now reconquered. They are bound to make trouble if they come back here, so, if you can bring yourself to attend the Assembly, I trust you will vote for their execution. It is the least you could do for your father.*

On my way to the Assembly, I passed the parade of Aeginetans awaiting sentence. One of them stopped me and called, "Aristophanes, isn't it? I thought so. I've heard great things about your work. I've always followed your doings because your father has my old farm. I hope he's looking after it." Of course, I couldn't vote for execution after that, but the vote was carried anyway.

*Farmers* failed at the Dionysia, a bit of a let-down after my two consecutive successes at the Lenaea. I have to admit the plot was not that clever. It was about the joy of farmers returning to the land after our win at Pylos had put a stop to the annual Spartan invasions. Theirs was a tough life. Many city dwellers had small farms in the countryside where they grew a few vegetables and perhaps ran some chickens or a sheep or two just to save a little money, but full-time farmers had a lot to contend with in the way of stony soil that made for difficult tilling for crops and scarce pasture for their cows, donkeys, sheep and pigs. Not only was their chosen vocation hard and unrewarding, manifested in an increasing gap between their living standards and those in the industrialising city; they had to put up with sophisticated urbanites mocking their slow speech and with being regularly cheated in the marketplace. They were solid citizens and I really admired their grim adherence to common sense in the face of modern fads. They hated the Spartans for destroying their land but, except in particular areas like Acharnia, they would have been happier to be at peace.

They made a striking contrast to the urban demagogues and I managed to get in a few digs at Cleon and at the sophists again – and, just to be even-handed, at Nicias too – but I had been so obsessed with *The Knights* that I didn't give the play much attention till the last few weeks. My joke about the comic poet Cratinus being asked what the state needed most and answering, "a bottle of wine" went down quite well, though it would come back to bite me the next year. Overall, there weren't a lot of the twists and turns and verbal jousts that audiences really love. I did, though, come up with one line that would do credit to any tragedy: "Hail, gleaming plain, bosom of fine land." That stuff is not so hard.

The failure made me all the more determined to win another Dionysia. I cast around for a plot that would capture the public imagination and worked through various spoofs of famous tragedies, a satire of the jury system and several themes involving escorts and whores, none of which seemed very promising, until I realised the philosophical claptrap Praxagora and Human Artemis brought back from their seminars most days offered the best material in town. In *The Good and the Buggered* I'd been too gentle. Most of all I'd allowed the sophists to be defeated easily, suggesting they might not have been much of a threat. In the three years since then they had gone from strength to strength with new charlatans arriving from Asia by the boatload. Even some citizens had shamelessly taken their ideas up and started relaying their ridiculous teachings for outrageous prices. I thought this time I would show what happens when they gain control.

I decided to show how a man successfully escapes his debts by sending his son to learn from the sophists how to argue with his creditors, and actually gets away with it. There can be no better way to make the city see its danger than showing what it might lead to. If it looks exaggerated now, who knows if it will soon? The only question nagging at me was who the representative target should be. They were all pretty interchangeable and any of them would do, but I needed someone easily identifiable through their dress or ideas or both. I thought of Socrates.

The war seemed to be at a bit of a stalemate. Brasidas had ventured as far as taking Megara, which is only about a day's march away; we didn't dare oppose him because we would have been staking our whole army while he was only risking a small part of Sparta's resources. Then he took the war north to try to take pressure off the Peloponnese and Thucydides went after him with the fleet but arrived too late to do any good. He should probably have stuck to his boring scribblings about the war. For reasons I will never understand we then decided to invade Western Greece and I was called up once again, though it was certainly not my turn. It must have been Cleon's subtle revenge. I noticed the chief of my tribe had suddenly acquired an expensive gold ring.

# 22

We went by land this time, a five-day march. Fortunately, our armour and other equipment were carried on donkey-drawn carts until we were almost there. When we got there, we didn't have much trouble seizing the temple at Delium and fortifying it. "Mission accomplished," announced General Hippocrates, as he organised the garrison we were leaving behind and we started the lengthy trek back to Athens. We had only gone a mile or two when the Boeotian army suddenly showed up and blocked our way. It was too late to start a battle, so both armies made camp for the night. We were about equally matched in heavy troops: there were around seven thousand hoplites and one thousand cavalry on each side; but the seven thousand archers and javelin throwers our local allies had supplied were seriously outnumbered.

When I had pitched my tent for the night, I found I was next to the one shared by Alcibiades and Socrates. Popular rumour, no doubt spread by Alcibiades himself, said he had saved the philosopher's life at the battle of Potidaea a few years earlier and they had shared a tent on campaigns ever since. I never believed the story about the life saving and everyone knows why they shared a tent. Alcibiades' mother was a cousin of Pericles, but I was suspicious of the Spartan connections on his father's side, suspicions that were to be proved correct a few years later. When he saw me, he came over, picked me up by the tunic and, swinging me from side to side, asked me if I'd like to get on his back so we could do another horse dance. He then announced he had an especially bouncy trotting style and started to toss me up in the air and catch me just before I hit the ground. "You know what happenth when you make fun of me," he lisped in that affected way of his. "Well, thith is what happenth when you make fun of my friendth." Here we go again, I thought. Comic poets should get danger money.

"I wasn't identifying any of your friends," I told him. "It was only a bloody chorus." "Good, becauth thith ith going to be a bloody chowuth too," was the reply. I looked to Socrates for some support; he was supposed to be good at getting people to stop and think about what they were doing, which was exactly what I wanted Alcibiades to do, but the old fool was walking around deep in thought, neck craned and staring straight ahead of him, more like a pelican than anything human. When he happened to turn towards us, he just looked straight through me. That was the moment I decided I should definitely use him in my play. I emerged from the encounter with a sore neck and a bleeding nose, but as we'd be fighting to the death next day, it seemed silly to fuss about minor injuries.

That night I dreamed about Socrates. The tent he shared with Alcibiades had become the canvas building at centre stage with a big sign over the door saying 'Thought Machine.' Inside, Socrates and another philosopher (I couldn't quite see who) were conducting strange experiments with insects while clouds floated above them, in front of them and around them. Alcibiades was knocking on the door asking for instruction, with enthusiastic encouragement from his father.

We were roused at dawn and lined up to face the enemy. It was a very peculiar formation. Our right wing, which I was to be part of, overlapped the Boeotian left by about five hundred men. Because they had more troops than us in total, this meant their right wing overlapped our left by even more. I thought this was not a very clever way to prepare for battle and that General Hippocrates could have used a professional choreographer like me. In the centre, he was giving us the usual pep talk, and on my way to my position I thought I should stop to hear it in case there were lines I could use in future plays. I made a few notes, though there was nothing special, and just when he seemed to be getting to the crux of the matter, he was interrupted by a lot of shouting and movement. The Boeotians had launched their attack.

I made my way as fast as I could towards the right wing, but my path was blocked by fighting men and I had to divert to the rear and go round the back. By the time I arrived our right wing had pushed forward a little and, as I hurried to join them, I saw a chap about my height who seemed to have been overlooked by my colleagues. He was still alive and perhaps a threat from their rear, so I decided I'd better try to take him out and started to brandish my sword a little nervously. When I got within a couple of paces, he gave deep sigh and said, "Bloody fox's earth." He pulled himself out of the deep natural hazard he had slipped into and immediately blocked out the sun. I decided he must have been a near relative of Massive Rower and confess I would have run away if one of our hoplites had not arrived from behind him at just that moment and run his sword through the giant's neck, not a pleasant sight even if your life is being saved, and a little messy – a mess I contributed to by vomiting uncontrollably. To this day, I don't know who my saviour was, but he recognised me. "Hey, it's Aristophanes. Guys, go easy! We're back through to our own troops." He was part of the endmost ranks who had encircled the enemy flank and were coming back towards the centre. If they had gone any further they would have been fighting their own men without knowing it, as the arms and armour on both sides were pretty much identical. It wasn't a very distinguished way to do it, I know, but I felt I had once again made an important contribution to the Athenian war effort.

Our success on the right wing did not last very long; the Boeotian cavalry arrived and stopped us in our tracks. Meanwhile our left wing had been encircled, as any comic poet could have predicted. The toughest fighting seemed to be in the centre, but when they saw both wings defeated our men there gave up. Apparently Cleon's chum Cleonymus had dropped his shield and fled at the first encounter, the ultimate display of cowardice. I had a sneaking sympathy for him, because no one could run very far carrying one of those heavy wooden shields, but it would still make for some good mockery in future plays. Anyway he should have waited till things got properly dangerous.

The battle was a disaster for us. We lost over one thousand two hundred men, including General Hippocrates, twice as many as the Boeotians. General Demosthenes arrived with his army but failed to link up with us in time and was defeated himself soon after he landed. We joined his troops to march home and on the way back he caught sight of me and greeted me like an old friend. "Our little rowing singer! What are you doing here?"

I explained about Cleon's revenge and he shook his head. "You are too valuable to the city to risk in the war," he said. "We should make people like you exempt from military service. I really enjoyed *The Knights*. It does us all good to be represented as slaves now and again. I hope this petty revenge doesn't put you off making fun of Cleon."

"Thank you, sir. It won't."

"I'll try and make sure it doesn't happen again." He did, though it took a couple of years to get the poets' exemption law passed. In the event it didn't matter because our defeat led to a one-year armistice which held pretty well for two years and allowed peace negotiations to start in earnest. I never went to war again.

When I got home Xanthias was out and Praxagora was in, spinning wool with Human Artemis. I thought this was a good sign, even the next day when a neighbour said, "Praxagora was so excited when I told her I'd heard you were coming back."

# 23

Soon after my return, I sought out Euripides to see what he thought of my plan for a play about the sophists. He didn't seem to be in a very good mood and I was disappointed with his reaction.

"You mean like Cratinus' attack on Hippon? Or Hermippus' *Bakery Women*? I thought they were both very ordinary by the way. And anyway, you've already done that with *The Banqueters*. Can't you think of something more original?"

"That's the point. Making fun of them and seeing them brought down on stage hasn't had any impact at all. There are more sophists around than ever and they are more influential too. I thought I'd show what happens if we let them win."

His left eyebrow reached new heights. "Um, I'm not sure why that would work. I thought you might do something based on the section of *The Suppliants* you helped me with after *Hecuba*, you know, that there are three types of citizens: the useless rich trying to get richer, the envious poor, and the majority in between. You could set up a really good Contest between the first two groups with the chorus representing the third."

"Maybe I'll do that another time. Right now I think the sophists need to be put in their place. I am going to use Socrates as the archetype."

"I wouldn't do that."

"Why not?"

"He's a bit different from the others. He doesn't take money for his teaching and he doesn't pretend to know everything. He just asks questions. You should use Cratylus or Gorgias or someone like that."

It was the first time Euripides had been anything but encouraging to me. I decided to ignore his advice, even when Pherecrates also told me not to use Socrates. There were lots of reasons why he was my choice. He had awful friends, not just Alcibiades but closet oligarchs like Charmides and Critias, and his advocacy of 'mentoring' of young boys by old men was so public it was embarrassing. And even if he didn't take money for teaching, he made damn sure he was well looked after by the rich men he engaged in his discussions. Most of all, he was physically distinctive, fat, pug-nosed, scruffy and usually barefoot. His appearance would get some laughs by itself.

Those were all good reasons, but to be honest the thing that really made up my mind to stick with Socrates was a visit from Anytus, one of Alcibiades' lovers. He told me he was very worried about what Socrates was teaching his son, and wanted to discredit him. He suggested that if I wrote a play making Socrates look like a dishonest charlatan, he'd fund it. I knew the real reason was simply his jealousy over Socrates' relationship with Alcibiades, but I wasn't going to argue if it meant I could get funded without an awkward discussion with Euripides. Artemis was looking after me again.

I had a play in each festival again, even though the expense of the war meant more sponsorship was needed to replace our ships and maintain the walls and there were only three comedies at each instead of five. My *Merchant Ships* came second at the Lenaea. It was about the ships that brought us our supplies of grain and timber during the war and, because of the armistice, I was able to dwell on the sufferings and shortages the war had caused the Spartans as well as us. I worked in some powerful mockery of litigious sycophants in general but didn't go too hard after Cleon, feeling I had done enough for the time being. I'd been hoping for a hat-trick of Lenaeas but it wasn't a great play. Criticus observed that the psycho-emotional impact of my paradidactic phenomenalism was less rebarbative than in my previous works, and, who knows, he might have been right. I wasn't too upset at coming second as all my thoughts were concentrated on making a success of *The Clouds*. And of course, the money was still useful.

*The Clouds'* plot was quite straightforward: a foolish but cunning old man has heard how sophists can win any argument, irrespective of the merits of the case, and decides to go to Socrates' school, The Thought Machine, to learn the new rhetoric and persuade his creditors to cancel the debts incurred by his wastrel son on horses and his spendthrift wife on clothes and perfumes. When he comes to enquire at the door, a student tells him of recent scientific experiments conducted by Socrates and his colleague Chaerephon, including a new unit of measurement for

114

ascertaining the distance jumped by a flea by putting wax on its feet, to be known as a flea's 'foot'; the exact cause of the buzzing noise made by a gnat – its bottom acts as a trumpet; and a new use for a large pair of compasses to steal cloaks belonging to passive homosexuals from pegs over the gymnasium wall.

Once the old man is enrolled in the school, Socrates makes him get into a bug-infested bed and the chorus encourages him to do some thinking. He wails tragically about bedbugs and Socrates asks him why he isn't thinking. "But I am thinking – about bedbugs."

"What have you come up with down there?"

"My prick." Socrates tells him to apply his mind to his objective of not paying interest. His first plan is to hide the moon so monthly interest never becomes due. Then to avoid a lawsuit he would focus the sun through glass on the relevant papers and burn them up. If he was about to lose a case for lack of witnesses, well then, he'd run away and hang himself. He proves such a hopeless student the school throws him out and he decides to send his son instead. The son not only gets rid of the debts with the brilliant rhetoric he learns but demonstrates that it is right for children to beat their parents, which he does with enthusiasm. Consistency not being important in comedy, he also justifies incest. The Celebration at the end is a triumph for the son over his father, who deserved it, and for them both over their creditors, who probably didn't, but it is also the triumph of false reasoning over all the moral principles that made this city great. I was confident the audience would sit up and take notice.

Given the various acrobatics my Socrates was to get up to, I was delighted we were assigned Archinous. His antics as Socrates were so funny, they stopped our rehearsals twice. Other than the slapstick, the whole thing was pretty ethereal. The new thinkers indulge in blasphemy about our old gods, replacing them with hot air, the chorus are clouds, Socrates enters about a metre above the ground, and the ideas are far removed from earthly reality. I had taken a bet with Carcinus, the distinguished admiral and tragic poet, that I could write an excellent tragic Entry of the Chorus. The clouds sang of their homeland and nature in verse that any tragedian would have been proud to have written:

*Eternal clouds, arise we,*

*Show our sparkling shapes,*
*On ocean and on mountain,*
*On forests, fields and lakes…*

I again split the Address into two parts separated by some Farcical Scenes. In the first, the chorus criticises the audience for not recognising the good that clouds do by creating storms when there is a stupid expedition planned or as a warning not to elect Cleon, an error the city could easily undo by punishing him for corruption. They invoke Apollo and Artemis, and then the chorus leader sings that the moon has been complaining that she gets no recognition for saving expenditure on torches and that the changes Athens had been making to the calendar mean the gods don't know when to come and collect their sacrifices. I used an unusual combination of aeolics (tum-ti-ti-tum) and dactyls (tum-ti-ti) in the Ode, while keeping to the more conventional anapaests (ti-ti-tum) in the earlier parts and trochees (tum-ti) in the half-chorus Addresses. In the second Address the chorus threatens dire weather if the play doesn't win.

# 24

I wish the judges had taken the Clouds' threat seriously. In the event we came third out of three and the weather continued fine. If I was disappointed not to get the prize at the Lenaea, I was devastated at this. I'm still inclined to think *The Clouds* was the best play I ever wrote, and the applause had made me think the audience did too. Even Socrates claimed to like it. He hardly ever went to comedies, but he had heard this one was going to be about him, so he stood up and waved when Archinous made his aerial entry. Apparently, he said he enjoyed being laughed at and thought it was just like being at a party. The Entry of the Chorus made the tragic impression that it was intended to; the audience gasped and started to wonder if they were at the wrong drama. At least I had won my bet with Carcinus. He and his three sons, all tragic poets, would now perform an absurd dance in my next play. Cratinus had won the competition with a play in which he got his revenge for my joke about the wine bottle by sending himself up as an even greater drunkard than I had. I thought this was a bit mean as I had given him full credit for his past glory in good tragic style: "He once rode the sea-swell of applause and roamed through the wide plains, sweeping majestic oaks, plane trees and enemies from their moorings and carrying them off uprooted." He knew I had been working with Euripides and coined the word Euripidaristophanise to describe the way we both used words. When I saw Euripides himself immediately after the judging, he came very close to saying, "I told you so." Pherecrates didn't but I knew that was what he was thinking.

I was seriously depressed wondering what had gone wrong, and didn't go out much for weeks. Praxagora was wonderful, so kind and understanding I didn't even think of visiting Cunna, not even for sympathy as I would have before. Xanthias did his best to tiptoe around respectfully, which at least made me smile, and Human Artemis suspended her criticisms of my approach to river entry.

When I finally decided to go to the pub, I discovered I was the only person who didn't know why *The Clouds* had failed, though no two people had the same explanation and not all of them made sense.

"The audience didn't want another play about sophists." But Ameipsias came second with one.

"People like Socrates." I'll bet half the judges didn't know anything about him except that he was a sophist.

"Archinous let you down." No, he didn't. He was just as funny on the night as he had been at rehearsals.

"The judges were Cleon fans." Horrible thought.

"People thought you were getting cocky and needed a failure." I had just had one with *Merchant Ships*.

"The third line of the Antode contrasted too strongly with the beginning of the Counterflow, producing a kind of catalectic exegesis that some in the audience might have struggled with." Criticus, of course.

In the event the most plausible explanation came from Pherecrates a week or so later. I had gone too far in allowing the sophists to win and having a Celebration that rejoiced in having overturned the natural order. Combining that with the way I was using Euripidean language in comic situations and clever puns everywhere, people thought I was a bit of a sophist myself and was advocating for them. In short, showing the success of the sophists had frightened the audience as I intended, but it rebounded on me because they thought I must be one too! It was a sad irony that my best play should fail because it was too effective. There was so much good material, especially about the experiments, it deserved a better hearing and I determined to rewrite it with a different ending.

Politics were quiet that year, partly because Cleon had not been re-elected general, which made for more restrained debates. Hyperbolus was quiet too, there being no scope for warmongering rants now, and few political arguments going on in the baths he derived his policies from. Cleonymus was in disgrace for dropping his shield at Delium, so he stayed out of the public eye for a while. Thucydides was exiled for arriving too late with the fleet to fight Brasidas' army in the north, but other than that there was not much happening at assemblies, so Lysander and I decided to entertain ourselves with a day at the law courts instead.

One of the ways Cleon had bribed people to vote for him the previous year was by proposing an increase in the pay for jury service to three obols, which was just about a living wage. Pity he didn't do as much for the disabled who were forced to try to survive on just one obol a day. The attraction of jury pay was obvious from the crowds of old men (they were nearly all old) pushing and shoving to try to get on one of the day's trials. Each year, six thousand citizens over the age of thirty were registered as jurors, six hundred from each of the tribes who were always vastly oversubscribed with volunteers. Apparently, some people volunteered under several different names to make sure of getting picked. But that wasn't the only competition. Each juror was assigned to a particular court which wouldn't be sitting on all court days, and when it was it might require two hundred jurors for small private suits or five hundred or more for major public ones, at the discretion of the magistrate, but never enough to accommodate everyone who was eligible. As a result, if you wanted to improve your chances of actually being on the jury and getting paid, you needed to get to the courts early. By the time Lysander and I showed up, all the juries were full and crowds of disappointed old men were making their way home, probably wondering where their next meal was coming from.

The magistrate has to make sure that all cases are settled in one day, but other than that he gives no advice or commentary to the jurors. The plaintiff always gets to speak first and then the defendant, both timed with a water clock. They are followed by any witnesses they call, who are allowed less time. There is no summing up and the jurors are supposed to vote immediately after the evidence is over, though a lot of muttering and occasional shouts tend to drive them towards some sort of consensus. A tie in votes means acquittal, but that is very rare. If it is a criminal case, the penalty is usually predetermined, while in a civil case the successful plaintiff can specify the damages requested and the jury votes on that. It all works very well and is a great manifestation of our democracy, as long as the jurors are smart enough to tell when someone is lying. Sadly, that is not always the case.

The first case we saw was about a maritime loan. The plaintiff had received less than he was expecting for his investment because the merchant he was funding claimed the cargo had been damaged. The plaintiff brought witnesses to show the wine claimed for had actually been sold at very good prices through another merchant. Lysander and I thought the evidence and the rival calculations of damages were quite interesting, but the largely closed eyes of the jurors suggested they didn't and we wondered just how much of it they understood or wanted to.

They certainly sat up for the next case. It was brought by the daughter of a citizen, using one of her cousins to present her case in court, which a woman could not do herself. She claimed my father's friend Eucrates had offered her one thousand drachmae for an exclusive relationship, but after paying half, he'd changed his mind. She wanted the rest of it. The jurors let him off, probably imagining that in the same position they would like the same freedom, however improbable it was that they'd ever be in anything like the same position. They couldn't let him off the new ammunition I had when I would next need it in a conversation with my father. Would he try and defend his best friend? If so, he'd have to be more forgiving of my relatively minor peccadilloes.

The third case was the most entertaining, even though it involved Cleon at his worst. He was prosecuting Laches for embezzlement in Sicily in his usual loud, uncouth, red-faced way, full of outrageous exaggeration and mudslinging. We were delighted when Laches got off. We left during the last case in which an old man was suing a much younger one for seducing his young wife. It was an unusual response as most cuckolded husbands would just have accepted some money as compensation rather than undergo the publicity, but there was no doubt which way the ageing jury would go, so Lysander and I left.

Before going our separate ways we had a glass of wine in the pub and talked about the day, not so much about the cases as about the jurors.

"It's so sad to see them like that. Some of them fought against the Persians at Marathon," Lysander observed.

"No, they didn't. That was almost seventy years ago."

"Well, jolly nearly. And they would have. Probably."

It was clear to us both that the loyal, crusty old men deserved better from the city. And maybe the city deserved better from its juries. An obvious plot for a comedy!

# 25

It may have been because of continuing hostility to *The Clouds* that the archons didn't select me for the next Dionysia, or possibly because they didn't quite trust what I might put on when foreigners were in town. As a strange form of compensation, they accepted both my entries for the Lenaea. Philonides had agreed to sponsor one, which was a relief because I needed an experienced producer like him to manage one production if I had another one to manage myself for the same festival. I was also hoping to cultivate him as a regular sponsor, so I wanted to do the right thing by him. I knew Euripides would also be willing to sponsor me, but only if he thought I was making a point that mattered to the city. One play I had was a simple comedy with a few political insults but nothing too serious in the way of critiquing our city and its foibles, so I gave that to Philonides. The other was a critique of the jury system and I knew Euripides would be interested.

Philonides' play was called *Selection*. It was about the process by which the archons selected plays for performance at the festivals, comic poets and their producers giving a broad outline of their plot and some highlights in the hope of being selected. You can imagine how easy that was to put together – just a series of caricatures of my comedy competitors putting forward ridiculous ideas and doing it badly. I showed old 'Bean Soup' Hegemon proposing an idea for a play about the inadequacy of army rations, Cratinus too drunk to present his idea for a chorus of pretty young boys, Pherecrates with a highly moral domestic situation comedy, Aristomenes with an idea centred entirely around finding new ways to blaspheme, Bloody Eupolis with a play which turned out to have been written by someone else, and of course the great Aristophanes himself, whose satires on sophists and Cleon were made to appear clumsy and ignorant – which was disturbingly popular with the audience. That play won and I hoped that I had disarmed some of my critics.

*The Wasps*, my play about the jury system and how demagogues could and did abuse it, came second, though it was so much better and more important. The chorus was formed of the pathetic old men Lysander and I had observed. After they had been on stage a while, they whipped their cloaks aside to show a yellow and black striped tunic and their phallus thrust back between their legs as a dangerous looking sting – a stunning moment for the audience. The lead character was one of these old men, desperately keen to be on a jury every day, and he was named Cleon-yay. His son, who was trying to get him to overcome his addiction to the courts, was Cleon-boo.

The Contest gave me a chance to set out the argument in full. Cleon-yay gives his reasons for his addiction: he enjoys the flattering attentions and gratitude of rich men who appeal to him for a favourable verdict, though he seldom feels he has to do what they ask. He can interpret the law as he pleases since his decisions are not subject to review, and his juror's pay gives him independence and authority within his own household. Other benefits include looking at little boys naked as part of the registration process, getting top actors and pipers to perform for the court, awarding orphaned girls to whomever he feels like and being flattered by political heavyweights. Best of all is the respect he gets at home for coming back with his pay.

Cleon-boo counters that jurors' pay amounts to under a tenth of the state's income; the demagogues and sycophants get a good slice of the rest and they also receive huge money bribes and luxurious gifts from allies who know that they are where the power lies. The deserving old men get miserable pay on the days they get anything at all, and an effeminate youth, paid twice what they are, can threaten their jury pay if they turn up late, and will then split defendants' bribes with his mates. Demagogues want to keep the old men poor so that they will depend on jury pay and vote as directed. Jurors just get 'the drip of oil from the wool.' If each city paying tribute supported just twenty of these men, the whole city would be much better off.

Cleon-boo wins the argument, despite his father's volley of unfounded accusations against him of the type Cleon was always making. To make up for his father's loss of entertainment as a juror, Cleon-boo stages a trial at home, a dog called Labes being accused by a shrill, shouty dog in a Cleon-mask of stealing a Sicilian cheese from the kitchen. The name of the dog, a reference to both dogs' suburbs, and the source of the cheese made it obvious I was referring to Cleon's unsuccessful prosecution of Laches. Cleon-yay immediately pronounces guilt, but Cleon-boo brings various kitchen utensils as witnesses for the defense (played by good slapstick actors) and says a few words in praise of the accused and his unfortunate upbringing. Puppies, representing the children of the accused, are ushered in to soften the heart of the old juror with their plaintive barks. Part of Laches' defence had been that he hadn't learned how to account for his expenditure, which I changed into the tragedy of him never having been taught to play the lyre. Cleon-yay still wants to find him guilty but is fooled into putting his vote into the wrong urn. The old man is deeply shocked by his first acquittal, but his son promises him a good time – new clothes, new shoes and plenty of parties.

The rest of the play shows Cleon-yay being prepared by his son for the first of those parties. He is rollicking drunk and has a naked flute-girl on each arm and his uncouthness, bumbling and greed provided plenty of opportunities for Archinous' slapstick skills. The play ends with a dancing contest between Cleon-yay and Carcinus and his three spindly sons, the result of our bet on *The Clouds'* Entry song. The chorus leads them offstage, singing and dancing, another innovation of mine.

In the Address, I took the opportunity to complain about how *The Clouds* had been treated at last year's Dionysia: I pointed out that I was always willing to help my rivals with materials, I never got big-headed when I was successful, I never used my fame to pick up boys (Bloody Eupolis had boasted that he did), I never agreed to insert material to help a lover in his ambitions and I always went for the big targets; despite all this, I told the audience, *The Clouds* came third, because you simply couldn't appreciate it. "In future you should be sure to encourage innovators like me."

I had arranged to meet Euripides in the pub a few days later but he hadn't arrived when I got there. It was crowded and I was relieved not to see Criticus there either, but in the event, I rather missed him. Nobody had much to say about my success with *Selection*, but everyone had a strong view as to why *The Wasps* didn't win.

"You shouldn't have gone after Cleon again."

"Would it have been funnier if I hadn't?"

"No, but it would have been different."

"You should have made more jokes about Nicias and Demosthenes."

"Would that have been funny?"

"No, I suppose not."

"There was too much slapstick."

"Would it have been funnier with less?"

"Not really."

"You should have made the moral lesson more explicit."

"Would that have been funny?"

"Not really."

"You should have made more of the Address and talked about the armistice."

"Would that have been funny?"

"I suppose not."

"You should have staged a fight amongst the old men. That would have been powerful."

"Fuck off, I'm a comic poet."

I was storming out when Euripides arrived and I took him to another pub, though I fully expected him to go back to our usual one when we parted. I knew he'd been very happy with *The Wasps,* as he had worked through some of the script with me and was as proud when we came second as if he had written the whole thing himself. He knew having two plays on at once had exhausted me and he told me to take the opportunity of not being involved in the Dionysia to have a good rest and try not to think about the theatre at all. It would be best if I missed the next Lenaea too, so I could recharge my energy properly. I pointed out that if I wanted to get nominated for next year's Dionysia, I would need a good plot to submit to the selection process. If I wasn't putting in for the Lenaea and didn't get selected for the Dionysia, that would mean two years between plays. I wondered vaguely if Praxagora would treat that as the two years without a win and make me give up writing altogether in line with our deal.

Euripides didn't see it as a problem. "Look, the city is enjoying its break from war and politics, so an obvious theme is peace. I'll get us through the selection with some bits of my material on the horrors of war which you can twist a little to make them funny. You can point out that generals get the glory; soldiers the dangers and privations. You can lift that straight out of my *Andromache*. You can illustrate that there are lots of rational arguments in favour of peace but none in favour of war, as you and I noted in *The Suppliants,* by having warmongers make the silly types of arguments you're so good at. I'll get old Hermes to be chorus leader. He's looking for something to do and is always reliable. He'll be great. All you have to do is come up with a plot. Let me know when you have and we'll work through it together."

I hadn't got far thinking about it when I arrived home and Praxagora told me she was pregnant. Human Artemis looked uncertain as to whether this was another river-based folly of mine and Xanthias could not resist punching me on the shoulder with a cry of, "Bugger me, you arsehole!"

# 26

I spent the next few months trying not to think about comedy. Praxagora and I became good friends and we had begun to teach Xanthias a little Greek. We set Human Artemis a full program of baby clothes making, which kept her out of my way and probably saved a little money. I taught Praxagora a few dice games, she taught me some of the folk songs from her island home and we read Homer to each other. I even told her about Cunna, and she told me about an Ethiopian slave on the next-door farm in Aegina which explained a lot. It was a happy time at home and I didn't go to the pub much and didn't visit Cunna at all until a few weeks before the birth, and then only twice and with Praxagora's encouragement.

Euripides' confidence was justified. We were the first play selected for the Dionysia, though I can't claim the plot outline that we presented at selection was very clever. The basic idea was that the hero decides to go and dig up the goddess Peace, who has been buried somewhere in the heavens, so he can bring her back to earth. There are various comic exchanges with the gods he comes across up there, but eventually he triumphs with the help of people from all over Greece and celebrates in the usual way. Frankly it wasn't that funny, so I knew I would have to liven it up with lots of slapstick, sex jokes, scatology, and foreigners talking in strange accents. It was promising that we were assigned Apollodorus as our lead actor, an up-and-coming declaimer whose rants could be heard for miles and whom many thought was getting to be better than Bronchus.

They say good things come in threes and, to add to my excitement at impending fatherhood, two more good things happened. Demosthenes got his law passed exempting a certain list of poets from military service and Cleon was killed on a campaign at Amphipolis in the north. He had captured a couple of major cities and was advancing on Amphipolis when Brasidas led the Spartan troops out to oppose him. Cleon had been waiting for reinforcements, but his men were so restless under his rotten leadership he felt he had to advance towards the city, thinking he could always draw back. When he saw the feet of men and horses showing under the city gate, he took fright and ordered a retreat. Brasidas attacked and in the battle that followed, four hundred of our men were killed and just seven Spartans. Cleon was running away when he was felled by a spear. Brasidas died in the battle too and was buried as a hero; Cleon wasn't.

My feelings about Cleon's death were ambivalent at first. When people die it is only right to try to remember their good points and I tried very hard. He did die fighting for our city of course, even if he didn't do it very well. He had been successful at Pylos but that was entirely due to luck. On the other hand, he had always opposed peace. Brasidas loved war because he was good at it; Cleon loved it because it helped to cover up his misdeeds. He had won popularity with a capital levy for redistribution to poorer citizens and most of the proceeds ended up in his pocket; he had taken personal bribes instead of the tribute due from our allies; he had sued people on trumped up charges and then blackmailed them; he had regularly misled the Assembly; and he had embezzled whatever public funds he could lay his hands on. It just didn't balance and I decided all Athens had to regret was the loss of a good butt for comedy.

As I was musing on this one day near the marketplace, I saw Demosthenes and Nicias together and hurried over to thank Demosthenes for getting the exemption act passed. "We should have done that years ago," he said. "Nicias, have you met Aristophanes? He's the guy who showed us as slaves in the Dionysia."

"Of course. I enjoyed that," Nicias smiled. "It's the sort of thing that could only happen in Athens and sends an important message about avoiding hubris. But for the grace of Zeus any of us could be a slave. You are welcome to do it again any time."

"You can play some slave parts yourselves if you like." It was a mischievous remark and I don't know why I suggested it. To my horror they both thought it was an excellent idea. "Oh yes, and give us something humiliating to do," added Demosthenes.

When Praxagora gave birth, I was firmly under the impression that I was the first person in the history of the world to achieve fatherhood. I was spending a lot of time at home, so it should have been a productive period for composing *Peace* but I spent most of it admiring baby Ararus, whom we had named after the little boy who had carried off my mother. I did so wish she had been there to greet him. It is amazing how fascinating a small, largely inert, lump of pink flesh can be. I was even proud to note he had inherited my baldness, though that didn't last long. It was difficult to get enthused about the play in any case. It was an essentially happy story, not trying to right any major wrongs, and any political satire would have to be in throw-away lines as I couldn't see a way of working much of it into the plot.

I felt a bit more inspired when Bloody Eupolis won the Lenaea with *Maricas*, an attack on Hyperbolus, copied largely from my attack on Cleon in *The Knights*. When I confronted him with this, he reminded me that he'd helped with part of the chorus of *The Knights*, but I told him that was not at all the same thing as lifting great chunks of text with only tiny changes. He also pointed out that his play had been the first to introduce market women and had the nerve to ask why I didn't do something original like that.

From the beginning of winter, there had been a sense of relief all around the city that there might be no campaign next summer. Both sides were ready for peace. Despite her success in the north, Sparta had not got over the raids on Pylos and the loss of the prisoners on the island. Her slaves were deserting and her regular invasions of Attica had long been ineffective. For our part, we had rather lost confidence after Delium and Amphipolis and several of our allies seemed to be on the point of deserting. It helped that Brasidas and Cleon were dead. Alcibiades seemed to have taken up the mantle of warmonger in chief, advocating an aggressive foreign policy and undermining attempts to make the treaty work by creating an anti-Sparta alliance in the Peloponnese, but public sentiment was largely against him and a formal peace treaty still looked close. Whether it would be achieved before the Dionysia was another matter. If it was, I'd have to do some quick rewriting as it wouldn't make much sense to have the hero bring the goddess Peace to Athens when she was already there. I thought of an alternative plot in which Cleon and Brasidas are in Hades and start a war there to make up for the lack of fighting on earth. I sketched out some scenes and funny lines and hoped I wouldn't have to write it all.

Determined to beat Bloody Eupolis, and for want of any serious political targets, I put a lot of effort into the choral writing and I think *The*

*Peace* contained some of my best imagery. I knew it was going to be hard for Nicias and Demosthenes to come to rehearsals, so I gave them just a short scene at the beginning, about sixty lines between them. Of course, they weren't expecting to be paid which meant we could employ the usual three actors and have a couple stand by as understudies for the first scene in case duty called the leaders away.

Another complication was the machine. Euripides had always been a big fan of it and used it a lot to resolve his plots. I'm not such a fan. In tragedies you generally just have gods being lowered delicately to the stage, whereas in comedies you have bumbling humans getting up to all sorts of silly antics, which is much more difficult to pull off without a serious accident. In this case, the hero was to make a funny speech as the machine lifted him up towards heaven in a spectacularly bumpy ride. Slapstick wasn't Apollodorus' strength and he found it difficult to make the words I gave him fit the trajectory they were meant to be describing. When he said he was going up, he was actually going down, when he said he was going left, he was actually going right and so on, and he ended up getting so confused he forgot his lines altogether. In the end I had to turn the speech into a collection of individual phrases which could be used in pretty much any order and still fit the metre. That seemed to solve the problem, but at the cost of some of my better lines.

Demosthenes and Nicias had asked me to give them something demeaning to do and I certainly did. To get to heaven and bring back Peace, the hero chooses to ride a dung beetle on the sound ecological grounds that the creature's recycling system means there is no need to carry food for it. The play opened with the two great men kneading dung cakes to feed the beetle to start the journey. I used the same trick as in *The Knights*, inserting lines from their recent speeches to let the audience know who they were, but after a couple of exchanges, people started to recognise their distinctive, aristocratic voices and gradually began to rise and applaud, whether for their achievements or their willingness to participate in a ludicrous event – or perhaps for my originality in engaging them – we'll never know. Apollodorus was brilliant with my 'list with a twist' of things you can do in peace: "rejoice, yell, laugh, travel, not travel, fuck, oversleep, go to festivals, feast, gamble, live it up, and shout 'Whoopee!'" and later with some sentimental poetry about the smells of peace: "the harvest, parties, festivals of Dionysus, pipes, tragedians, Sophocles' songs, thrushes to eat, Euripides' witty sayings," degenerating to "the boobs of women running in the fields, a drunken slave girl and an empty wine jug."

We were so close to real peace I wanted to get the audience truly enthused about it and made the Celebration at the end rather special. In the first place it was Panhellenic, not a selfish one as in *The Acharnians* or even just an Athenian celebration, though of course Peace herself was to be based in Athens. We engaged the audience by giving them some of the food from the dinner and Peace handed over one of her attendant demi-goddesses (played by a flute girl) to the council members in the front row.

Overall I thought I had done rather well with an unpromising theme, so it was disappointing to come second and maddening to be second to Bloody Eupolis who had now won both festivals that year. Even more annoying was that his play was about sophists and not nearly as good as my *Clouds* which had only come third. He attacked Critias in particular but also got in a few jokes about Alcibiades and his gang. I vaguely hoped he'd get the same rough treatment from them as I had, but didn't expect it; he was smooth enough to pass for one of them and his jokes were lame anyway. Our conversation at the after party was rather strained. He asked me why my verse was so uncouth. "To speak is a gift of Nature; to speak well is a gift of Art," was the way he put it. I asked him why his material was always so superficial. Wasn't he interested in helping the city change for the better? He tried to quiz me on my ideas for future plots but I wasn't going to trust him so I gave him a few themes I was never going to use.

I wasn't sleepy, so I stopped at the pub on the way home. There were only a few people still there and they were surprisingly complimentary, perhaps because everyone was relaxed and confident that a real peace was just around the corner. They said nice things about the ascent to heaven, the choral odes and the innovative Celebration. They asked me how I'd got Demosthenes and Nicias on stage and didn't know whether to believe me when I pretended it was their idea. And of course, once the compliments stopped, the critique started. The play had been rather hard on Athens; was it fair to be so critical of some of the things we had done in the war and the way we had treated our allies? The role of the chorus was confusing; were they all farmers? How did they suddenly change from being Athenians to being Panhellenic? Peace isn't a proper goddess. How did all those other people get up to heaven? The last thing I remember about that night is mumbling, "Fuck off, I'm a comic poet," again and again, and then I must have drifted off to sleep.

When I got home in the morning there was a golden model of a dung beetle waiting for me, a gift from Nicias and Demosthenes. Praxagora was sufficiently impressed not to quiz me about the night before and we settled comfortably back into our little family life for a while. Xanthias and Human Artemis seemed perfectly contented as well.

About a week after the Dionysia, Nicias signed the peace treaty with Sparta. Life was good.

# CLINGING ON

# 27

I was a bit surprised when Asclepius, the god of medicine, drove past me in a golden chariot, shouting, "Come to me! I can cure you! Very cheap!" In the first place it was supposed to be a torch race with no chariots allowed. And then it wasn't often that gods appeared in the streets and this was the first time I'd seen one. I also thought it strange he was flogging his curative powers directly rather than through one of the innumerable quacks and charlatans who sold expensive and useless remedies in his name. And why was my mother sitting beside him? I was about to point all this out to Lysander when I realised he was still talking.

"...of course, girls are usually much cheaper because you don't have to pay for their education, but you still have to manage their religious observances which can be tricky. It's OK if they just do the Brauron temple bit where all the little girls run around pretending to be bears, because they do that naked, but if they get selected to weave Athena's robe, you have to pay a fortune for them to live in the Acropolis for a year. And then the phallus-shaped loaves to carry in the procession are supposed to be gold-plated which is really expensive. And if you can't find someone to marry them, they'll stick at home feeling sorry for themselves and living off you and your family for ever. No, you should consider yourself lucky to have boys."

We had been celebrating the birth of my second son, Philip. When he had reached the ripe old age of five days I did the traditional thing of carrying him round the house and five days after that we officially named him. Calling him after my father was Praxagora's choice, not mine. She was hoping for some sort of reconciliation between my father and me, though I couldn't see any grounds for expecting one. Lysander and I were celebrating after the naming anyway. After a few drinks at the tavern, he had suggested we go and watch the torch race.

Before leaving the tavern, we had a few more drinks in honour of Philip, and Lysander asked me how he looked. I said he was just like all babies – shrivelled features, misshapen head and a look that veered unpredictably between bewilderment and contempt. I didn't mention that he was considerably darker and hairier than me or his elder brother Ararus – or Praxagora for that matter. I needed time to think about how to deal with that and comments from Lysander were unlikely to be helpful. It was all a bit worrying and Lysander picked up on my mood. "You're supposed to be happy today," he told me. "You look as if you'd rather not have had any children. Take this." He slipped me a small sachet of white powder. "It'll make you feel on top of the world." I was too preoccupied to ask what it was and swigged it down with the remains of my wine.

Until the appearance of young Philip, my domestic life had continued peaceful and happy. Praxagora was a devoted mother to little Ararus; her voice had become less shrill and she would sing to him for hours while he sat and gurgled or played with the little wooden toys Xanthias had made for him. Xanthias had shown a lot of skill at woodwork. He was still largely silent but seemed to understand anything we said to him and participated in quite complex conversations with grimaces and gestures. For some reason he seemed to avoid Praxagora except when he took her out to shop or listen to philosophers, and she seemed to avoid him as well. Human Artemis had changed a lot – and for the better. She seemed less concerned about river entry procedures and was good with the baby and at helping Praxagora make clothes. She did the spinning and seemed to get faster by the day, while Praxagora concentrated on weaving which she thought was more suitable for the lady of the house and certainly less monotonous.

There wasn't much to inspire a comic poet now that we were at peace. Argos was threatening to take over the Peloponnese and Sparta sent ambassadors to ask for an alliance with Athens to stop them. That would obviously have reconfirmed our peace treaty with Sparta, but Alcibiades, who had been made a general at thirty, the youngest age possible, was keen to draw attention to himself because he had been left out of the original peace negotiations, so he managed to undermine the deal. He conned our Assembly by telling the Spartan ambassadors to deny they had negotiating powers and then denounced them for lying about it so the Assembly would vote for an alliance with Argos instead. Nicias tried to counter him by sending an embassy to Sparta to reinforce the peace terms, but it was unsuccessful. Nevertheless, no one much wanted to revive the war with Sparta and the only sanction Alcibiades could manage to get imposed on the Spartans was getting them banned from the Olympic Games because they had refused to pay a fine for breaking the truce. As a brilliant snub to Alcibiades, a Spartan won the chariot race by entering under a false identity. Alcibiades' tricky behaviour didn't impress many Athenians and he was not re-elected general. People suspected he wasn't truly committed to our great democracy in the way people like Nicias and Demosthenes were.

With no other politicians behaving too badly, and with no external threats to warn the city about, I struggled for good material for my plays. For the Lenaea, Callistratus, who had forgiven me for all the past embarrassments, probably because he knew I had more winners in me and he couldn't be so confident in my competitors, put on *Campsite Grabbers* for me. It was about competition for the best spots at an overcrowded drama festival. There were some quite funny scenes as the chorus, half male, half female, fought over their preferred sites, and I was able to parody various playwrights who passed them on the way into the theatre, but it wasn't that good. Euripides enjoyed my send up of him, especially when the character representing Bloody Eupolis told the chorus, "I can easily imitate Euripides' polished style, but not his vulgar ideas." He thought it was a good send up of Bloody Eupolis too, with his slick verbiage.

We were back up to five plays now at each festival and some new poets were emerging. *Campsite Grabbers* lost out to Platon's *Hyperbolus*, a competent political satire but one that seemed to me a bit pointless as Hyperbolus hadn't been very visible since Cleon died. Platon also beat me at the Dionysia by coming second with his *Security Guards*. Bloody Eupolis won with *Cities*. It was appropriately sympathetic to Athens' allies, who were the cities in the chorus, but the only jokes were about Lycon's wife and I thought them a bit cruel. One character says she ruins every man in Athens and another asks if she is cultivated or unploughed! Poor old Lycon's drinking problem got worse and he didn't show his face in the Assembly for weeks. My own entry was *Heroes*. The chorus was composed of different but easily recognisable heroes from legend, and the real comic hero, helped, or more accurately hindered, by Hermes and Dionysus, has to decide whom to promote to demi-god. It was quite funny in parts and I thought it deserved at least a place, especially as for the next few days I heard plenty of people singing the chorus' Entry song:

*We are the keepers of evil and good,*
*We hunt bandits and thieves,*
*And bring them disease:*
*Burst spleens, coughs and dropsy,*
*Catarrh, mange and gout,*
*Madness and fevers,*
*Plague, cancers and shivers*
*That sorts them all out.*

Torch races are always quite good to watch, especially for anyone interested in staring at the fit young men who compete to carry fire from altar to altar, depending on which god was being celebrated, in this case Hephaestus. It was one of the more expensive public charities and a rich citizen was chosen annually from the ten tribes in turn to bear the expenses of the torch races, including the training of the competitors. My father's friend Eucrates had been assigned this role. I had no doubt he would have gone to a lot of trouble to try to get out of it but clearly hadn't succeeded. The first part of the event was the true race and the runners came round the circuit a few times so you could see a lot of it from just outside the temple of Hephaestus in the market place where Lysander and I were sitting. After the competition, the four fastest runners formed a relay team to carry the sacred torch once more round the circuit to the temple, while the four slowest got flogged.

Lysander hadn't noticed my abstraction and was still trying to cheer me up. "With boys, you just have to take them to the three days of the Anthesteria Festival before their third birthday and give them their first taste of wine. You'll be doing that for Ararus soon. And I assume you'll send them both to our old school – unless you want them to learn from the sophists." He laughed, being well aware of what I thought of sophists. "And you'll enrol them in our club when they're five. Then there's nothing much to do for them, other than make sure they go to school, until they reach the age of full citizenship at eighteen which is the big event – major sacrifice, special haircut and so on. Yours was a bit of a disaster as I recall." He was right. My father hadn't come so Lysander was the only guest, and Ismenias had refused to buy decent wine and had cut my hair so badly I'd had to wear a cap for two months. I think that's why I went bald.

The runners had just been sorted into relay team and flogging victims when an extra torch suddenly appeared behind where Eucrates was sitting and set fire to his elaborate race-master's cloak. It was the woman who had sued him unsuccessfully for breaking off their sexual contract. He leapt up, swung a wild fist in her direction and missed, ripped off his burning cloak and made a hurried dash behind a pillar in a rather inadequate tunic, shouting through tears of embarrassment for his slave to bring him another cloak. The woman escaped in the confusion, no doubt helped by some of the many people who disliked Eucrates and admired her courage. She got a laugh that most comic poets would envy and no one came forward to identify her when Eucrates tried to prosecute her the next day.

I hadn't found Lysander's arguments about the advantages of being a father of boys very convincing, and attributed them to the fact he had two daughters and no sons. I told him about Asclepius and his chariot and my mother but they had gone now and Lysander claimed he hadn't seen them. I was also starting to feel a bit weird. Colours seemed much brighter and noises louder, and I felt suddenly confident that the world was not a bad place and I could deal with whatever fate threw at me. "Where did you get that powder?" I asked.

"Oh. It comes from some sort of fungus. I can't quite remember its name. It begins with a psi. Psilo-something, I think. I saved some from the Eleusinian Mysteries last spring. Earth festivals like Demeter's tend to rely on these things to get everyone in the mood. Apparently, it's what the Bacchic worshippers in Asia use for their orgies – you can't get that crazy just on wine. I find it makes everything more interesting, even torch races." I had never been to the Eleusinian Mysteries, not having had a parent to introduce me and pay the entry fee, but I did know that everything that happened at the annual three-day ceremony was top secret, so I didn't ask any more in case I got Lysander into trouble. I was feeling good though, and ready for anything, even Praxagora.

"I'll confront them tonight," I said firmly. "You see if I don't."

"You do that. Be tough. Show them who's boss, whoever they are. Who are they, by the way?"

139

"Well obviously…" I stopped, remembering I really didn't need to tell Lysander my concerns. I could deal with this myself.

"OK. Don't tell me. I can guess."

"Don't you dare."

I marched home to confront the pair. As I should have guessed by now, neither of them were there. I suppose I could have had sex with Human Artemis, as both the little ones seemed to be asleep, but my feeling of invincibility didn't quite extend to that, so I just went to bed. I fell asleep quickly and had some very vivid dreams in one of which I saw the cloak being set on fire in the torch race, only the cloak was my father's and the culprit Praxagora.

I don't know when Praxagora got home.

# 28

I awoke to a world that had taken on pastel shades. I felt more relaxed than I had for a while and lay in bed admiring the drapes and the furniture under the strong impression that I had never seen them before. Praxagora was not in the bedroom but I heard female voices making baby noises, so I knew she was back and Human Artemis was in too. I didn't want to spoil my ultra-relaxed mood with a row but when she came in to see how I was, I thought I ought to get it over with and asked where she had been the previous night.

"Gorgias is back," she told me, "and I went to his afternoon session which overran a bit. You must have got back from the torch race very early. It was still light when I returned and you were fast asleep. How was it?"

"Where's Xanthias, then?" I mumbled, ignoring her question because I couldn't at the moment think of an answer.

"I gave him a couple of days off. It seems an old friend of his has just arrived from wherever it is he came from and his new master took him straight off to a farm. Xanthias has been so good recently with his woodwork and entertaining Ararus while I'm busy with the baby, I thought he deserved a break."

"Who took you to listen to Gorgias?"

"Oh, Xanthias arranged all that. The neighbours have gone to Salamis for a week and Xanthias arranged for their slave Sosias to look after me when I needed to go out. I gave him a little wine as a thank you."

I couldn't argue with that and was wondering how to introduce my concerns about Philip's appearance when I remembered I had an important meeting with Callistratus at the theatre. He had been as disappointed as I had at my recent failures and had said we needed a new plan. I floated along to the theatre where I found him pacing up and down. His eyebrows told me I was very late. We talked for a while but neither of us was very inspired. He suggested I give him my political plays to produce, while Philonides would do better with my literary satires and mythology-spoofs. I was a little surprised, knowing how nervous he had been about my political works after *The Babylonians*, but I think he knew I wasn't likely to be doing much political satire the way things were in Athens at that time. I wondered if he was punishing me for being late or if he was unsure if I was worth supporting any more. Either way I thought it was a bit ungrateful. He was still getting recognition and a little income for *The Acharnians* which was regularly performed at rural festivals along with my self-produced *Knights*. There was no point arguing though. Between Philonides and Euripides, I could be confident of funding if only I could think of something new worth producing.

An additional worry was the promise I'd made to Praxagora. I was coming up to two years without a win which meant I was due to give up playwriting and find another source of income. Remembering the trouble I'd had finding an acceptable job just after we married I decided to make an extra effort to win before the two years were up. Still stuck for ideas, I thought my best chance would be a rewrite of *The Clouds*. There was a lot of great comedy in the original and some excellent songs, well worth reviving. Unlike the first version, in which too few people had seen the irony and thought it was pro-sophist, I'd change the plot and have Socrates soundly humiliated instead of successfully helping the old man get out of paying his debts.

With all this and more on my mind, I decided I needed a chat with Pherecrates. I went round to his house, but he was out, so I decided to wait outside. It was a long wait, only partly relieved by the Fatties rolling along the street, giggling at some silly trick they had played on a male whore and singing one of Bloody Eupolis' choruses. When Pherecrates finally arrived, I didn't recognise him. I hadn't seen him for a while and I'd heard he'd been ill. I hadn't heard that one effect of his illness was that his eyebrows fell out, so it was now completely impossible to tell what he was thinking. He poured me a large glass of wine and I told him about my discussion with Callistratus and general lack of inspiration. He didn't seem to think it too much of a problem.

"You're good. You know you are, and so does most of Athens. There are lots of opportunities. Your literary spoofs are excellent and you could make a whole play with them. There are plenty of myths you could parody.

Personally, as you know, I like writing domestic comedy – plays about the typical life of Athenians behaving badly. I've never written anything very political since I got beaten up by Cleisthenes and Melanthius' friends after my *Petale*. I do enjoy the political stuff though and if you can think of a good subject, I'd like to help you with it, provided you promise I won't get any of the credit."

"You mean like *The Clouds*?" I asked hopefully.

"No, not really. That was more of an attack on the new philosophers and didn't seem to resonate with the judges. If you're not doing something political, just think about ordinary Athenians doing ordinary things and getting into some kind of trouble."

I tried again. "I thought I might have a go at rewriting *The Clouds*. The audience seemed to like it better than the judges did and if I make sure Socrates loses in the end, the judges won't have any reason not to reward it."

"Well, you could do that I suppose, but I wouldn't advise it. You've a far better chance with something fresh."

I decided to change the subject. "What if I don't have a win next year? You know I promised Praxagora that I'd give up writing."

"Don't worry, you'll win."

"But if I don't? I had a good look around last time she threatened to stop me writing and I couldn't find any way of making a living. I looked at all the crafts in the marketplace and the only one that appealed was being a barber and that's supposed to be just for slaves. Is there anything else you could suggest – working for the city in some capacity perhaps?"

"Well, you know most of the people who work for the city are slaves too. They have to be in case the city suspects something wrong is going on and needs to investigate. You can't torture free citizens."

"But someone said there were over one thousand citizens with official positions every year. There must be some reasonable jobs in that lot."

"We're a democracy, remember? A basic principle is that any citizen is capable of taking responsibility for anything. That's why pretty much all state jobs are short-term, unpaid and selected by lottery. You'll soon be old enough to serve on the Council if your tribe nominates you, and they probably will as most people get a chance at some point. But that's only a one-year appointment and each tribe only runs the show for a tenth of the year. And of course, it's unpaid and you can only serve once, so that doesn't solve your problem. Most of the positions reporting to the Council, looking after the navy, the building program, religious festivals and so on are unpaid committees, supported by a slave secretariat. For the top jobs like generals and treasury officials you need to be elected, which means you have to be rich for the election campaign in the first place, and you wouldn't get the job if you weren't because the city needs to be able to reclaim the funds from your estate if you are found to have embezzled anything. Pretty much the only paid positions in the public service open to citizens on the basis of merit and hard work are on the building program and they are all one-off."

"That might be quite promising. How do I get into the building program?"

"It takes a while and lot of focus and dedication. You won't even have time to go to plays, let alone write them. You start as an apprentice to an architect. That's not too expensive; Praxagora can easily afford that if she wants. You spend a few years following their every movement and running humiliating errands for them and learning every aspect of projects – drawing plans, learning measurement techniques and principles, allocating tasks to contractors, making sure supplies have been ordered in good time, checking the quality of the materials and workmanship, managing payments under strict contractual terms and… and various other things I can't remember right now."

It didn't sound attractive so far, but perhaps it would get better after the apprenticeship.

It didn't. "And then when you have shown you can do a good job, and if the right project comes along, and if there aren't too many other people after it, you might get allocated total responsibility for a small part of a project – half a column, say, or a corner of the building. You'd have to put in a budget and if it was too high you probably wouldn't get the job and if it was too low, you'd have to fund the overrun yourself. Then you'd take bids from subcontractors to do the work, draw up contracts, oversee their performance and pay them when you're satisfied."

"Sounds pretty dull. How do you get to be an architect? Designing a new buliding must be very challenging and rewarding."

"I'm sure it is. And you're creative so you might be very good at it, though there's a bit of a difference between a play and a temple. But getting

144

to be an architect comes last, after working up to it in the way I've just described. Architects tend to be old and grizzled and bad-tempered because it has taken them such a long time to get there. And even when they are recognised as excellent in their profession, there is still a lot of competition to win projects and a lot of financial and bodily risk if it goes wrong or if you overspend."

"So! A barber it is then."

"No, a playwright. Stick with it. I'm sure you'll have some more successes. You'd be wasting your talent doing anything else. Anyway, congratulations on the new baby. Does he look like you?"

I must learn not to show my emotions so much. Just as Lysander had, Pherecrates picked up on my reaction and his next question was, "Something is bothering you. A problem with the baby? I hope he's healthy."

I told him the baby was fine and, embarrassing though it was, told him it looked awfully like Xanthias. To my surprise he laughed. "Oh, is that all? I thought it might be something serious. Lots of families are bringing up children as citizens who were really fathered by slaves."

"I didn't know that."

He would have used an eyebrow at this point if he'd had one. "You are so naïve. Everyone knows that the master and his sons sleep with female slaves all the time. That's generally how boys learn about sex, even if you didn't. We discussed that before, remember? The only thing that is off limits is male citizens and male slaves. Citizens are expected to keep all the same sex stuff among their own class, including only using male prostitutes who are citizens."

"I didn't know that either."

"So, anyway, what's surprising about the mistress of the house having a bit of fun too? It doesn't always result in babies, but you'd be surprised how often it does."

"I expect you're right, but what should I do about it?"

"Do? Well there's not much you can do now. Bastards are generally aborted, but you told me Praxagora has always wanted a lot of children and she obviously thought she could get away with it. You can't really ask Xanthias to pay compensation because he won't have any money. If he was a citizen, you could prosecute him, though that is often more embarrassing than it's worth, but you can't really prosecute your own slave. You'd have to pay the fine to yourself if you won. You could sell him of course, but it might happen again with another slave. Anything else you do to punish him will just draw attention to the problem and he'll probably make sure it does. Better just to say nothing and treat the lad as your own. That will mean he's a full citizen. Otherwise he'd be sent to live with all the other bastards at Heracles' gym outside the city and I don't think Praxagora would thank you for that. Anyway, he might turn out to be a terrific success. He probably will if he inherits Xanthias' ingenuity and Praxagora's pragmatism and combines them with a good traditional education."

"And Praxagora?"

"I wouldn't raise it with her if I were you. There's not much that can be done about it now and if you make a fuss about it, she'll probably try to stop you going to Cunna."

Cunna! That's who I should talk to, I thought. I thanked Pherecrates for his advice – after all, it wasn't his fault that I didn't like any of it – and headed off to Aspasia's, hoping I'd find Cunna a little less depressing.

# 29

As I might have expected, when I got to Aspasia's Cunna was busy. Aspasia greeted me herself and led me over to a couch next to hers, clearing away a pile of scrolls she had been reading.

"Cunna shouldn't be long," she said. "Theogenes never takes long. But that gives us a chance to talk. I do so love having poets come and visit and it's quite rare nowadays. Pherecrates drops in sometimes for a chat, Eupolis came once but the girls and I didn't like him and I think he could tell. Euripides came once too and for some reason it didn't work out. Sophocles used to be a regular, but I think he's gone off women. And of course Agathon and a lot of other poets were never interested in us in the first place."

I was pleased with what she had said about Bloody Eupolis and assured her I would continue to be a regular as long as she and Cunna were there. She continued, "About the only conversations I get are with philosophers and politicians – the boring and the buggered, I call them." Great Artemis! The boring and the buggered! Was this really the refined intellectual Aspasia talking? Good for her! "So tell me what you are working on. I loved that line in *The Knights* about me and Pericles. You were right; today's politicians aren't my people and they can't hold a candle to Pericles."

I told her I was rewriting *The Clouds,* but she didn't seem too impressed. I tried to explain why I thought it would do better next time, but she wasn't convinced. "You should do more domestic themes. Take an interesting household with an intelligent and beautiful mistress and show some of the idiotic visitors they get."

I knew exactly which intelligent and beautiful mistress she wanted to see represented on stage, but I wasn't sure it was such a good idea. "That's interesting. Pherecrates suggested the same thing – domestic comedy," I offered. "There doesn't seem much to do in the way of politics, and audiences get plenty of myths in the tragedies, even without half the comedies spoofing myths as well. So I'll work on a domestic comedy as well as *The Clouds*. It's very important I win." I thought of telling her why but decided against it. I'd tell Cunna, but there was no point lowering what appeared to be Aspasia's high regard for me if I didn't have to.

"Of course, you'll win. My house doesn't accommodate losers – except some politicians of course." She gave a little chuckle and a wink. She must have heard something I missed because she exclaimed, "Ah, Cunna's free now. Here she comes. It's been so nice talking to you, Aristophanes. Drop in any time, even when Cunna's not available."

As she took me through to her room, Cunna said she was sorry to have kept me waiting. "I have to be nice to Theogenes. He thinks he is Ariadne's father." Ariadne was her daughter, almost ten years old now.

"Well, is he?" I asked.

"I doubt it. She's pretty and he's hideous. But it's always good to have a lot of people feel responsible for your children. Archeptolemus and Theramenes think they're her father too, so she should be well provided for."

I didn't really want to hear about all the minor politicians she was entertaining on Ariadne's behalf, so I changed the subject and told her about Philip and how he looked suspiciously like Xanthias. She seemed no more disturbed than Pherecrates had. "Are you surprised?" she asked. That sort of thing happens all the time and in the best run families."

"I was a bit surprised – and disappointed as well. I always thought Praxagora was faithful."

"Well, you're not. Why should she be?"

I didn't have an answer to that, so I told her how Pherecrates had said there was nothing I could do about it.

"You could always stick a radish up his bum. That's a traditional way of dealing with adulterers in my country. Apparently some of them quite enjoy it at first but it gets a bit warm after a while."

That was all news to me but sounded quite funny. I decided to include it in my rewrite of *The Clouds*, which led to a conversation about plays. She didn't seem enthused about the rewrite. "You should do something original," she told me. "That's what people like. I never heard of a prize going to a rewrite."

"But there's not much new to write about. We're at peace. The only politician behaving badly is Alcibiades and I'm not keen to be beaten up again. Aspasia suggested I write a comedy about this place, but I can't do that."

"Why not?"

"Because I couldn't do it without making her look silly and I don't want to do that."

"What about another domestic comedy then?"

"But if I do that, Aspasia will be offended I didn't use her idea."

"Zeus, you're being difficult today! How about myths?"

"Yes, I suppose that's about all that's left. And I think Euripides would fund me if I promised to parody him."

"That's it then. Go and talk to Euripides."

I dropped in at Euripides' house on the way home, only to find he was away at his holiday home on an island on the far side of Salamis. I left a note, asking him to get in touch when he got back. No one seemed to know when that would be. I spent the next few weeks playing with Ararus and trying to communicate with baby Philip. I was finding it quite hard to concentrate on the revised *Clouds*, having had such discouragement from everyone I had mentioned it to. I wondered now and then what myth I'd write about but decided I'd wait till I'd discussed it with Euripides. There was still nothing to inspire me in current events. Alcibiades was trying to stir things up in the Peloponnese again and Sparta had sent out a large army, no one knew why. They found the omens were unfavourable and promptly marched home again. Argos invaded Epidaurus but no one at Athens cared very much.

After what seemed like forever but was probably about a month, I received a note from Euripides asking me to meet him in the pub at sundown that day. I got there a bit early, which was a mistake because Criticus was lying in wait for me. After telling me how great he thought I was, he rather spoiled it by saying I could never write something as good as *The Knights* again. He came up with various reasons my recent efforts hadn't won, all of which I've forgotten, except, "Perhaps the semantic relationship between your fantasies and the world of logic and experience is not sufficiently defined in terms of the human comic impulse?"

Of course, this was the time for my now traditional response. "Fuck off, I'm a comic poet," I told him. He laughed, obviously thinking I was teasing him. I wondered how to make him realise I really didn't enjoy his drama classes, and I was unsure how to end the conversation if that attempt hadn't, when, to my great relief, Euripides showed up. He nodded brusquely to Criticus, grabbed my arm and took me off to a dark corner, signalling to the landlord for two tumblers of wine and something else I couldn't interpret.

He greeted me like an old friend, which I suppose I was becoming. He said he had found his island so conducive to writing that he almost decided not to come back to Athens. But certain things drew him. He winked, and asked me how I was doing. I didn't see any point in telling him about Philip and being told once again that there was nothing I could do about it, so I went straight to the point and told him about my urgent need to have a winning play. I skipped quickly through the reasons there wasn't much scope for a political comedy and the awkward situation with Aspasia if I followed Pherecrates and did a domestic one. I also told him I was rewriting *The Clouds* and got no more encouragement from him than I had from anyone else. It became apparent to us both that spoofing myths was the only sensible option, though I was looking for an intrinsically funny plot, while he was more focussed on opportunities to see his own plays parodied.

"How about Daedalus?" he suggested.

"That wouldn't be very interesting. Just a man and his son Icarus flying around on wax wings until Icarus gets too close to the sun and his wings melt. And we'd need two cranes and a very credulous audience."

"No, not that story. In fact not even a story about Daedalus. It's just a metaphor. Daedalus was a bit of a magician with lots of tricks up his sleeve and people who use his tricks call themselves a Daedalus. For instance, you could tell how the despicable traitor Eurybatus pretends to be Zeus and uses Daedalus' magical arts to adopt different forms to pursue Leda. He could try lots of things before finding that Zeus' approach, being disguised as a swan, was the only one that works."

That sounded OK to me and I could see the possibility of making it a sort of allegory about tricky Alcibiades pursuing the king of Sparta, though it wouldn't do for that to be too blatant. I was about to explore the idea further when Euripides suddenly got up and said, "Sorry, I can't wait any longer. Two months with no women is a long time." He disappeared towards the back of the tavern.

*Daedalus* was accepted for the Dionysia, probably more because of my reputation than because it was a very promising idea, but I worked hard at it and was disappointed to come second. Leda's cuckolded husband got a good laugh when he observed that, "All wives have a lover as a side dish," but the line was written with some bitterness. Our chances weren't improved by the fact that Leucon had put on a similar play at the Lenaea a couple of months previously – something the archon should have warned me about. I'd had to do a fair amount of rewriting and our early rehearsals were largely wasted. I also attributed some of the problem to the fact that the audience had had to sit through a trilogy by Agathon the same day, featuring such idiocies as, "It is a part of probability that many improbable things will happen." For the sake of Artemis! It was like listening to those philosophers for six hours. At any rate I'd beaten some good competition including Hermippus with his *Bakery Women* and Phrynichus with *Tragic Actors*, two quite different domestic comedies. But it hadn't solved my problem of having to give up writing and I'd been beaten by Bloody Eupolis again with his *Vigilantes*, which frankly wasn't very funny except in the parts he'd borrowed from my *Wasps*.

The discussion in the tavern afterwards seemed to be more about why Bloody Eupolis was so good than about how I'd deserved to win. There seemed to be a consensus that he was especially clever for inventing what had come to be known as the Eupolidean metre (ti-ti-tum-ti, tum-ti-ti-tum, ti-ti-tum-ti, tum-ti-tum). It had become popular with other comic poets, including Pherecrates and Leucon, and, the group agreed, I should use it myself. I pointed out that it was hardly a metre worth talking about as it was so flexible. Any of the 'ti's' in the first and third feet could be replaced by 'tums', so what is the metre exactly? And anyway, I had used it in *The Clouds* and look what happened to that.

As I was leaving, I was grabbed by Criticus who wanted to make sure I'd got the message. "Of course, with the Eupolidean meter you could synthesise the verbalising elements of your fantasy with the rhythm of the hum…" I cut him short by flashing open my cloak to display a wax tablet pinned to the inside bearing the words, *Fuck off! I'm a comic poet.*

When I got home that night, I found a wonderful thing had happened: my father had died.

# 30

It was Xanthias who gave me the news and in the way only he could. First, he picked up a stick, bent forward and started to hobble around while pointing at me, so I knew we were talking about my father. I nodded to him to get on with it. He dropped the stick, stood at attention, folded his arms across his chest, closed his eyes and looked, if not peaceful, as peaceful as nature had allowed him to look, and a lot more peaceful than my father usually did.

My first thought was that I was now at risk of getting Ismenias back. I would have to sail to Aegina and see if I could make any arrangements that would keep him and Nerita there. I now had the responsibility of caring for the pair, who were long past their sell-by-date. As far as I knew my father had no assets other than a modest-sized farm and if I sold that it would give me a little financial independence so that I could keep writing; on the other hand, it would mean the two of them would have to come to live with me in Athens.

Praxagora showed me the letter from her parents giving the news. They suggested that it would be important for me to visit my father's estate (*estate?*) and hoped Praxagora would come too. She decided not to, not wanting to take the little ones on a sea voyage in winter, but she thought it might mean that I would no longer be dependent on her. I told her not to get her hopes up.

When I arrived at the farm on Aegina, Ismenias and Nerita were nowhere to be seen. I was greeted by Clione, the slave girl my father had been bedding ever since my mother died, or possibly before.

"I been father, now I you," were her first words. "Happy us. Start now?" were her next ones, accompanied by a meaningful nod towards my father's bedroom.

"No, no, let's wait a bit," I stammered; she was at least twenty years older than me and had lost all her teeth and most of her hair. "I don't feel very well just now, after the sea trip."

"Ah, I see. You like Nerita, isn't it? You think she prettier from me."

"No, I really do feel ill." The thought of sleeping with either of them made the statement truer than it would have been a few minutes earlier. And pretty wasn't a word I could associate with either of them, so I changed the subject and asked where Ismenias was.

"He in town. Get papers banker. Back soon. Ah, here come."

This was probably the first time I'd ever been glad to see Ismenias. He was staggering under an enormous bundle of documents which he deposited on a table before turning to embrace me and tell me how very honoured he felt that he was now serving such a fine fellow and famous poet, and that he hoped his attentions would be everything I desired until he joined my father in Hades. Perhaps, I thought, now I was really the boss, if I did bring him back to Athens, he wouldn't lock me out at nights, but I wasn't altogether confident.

Ismenias took me over to the table where he had dropped the documents. They turned out to be the title deeds to farms or to houses in the town. It seems my father had been running a very successful protection racket. After the Aeginetans had been expelled from their island, a few of them managed to hide until the official round-up was over and many tried to come back after a few years. Either way they had to pretend to be Athenians and a discerning listener, such as my father, could always tell an Aeginetan by a slight idiosyncrasy with the letter 'th'. My father was quick to exploit this and roamed restlessly about the island for a few years, listening. When he found someone who was clearly an Aeginetan he offered them a choice: either he would turn them in to the authorities for almost certain execution, or they could sell him the title to their property at a price he would specify and pay him a rent calculated to allow them a modest living; in which case he would undertake to swear he had known them in Athens if their origins were ever challenged. Unsurprisingly, no one took the first option and my father had acquired twenty or so farms and several houses in town at outrageously cheap prices and collected enough rents to account for the three gold talents Ismenias showed me, hidden under the couch in the bedroom my father had shared with Clione. I was relieved to find Praxagora's parents were not among his victims, but decided not to call on them, being a bit uncertain as to how my new position would be received by the inhabitants, true Aeginetans or not. My father had been smart enough to overwork his own slaves, temporarily hired ones, and his tenants to supply Athens with produce during the annual Spartan invasions, which increased the income he received directly and through his rents. I reckoned he owned around a fifth of the whole island and the rental income was more than enough to cover my modest expenses (mainly Cunna) and even enable me to produce the occasional day at a festival.

My decision about Ismenias was relatively simple. I pretended to give him one of the gold talents as a reward for past work, and he pretended to give it back to me as the price of his freedom and Nerita's. I told him I was prepared to throw in Clione as well, for fear of the alternative. I then allowed the three of them to stay on my father's farm until the last of them died but offered no further support. I was well aware that they would have to spend an increasing amount of the farm's income buying slaves and maintaining them, as they were all too feeble to do much of the farm work themselves. In the event, the farm reverted to me within four years.

I travelled back to Athens with all the title deeds, the gold talents and quite a lot of cash in four-drachma coins. I decided to keep the cash at home, hidden in a large jar in my bedroom, so I could use it at short notice for Cunna or as a deposit on plays I might commit to produce. The three talents I took down to the Peiraeus under Lysander's promised guidance.

We went straight to the table of a banker whom Lysander told me was reasonably honest. He offered to look after all my money for nothing. I wasn't going for that, though I suppose some people do. I was about to take my money home and ask Praxagora or Pherecrates for ideas when Lysander intervened: "Put it to work for him, like you do for me."

"Wouldn't it be better just to keep it safe for him?" the banker asked.

"No. And you know I don't think so or why would I have insisted you put my money to work for me?"

The banker shrugged indifferently. "Well, I suppose I could get him six percent on a mortgage on land."

Not knowing if this was a fair offer I signalled urgently to Lysander. We moved a few paces away and whispered to each other. "What do you think?" I asked.

"It's obviously a rip off. He gets twelve percent. You should ask for nine and settle for seven." I asked for time out, during which, with the help of a friend of Lysander who was close by talking to another banker, I worked out that seven percent on two of the talents would bring me an income of a little over two drachmas a day – about twice the average wage. Added to the rental income, this was unimaginable wealth. I could become like Alcibiades, though I hoped I wouldn't. We went back to the banker and after a long explanation as to how anything above six percent would put his family on the street he contradicted himself by saying he could only give better rates to people he had known a long time. As he was going to have the money, it wasn't clear why he had to trust me or why I should trust him. He offered me six-and-a-half, but I stuck out for the seven as Lysander had said I should.

I gave him two talents and the other, still under Lysander's guidance for want of an alternative to hand, I invested in three maritime loans, one for three thousand drachmae, which bought me half of one voyage, and two for one thousand five hundred each, buying me a quarter in one case and a third in the other.

I went home, satisfied that if I hadn't made the best possible decisions, at least I could afford not to. And, as I seemed to have put my money pretty much where Lysander put his and he was familiar with this stuff, it was probably going to be OK. Even if it wasn't, the rental income would cover most of what I would need. I thought I might use the spare drachmae to catch up on my presents for Cunna and went to check exactly how much they amounted to. I found them gone.

First, I checked underneath the vase in case I had decided to put them there. It was a pretty forlorn hope as there were so many the vase couldn't have perched on them and I seemed to remember pouring them into the vase anyway. With modest expectations I searched the rest of the bedroom and then, with expectations more modest still, the rest of the house, though I did pay extra attention to Xanthias' sleeping quarters. It was a big enough pile to be difficult to hide and I found nothing. Even so, I thought, there could only be one culprit.

When Praxagora returned, I asked her if she was happy with Xanthias. She looked a bit startled at the question and asked why I wanted to know all of a sudden.

"Because I'm about to sell him," I told her. "He's pinched my cash."

"Oh, don't do that. It would be very unfair."

"So! You'd defend him, would you? I thought as much. He's special to you, isn't he?"

"No more special than any slave should be to his mistress. But the fact is he didn't take the money; that was me. I was going to put it back, but I needed it urgently this afternoon and I didn't have enough of my own at hand."

"Urgently? Why?"

"For Hippias, the poor soul. I can't tell you how much I admire that man. He's an authority on everything, you know. He said so himself. He's so clever he said he would go to Olympia and speak to any audience on any subject they propose to him. He has what he calls a 'binding principle' which is self-sufficiency. He thinks we should only use what we make ourselves, which is all very well but you should have seen what he was wearing. The left arm of his tunic was a foot longer than the right, his cloak was fraying where the stitching was coming apart and the soles of his shoes had somehow disappeared. Of course, I had to do something and I bought a smart new outfit and gave it to him just as he started his lecture. He didn't seem very grateful, though. I wonder why."

Before I could enlighten her, Xanthias arrived in person with an invitation I couldn't refuse.

# 31

Perictione was getting married again. She was one of the true aristocrats, descended from Solon, the great lawgiver. Her first husband Ariston could trace his lineage to the early kings of Athens and Messenia, and her new husband was her uncle, the equally distinguished Pyrilampes. He had been a friend of Pericles and served many times as ambassador to the Persian court. His son from a previous marriage, Demus, was famous for his beauty and was destined to get more attention at the wedding than the happy couple.

It was only recently I had started to be invited to events like this. The guests were drawn almost entirely from the aristocracy. Perictione's brother, the well-known politician Charmides, was there, and another uncle, the even better-known Critias. Alcibiades was there of course, along with some of his long-haired friends. Demosthenes was unwell but Nicias represented the old-style politicians; Hyperbolus hadn't been invited and nor had any other demagogues. Other than Agathon and Bloody Eupolis, I was the only creative artist; most other poets weren't considered distinguished enough and Sophocles and Euripides tended to avoid large gatherings, though Agathon didn't.

After the sacrifices and the ceremony, prodigious quantities of the best Chian wine were circulated and the party broke into small groups. Agathon was chatting up Demos but didn't seem to be getting anywhere, so several other men were waiting to take his place. Alcibiades and Eupolis seemed to be hitting it off, but the politicians generally avoided each other and each formed the centre of a mostly female group of admirers. A young boy, probably eleven or twelve years old, neatly dressed with a round face, an untidy mop of hair and slightly bulging eyes, was sitting by himself in the corner. He had a strangely surprised expression which intrigued me, so I went over to talk to him. It turned out he was Perictione's son by Ariston and was called Plato.

"What do you think of think of all this?" he asked, in a beautifully mellifluous but adult tone. I later heard the story that bees had settled on his lips when he was in the cradle, which was supposed to account for the sweetness of his voice. He was a serious young lad; his permanent look of surprise made you think he was questioning everything you said and very often you'd be right. After astounding me with his knowledge of various sophists, he started grilling me about Socrates, about whom he seemed to have a lot of information. "It's not so much what he says himself as what he gets other people to say that is so impressive. I heard about your *Clouds* and I understand it was very funny, but I don't believe Socrates was the right target. I hope you'll attack some of the real rascals in future." I promised I would, though I wasn't sure how.

Our conversation continued till long after the guests started to leave. He put his hand on my thigh and said his mother had told him it was time he found a mentor. He had been thinking of asking Socrates, but he seemed to have quite enough young boys to keep him occupied and he thought I'd be more caring and informative. I hesitated. I didn't feel I wanted to be responsible for the development of someone as smart and well-connected as Plato, nor was I keen to add a young boy to my love life, being quite satisfied with Cunna and Praxagora and vague intentions towards Human Artemis. I told him I would be happy to be his friend and to talk to him as often as he wanted in the way we were then, but if he was looking for an older lover, he should try someone else. He seemed happy with this arrangement and it was the start of a life-long friendship.

His comment on *The Clouds* made me realise I should stop messing around and either complete the revised version or give it up and do something new. I had made lots of changes to the original but didn't see how I could change the main butt to someone other than Socrates. The audience was quite well-informed but there was not much chance more than a quarter of them would recognise any of the other sophists. And anyway, I wasn't going to be told what to write by an eleven-year-old. The changes I had already made were designed to get over the original audience's failure to grasp the irony and make it quite clear that sophists were a bad thing by having Socrates lose the battle to save Strepsiades from his debts. As well as completely rewriting the ending, I added a new character called Better Argument to counter sophistry, now represented by Worse Argument, and composed a new Address, explaining why I thought the play had failed before and observing that it deserved much better this time. I still wasn't quite happy with it and a little deterred by the total lack of support I had so far, so I asked Pherecrates to have a look at my revised script. He was busy with a play of his own, but still managed to find the time to read it in a couple of days.

His reaction was very disappointing. Rather than look at the cleverness of the overall concept and the way the drama now unfolded under the new plot, he homed in on inconsistencies. "Whose side are the clouds supposed to be on?" he asked. "Socrates is meant to be their enemy, but he is the one who invokes them and they then start encouraging Strepsiades to avoid his debts. And why does Strepsiades have to be taught to respect the old gods when he has already made a case for Zeus against the sophists? And how come Strepsiades still blames…"

"All right. I can fix all that up. There are bound to be a few glitches when you change the plot so radically. But what do you think of the play overall? Do you think it's funny? Do you like the Better Argument? Do you see what I've done in the Address?"

"Frankly, it's not one of your best. It's quite funny but not as funny as the original. And putting all misconceptions aside, that still counts, you know. You'd be far better off coming up with something original. It's worked for you before and it will again."

I decided to give it one last shot. I took the script to Euripides for a second opinion. Unfortunately it was like the first opinion – if anything, more nitpicky. "You talk about the teachers as things to be learned and then you put them on stage. The Better Argument has the same views on the benefits of austerity as Socrates. The nature of Socrates' interest in sex is implausible – and believe me I know about implausible interest in sex. Stop wasting your time trying to save the play's life. It's dead. Do something new. Now I think you could make a very good comedy out of the story of Danaus, perhaps spoofing the tragedy I wrote about him."

So for the next few weeks I tried. It wasn't a bad story in fact. Danaus was the son of the Egyptian king and he had fifty daughters by ten different mothers. The king of Arabia just happened to have fifty sons by a similar distribution of mothers, and commanded Danaus to marry his daughters to them. Danaus preferred to build a ship and flee with his daughters to Argos, where they were given asylum. The king of Arabia followed them and offered the Argives protection against their enemies, in exchange for which he was granted his wish for his sons to marry Danaus' daughters. Danaus told his daughters to murder their husbands on their wedding night; forty-nine of them did, one sparing her bridegroom after he agreed to allow her to remain a virgin. The surviving husband got his revenge for the murder of his forty-nine brothers by murdering Danaus.

It was a simple story that had been used by Aeschylus as well as Euripides, giving me plenty of scope for parody and lots of jokes about wedding night activities. Obviously comedies don't really accommodate mass murder, so I'd give the bridegrooms some humiliating punishment instead, resulting in permanent impotence. Danaus would make just the kind of anarchic hero I liked to feature and I could split the chorus between the sons and the daughters, with some dances representing chase and escape. The Celebration would feature the daughters' relief at ending the sons' sexual attention, but only after gratifying themselves.

It got accepted for the next Dionysia and I had pretty nearly finished the work when I failed to avoid Bloody Eupolis at the theatre, where we were both arranging times for rehearsals. He seemed a bit down and appeared unusually glad to see me. He told me he had been having trouble at home and his current play *The Friends* was not going well. I wasn't surprised; from what I'd heard it was just more attacks on poor Lycon's wife. This time he called her the town donkey.

"Look I know you've got a couple of new plays up your sleeve. Can I borrow one? I'll pay you back when I've got things sorted out and am feeling creative again." This was a strange request from an arrogant swine. I couldn't help feeling a little glee that he was reduced to making it. I was a bit puzzled, though, because he had talked about *The Friends*, which I knew he had been working on for ages, but the play outline he had submitted to the archon was about some Egyptians. I explained that I didn't have anything finished and was spending all my time on a myth parody, which wasn't his type of theme. He suggested he might finish one of my incomplete ones, but I pointed out our styles were very different. He said they weren't that different and he'd prove it one day. It wasn't long before I found out what he meant.

This being a comedy and women needing to conform to their comic stereotype, in my version of the story Danaus' daughters were not inclined to play hard to get but were exceedingly manipulative and saw no need to treat their partners well once they had had enough fun with their bodies. Their attitude was conveyed, rather well I thought, in a half-chorus:

*I'm going to Argos, so follow me quick,*
*I can't bear a minute away from your prick.*
*I've a palace of pleasure to circle your head –*
*Enough to get started – and then off to bed.*
*Follow me there and then put out the light,*
*We'll see who's master on our wedding night.*

When Xanthias came up to me looking anxious a few days before the festival and said, "Palace of pleasure, ho, ho! Put out the light, ho, ho!" I was amazed.

"That's brilliant, Xanthias. I had no idea you could speak so much Greek. You must have been working hard at it. Well done. I'll teach you some more of my verses if it's such a good way for you to learn."

So far from accepting my compliments and offer of support, Xanthias looked even more anxious. His cheeks and a large part of his nose disappeared entirely into his beard and his eyes peered at me over the top as if I was a complete idiot. "Eupolis," he said. "Bloody Eupolis." I had obviously taught him that too. He grabbed one of my arms and started dragging me out of the house and pulled me all the way to the theatre, where the wretched man was having his final rehearsal. It was considered bad form for playwrights to attend one another's rehearsals, so I stayed outside the theatre but moved round to be level with the stage so I could hear everything. It didn't take long to discover that Bloody Eupolis had not only pinched some of my best lines, but the entire theme. As I had suspected, the talk about *The Friends* was a ruse. What I hadn't suspected was that his *Egyptians* was the same story as my *Danaids* but without the clever twist I had given it.

When my indignation had abated somewhat, I began to think seriously about what I could do. Eupolis was scheduled for the first day of the plays and I for the fourth. No matter how much better my play was, the audience wouldn't take kindly to seeing the same myth parodied twice at one festival, let alone having to listen to some of the same verses. I could complain to the archon, but he really shouldn't have let this happen in the first place, so he was unlikely to be sympathetic. Nor was there much he could do at this stage, other than cancel Eupolis' production which would have made him look silly. I had no option but to scramble something else together in the ten days before I had to produce something. I decided on a rewrite of *Peace*, not because it was a good idea – it would be pretty meaningless now after a few years of real peace – but because I had been assigned most of the original cast and it was the only thing I thought I could revise and rehearse in time. I made a few changes: Eupolis and Platon had both made fun of Peace being a mute statue, so I gave her a speaking part, and I did the same for Agriculture, as it would have been more front of mind and less a matter for nostalgia than at the time of the first production. It was under-rehearsed and came nowhere. I can't honestly say it deserved better. It wasn't for another twenty years that I actually put my *Danaids* on stage.

At the Dionysia, I couldn't confront Bloody Eupolis on the first day because he was behind the scenes preparing *The Egyptians* and went straight to a party afterwards at Alcibiades' house. He didn't turn up for the rest of the festival, obviously hoping to avoid me, but he had to be there at the end for the judging. When I confronted him, he put on his superior look and tried to convey injured innocence.

"How did you decide on that theme?" I asked.

"Oh, that. That was Euripides' idea. He's been encouraging me to put on a myth parody and we thought the Danaus story was a good one. I don't think anyone else could have done such a good job with it as I did." He had come second but his effort hadn't deserved to. Mine would have won.

"Where did you get the daughters' song to the sons? I know it's not original."

"Oh, I heard someone singing it in a barber shop and borrowed some of it. It was obviously quite well known." Now this could have been true, though I knew it wasn't; while the actors, the chorus and the stagehands were all sworn to secrecy before a production, there were almost fifty people who had heard the song and one of them might have enjoyed it so much that they couldn't help themselves singing it. The barber shop was a bit of a giveaway though. The singer would have had a dozen voices asking where he got the song from and, even if he had tried to make up a story, it would have become obvious it was a new one. Bloody Eupolis had probably paid someone to bring him part of my script, but it would be impossible to find out whom. I resolved to get my revenge before long.

First, I went to Euripides and told him I was furious that he had made the same suggestion to my chief enemy as he had to me and accused him of giving the swine the song. He burst into tears. "I didn't. Of course, I didn't. I wouldn't. I hate Eupolis. His language is horribly slick and his parodies of me are pathetic. You're the only comic playwright I want to work with. How could you think I'd do something like that to you?"

When I had dried his tears and apologised for suspecting him, we went to the tavern and, before he slipped out the back as usual, he had invited me to spend a few days with him on his island near Salamis, talking and writing. "And I've got a very nice surprise for us there," he added.

# 32

We had to wait a few weeks before we could go to Euripides' island, as the Assembly had voted to approve Council's recommendation that no one sail west from Athens until the fighting in the Peloponnese had stopped. Sparta, Corinth and Boeotia had taken it into their heads to attack Argos. Sparta would have won easily as they had completely surrounded the Argives with the largest force they had ever put in the field (not that the Argives knew they were surrounded), but just before the battle two of the Argives and the Spartan king made a private peace and the Spartan troops went home. The Corinthians and Boeotians were now seriously outnumbered and had no option but to do the same. A private peace! My idea from *The Acharnians* finally put into practice.

We were all set to leave when, instead of lifting the travel ban, the Assembly extended it until we knew if Alcibiades was going to be successful in yet another attempt to stir things up. He had turned up at Argos to try to persuade the Argives and some of our own Athenian allies to attack Arcadia. I don't know where he got that idea from, but it made no sense to anyone in Athens. Fortunately, the Argives didn't join in, not being confident in Sparta abiding by the private peace. We didn't join in either but sent some troops to defend Argos in case the Spartans attacked. The Argives were right to be suspicious; Sparta did attack and over a thousand were killed on the Argive side, including the Athenian general whose name now escapes me. I don't think it was because of the private peace though.

Finally we set off on our planned forty days' working holiday. Euripides' island was quite a large one, being a little over a mile in circumference, and he had it all to himself and the two male slaves he kept there, not trusting himself with female ones. His residence was on the sheltered side of the island, not far from the mainland and convenient for getting supplies in the little boat drawn up on the beach. On the other side of a small hill, with a view of the open sea, was his writing studio which contained a large desk, two chairs and four chests of manuscripts which I discovered included five of the seven Homeric poems, works by Hesiod and Herodotus, and play scripts of his own and others including, I was glad to see, Aristophanes.

We spent the first week or so wandering around the island talking, occasionally interspersed with an hour or two's composition. Euripides had suggested I write about how the seasons stop functioning and fruits and crops appear at strange times of year. The sudden availability of out-of-season produce causes a massive increase in consumption, leading to a prosecution banishing the seasons from Athens with the result that nothing grows at all until the hero brings them back. It included some satire on immigrant gods and cults, notably Sebazius, the Phrygian flautist. I got in some jibes at Callias for wasting his money on sophists, Chaerephon for his devotion to Socrates and Theogenes for the monstrous way he emptied his bowels, but Euripides' motive was simply to see more parody of his own work. He offered to help me with it and did so to the extent of writing almost half of *Seasons* himself. In the meanwhile, he was working on *Heracles* and I provided regular advice and a few innovations he rejected. The story was about Heracles trying to capture the dog Cerberus from the underworld. When he gets home, having completed that labour, he finds his father Amphitryon, his wife Megara and his children have been sentenced to death. He is in time to save them, but then the goddess Iris and a personified Madness cause him to kill his wife and children in a frenzy. I wrote about his successful return from Hades and the beginning of the rescue scene, though Euripides changed some of my lines, but I didn't feel ready to cope with the gory ending. Talking through his approach with him whenever he took a break from writing, I learned a lot and was to use that knowledge in the one tragedy I wrote myself – of which more later.

One night as we were going to bed, Euripides told me to get a good night's sleep, as I'd need all my strength in the morning. I wondered what he meant. He was a bit old to be planning athletic pursuits. Perhaps he just envisioned an extra hard day's work. I had forgotten about it the next morning and was about to go down to the studio to resume writing when Euripides jumped up excitedly, pointed to the sea between us and the mainland and cried, "Here they come! Come onshore, my beauties."

The little boat was rowed by a couple of slaves and on board were four females. As they approached, I noticed they were young and lovely. One in particular stood out; she had curly golden hair, a gorgeous figure, and long, elegant legs and, I noticed as the boat drew close to shore, perfectly formed features, neatly made-up and displaying carefully painted dimples. Even in the awkwardness of disembarking, she maintained a dignified aristocratic air and a winning smile. I didn't recognise any of the ladies, so they weren't from Aspasia's, but one might have been the Pellene who had left there in a huff after Ariphrades had shocked her modesty with his tongue.

Three of them, including the possible Pellene, advanced on me seductively. They took it in turns to paw me in increasingly private places, while the other two danced around hoisting their robes and cavorting in poses that left nothing to the imagination. I was sufficiently occupied not to give any thought to what Euripides was up to but assumed he had gone back into the house with the prettiest one. This assumption was confirmed by a furious yell. The pretty one came running out of the house, pursued by a large pot, flung by Euripides. She just managed to duck, but in the process her wig fell off. She was Alcibiades.

Rather to my regret, my companions left me alone and after applauding Alcibiades for the success of his trick they boarded their boat and set off again. I could hear them laughing all the way to the far shore. Euripides was sitting on the beach, picking up handfuls of sand and small pebbles and running them through his hair, just like one of his own tragic heroines. When he had recovered enough to speak, he said, "This will be all over town soon. How will I ever be taken seriously again? Anything I write about female passion and suffering will just invite people to think about my own excessive passions. Add to that my being taken in by Alcibiades and I'll be thought of as so obsessed with sex that I'm anybody's fool." When he had calmed down a little, I told him not to worry. Audiences didn't care too much what playwrights got up to as long as their works were good. This wasn't true, but it seemed to cheer him up a bit. He asked me to plead with Alcibiades not to let it go any further. I didn't think that would do any good, but promised anyway. When I got back home and confronted Alcibiades, it was just as I expected.

He laughed and pointed out that the girls he had hired from Orchilochus for the day weren't likely to keep quiet about it – "And they're pretty well connected, you know," he added with a mean chuckle. Euripides got more support from Aspasia who was horrified to hear of the trick and offered Euripides free access to any of her girls for a year. Of course he didn't want it.

Soon after my return I bumped into Callistratus on his way to the theatre. He greeted me like a long-lost friend, which I suppose I was, though he had been pretty cold at our last meeting when he told me he'd only produce my political plays, knowing perfectly well I had no plans to write any.

"Ah, Aristophanes, just the man," he cried. "I was just going to the theatre to see if there was any new writing talent about. The stuff people have been asking me to produce is simply awful. I don't think much of young Platon, I can't bear Eupolis and that Criticus wouldn't know a joke if it jumped out of a wooden horse at him. I really miss our happy days working together. And I didn't mean what I said about political plays only. It could be anything. So, what have you got for me?"

I was pleased I was back in Callistratus' good books; he was a decent sort and we'd done some great things together. But all I had to offer was *Seasons* and I didn't need a producer anyway now I could afford to finance my own work. On the other hand, he was a good producer and an excellent chorus leader and letting him produce would free me up to spend more time writing comedies and learning the tragic craft from Euripides. I agreed and *Seasons* won the Lenaea. Euripides was secretly overjoyed but refused to take the credit that was his due lest it do further damage to his reputation.

About this time Praxagora told me I should think about what our boys were going to do. She had started to worry that now we were in a position between the two of us to support them indefinitely they might end up as useless layabouts like Callias or hell-raisers like Alcibiades. She wanted them either to become sophists or be taught a craft. The idea they might become sophists horrified me. It might be lucrative but, in my view, it was a shameful exploitation of gullible people like Praxagora. In any event there was little we could do to train them in sophistry at their tender ages of three and one. She said that I should get on with looking for crafts they could learn in case the sophistry path didn't work out.

I reminded her of my day in the market looking for a suitable career and how it was so hard to make more than a very basic income from personal exertion – except possibly as a barber. She said the money didn't matter, it was just important to give them a purpose in life and keep them from roaming the streets looking for mischief. The fine arts – pottery, painting, sculpture and music –offered a chance at fame as well as an income if you were good enough. She urged me to investigate and see if the boys might get an apprenticeship with a good teacher when they were a little older.

This all seemed rather premature as the boys couldn't be taken on until they were at least eight or nine, even if we wanted them to miss a lot of schooling, but I thought that rather than argue with Praxagora I might as well do something I'd probably have to do at some time anyway. And it might give me good material for a play. I promised I'd start my investigations the next day and then turned my thoughts to revenge on Eupolis.

# 33

That night I dreamed I was in the workshop of my namesake, Aristophanes the potter and painter, with a suddenly teenage Ararus. Aristophanes was laughing as he painted his trademark heavy lines around all Ararus' features. "Do you want an apprenticeship too?" he asked, advancing on me brandishing a brush dripping with red paint. In the meanwhile the human characters on the vases he had already painted had turned into birds who were flapping around the workshop trying to untangle themselves from the heavy lines that surrounded them. Dreams don't recreate the past, they create the future. Was this what my sons would do, paint pictures of birds? Would that be a satisfying life for them?

I woke at the first touch of Aristophanes' paint brush, which turned out to be a peck on the cheek from Praxagora. "Time to get going," she instructed me. "You've got a busy day coming up." I don't know if she expected me to come back with craft apprenticeships lined up for our two infants and babies yet unborn, and anyway I wanted time to concentrate on my revenge on Eupolis, but I thought I'd better make myself scarce. I rose, grabbed a pomegranate and a handful of figs for breakfast, and headed off.

I couldn't face the idea of making a fool of myself by asking various craftsmen about possible apprenticeships for the distant future, so I decided that I would tell Praxagora I'd spent the day enquiring how Ararus could make a career as a sophist. I could make that up. I headed for a quiet corner of the Arcade where Lysander and I sometimes met when the taverns were shut, and ate my breakfast there. It was a good place to observe the world without being noticed; you could see busy people coming and going between the temples and law courts and offices that filled the space between the Arcade and the marketplace, a corner of which was visible across the Panathenaic Way. I sat and gazed and tried to think about Bloody Eupolis. It was clear to me that a suitable revenge would involve getting him to produce a play that would get him into trouble, but I couldn't think how.

Hoping an idea would come to me, I started thinking about my next productions.

I was planning to enter a play in each of the two festivals coming up and had worked out the outlines but needed to come up with some more dramatic twists to make them work. *The Centaurs*, which I was aiming for the Lenaea, was about an exceptionally smart, civilised and immortal centaur called Chiron. The other centaurs, being descended through a family line which started with a king raping a minor cloud goddess under the mistaken impression she was Hera queen of the gods, were bestial, ugly and mortal. One other centaur shared Chiron's looks and demeanour, though not his immortality, and his name was Pholus.

On his way back from capturing the enormous Erymanthian Boar, Heracles stopped by Pholus' cave for a swig of wine. When the other centaurs smelled the wine they went nuts and charged into the cave where most of them were killed by Heracles with arrows soaked in the poisonous blood of the Hydra, and the rest fled. Poor old Chiron was asleep nearby by and got hit by an arrow; the wound was so painful he traded in his immortality and was glad to be allowed to die. Pholus picked up an arrow and cut himself with it by mistake. Same result, though he had no immortality to renounce.

I had decided to set the play in Cyllus' Wallet, a space behind the Areopagus well-known for casual sex encounters, largely involving women desperate to get pregnant. The centaurs would obviously go in for a lot of dirty dancing. In my version it wasn't the smell of the wine that attracted the centaurs' attention – Heracles drank all that too quickly – but a lamb Pholus had brought for sacrifice. This was a parody of the festival at which fathers introduce their sons to their club that I had represented in my first play, *The Good and the Buggered*. It was customary for the assembled club members (in this case the centaurs) to pretend to humiliate the presenting father by pointing at the lamb he had brought and shouting "Too small! Too small!" Of course, the phrase created an opportunity for a string of dirty jokes. I'd thought of making the sacrifice a piggy, but the club parody wouldn't have been so clear.

I was pretty happy with where I'd got to with the plot and some of the key situations, and confident I had more than enough to make a compelling case for selection by the archon. I had got less far with my thinking for the

Dionysia. I planned to present *Anagyrus*, the name of a southern suburb of Athens, called after the foul-smelling wasp that attacks the fruit trees growing there that supply most of the city. The hero, also called Anagyrus, finds an old man cutting trees in his orchard and plans revenge which takes a rather complicated form involving the old man's mistress and Anagyrus' son and results in them all dying horrible deaths. As with *The Centaurs* – and in fact with most myth and legend parodies – I had to find a variation on the story with less death in it, but it would be a good opportunity to parody Euripides again and he still needed cheering up. I would put in a bit of social satire about the poor going to the baths at the same time as the rich in order to use their sponges. And I would get in a lot more digs about Bloody Eupolis' plagiarism, pointing out the *Brigadiers* he had put on the year before last was the third time he had based an attack on Hyperbolus that was derived almost entirely from mine on Cleon in the *The Knights*.

I was beginning to try to solve the *Anagyrus* plot challenge, and wondering if I was fated to spend the rest of my life dreaming up bloodless but comic forms of revenge for the stage and for Eupolis, when loud shouting broke out about twenty paces or so from where I was sitting. The painter Micon had been painting a mural there and four or five long-haired thugs were pulling him around, twisting his arm behind his back, tripping him up and generally behaving in a way that showed a distinct lack of approval or affection. They looked like friends of Alcibiades and I thought I recognised Callias in the middle of the melee.

When they decided they had done enough, they ran off with loud shouts of glee, evidently feeling they had done a great job. It seemed they had. I moved over to where Micon was lying on the ground, covering his bleeding face with his hands. "Ow! Ooh! I think I've gone blind," he moaned. I pulled his hands away from his face. "Ah! That's better. I can see a bit, but it's all blurry."

"You're probably a bit dizzy from being hit on the head. You'll get over it. No bones broken that I can see. So, what was that about?"

"Don't ask me. I was just sitting here, quietly getting on with my painting when they jumped on me. They said something about Alcibiades, but I couldn't make out what."

I looked at the mural and saw immediately why Micon had been beaten up. It was a painting of Zeus disguised as a swan in the act of raping Leda.

The beautiful Leda was a perfect image of Alcibiades, especially perfect to one who had seen him dressed as a girl as I had. His friends obviously thought being raped by a god wasn't the sort of image Alcibiades liked to have and had taken it out on the unwitting painter. I explained this to Micon and suggested that to avoid similar problems, he should get an escort or a friend's wife to sit for him and try to represent her features accurately, it being unlikely that they would look quite so like Alcibiades. He seemed grateful but said he didn't feel like working any more that day, packed up his paint and brushes and limped away.

Watching him go, I realised he had just given me an idea for Bloody Eupolis. The most certain way to get him in trouble was for him to produce a play insulting Alcibiades. The challenge was how to get him to do it. He was unlikely to ask me to write something for him again, knowing how I'd reacted to his theft of my *Danaids* material. However much he relied on outside help, he would know exactly what everything produced in his name would be about, so I'd have to find a way round that. I decided the only thing I could do was see what plays he had lined up and hope for inspiration.

I went to the theatre and looked at the list of competitors selected for the Lenaea and Dionysia. The lists included the names of the actors who had been allocated to each production and I saw that my old friend and colleague Archinous was assigned to Eupolis' *The Dippers*. I was surprised because I knew Archinous didn't think much of Bloody Eupolis' plays and had often told me he wouldn't work with him again. Remembering how his partiality for cheap wine had ruined the final rehearsal for *The Good and the Buggered*, I tracked him down waiting for the taverns to open and when they did, bought him enough wine to keep most people drunk for a week.

"How's *The Dippers* going?" I asked when he was suitably mellow.

"Bloody awful," he shouted in reply.

I asked him to keep his voice down – the tavern was quite full already – and what was wrong.

"That cowsucker Eupolis is gape-arsed impossible. He won't let me use the crane and you know I always insist on that. He gives me words so pissing delicate and refined they feel slimy in my mouth. And what's with this fancy Eupolis meter? Pretty much anything seems to fit it, except when I do it and then he bawls me out. It's undignified and I'll never sign up for him again. If I'm allocated, I'll pretend I'm sick."

"But you never liked his plays. In fact, you told me you wouldn't work with him again. What happened?"

"Well, you might as well know, at the end of the selection process, the archon told me there had been complaints about my drinking during rehearsals. Some people are so unreasonable. He was going to give me one last chance to prove I could go through the whole preparation process sober, and if I didn't, I would be suspended from both major festivals for three years. Well of course I didn't want to spend the next three years playing at rural festivals and private dinner parties, so when I was allocated to Eupolis I couldn't just find an excuse to get out of it as I would have otherwise. But it's even worse than I knew it would be."

"Would you like to get your own back on him?"

"Of course – as long as it doesn't get me into more trouble with the archon."

"Would you like to see him beaten up by Alcibiades' friends?"

"But he's a friend of Alcibiades himself."

"We can soon put a stop to that."

I made him give me an outline of the play's main scenes and the meters they were composed in and told him I'd write a few lines insulting Alcibiades. Before he lapsed into incoherence, I impressed upon him the need to keep the material secret in rehearsals and only insert it in the final production. Not being sure he would remember, I decided not to give him the lines until after last rehearsals.

The *Dippers* are priests of the Thracian goddess Cotys, another of those eastern religions which seem to be largely an excuse for an orgy. They were originally called dippers because they baptise new initiates in a vat of wine before getting down to the indiscriminate sex, but the word also suggested the long-haired youths who dipped their hair in a variety of dyes before their orgiastic festivals. The cult was starting to be taken seriously by some quite sensible citizens and I had to admit Eupolis was quite right to make fun of it before the rot spread much further. The play didn't sound as if it was going to be very funny as it just showed a lot of non-descript characters going wild; it had been done before and would be done many times again – in fact I would use a similar theme in my one tragedy. To spice it up, I made it a lot more fun for the audience by having Archinous identify the leader of the crazy cultists as the son of Cleinias. Everyone knew that meant

Alcibiades, whose social antics and anxiety to start a war were making him increasingly unpopular. When Archinous imitated his lisp, the audience roared. In the lines I added he even admitted to being a traitor – a charge that turned out to be prescient.

It worked! That Lenaea was the first time I'd ever been glad to come second to Bloody Eupolis. My *Centaurs* would probably have won if I hadn't made *The Dippers* so popular by sending up Alcibiades. I was less pleased that *Anagyrus* came second at the Dionysia to Phrynichus' play *Lady Mowers*, a trivial production if ever there was one.

I was expecting Eupolis to get his beating any day, and he was expecting it too, which made it more satisfying for me. He seldom left home then and didn't submit any plays for the next year's festivals. Alcibiades was clearly biding his time. I knew he hadn't forgotten about it when I received an extraordinary invitation from Agathon to come to a symposium he was giving in a few days' time. Agathon wasn't really a friend – in fact we'd hardly spoken since our schooldays – and, when I saw the guest list, I felt proud to be included until I read further.

*Of course, I was going to invite Eupolis,'* Agathon wrote, *'because he always speaks so well at these occasions, but I'm hoping Alcibiades will come and I know he won't if he knows Eupolis is going to be there. Socrates is definitely coming and so is Doctor Eryximachus and Phaedrus and Aristodemus. The theme of our conversation will be love, so try and come up with something witty and clever for a change. And don't be vulgar.*

# 34

A couple of days later an excited young Plato ran up to me in the Arcade where I was waiting for Lysander to go for a drink. "You've been invited to the great symposium with Socrates," he cried, his eyes almost popping out of his head, but still managing to make his congratulations sound like questions. "Well done! I'd love to help you with your speech."

"How did you know? And you're fourteen years old and I'm a well-known writer, so why would I want your help with my speech?"

Plato looked a bit crestfallen and I felt I'd been a bit harsh, so I put an arm round him, then took it away quickly in case he misinterpreted my intentions, and told him I'd be glad of any suggestions.

"Well, I have been following Socrates around a lot. My mother doesn't mind as long as I don't miss too much school. She thinks I'll learn a lot from him and I already have. That's how I know about the symposium. Socrates isn't very organised about appointments and things like that, so my uncle Critias keeps a diary of important events for him and I always try to get a peek at it so I can listen to him when I can. Critias had included the whole guest list."

"Well, what do you think would be a suitable theme for my speech?"

"I'll give it some thought and get back to you," he said with irritating self-assurance. "Meanwhile you look a bit miserable. What's bothering you? At least you're not scared for your life of Alcibiades' thugs like poor Eupolis."

I could have done without the 'poor', preferring 'bloody' myself, but I couldn't help smiling at how public Eupolis' terror was. Plato was looking at me intently. I had no desire to tell him about my domestic worries but thought he could help me with some things that were puzzling me. "Have you ever heard of Prodicus?"

"Yes, he's a friend of Socrates. He likes asking questions just like Socrates does."

"And Thrasymachus?"

"The new rhetoric fellow? Of course."

"And Callicles?"

"I can't bear him, he's a horrid man. He thinks it is all right for the strong to dominate the weak and unfair for the weak to pass laws against oppression. He doesn't believe our sense of right and wrong is divinely inspired and says all our institutions are there just to further some people's self-interest. He claims the self-transformative potential of mankind makes divinity redundant, but he's wrong of course. Worshipping the gods is fundamental to civic order, irrespective of any transcendent verities. And besides everything we see or touch or hear is an imperfect attempt to replicate the ideals which are outside our physical frame of reference." Not for the first time, I found myself struggling to make sense of the child's deep philosophical thought but didn't let on.

"Why are you so interested in all these sophists?" Plato asked. "Are you trying to find a different character to make fun of as you did with Socrates in *The Clouds*? That's a good idea, by the way. Or are you going to do something new about sophists?"

"Yes, that's it," I lied, "something new about sophists." After a bit more chat about what was wrong with Callicles, we parted, Plato promising he'd be back with ideas for my symposium speech in a day or two.

The real reason I had been asking about sophists was because of my disquiet about the time Praxagora was spending out with Xanthias. Once she had come back wearing his cloak and claimed she had been helping a friend in labour and had borrowed the cloak to keep the baby warm. I found that a bit easier to believe than all the times she said she had been listening to sophists, but if Plato was aware of them, they must exist and she must at least have done her homework. When I confronted her, she refused to discuss the possibility that she was having sex with Xanthias, claiming she thought him ugly. Then she started going on about my relationship with Cunna and the conversation took a similar turn to the last time the subject came up. "You can have as many men as you want," she told me. "Find a young boy to mentor and I would even be proud of you. It's that you need other women that I find upsetting." We had no sex for months then and I spent a lot of time with Cunna until one evening when I was drunk and exceptionally charming and Praxagora seemed flushed and excited when she came back from that day's sophist. That resulted in our third son, Philetaerus (meaning Dear Comrade). For some reason she never explained, Praxagora chose to call him Nicostratus (Victorious Army). He grew up answering to both names, but I think he preferred mine.

My concern about Praxagora and Xanthias should have allayed my enthusiasm for carrying out my original intentions, now nearly ten years postponed, with Human Artemis, but it hadn't. It wasn't that I found her especially attractive. She wasn't, though she washed more now she was looking after the little boys and was a bit less smelly. It wasn't lust that was driving me, more a sense of a long-standing obligation, a promise I had made to myself and had never got around to fulfilling. So when Praxagora told me she was going to help yet another friend in labour and expected to stay the night and would send Xanthias home once she got there, I saw my chance had come. I gave Xanthias the evening off and told Human Artemis that she must stay at home that evening as I had something very important to impart to her. Xanthias seemed delighted and said something I think was about dogs. Artemis just stared right through me. My courage nearly failed at that point and I went to the tavern to recover it.

When I came back a couple of hours later, I felt ready for Human Artemis – or indeed for anyone of either gender who might present themselves for my care and attention. But there was no one at home. I checked all the rooms and looked under the furniture and in cupboards, but it was clear that on this my big night with Human Artemis I was the only adult in the house. The last place I looked was my own bed – with hindsight that might suggest a lack of confidence, I suppose – and there was a note.

*Gone to Alcibiades. He knows how to treat a real lady. Be kind to Xanthias. You can trust him. And be careful how you go with rivers. Artemis.*

At that time Alcibiades had been up to some of his more outrageous tricks. After his wife's failed attempt to divorce him, he had got heavily involved in politics again, advocating a return to war on the flimsiest pretexts. There had been a major debate in the Assembly as to the treatment of Melos, an island colony formerly belonging to Sparta that had refused to join Athens under the terms of the treaty as islands similarly placed had.

The debate was a good Contest between those who argued that might was right and we should punish Melos severely because we could, and others taking a more pragmatic view and concerned that harsh treatment would encourage more allies to desert. I would have enjoyed writing both sides of the case, but Alcibiades of course wanted the harshest possible treatment for the Melians and his view carried the day. Melos was captured after a six-month siege; the men were executed and the women and children enslaved. Alcibiades bought a very beautiful woman from Melos as a concubine, which I suppose might have been his original motivation. Soon afterwards he created a scandal at the Olympics by entering seven teams of his own in the chariot race. He came first, second, and fourth and boasted about it for weeks. He was also rumoured to be trying to start another war, this time in Sicily. He was inevitably pretty full of himself and unlikely to be very tractable, but I felt I couldn't just let him steal a slave from me without remonstrating.

As I expected, he thought the whole thing was a huge joke and suggested I buy another slave. "If she's pretty enough, I'll take her too. Better get an old hag," he chuckled. "But here's a deal. If you promise not to make fun of me again in your plays, I won't make fun of you by telling everyone about Artemis running away to me." I had to agree, but I wasn't planning to make fun of him anyway – at least until I saw what happened to Eupolis.

A few days later I came across Alcibiades' Melian concubine heavily pregnant and begging in the streets, having been thrown out by Alcibiades when Artemis turned up. She had no commercial rights, even to herself, so she couldn't even be taken in as a slave in another house without being sold by a third party. I took her to the slave market and found a kind buyer, having turned away several who offered more but would have been less sympathetic to an unfortunate like her. I gave the money, which really belonged to Alcibiades, to a veteran who had been wounded in one of Alcibiades' unnecessary campaigns, to enable him to buy the strong male slave his mutilation meant he needed.

In the event, Artemis came home within three months looking as scruffy as a half-plucked chicken. She had been abused daily by Alcibiades and claimed to be shocked at some of the other goings on in his house. Praxagora wouldn't have her back and went to see Alcibiades' wife

Hipparete to tell her she could keep her. Unfortunately, Hipparete not only wouldn't oblige but told Praxagora the circumstances of Artemis' leaving us, which led to the usual deprivation. My visits to Cunna were pretty regular at this point, but the idea of women refusing to have sex with their husbands struck me as a good idea for a play. Praxagora insisted on selling Artemis and replacing her with a male slave. To my surprise, Xanthias seemed happy about that and even happier when Praxagora chose a slave as different from Xanthias in appearance as it is possible for one human being to differ from another. Tall, gangly, fair-haired, clean-shaven and speaking perfect Greek in a rather high-pitched voice, when Praxagora and Xanthias brought Manodorus back from the slave market I asked where he had come from. "Far west," he giggled, standing awkwardly on one leg. Praxagora laughed too, as if it was the funniest thing she had heard for a long time. I wondered why.

When I told Cunna about the end to Artemis' adventure she couldn't stop laughing. "At least it means I'll get to see more of you," she said sweetly, knowing how I had generally tried to stay away from Artemis. "But what about Xanthias? He'll be deprived too, now that Artemis is gone."

"Well, I offered to pay for prostitutes for him once a month, but he shook his head and said something about dogs. One night I followed him and found he was spending his free evenings at Cyllus' Wallet where a lot of upper-class wives enjoy a bit of rough."

"That's all right then," Cunna smiled. I wasn't sure about that, but I let it pass. I told her about how Praxagora wanted the boys to be craftsmen or sophists and she asked why they couldn't be playwrights too. I said I could see no reason as they wouldn't need to earn a living and Ararus was already showing extraordinary talent at saying things in verse including some quite complex choral metres. We then talked about the symposium I had been invited to. She was impressed that I was mixing with intellectuals, though none of them were her men friends. I told her I was struggling to think of what to say and she suggested something about how we were all incomplete halves of a being until we found our other half. It didn't seem very clever to me at the time, but I thought I might have to go with it unless Plato came up with something better.

# 35

Plato didn't come up with something better. In fact he came up with pretty much the same idea as Cunna, people being incomplete till they find their other half. Continuing to lack inspiration myself, I had been relying on him to produce something relatively finished which I could edit a little, adding a few jokes, but he hadn't done that either. "Sorry, I was hoping to give you a first draft, but I got caught up with a discussion Socrates was leading about the immortality of the soul and I had to write up my notes on that, so I didn't have time. It doesn't matter though; you're an experienced writer and I'm sure you can knock something up."

I had until the following evening to prepare but, try as I might, the words came with difficulty and I struggled to make sense of the whole idea. For one thing, if you put two people together of whatever gender and in whatever configuration, there would always be at least one orifice unoccupied and in some combinations several. How could that be clever? I wanted to make it funny but was in danger of making it ridiculous. By the late afternoon of the next day, just a couple of hours before the symposium was due to start, I had come to the view that working on it further was not going to improve it, so I'd have to rely on on-the-spot inspiration, which indicated a preliminary visit to the tavern. I sought out Lysander and told him I felt very unprepared.

"I need to be inspired tonight," I told him. "Come and have some wine and help me get in the mood."

"Are you sure wine's the answer? You'll get plenty of it at the symposium and if you start now, you'll probably go to sleep or do something absurd."

"That's all very well, but frankly I'm more nervous and less well-prepared than I've ever been before a performance. The way I'm feeling I'll probably just freeze when I'm called on to speak."

"How about some mushrooms then? They made you feel pretty confident last time."

I wasn't altogether sure about this. Yes, they had made me confident, but they had also made me see Asclepius and my mother riding around in a golden chariot, and since that time I'd become convinced that it might have been an hallucination. I expressed my doubt to Lysander and he told me not to worry.

"That was a different mushroom, psilo-whatsit. This powder," he said, pulling out a little sachet, "comes from a different species, called fly agaric. It's gentler and shouldn't give you hallucinations, but will still do wonders for your confidence."

I wasn't completely convinced but then I thought of going to the symposium in my present state of nerves, so I took the powder. Lysander sat and chatted for a while and when he left, I was still feeling as nervous as before. I had an hour or so to kill so I went and sat in the marketplace for a bit, thinking that the noise and bustle at the end of the day might brace me a little. As I sat there, I felt my confidence in my speech growing just as Lysander had said it would. I was no longer worried about being underprepared and started to look forward to receiving the plaudits of Socrates, Agathon and even Alcibiades for brilliance, originality and spontaneity.

Just as I was about to set off for Agathon's house, my attention was drawn by some strange noises from the bird stalls nearby. Philocrates, the largest bird retailer, was having an argument with the combative little Asopodorus. Others were coming up to watch. Sporgilus the barber was there, along with Spintharus from Phrygia, Lycurgus just returned from an embassy to Egypt and Socrates' friend Chaerephon. As I watched, I seemed to be back in my dream about the potter-painter Aristophanes: all the human figures except Philocrates himself started turning into birds. Asopodorus became a jackdaw, Sporgilus a sparrow, Spintharus a finch, Lycurgus an ibis and Chaerephon a bat. As others arrived on the scene, the same thing happened to them. Menippus became a swallow, Syracosius a magpie, Opountius a one-eyed crow, Cleocritus an ostrich and the stupid Meidias a quail. Others changed into birds before I could recognise their human forms. I saw a hoopoe, a lark, a partridge and a goose. I had a nagging feeling that there was something else I was supposed to be doing but I couldn't think what and this was too good to miss. It seemed to me that the bird each person was represented by was particularly apposite, so I went through them one by one making the connections. Most were to do with their appearance or behaviour; Opountius was hideous, hence the one-eyed crow, the quarrelsome Asopodorus was a typical jackdaw and so on. I was puzzled by Meidias being a quail but then I remembered the popular boys' game of quail-tapping, where one contestant put his quail on a board and his opponent hit it on the head. If the quail moved, the striker won; if it stayed put, the owner. I didn't know if whoever was responsible for this spectacle was implying Meidias was as slow to react as a quail or that he had been hit on the head too often. Either way it was a good bird to choose.

I must have closed my eyes at that point because I suddenly saw the entire Boeotian army at Delium turned into vultures; they were picking away at a prostrate Athenian who looked like Chaerephon. That made me think of his friend Socrates and I opened my eyes with a start, suddenly remembering what I was supposed to be doing. It was dark and the birdmen had vanished, leaving only Chaerephon who was lying on the ground contemplating the stars with a look of intense concentration. Whether he was conducting a scientific experiment or dead drunk I didn't have time to find out.

Fortunately, Agathon's house was fairly central but when I arrived the symposium seemed to have been going for some time. Socrates was cuddling Agathon, to the disappointment of a rather mature looking flute-girl, while the ugly nymphomanic dwarf Aristodemus was kneeling between Socrates' legs with his head nowhere to be seen. Another flute girl was entertaining Doctor Erixymachus in a similar manner and Phaedrus was asleep with a happy grin on his face. No one took any notice of me and just carried on with what they were doing until there was a loud noise from outside and Alcibiades burst in. He was dressed extravagantly, even for Alcibiades, with multi-coloured ribbons in his hair and a massive garland of ivy and violets. "Can I join you?" he asked. "Would you dwunkardth like to dwink even more with thomeone who ith even more dwunk? Or thall I just put the twophies on the head of the beautiful Agathon, which ith what I bwought them for?"

Against what would have been my better judgment, the group welcomed him in. Socrates hurriedly pushed Aristodemus away and he crawled under the couch heading, I assumed, for Agathon's back door. Agathon tore himself away from Socrates and stood up. Alcibiades took off his garlands and ribbons and held them towards Agathon, pretending not to have seen Socrates, before dragging Agathon back to the couch and sitting down with his back to Socrates who was on his other side. He kicked off his shoes, made a great ceremony of crowning Agathon and then pretended to see Socrates for the first time and expressed great indignation that he had been sharing a couch with Agathon. Socrates apologised to Agathon for Alcibiades' behaviour and explained to us all, tongue only half in cheek, that whenever he 'spent time with' a beautiful young man like Agathon, Alcibiades' mad passion for him (Socrates) sent him (Alcibiades) into a rage of jealousy. He claimed to have been living in a state of permanent terror in case Alcibiades caught him in a situation just like this. Just then a squeal and a giggle from a flute girl standing behind them suggested that Aristodemus had mistimed his emergence from underneath their couch and got himself entangled in her robe. A little later the giggle turned into a contented purr; Aristodemus was showing his versatility. Alcibiades started to turn to investigate but Socrates embraced him enthusiastically and held him tight. Alcibiades seemed sufficiently glad to have regained Socrates' attention that he started taking the ribbons back from Agathon and setting them lovingly on the philosopher's head, patting Agathon's thigh all the while to show there were no hard feelings. He then started to sing Socrates' praises in an embarrassingly over-the-top fashion, starting with his provocative way of arguing and his remarkable self-discipline (not altogether appropriate I thought), and coming to a ridiculously flattering description of how he had conducted himself at the battle of Potidaea, where he claimed the philosopher had saved his life. This was a highly dubious story of which I had already heard several conflicting versions, but I didn't want to attract Alcibiades' notice more than I had to, so I kept quiet. It was a relief when he concluded by describing the determined and courageous look on Socrates' face as he marched through the lines at Delium. I had seen that face at exactly that time and would have described it as resembling a pelican giving a carefully constructed impression of a frightened hare, but I still said nothing.

I was wondering how such a scruffy, ugly, dirty old fellow like Socrates was able to attract beautiful young men like Alcibiades and

Agathon when the philosopher announced that it was my turn to speak. This put me at rather a disadvantage, not having any idea what someone might have said before, and the great wave of inspiration that a few hours earlier I had been so certain would rush on me was showing no signs of coming to my aid. I was relieved therefore when Alcibiades intervened.

"What! Lithten to a comic poet when we could be dwinking! Lithten to an idiot talking about love when we could be making it! Wathte an evening in chatter when we could be wevelling like the godth! I wouldn't have come if I'd know it wath going to be one of thothe dull eveningth. Come on, Agathon, thurely you can give better partieth than thith." With these words he signalled to a slave to bring him a huge wine cooler, holding about four pints. He swigged it back and told the slave to refill it for Socrates, observing that no amount of wine would make Socrates the least drunk. Socrates knocked back the wine just as fast and appeared none the worse for it.

Alcibiades then turned his attention to Agathon, perhaps hoping to make Socrates jealous, or, more likely, because that was what he had had in mind when he arrived, while Socrates proved he was as unaffected by the wine as Alcibiades had said he would be by starting a strange conversation with Erixymachus about the physical symptoms of love and how a good doctor might distinguish them from lust.

I closed my eyes and tried to work out what bird would be right for each person. I had already compared Socrates to pelicans and storks several times in my plays, but I couldn't work out whether it was Alcibiades or Agathon who best deserved to be represented by a peacock. I must have nodded off for a while because when I awoke the cocks were crowing and almost everyone else was either sleeping or had left; the only people still awake were Agathon and Socrates, both, amazingly, still drinking. I lay half-dozing for a while, scarcely taking in their conversation, until I heard Socrates say something about comedy. I assumed he was going to say something rude about *The Clouds*, so I listened more intently.

I'm glad I did because he wasn't talking about *The Clouds* at all. He was explaining his view that the ideal form of comedy and the ideal form of tragedy were divine sisters and the passage between them must be easy for a true lover of either. I didn't like the metaphor much, but it was exactly the point I believed myself. I had promised myself I'd prove Sophocles wrong by writing a great tragedy and talked it over so many times, mainly with Euripides, that I considered myself a bit of an expert on the topic. I was planning to join the conversation when Socrates put an end to it. "It's fully light now. I promised I'd meet a group at the baths this morning to talk about the role of philosophers in the ideal state and they're probably already waiting for me. I must go now. Agathon, may the gods reward you for your hospitality – and for all the other pleasures you provide for a sad old man like me. I look forward to your next play and our next divine encounter." So off he went, having been up all night drinking and making love and expressing deep thoughts, still ready for another day's philosophising. What a weirdo!

To my own surprise, as the old man left, I got up, patted him on the back and said, "That's it, old friend. Tragedy and comedy. Closely related. Easy passage. You've got it, chum. Well done!" Socrates said nothing. He just looked through me, kissed Agathon and went on his way.

All was quiet then, just me and Agathon still awake and presumably he was ready to sleep. I wasn't, having had a few hours of shut eye and weird dreams by then, and still feeling a bit of a tingle from Lysander's powder. I was keen to discuss the extraordinary evening with someone. I went to Aspasia's house, not really expecting to find Cunna up and free at that hour, but Aspasia herself met me at the door and reminded me Cunna was going to visit her family in Asia and told me she had just left. I knew Euripides had gone to his island and armed his slaves with spears and bows and arrows and instructions to repel all visitors, so I couldn't talk to him. I went round to Perictione's place, only to be told Plato was busy organising his possessions prior to a lengthy educational trip overseas with one of his uncles. Lysander was a possibility, I suppose, but I thought my strange evening deserved more than cynicism and contrived jokes, funny though they might be at other times. So, I just went home. Praxagora and Xanthias were already out. I spent a few unproductive hours thinking how I could turn my visions of birds into a play, and when they came back, I gave Praxagora a brief summary of the evening, not drawing too much attention to my part until the farewell. Her response was only moderately enthusiastic. "You called Socrates 'chum' and patronised him? Well, I don't think many people will ever do that, so I'm quite proud of you. But obviously you're wrong to treat him with so little respect. You should listen to him and the other philosophers before you make fun of them."

This was unfair because I always did my homework and listened to sophists, politicians, generals, poets and anyone else before I made fun of them. But I still wasn't sure if I'd struck quite the right note with Socrates.

# 36

"It'll be tough on the barbers," someone said.

"Yeah, if it was Goldilocks it wouldn't affect them."

"And the general's bald anyway."

I had dropped into the tavern on my way to the marketplace to take part in the ostracism vote, hoping to find out what was going on. Every year the Assembly has to vote on whether to ostracise someone without anyone having to suggest who it might be. Most years the answer is no but this time Hyperbolus had made sure it was yes, which meant that two months after the vote, all citizens had a chance to say whom they'd like to see banished for ten years. Provided at least six thousand citizens vote on ostracism day, whoever gets the most votes gets banished. Whenever the Assembly votes for an ostracism ballot, you can be pretty sure there is an orchestrated campaign behind it with a specific target in mind and this time most of us thought the target was Alcibiades, either for his permanent desire for war or for some of his shocking activities at home, but of course you just don't know whom the banishment will fall on until the vote takes place, and there is always a lot of manoeuvring behind the scenes.

"Why isn't it Goldilocks anyway? He's the one I'd like to see the back of," someone offered. A murmur of assent ran through the group; he was not alone in that.

"He's too smart and he's got so many powerful friends he can afford to bribe every citizen in Athens; it was never going to be him. That's why the general got involved and they did a deal." This from a one-armed veteran who, judging by the attention he was getting from the group gathered around him, was clearly thought to know what was going on.

"What deal?" I asked.

"Haven't you heard? We are all supposed to vote against mini-Cleon, so neither of them will get the most votes."

I was beginning to make sense of the conversation. Goldilocks was obviously Alcibiades and the mini-Cleon the barbers would miss had to be Hyperbolus, but who was the general?

"Well, it's not going to be Demosthenes, is it?" the veteran told me. "Everyone loves him and he isn't the one who has got his name on the peace with Sparta. And nobody cares about Lamachus very much. There's a lot of people who'd rather be at war you know, not just Alcibiades and Hyperbolus. They might have had enough votes to get rid of Nicias. And Alcibiades wasn't going to take any chances."

"But that would be awful!" I cried. The thought of losing Nicias when we had an opportunity to lose at least one out of Alcibiades and Hyperbolus made no sense. That's the trouble with democracy; it can be so unpredictable.

"Lucky it's not happening then," the veteran grunted. For some reason everyone chuckled, but I couldn't leave it like that. The whole thing sounded too chancy. Surely there were other candidates we might be considering.

"What about Theramenes?" I asked. "He's a bit of a stirrer. Aren't people sick of him?"

"They will be one day," he prophesied, accurately, "but he's very smart and he's lying low at the moment. He reckons whoever loses is one less opponent for whatever it is he's planning. Right now ostracising Hyperbolus suits him well. And it would serve him right for starting the whole thing."

Neither the military peace nor the peace among our rabble-rousing politicians had lasted very long. Of course Alcibiades was at the centre of it all, though for anything involving war, Cleon's disciple Hyperbolus joined him enthusiastically. First they took advantage of the fighting that was continuing between Sparta and Argos. We refused the help Argos had come to ask us for and when Sparta knocked down their newly constructed city walls, so far from offering any support, Alcibiades rounded up three hundred Argives he claimed had been working with Sparta and imprisoned them on various islands of ours. It may have been this sort of bellicose behaviour that led to the ostracism fiasco and Alcibiades may well have been the original target. Between the original vote to have an ostracism and the ostracism vote itself so much plotting and backroom bargaining had been going on that most citizens were as confused as I was about whom we were supposed to ostracise. I would have voted for Alcibiades anyway, but I wanted to see what he did to Bloody Eupolis first.

I left the tavern and, sure enough, when I joined the crowd of citizens shuffling into the corner of the marketplace that had been closed off behind wooden panels for the vote, I could hear citizen after citizen saying Hyperbolus' name to the clerks, who inscribed each nomination on a shard of pottery. At nightfall when the shards were counted, it turned out nearly ten thousand citizens had voted, three quarters of them for Hyperbolus. He had ten days to get out of town. Not a bad result. In the event it wouldn't have made much difference if it was Alcibiades, as he was soon to desert us for ten years anyway. There haven't been any ostracisms since then, which in my view is a bit of a shame, but it does put the onus on us comic poets to keep dangerous people in line, and I suppose that's not a bad thing for the profession.

The one-armed veteran in the tavern was not only right about Hyperbolus but he was right about there being a lot of citizens looking to start the war again. A pretext came in the form of a request from Egesta in Sicily for help against its aggressive neighbour Selinus. The first I knew about it was a letter from Plato, whose uncle had taken him on a round trip of the Western Sea on the way to an extended sojourn in Egypt. Writing from Tarentum, he told me Egesta's request was on its way and that we would be mad to respond to it. The big game was Syracuse itself which had ambitions to take over the whole island. It was very powerful and had plenty of local allies and was certain to get help from Sparta. Athens, Plato said, must realise that if it gets involved in Sicily, it will almost certainly lose and strengthen Sparta. He added that even if we won, he couldn't see how it could do us much good anyway.

It was as he feared. We totally underestimated what we were taking on. When the ambassadors from Egesta arrived, Demostratus proposed we send troops to support them. When he described the scale of the undertaking he was proposing, it became very clear that he aimed to establish a large presence on the island to stop Syracuse's expansion and ultimately conquer Syracuse itself. Alcibiades followed with a speech in honour of himself, his war record and how his 'dithtinguithed lifethtyle' brought glory to Athens, and showed his ignorance by concluding, "Thicily ith dithorganithed and badly equipped; thucceth will be eathy. Thafety lieth in ecthpanding our empire."

Nicias was the only person who made the argument against getting involved. He said the plan was ill-timed and too ambitious. "You are leaving a lot of enemies behind you and making new ones there," he said. He thought that Alcibiades was still too young to be much good as a general and only wanted the war so he could pay for his horses. He argued that we would need far more ships, land troops and provisions even than Demostratus was asking for. And, he added, even if we sent enough troops to conquer the island, he didn't see how we could control it afterwards.

So far from bringing the Assembly to see sense, Nicias' words seemed to make people more gung-ho. They voted for a huge contingent to be dispatched in sixty ships, under the leadership of Alcibiades, Nicias and good old Lamachus, my military butt in *The Acharnians*. Nicias was obviously unhappy that his good intentions had rebounded so badly. There was some talk he might use the new public indictment law, under which decrees of the Assembly can be challenged in the courts, but there was no real prospect of success and his enemies would have accused him of cowardice.

All the same, the ill-fated expedition was thrown into disarray before it started by a very public act of sacrilege. As all Athenians know, nearly everyone's house and quite a few sanctuaries have four-sided pillar-statues with the face of the god Hermes by their entrance to remind those going in and out that Hermes is in charge of the premises. One morning, just a few days before the fleet was due to sail, the city woke to find that all but a handful of these herms had been defaced – a terrible omen for the expedition.

Of course, when things settled down after a few weeks, we all acknowledged that it was most unlikely to have been the work of any of our citizens. Most would have at least some fear of Hermes' vengeance and the penalties for getting caught were certain to be horrendous. Much more likely it was the work of foreign agents, probably from Sparta but possibly from Syracuse. Before the city admitted this obvious conclusion, though, there was chaos, gossip running wild and everyone finding different suspects to point the finger at. I think Socrates and I were the only people who had been at Agathon's symposium not to come under suspicion. Things got worse when the council offered rewards for information leading to convictions. Alcibiades was an obvious suspect because he and his gang were wild enough on one of their big nights to do something like that and it was rumoured that they regularly offended the gods by performing a comic version of the secret Eleusinian Mysteries in their homes. On the other hand, he was all set on leading the attack on Sicily, and it didn't make any sense for him to jeopardise that, however much he might be inclined to show his contempt for the gods. But as you can imagine, that didn't change the general view in taverns and barber shops that nothing like this could have happened without at least some involvement of Alcibiades. A rumour went round that Eupolis was about to denounce him. I have an idea I might have started it. In any event, Alcibiades insisted he wanted to clear things up before the expedition and demanded to stand trial. His aggression towards Sicily and the big promises he had made about the campaign had made him pretty popular though, and his enemies couldn't bear the idea of a public acquittal, so they blocked the trial and bided their time.

Meanwhile, the priests of the Eleusinian Mysteries, backed by a few religious extremists, decided the sacrilege was the work of rationalist philosophers. Diagoras of Melos was prosecuted but acquitted because of a lack of evidence, and several others went into hiding. Another group started a rumour that it was the beginning of a plot to replace the democracy with an oligarchy and informed against anyone who had ever shown a less than whole-hearted enthusiasm for the way our democracy worked. I was afraid I'd be caught up in that for all my satire and went to hide in one of my father's empty properties in Aegina for a few days. Quite a few other comic poets fled the city for longer, which reduced the competition for a while, but I was sufficiently satisfied that my service to the democracy had been for the good that I felt safe to go back to Athens as soon as the fleet sailed.

I missed the departure of the fleet, but I gather it was quite spectacular. The sixty fighting ships were accompanied by four thousand hoplites on forty transport vessels, all looking their best in shining new armour, dozens of supply ships, smaller boats carrying archers and javelin throwers and so on. Everything you might need for a military adventure you might think. Before the fleet left, "Taking a huge amount of Athens' money and manpower," as boring old Thucydides observed in his history, there was a bit of chaos on the quayside. Alcibiades refused to sail until he was certain Bloody Eupolis was on board (the poets' exemption from call-up had lapsed when peace was first declared). After a search it was discovered that the wretched plagiarist had hired an actor with whom he was in some sort of relationship to take his place on Alcibiades' flagship. Alcibiades wasn't having any of that and the whole departure was held up until a shamefaced Eupolis took his proper place.

By the time I got back to Athens the fleet had already reached Corfu where some of our allies met them with another thousand hoplites and thirty-four more triremes. Good luck to them all, I thought. I could now concentrate on *The Birds*.

# 37

It was Pherecrates who gave me the idea, though he didn't realise it. For months I had been wrestling with the problem of how to introduce my extraordinary birdmen into a play. I wanted to make the theme relevant to current events without being too political; with Hyperbolus banished and Alcibiades off limits, there still wasn't much scope for direct personal satire, and the only event the city was concerned with was the invasion of Sicily, which wasn't very funny. We were talking about the different genres of comedy and Pherecrates claimed they all related in some way to the stories of tragedy, though some so remotely you wouldn't really know. I asked how his domestic comedies related to tragedy and he said they were the other side of the same emotional coin. He said when domestic comedies used tragic themes and transposed legends into day-to-day settings, they shone a heroic light on the hopes and fears of ordinary people doing ordinary things and helped the audience to forget just how ordinary they were. Myth parodies by contrast were a way of ignoring the present altogether and escaping into the world of kings and gods and monsters.

"But what about the plays I used to write before the Peace of Nicias?" I asked. "You know, like *The Acharnians*, *The Knights*, *The Clouds*, *The Wasps* and so on. They were all set in Athenian homes and public places and only used tragic parody for random jokes, not as an allegory for the whole plot. Would you call those domestic?"

"Yes, I think I would, though they were more political than most domestic comedies and a lot more political than anything you'd want to write now. Your plays worked – and sometimes didn't work – because they launched a major attack on something real that was part of people's everyday lives, either an individual like Cleon or Socrates or an institution like the law courts or the Assembly. And, as you say, you used tragedy to point up particular scenes and characters. You did that exceptionally well, of course. But now is not a good time for that seriously critical sort of stuff.

The only leaders worth making fun of are on their way to Sicily and until we see how that turns out, the next few months are dangerous ones for the city. It behoves us comic poets as opinion-leaders to keep the city's spirits up until we hear news from there. That leaves us with a simple choice: a realistic domestic comedy without a critical message or a purely escapist myth parody."

I thought about this for a few days and became more and more convinced that Pherecrates was wrong in classifying everything as domestic/realistic or myth parody/escapist. It had to be possible to alleviate the cares of the world without just confining oneself to a day in the life of your average citizen. And there must be a way of escaping that everyday life without becoming completely irrelevant. Come to think of it, in some of those comedies of mine that Pherecrates was calling domestic, the heroes escaped by doing something totally unrealistic – a private peace, private law-courts, defeating creditors through false education and so on. I needed something that started with normal citizens with normal cares going about their business and then escaping from those cares in an original way and one that somehow involved birds.

After a few weeks of anxious thought and a number of conversations with Pherecrates, Euripides and (most usefully) Cunna, the plot of *The Birds* took shape: two perfectly ordinary Athenians, with a perfectly ordinary desire to escape the city's many imperfections, including the state of politics, litigation, sacrilege, rumours of oligarchic plots and so on, get carried away to a non-existent kingdom in the clouds that happens to be run by birds but in other respects bears an uncanny resemblance to Athens. The remoteness and improbability of the birds' city would take the edge off criticisms I was really directing at Athens. It also gave me a chance to work with Callistratus again; I'd helped him out when he was desperate by giving him *Seasons* when I didn't need to, but this was a play that would really benefit from our combined talents. The archon thought so too and we were accepted for the Dionysia.

Earlier the same year I had a play on at the Lenaea: *Amphiaraus*, produced by Philonides. It was a sort of mixture of domestic comedy and myth parody that I wrote just to prove to Pherecrates that the two could be productively combined. A contemporary Athenian and his wife visit the oracular healing shrine of a Theban hero, perform various sacrifices to summon visions, and undergo a series of extremely uncomfortable cures for a problem which might have been a disease but might simply have been a lack of friends – I kept it ambiguous. The play came second which was probably better than it deserved. Euripides was annoyed because I parodied Sophocles more than him.

*The Birds* was a much better effort and, though it also came second, I still rate it as one of my best. It was quite expensive; even though we only used three actors they had to play seventeen roles between them, so we needed a lot of mask variations in addition to the costs of lavish bird dresses with real feathers and cleverly moulded beaks for the chorus. It was my longest play because I couldn't stop coming up with more Farcical Scenes as the city in the sky deals with undesirable Athenians in just the way we should be dealing with them in the real Athens. All the same, the plot was tighter than I'd ever achieved before with the final revelation held back to the end, and though there was clearly a principal hero, the story was sufficiently convoluted to need to be carried by the whole cast and the chorus. I rewarded them all afterwards much more generously than I had to.

I named the kingdom in the sky Cloud-Cuckoo-Land and ever since people have used that to refer to fantasy places. I gave my Athenian heroes suitable made-up names, Friend-persuader and Hopeson, but couldn't resist calling their slaves after my own, Xanthias and Manodorus. I trained the actors to mimic their speech and the contrast in their voices brought a lot of laughs. To make the transformation to birds more effective, I adapted the Procne myth. This meant upsetting Euripides by parodying Sophocles again, but the suitability of the story was too good to miss. Procne was the daughter of King Pandion of Athens. When she married Tereus she missed her sister Philomena so much Tereus offered to go and fetch her. On the way back he raped her and cut out her tongue to conceal his offence, but she was still able to tell Procne what had happened through clever embroidery. In revenge, Procne killed her own son Itys and served him to his father Tereus for dinner, whereupon, to round things off nicely, Zeus turned all three characters into birds: Tereus became a hoopoe, Procne a nightingale and Philomena a swallow.

Fleeing Athens, which they had started to dislike, our heroes come to Tereus the Hoopoe's house where they are greeted by a slave, who has also been turned into a bird just in case Tereus needed a butler. A badly moulting Tereus appears and, once he is assured the Athenians are not jurors, suggests various cities they might choose to move to. (The cities are named after various people I wanted to make fun of, so unsurprisingly none of them appeal). They start to discuss the life of birds and Friend-persuader suggests how powerful birds could be if they settled down in a city in the sky, where they could control human life and prevent sacrifices reaching the gods. Tereus likes the idea and goes to get Nightingale Procne to wake up the other birds, whom he has taught to speak. He sings a beautiful song for Procne and, to the notes of an unseen flute, Procne sings another to summon the birds.

The chorus of twenty-four birds of different species make a spectacular entry with beaks on their masks, feathers on their arms, hooked talons and feathered headgear. I was especially proud of the verses I composed for the play. Euripides forgot his disappointment at not being parodied enough and actually did me the honour of copying much of Tereus' song to Procne in his own *Helen* a couple of years later. The chorus' Entry song was full of complex and ever-changing rhythms, mimicking bird song and adding another dimension to their garish feathered costumes. I put in two Addresses with quite different and very sophisticated metres. I don't think I ever produced such good music before or since.

In the Contest, Friend-persuader, with many unhelpful interventions by Hopeson, reminds the birds they used to be all-powerful but now they have lost their influence and are just hunted and cooked. To regain respect, they should build a new city, claim power back from the gods by threats and get mankind to start sacrificing to them. The birds are enthused and start preparing war on the gods while the chorus explains that birds are not only gods but older gods than the Olympian ones (the real gods don't mind being made fun of at festival time). There follows a list of the benefits birds bring us: being used as gifts to young boys for seduction, indicating the change of seasons, playing a key role in divinations and lending their names as metaphors for many things. Birds can get away with plenty that humans can't, such as beating up their fathers and betraying the city. At the Dionysia they can fly off to miss the boring tragedies, enjoy lunch, and return for the comedy; they can nip out for a fart or a shit, and they can go off to have sex with the wife of anyone they see in the audience.

In the Farcical Scenes, Friend-persuader tells Hopeson to get on with overseeing the birds building the city while he vets people wanting to move there, rejecting with clever insults a range of absurd caricatures including a pompous poet, a collector of oracles, an astronomer, a tax-collector and a decree seller. After a witty piece from the chorus about the fun of being a bird and a threat to the judges of a major shower of droppings if the play doesn't win, the newly completed city is threatened by the gods. A naïve goddess Iris appears on the crane and argues with Friend-persuader about who the real gods are. A herald returns from earth to say everyone has gone bird-crazy down there, all behaving like birds and adopting bird names. Ten thousand of them are on their way to Cloud-Cuckoo-Land! (Here I named all the people I had seen in the market before I went to Agathon's symposium and the birds they had transformed into). The chorus sings the glory of the place, while Friend-persuader sends his slaves to get wings for the new arrivals.

More Farcical Scenes follow, including a man who wants to live where it's all right to beat up your father (a thought I could identify with), another pompous poet who wants wings so he can capture verses from the sky, and an informer who wants wings for snooping. All are chased off before Prometheus arrives, hiding from the Olympians under a parasol because he disobeyed Zeus in giving mankind fire. He tells Friend-persuader the gods are starving in the absence of sacrifices from men and are coming to negotiate a truce.

In the Celebration, three delegates arrive: a solemn Poseidon with bare feet, a crown and a trident, a big, stupid, greedy Heracles, and a god worshipped by barbarians whom Poseidon tries and fails to dress properly and whose interventions are incomprehensible. Heracles keeps talking about food and wants a fight, but Poseidon is there to negotiate. They meet Friend-persuader who is grating silphium on some treacherous birds he happens to be roasting, and he tells them the gods would be better off handing over power to the birds who could help them detect mortals who are perjuring themselves or failing to offer due sacrifices. Eventually the gods agree to terms and it all ends with the traditional wedding song as Friend-persuader goes off with one of Zeus' mistresses.

In the event, we were beaten by Ameipsias' play *The Revellers*, though I don't think we should have been. Criticus must have noticed something in the script I hadn't been aware of because he told me he could tell I had become a follower of Gorgias. I gave him the usual reply. Praxagora complained that if I could introduce Xanthias and Manodorus into my plays I should be able to feature her. I promised I would.

Meanwhile, the news from Sicily was not good. The Sicilians were ready for us and, so far from being welcomed with open arms by all the cities who feared the ambitions of Syracuse, our army was turned away time and again and only found allies in two small towns not far from Syracuse itself. The whole summer was wasted and we had to finance the army over the winter till the next campaigning season while they settled down to a lengthy siege of the city. While this was going on, Corinth had agreed to help Syracuse and tried to persuade Sparta to do so as well. Sparta didn't commit until we provoked them by sending more troops to Sicily and then breaking the Peace of Nicias by siding with Argos against them. We were at war again with Sparta, though this time a long and expensive way from home.

There was disturbing news about Alcibiades. Just before he got to Sicily, he heard a ship was waiting to take him back to Athens to be tried in relation to the mutilation of the herms, so he escaped on the voyage and was found guilty in his absence. The Athenian authorities offered the huge reward of one gold talent to anyone who could claim responsibility for his death, but he made his way to Sparta and supported their war effort as enthusiastically as he had just been supporting ours. He urged them to send troops against us in Sicily, stirred up trouble among our allies in Asia and helped build a fort just a dozen miles from Athens from where the Spartans could destroy our crops again, as they had been doing annually before the peace. Not satisfied with trying to destroy our army and our farms, a rumour went around that he was trying to destroy our democracy too, by encouraging an oligarchic plot in Athens. Armed troops were stationed in the temple of Theseus for fear of an uprising. I'd never liked Alcibiades and thought he was a threat to our peace and well-being in many ways, but even I could never have imagined he could stoop so low.

With Alcibiades out of the way, I assumed Bloody Eupolis was not being dealt with and was wondering if I would need to resume my campaign for revenge when he got back. That question was soon answered when we started to hear rumours of Eupolis' death. There were multiple versions of what had happened but the most credible one was that Alcibiades couldn't wait till he got to Sicily and had him thrown overboard on the way. As when Cleon died, I couldn't mourn much because he was not a good man. On the other hand, I hadn't been in any way responsible for Cleon's death and I seemed to have had quite a lot to do with Eupolis'. Initially I assuaged my guilt with the thought that he had lived long enough; he didn't seem to have much more to offer, having obviously run out of creative ideas as shown by his plagiarism and requests for me to 'lend' him plays. No one was using his silly metre any more. I was wrong-footed again when his estate put on his last play posthumously. *Suburbs* was simply brilliant. He had been writing it while hiding away to avoid sailing with Alcibiades and it reflected his pessimistic view of the expedition. A miserable and demoralised Athens hears bad news from Sicily and has to choose which of the old heroes like Solon, Peisistratus and Pericles will be summoned from the underworld to rescue her. It was by far his best play.

# 38

"She is rather badly hurt, I fear. It was my fault. I was supposed to be responsible for her safety and well-being in line with the traditional obligations of slaves in this metropolis towards their esteemed mistress, but any properly impartial witness would acknowledge that the cart in question was indubitably out of control and such acknowledgement would be irrefragable by all thinking judicially-oriented arbitrators. Those quarry slaves should never have attempted to abridge their journey by deviating from the customary route. I understand it's not impossible that she could be disabled for life. Wise and experienced as he is, the responsible doctor just doesn't know. Oh, master, I'll never forgive myself."

I had never seen Xanthias in tears before and, in the dozen years he'd been with us, I had never heard him speaking anything like perfect Greek. I tried to calm him down and asked him to elaborate. After a pause in which he stared at me as if he'd never seen me before, he resumed his more customary form of speech.

"Mistress Praxagora... cart... too fast... legs... hip. Gorgias..." he sobbed.

After more tears and broken phrases, I came to understand that Praxagora had been hit by a cart laden with massive stones while she was listening to Gorgias. The slaves dragging it from the quarry to where the Erechtheion was under construction had taken a short cut along the Panhellenic Way and lost control, so it plunged down the hill to the pottery district where Gorgias was giving one of his satirical speeches. Xanthias had gone to a stall to buy some fruit and returned just in time to see Gorgias' audience scattering. Praxagora, presumably too taken with the sophist's clever use of irony, had failed to scatter in time and had been struck.

Having told his story both well and badly, Xanthias grabbed my hand and we set off to find Praxagora. We hadn't gone far when we met her, lying on a stretcher carried by two slaves under the supervision of Lysander.

She was clearly in pain but quiet and gave me a rueful smile and gestured towards her rescuer, whose cloak she was swaddled in. He explained how he had been on his way to sacrifice at his family's grave near the pottery district when he heard shouting. He had gone to investigate and found Praxagora lying moaning on the ground with Xanthias bending over her. He thought she had broken a leg and possibly a hip, so he gave her his cloak to keep her warm and sent Xanthias to fetch Doctor Erixymachus and then to inform me. Erixymachus bandaged her leg and sold her an ointment to rub on her hip and said he hoped the damage wouldn't be permanent but there was nothing more he could do.

It was several weeks before Praxagora could walk at all and she limped for the rest of her life. It seemed to have quietened her down though. I bought a stretcher so that Xanthias and Manodorus could take her around while she was recovering, but she seemed to have lost interest in going out and was happy playing with our boys and reading Homer to them. She was more affectionate to me than she had been for a while. I didn't have a play on that year, having run out of inspiration again, and I spent nearly all my time at home with her and the family. I realised I was finally getting to know my sons as individuals and marvelled at how different they were from each other. Ararus was a natural leader, an excellent singer and a capable athlete, popular with his schoolmates; the swarthy Philip, to everyone's surprise, was becoming a studious intellectual with a gift for dance; and Philetaerus was a rough-and-tumble little chatterbox. Praxagora reminded me of my promise to put her in a play and came up with various unusable but amusing ideas for plots about strong-minded women. She hadn't mentioned finding apprenticeships for the boys for a while, which I was happy about until Philip started talking about rivers and I realised she was paying to have them trained as sophists. I decided I'd better start looking at crafts.

In the meanwhile, Xanthias had gone back to mumbled monosyllables and it was only a few days after the accident that I remembered the fluent manner in which he had first reported it. I asked him to explain. He started by burbling again and pretending he didn't know what I was talking about. I persisted and repeated some of the sentences in which he had first told me of the accident. He admitted he had been able to speak fluent Greek for some time, but only used it at Cyllus' Wallet where it was sometimes useful to pretend to be a citizen. The accident had shocked him so much that he didn't know what he was saying when he first saw me. He explained that he learned a lot of useful things because people didn't think he understood Greek. This shed some light on a few things he had done for me, so I told him that I was quite happy with him pretending not to know the language but that when we were alone at home as just the family he should converse normally. He did and our lives became easier.

The morning after I learned about the sophist training, I took Ararus with me and set off for the pottery district. As we were passing the law courts, I noticed a large crowd outside one of them and when we drew closer, I could hear the distinctive voice of Sophocles reciting one of his tragedies – *Oedipus at Colonus*, I think; that was his favourite. I asked a young man in the crowd what was going on and he explained that the tragedian was now eighty-three years old and his sons were concerned he was too senile to manage his own affairs. They had taken him to court to prove his incapacity so they could take over his estate, and he was proving he wasn't senile by this recital. Ararus and I stayed around for the jury's decision and of course they found in his favour. The crowd outside the court cheered when they heard the news. He was still popular and had just been voted onto a panel of ten to manage the city's affairs while our troops were struggling in Sicily. A joke was going the rounds that he could have appeared in Eupolis' *Suburbs* as a contemporary of some of the city's most ancient leaders. A rumour suggested he claimed to be relieved he was too old for sex. I wasn't sure about that one.

We headed for the workshop of Aristophanes the potter-painter, but he wasn't there. The head potter and workshop supervisor, a small, overweight fellow who turned out to be his cousin, told me he was running the business for Aristophanes who had been called up for Sicily. I explained that we were investigating future apprenticeships for my son and he offered to show me around.

The cousin had obviously decided to expand the operation. On my previous visit Aristophanes was working alone; fine vase painting took a long time compared with the rest of the process, so his wheel and his furnace weren't in use most of the time. Now though, there was quite a workforce: a clay preparer, a wheel turner, two furnace men removing a collection of small cups and bowls from the now cooling furnace, and no less than three painters hard at work decorating large vases, one of which looked almost finished. The potter showed us how clay was prepared with just the right amount of water and avoiding any air pockets which tend to cause explosions in the furnace. I had a go but wasn't able to knead the clay firmly enough to get all the air out. He then showed how us to make a bowl; the little apprentice spun the wheel and the potter's fingers worked faster than you could see them. He made three bowls and two small vases in less time than it takes to tell. Ararus stayed chatting with the wheel turner and trying to make a little vase of his own out of my unsatisfactory lump of clay, while the potter took me over to the painter who was just putting the finishing touches to a huge vase depicting the wedding of Achilles' parents, Peleus and Thetis. It had taken him six weeks, he told us, and I have to say, the detail was exquisite. The potter summoned all the workers to come and look before the two furnace men carried it carefully to the kiln, which was already heating up, and once there, they manipulated it inside with giant padded tongs.

"It has to go in the kiln by itself," the potter explained. If you put in another piece and it happened to explode, that's months of painting work wasted."

I found Ararus still over by the wheel and asked him if he had made anything he could show me. "I will later," he replied. We went over to look at the work of the other two painters, one of whom had fallen asleep. The awake one showed us how he mixed paints and told us the various herbs or shellfish the different colours came from. He let Ararus add some wavy lines to a piece of broken plate that was lying nearby.

All of a sudden there was a loud explosion. The furnace door blew off and flames leapt out accompanied by fragments of the large and beautifully painted vase. One of the furnace men was close enough to lose a lot of hair and sought relief from the clay preparer's water bucket while the rest of the crew ran to fetch more water to douse the flames before they did any more damage. I turned to Ararus and found he was crying. "Are you hurt?" I asked. "No," he told me, "but I had made a nice vase for Mummy with the clay you prepared and now it's gone and blown up." We left hastily, thanking the potter on the way out, and I crossed pottery off the list of possible careers for Ararus.

The news from Sicily didn't get better. Manodorus came from there originally. He had been captured by Carthaginians and sold in Egypt where he was bought by an Athenian who died soon after bringing him back to Athens, and whose estate didn't need him. He seemed to have a circle of friends who also hailed from Sicily and always managed to get news from there faster than official communications to the Assembly. I can still picture him now, standing on one leg, wringing his hands and grinning idiotically while he simpers the details of some new disaster.

The fighting round Syracuse had begun fairly well. The inhabitants were a little disorganised and our troops had managed to build a wall and fort around the city, though the Syracusans disrupted it by building another wall at right angles. We destroyed that and some of our men managed to get inside the city but were massacred there. The Syracusans regrouped and beat us soundly; poor old Lamachus was killed. Worse still, our support for Argos had encouraged the Spartans to attack us in Sicily, so Gylippus arrived with reinforcements which he supplemented with friendly Sicilians. We beat him back at first, but he counterattacked successfully. A stalemate ensued on the hills around Syracuse during which a Corinthian fleet arrived to support our enemies and more Sicilian cities sent men to join Gylippus.

Having heard this from Manodorus, it was no surprise to me when the Assembly received a message from Nicias that the situation was hopeless and Athens should either send a lot more troops or call him home. Once again the Assembly failed to take Nicias' broad hint and went with the more troops option. In a fit of pique at the Spartans for invading Attica in the spring – much earlier than usual – and blocking our food supply, we voted to send out reinforcements under Demosthenes and Eurymedon. It was ridiculous to be fighting a war against an enemy our own size or bigger far away, while our own land was being attacked. To make it worse, slaves started to desert the city to take refuge in the Spartan fort in Attica before escaping altogether.

Feeling a bit guilty about what had happened to Eupolis and thinking I should do my bit, I sought out Demosthenes and offered to go with him. He was a bit surprised at first, not knowing the poets' exemption had lapsed, but told me I was too important to risk on a tough campaign like Sicily, especially after what had happened to Eupolis. "We can't afford to lose any more of you," he said, and meant it kindly. Eventually he agreed I could come with him on the first leg of the journey, which was to blockade Corinth before heading to Sicily, and teach the piper of each ship some new rowing songs. It didn't quite work out, as the Corinthian and Boeotian fleets blockaded us first and we ended up in a frightening though indecisive sea battle off Naupactus. All the same, I got home safely after about fifteen days. When I got back, Manodorus told me that some Thracians had arrived too late to sail with Demosthenes. They could have been used to fight in Attica but at a drachma a day were too expensive, so they were sent away and committed various atrocities on the way home, including a massacre at a boy's school near Thebes. Many of the Thracians were slaughtered in their turn by the Thebans. War has some interesting side effects.

Unfortunately, Manodorus' news from Sicily was more predictable. We had won a small victory at sea but lost badly on land and Gylippus had captured our fort along with a lot of our weapons and provisions and blocked our supply lines. We just had to hope Demosthenes' arrival there would turn things around.

# 39

I only got away from home three times the year after the accident, once to sort out some tenants in Aegina who were behind with their rent, once as far as Naupactus with Demosthenes, and once for ten days' writing with Euripides on his island near Salamis. Noticing I hadn't had a play at either major festival, Euripides had come storming round to my house, banged on the door and, when Manodorus let him in, shouted "So you've retired have you, you lazy bastard. I knew your inheritance would be a problem. Come on I've got lots of ideas. Oh, what's the matter with Praxagora?" After I had explained her misfortune and he had pretended to show sympathy (he was better at sympathising with women in his plays than in real life), we agreed I'd submit a play on the legend of *Polyidus* and he'd help me with it, as he had already written a tragedy about it. This was obviously a way to make sure I parodied him and not Sophocles again; although both Sophocles and Aeschylus had also made plays of the story, it was a long time ago and Euripides' version would be more familiar to most of the audience.

Remembering Alcibiades' trick from a few years ago, Euripides decided to take his girl from the tavern, Myrrhine, with him and kindly suggested I bring Cunna, which I did. It was the first time I'd been with Cunna anywhere other than Aspasia's and she really seemed to enjoy the peace and freedom of Euripides' estate. We spent a couple of happy days walking around it chatting, and happy evenings with no time constraint. Unfortunately this was the first time Euripides had got round to actually talking to Myrrhine and, when he did, he found her quite interesting which upset him more than seemed reasonable. On the third day he told me he was going to have to send her away; she was too interesting to have sex with and too attractive not to. I decided it was only fair to send Cunna home too, which saddened us both.

With the girls gone we became very productive and all but finished *Polyidus* in four days. As with *Seasons*, Euripides did a lot of the writing again. He would give me a stage in the plot, I'd give it a comic twist and then we'd split up the writing, with him doing the long speeches by actors, me doing the Contest and all the choral songs, and both of us sharing the rest. The title character is a famous seer who impresses the king of Crete by noticing an unusual calf and is sent to look for the king's missing son, Glaucus. He finds the boy dead inside a beehive in a wine cellar and is locked up there himself for his pains. He kills a visiting snake whose partner turns up, sees her dead mate, disappears and comes back with a herb that brings him back to life. Polyidus then uses the same herb to bring the king's son back. Grateful though he is, the king won't let Polyidus leave Crete until he has taught his son the art of divination. He does, and then gets the boy to spit in his mouth which makes him forget everything he has learned. A silly story and rather a jolly ending for a tragedy, but it would do for the Lenaea comedy competition. In the event it came second to Pherecrates' *The Kitchen*. Platon's *Festivals* came third.

When we felt it was nearly done and we could turn our attention to something else, he asked me to write down the song to Procne from *The Birds* for him to incorporate in the *Helen* he was working on. In return, one evening after a good day's work, I thought I'd ask him for ideas on how to incorporate Praxagora into a play as I had promised.

"What has she done that's made the biggest impression on you?" he asked.

I thought about it for a while. The accident? The children? Then it came to me: "No sex!" I cried.

"You can't have a play about no sex. It doesn't make sense."

I explained that withholding sex was Praxagora's way of punishing me for anything she didn't approve of. He thought about it for a while, then became quite animated. "That's it! Brilliant! Women withhold sex and their husbands do anything they want. You can show them running the city and making all the decisions men wouldn't make."

It seemed a pretty good idea, but if I had a play about withholding sex and the main character was named after my wife, it would be embarrassing for both of us. "What else could I do that involved a strong woman called Praxagora?" I asked.

The reply was predictable. "Well, a lot of women don't approve of the way I portray them. They think showing them as passionate, strong-minded creatures willing to inflict a lot of damage on themselves and others doesn't reflect well on the sex and they'd like me to stop. So you could show them stopping me."

I'd been hoping to find a theme for a play about Praxagora and now he wanted me to do a play about him! But maybe Praxagora could lead the opposition, I thought. She'd like that, especially after his callous attitude to her accident.

Soon after the Lenaea more bad news emerged from Sicily. It was now quite clear where Manodorus' sympathies lay and he seemed delighted to inform us how the Syracusans attacked our troops by land and sea when Demosthenes was still a good day's sail away, and even more delighted when he explained how they had tricked us by launching a second attack on the same day, when everyone was seeing to their wounds. As a result, our original army was pretty reduced and dispirited when Demosthenes and Eurymedon arrived, and, though they had some initial success, the Boeotians, who had turned up with Gylippus and the Spartans, beat them back. Apparently our troops were in such disarray when night fell that several were killed by their own colleagues. It didn't help that both sides sang the same battle hymn. Manodorus tittered loudly at this point. I thought once again they could have used a comic poet to direct troop movements.

No doubt Nicias was even more inclined to give up after this disaster, but, of course he would have been blamed for the failure and probably executed on his return, so he had to press on. In the event it was Demosthenes who suggested they should come back and attack the Spartan fort at Decelea to save our countryside and recover our slaves. His request was refused by the Assembly.

After another defeat at sea, Nicias realised that without naval superiority our troops would be starved of supplies, so he staked everything on a massive naval mobilisation. He left a small garrison on land and put all the archers, slingers and javelin-throwers on boats; there were a hundred and ten vessels in all, including merchant ships and some disabled triremes. The idea was to fight a land battle at sea. They made grappling irons to counter the Syracusans' skill at ramming them, but the Syracusans covered their prows with hides so the irons couldn't grip.

The husband of one of Praxagora's girlfriends was with Nicias at the time and in his occasional letters home he was full of praise for Nicias' courage and perseverance. He reported how before the battle Nicias gave a pep talk to the troops and then spoke to each captain individually, addressing them by their father's names, then by their own, and finally by the name of their tribe. He told them they mustn't let themselves or their ancestors down and went on about how precious were the freedoms Athenians enjoyed which were now at stake. Personally, I thought it all sounded a bit unoriginal; the same sentiments are always expressed in a crisis.

By all accounts, the sea battle was fierce and raged for most of the day. Eventually the superior naval skills of the Syracusans and their knowledge of their own harbour and the surrounding seas prevailed. They broke through our lines and we were forced back on land with massive losses of men and ships. Our forces were trapped and Demosthenes wanted to escape by sea but the forty thousand survivors refused to go on board ship again. By the time they started the retreat on land the Spartans were blocking the way. Leaving many unburied dead and seriously injured behind, the Athenian army avoided the blockade by diverting south but once again there was confusion in the dark and a six-mile gap opened up between Demosthenes' rearguard and the rest of the army with Nicias. Taking full advantage of this, the Spartans surrounded Demosthenes and he surrendered.

You have to feel sorry for Nicias, who had opposed the expedition from the start and always been quite frank about how limited were the chances of success. Now with Demosthenes and his army gone, he had no choice but to offer peace terms. The Spartans rejected them, obviously preferring to wipe our army out. Nicias marched on but his men had no food or fresh water. Desperately thirsty, when they arrived at a large river the men hurled themselves in, providing the Spartans with an excellent opportunity to attack, which they did with great enthusiasm and bloodshed. A lot of our troops were killed and even more taken prisoner – seven thousand officially, who were kept in miserable conditions in Syracuse's quarries, and probably a similar number privately, who ended up as slaves. Nicias and Demosthenes were put to death by the victors and the few survivors of their armies fled to Catania.

The city was in despair. Our loss of ships and men was irreplaceable. Sparta was certain to step up its attacks in Attica, and who knew if the whole of Sicily might join them? The only person who seemed to have anything to smile about was Euripides who had heard that Athenian prisoners in the quarries were able to get better treatment or early release by reciting his works.

# 40

"I'll bet Alcibiades is behind it."

"You mean the Spartan alliance with Persia?"

"Yes."

"But that happened while Alcibiades was still on our side."

"I'll bet he was behind it anyway. And having him in Sparta obviously encouraged more of our allies to revolt, so Persia pretty much controls the other side of the Aegean now, while Sparta keeps attacking us over here."

"Yes, they say Lesbos has left the alliance too."

"Who cares about Lesbos? We should be much more worried about Euboea, which is right next to us and where we get a lot of our wood from. I've heard they could revolt any moment. Anyway, I'm sure it was Alcibiades who persuaded the Spartans to send their own ships to support our allies after we had stopped the Corinthian fleet getting involved. And he's over there right now, stirring up trouble in Miletus."

"Not any more he's not. Haven't you heard?" This from a quiet man who had been standing at the back of the group in the tavern with a wry smile on his face, as if he knew something the rest of us didn't.

"Heard what?" we all asked at once.

"Well, in the first place the alliance between Sparta and Persia is virtually over now after a row about what to do with the allies who were deserting us. Persia is after the tribute they've been paying us and wants them to join the Persian Empire, which most of them once belonged to, while Sparta wants them to be free and independent. And second, Alcibiades is right out of favour in Sparta and not just because he seduced the king's wife. They think he's a traitor and ordered him to be put to death, but of course he escaped as he always does. Now he seems to be on our side again and has been encouraging Persia not to give the Spartans any more money to pay the sailors or send them any ships. In fact, he told our generals in Samos that he could bring the Persians over to our side altogether."

"That sounds pretty good," someone volunteered.

"Except we'd get Alcibiades back," grimaced another.

"It's worse than that," our informant told us. "The condition of getting the deal with Persia is that we establish an oligarchy in Athens."

"Won't happen."

"Don't be too sure. Even without Alcibiades there have been rumblings for a few years now. Our friend Aristophanes here mentioned that in his play about birds, didn't you, Aristophanes? And that was two or three Dionysias ago."

"Anyway, we'll have to wait and see what the generals at Samos do."

The conversation seemed to have dried up, everyone having a lot to think about – not just whether the city might choose to give up its democracy at the whim of Alcibiades and his unstable diplomacy, but who might constitute the power centre of a future oligarchy, and how they personally would stand with them.

It had been a bad few months for Athens. Alcibiades seemed to change sides more often than the dice Achilles threw when he played with Ajax outside the walls of Troy. This time he had persuaded our ally Chios to join Sparta, who had sent a fleet to support them, and there had seemed to be little doubt our other allies on the other side of the Aegean like Mytilene and the rest of Lesbos would join in. If the alliance Alcibiades had fostered between Sparta and Persia had held, it would have meant we would soon have no allies on the far side of the Aegean and very little of the protection money (politely known as 'tribute') we had been relying on for the war effort. As a result, the Assembly had decided to use all our reserve funds on building more ships, but we couldn't afford a sustained campaign away from Attica. We had managed to block the Corinthian fleet near Euboea because they stupidly delayed their departure to celebrate a festival, which gave us time to stop them crossing the Aegean for a while, but they got past us eventually and Sparta's own fleet joined them. It had looked beyond question as though the glory days of Athens were over. The news about the collapse of the Sparta-Persia alliance was promising in a way but very upsetting to those of us who treasured our democracy.

A deep gloom settled over the tavern. Eventually someone broke the silence and turned the conversation to the damage the Spartan fort near

Athens had been doing to us by giving shelter to runaway slaves. "At this rate we won't have any slaves left," he said.

"And with our losses in Sicily and the rate at which our allies are deserting us, we won't be capturing any more," someone observed with a sigh.

"Poor old Nicias was right you know. We should never have committed all those men and spent all that money on that ridiculous adventure. At least we should have made sure we were still going to be able to defend ourselves at home."

"And keep our slaves."

The conversation was getting rather depressing again. I had a funny story to tell about slaves escaping to the fort at Decelea, and from there, they would be hoping, to freedom, so I thought I'd try to cheer everyone up. A few months earlier, Manodorus had joined the growing number of slaves running away, but before we had even got around to replacing him, he came back with his tail between his legs and told us he found the other slaves terribly rough and would much rather be with us if that was all right. As he explained it, standing on one leg as usual for his communications, "I was sorely discomfited by the unfortunate mannerisms of my fellow fugitive bondmen." As we had with Human Artemis when she ran away, Praxagora and I found it all too funny to punish him properly.

I was about to relate this tale but had only got as far as "My Manodorus…" when Lysander, whose entrance I hadn't noticed, tapped me on the shoulder. "I'm glad you've found something funny about Decelea," he said. "I've got news from there you are not likely to enjoy very much."

He led me away to a dark corner where he revealed all. "You know that banker we trusted? The one you invested two talents with at seven percent? Well, he's buggered off to Decelea too."

"But why?" I asked. "He seemed to be doing pretty well and could easily have bought his freedom if he stayed here."

"I guess he was just too greedy to want to pay for his freedom when he could get it for nothing by running away. He's from Samos and with the kind of money he's made here, he'd be a leading citizen. You've lost two talents and I've lost rather more, but fortunately, I only had about a fifth of my money with him. And you've got your rents from Aegina, which you told me were more than you needed to live off, and we've both been lucky so far with our maritime loans."

That was all true, but even so, suddenly losing two talents came as a bit of a shock, though a private one and trivial compared with the public disasters of Decelea, the loss of our democracy and the return of Alcibiades. Somehow, though, our cultural activities carried on. Sophists still roamed the streets, the Erechtheion building program continued, the Parthenon frieze was completed and I was working on the two plays Euripides had suggested.

# 41

In an ideal world, my play about the women's sex strike would have been shown at the Dionysia, where the best plays are usually presented. It was original, clever and hilarious. There was nothing much wrong with the play about women attacking Euripides, but it just wasn't quite as good. However, the world was far from ideal and our recent losses combined with continuing political unrest made it safer to have the sex strike play at the Lenaea where there would be no foreigners. One good outcome was that I was assigned Bronchus as lead actor for the Dionysia and I had the ideal part for him as Euripides' father-in-law, while Rhombus' range of tones was perfect for the female lead at the Lenaea.

Callistratus was my producer for the Lenaea and we worked together even better than before. The plot was sufficiently complex to require five actors. I decided to name the heroine Lysistrata (Army Disbander, a clear reference to the arch priestess Lysimache (Battle Destroyer)), and her offsider Myrrhine (Ladygarden), the name of the priestess of Athena Nike. I even called the play *Lysistrata* – the first time a comic play's title had been the name of the leading character. It was also the first time that respectable women had been presented in comedy. In fact only recently had comedies included real women at all; in my early days the only female characters were goddesses, then Pherecrates wrote a couple of plays about escorts and Eupolis one about marketplace women, but the women in *Lysistrata* could have been any citizen's mother or sister or wife. I showed them as intelligent, compassionate and resourceful, like my own mother must have been, rather than drunk and oversexed as was usual in comic plays. Euripides had been particularly insistent on that. The contrast with the chorus of foolish, incompetent and belligerent old men was very clear. Being the Lenaea, I could include a few Spartan men and women joining the Athenian ones, which was important to the plot.

The women's objective was to take over the city's government because men were doing such a bad job. There were two interlocking plots: they withheld sex to force their husbands to do whatever they wanted them to, and they seized the treasury on the Acropolis so as to control the city's finances. The first few scenes gave rise to plenty of opportunities for sexual jokes and innuendo. Some wives are late for the first meeting after exhausting nights, while others complain that the defection of our ally Miletus meant a shortage of dildoes for them to 'skin the skinned dog,' an expression coined by Pherecrates. Lysistrata gives very explicit instructions on how to make their husbands crazed with lust and describes all the sexual positions that they are not going to allow, from horseback (obvious) to the lioness on the cheese grater (similar but backwards with vigorous movement back and forth), with several others in between. I got a lot of laughs by referring to the horseback position as "the tyranny of Hippias." They then dance a spoof of the women's spring Adonia festival, in which they all wear masks, draw lots to find a leader, and form four concentric rings. The leader is blindfolded and touches three people from each ring who are now identified as men and equip themselves with strap-ons for the continuing revelry.

When the women hear a group of their older colleagues have captured the Acropolis, the Spartans among them leave for home and a chorus of twelve old men arrive, claiming to remember the occupation of the Acropolis by Sparta one hundred years earlier and carrying logs to burn down the gate if the women do not open up. This sets up a Contest with a chorus of twelve old women who are ready with water to put out any fires. They pre-empt things by pouring it over the old men. After a brief intervention by a magistrate, supported by the Scythian archers (our police), Lysistrata is arrested but quickly freed by her colleagues. She then makes a great speech about how much better women are at managing money than men and how men never listen to their advice, so they have decided to take over affairs to keep everyone safe. Only women will make the decisions as to whether it is necessary to go to war. She speaks movingly about young, childless women ageing at home while the men are away on endless campaigns, and reminds the magistrate that men can marry at any age whereas a woman has only a short time before she is considered too old. She then dresses the magistrate like a corpse for laying out, with a wreath and a fillet, and explains to him that he is in fact dead. Outraged at these indignities, he storms off to report the incident to his colleagues, while Lysistrata returns to the Acropolis.

The Contest is resumed as the old men accuse the women of collusion with Sparta and plotting to establish a tyranny. The old women respond by describing how they took part in all the religious ceremonies when they were young, most of which provide scope for some racy lines about phallus-shaped biscuits and grinding corn for the goddess. They point out how women now strengthen the city by breeding boys while men ruin it with their foolish decisions. Just as the oldies are settling down for a good physical fight, Lysistrata rushes in with bad news. Her comrades are now desperate for sex and they are beginning to escape and desert on the silliest pretexts. One woman says she has to go home to air her fabrics by spreading them on the bed, another needs to 'shuck her flax', a third uses a helmet to feign pregnancy and a fourth says she can't sleep near the Acropolis because of the owls. Lysistrata reads a mysterious oracle to persuade them not to quit. They return to the Acropolis and resume their diatribes against the old men.

A man arrives desperate for sex. He turns out to be Ladygarden's husband. Between them, Lysistrata and Ladygarden make him even more desperate and he begs for release, which he is only granted after he has promised to stop the war. Ladygarden continues to tease him with complex and quite unnecessary preparations of a place in which she will gratify him, before running off and locking herself in the Acropolis again. The old men commiserate with her husband.

A Spartan herald appears, with a large and extremely suggestive burden scarcely hidden inside his tunic, and asks to see the ruling council to arrange peace talks. He explains that Spartan men are now suffering in the same way. He is sent back to Sparta to organise a peace delegation. Meanwhile, the old women start to make overtures to the old men, who are happy to be comforted and fussed over. The two choruses strip off their clothes (stage nudity – they are wearing body suits with suitable designs on them), merge, and sing and dance in unison, promising the audience money and a nice dinner if the play wins. Spartan delegates arrive with their phalluses upright and Lysistrata introduces them and the old Athenian men to a gorgeous young girl called Reconciliation, whose naked body they all comment on with enthusiasm and some clever double entendres. They squabble briefly over which part of Reconciliation they'll go for (Spartans prefer the bottom, Athenians the vagina), but they quickly overcome their differences and all retire hurriedly to the Acropolis for the usual celebrations. Peace all over Greece is achieved again, thanks to the women's ploy.

We won and I really felt I was back on top of my game until I went to the tavern a few days later. People were very complimentary at first and a bored-looking man I hadn't seen before was quite enthusiastic. It turned out he was from Euboea and had fled after opposing the Spartan landing there. He had been disillusioned on arriving in Athens and finding we were on the verge of agreeing to overturn our democracy.

"I liked your play," he began. "I can understand why you chose not to say much about the dangers of oligarchy, but it was good that you showed the way to an understanding between Sparta and Athens. I hate the Spartans too, but they are less determined on war than their allies like Corinth. I also like the way women forced men to do the right thing without actually taking power themselves. That would have been too much of a stretch. In fact, I thought it was an important statement you were trying to make on more than one dimension."

"Thank you. It's really nice to be appreciated, especially by a visitor to our city."

"But of course there were a lot of inconsistencies."

"Name one."

"Well, the women wanted to admit all sorts of people to citizenship – resident foreigners, friendly aliens, people disenfranchised for owing money to the state, loyal allies and so on, but not women. That seemed most improbable."

"OK, name another."

"The choruses were confusing. We had old and young, men and women, but the distinction between the old and young women got very blurred and they all seemed to merge in the end."

"Any more?"

"Well, if you push me, I'd have to say the whole premise of the play was improbable, men so desperate for sex with their wives they'd do anything. This is Athens for Zeus' sake! There are whores, escorts, young boys looking for a mentor, women hanging out at Cyllus' Wallet and Aphrodite knows what else. No one can be seriously deprived of sex here for very long."

I had my '*Fuck off, I'm a comic poet*' notice under my cloak, but I didn't pull it out because I thought it would be a harsh thing to do to a visitor and it was his first offence. I didn't have to wait long though.

"Thank you for your comments. They are very helpful," I told the Euboean as I made my way to the door, only to encounter Criticus, who seemed to have fixated on one of the less important props.

"I loved the symbolism of the helmet as a pretend pregnancy," he gushed. "Were you saying that sex leads to war or that war leads to sterility? Or perhaps both? Or something else altogether? Perhaps something to do with Athena rather than Aphrodite?"

That was when I used the notice under my cloak.

# 42

"Who would you like me to marry?"

It was a strange question to come from my wife, so I asked for more detail.

"Well, you'll probably die before me and we are pretty well off, despite that bastard of a banker, so if we are going to keep our wealth in the family, I'll need a new husband to give me some legal status and the right to provide for the boys. It should be someone from among your relatives, but you don't seem to have any."

"Well, I trust Lysander."

"I don't – and anyway he's not my type."

I wondered exactly what her type was. Presumably somewhere between me and Xanthias, but that encompassed pretty much every degree of physicality and hairiness. Perhaps she just liked the extremes.

"Pherecrates then?"

"Haven't you heard? He's got married last month. His sixteen-year-old niece Persephone's husband was killed in Sicily and all their relatives got together and more or less forced him to marry her."

"He won't have liked that."

"He didn't. Kicking and screaming is the phrase that comes to mind. Now I'm off to see Prodicus discussing the difference between courage and rashness again. Manodorus, let's go or we'll be late." Ever since we acquired Manodorus, she had chosen him rather than Xanthias for her outings. I didn't want to speculate why, but felt quite safe that she wouldn't produce any children by him even if she wanted to.

I hadn't seen Pherecrates for quite a while and his marriage was news to me. I thought I'd better go and cheer him up. Of course I wasn't expecting to find him actually looking miserable because after the loss of his eyebrows it was impossible to tell how he was feeling about anything, but I was a little surprised that, after he had greeted me and I'd asked how he was, he replied, "Never better. Since I got married, I don't have to manage my household any more and can spend all my time thinking and writing. I think the plays I'm working on now are the best I've ever composed. Oh, you haven't met my wife, have you? Persephone, this is my dear friend Aristophanes that I've talked about so often. I hope the two of you will be dear friends too."

As he said this, a gorgeous apparition entered the room where we were sitting. Her long, flowing black hair, come-hither eyes, slim hips and deep, full bust would surely have been a challenge to anyone's celibacy, even someone as determinedly uninterested in sex as Pherecrates. She gave me a sweet smile and an embrace which made my knees wobble. "I heard someone come in, so I wanted to see who it was," she said. "I'm so glad it's you, Aristophanes. I've been wanting to meet you for ages. I think we could be great friends." The wink she gave me as she said this didn't do my knees any good, and I sat down hurriedly on the couch, hoping to conceal any evidence of the impact she was having. After some polite conversation in which I tried (not very successfully, I fear) to avoid staring at her, she left the room, saying she was in the process of teaching their slave Heracles some of the things she felt he ought to know, but that she hoped to see much, much more of me.

Once she had gone, my curiosity got the better of me and I asked Pherecrates how he was coping with the physical side of married life. He told me it wasn't a problem; he'd made arrangements that suited them both. He called for some wine and the slave that brought it had a physique that fully justified the name Heracles, though his ability to speak Greek – or perhaps any other language – made Xanthias' original linguistic facility seem the pinnacle of articulate sophistication.

We talked about the plays Pherecrates was working on. There were a couple of them, one called *The Kitchen* and the other *Human Heracles*. *The Kitchen* was set in the house where it was rumoured Alcibiades and his friends had been drinking the night the Hermes statues were mutilated and the plot centred on the owner having to mortgage the house in order to pay a heavy fine for his involvement. This was all clearly fictitious as no one had been found guilty of the sacrilege, and it would have been far too dangerous a subject if Alcibiades had been in Athens, but Pherecrates had developed the plot while the chances of his return looked very small indeed.

Now it seemed that the fluid state of political affairs meant there was a risk Alcibiades would come back so the play never referred to him by name. The central character was an escort whose clever tricks enabled her to gain possession of the house for herself.

For an asexual, Pherecrates was surprisingly fond of writing plays about escorts and had already done so in *The Sea* and *Petale* and possibly in others that had not been selected for production. I suggested that his heroine could have a more original occupation – a woman butcher or fishmonger, for instance – but he told me that was an absurd idea and it was better to stick to what women were good at. He did though accept my suggestion for the woman's name, Allnight, and my idea for a slapstick scene about a slave helping her put on her bathrobe.

When he told me he was writing a play called *Human Heracles*, I initially assumed it was about his own domestic situation, though I couldn't see how he could make that appeal to the audience over two or three hours. In fact it was a burlesque of the Heracles legend with his twelve labours carried out in contemporary Athens by a man who takes on the disguise of Heracles. Pherecrates took me through each of the labours and how he planned to represent them in a contemporary setting and, because he wasn't very practised in political satire, I was able to help him with some of them, including cleaning out the filthy Augean stables, dealing with the man-eating Stymphalian Birds and rustling the mad Mares of Diomedes. For the challenge of stealing the Golden Apples of the Hesperides, where in the original myth Heracles had relieved Atlas by taking over the task of holding up the sky for him while he stole the apples, I suggested he hold up the three Fatties while Atlas stole a huge quantity of cakes. In fact, obesity was a major theme of Pherecrates' play. Heracles was generally represented in comedy as a glutton and most of the labours culminated in him celebrating his success with an enormous meal. Of course he could not get the Belt of Hippolyta round his waist after eating Geryon's Cattle.

The scene with the Fatties and several of the other labours required some supernatural intervention and Pherecrates planned to make liberal use of the crane. I told him what Euripides had once said to me, that the machine represented the unpredictability of human affairs: tragedy shows how the unpredictability upsets matters and the crane, equally unpredictably, puts them right. As soon as I'd said this, I realised I was doing just what I disliked about Criticus. It would have served me right if Pherecrates had said, "Fuck off, I'm a comic poet," but he was too polite and just told me comic poets should use the crane whenever it might raise a laugh or if the plot was heading to a dead-end and needed a sudden twist that the characters on stage couldn't plausibly deliver without external intervention.

On my way out, I heard girlish squeals of delight coming from the women's quarters and understood I was leaving three very happy people.

A few days later, Praxagora received a message from her mother telling her that her father was dangerously ill and was begging to see her. She felt she had to go and she selected Manodorus to accompany her to Aegina. As far as I was concerned this wasn't an ideal time for her to go away, as I had put in a lot of time preparing *Lysistrata* and rather neglected my play about the women and their attack on Euripides. Now with the Dionysia only about thirty days away, I needed to concentrate seriously on that. I had agreed with Praxagora that she would make a special effort to keep the boys quiet while I was working, but I couldn't expect Xanthias to exercise similar authority, so I decided I had to move out myself. The obvious solution was to move in with Euripides, whose house in the city was quite large enough to accommodate me as well as his second wife Choerine and the slave she was now quite openly living with. Being there would also enable me to ask Euripides for ideas about which of his plots and passages he thought I should spoof in addition to the ones I had already drafted. I told Xanthias to look after the boys till Praxagora or I returned, and to try to teach them some skills that would come in handy in later life.

My time staying with Euripides went quite satisfactorily. I was at my most productive and I thought I'd stay there till rehearsals began in earnest, but it was not to be. One morning a flushed and anxious Manodorus appeared at the door to tell me he and Praxagora had returned and she wanted to see me as soon as possible. Of course I left with him but was puzzled about the urgency; it was improbable that she was missing me that much. I quizzed Manodorus but all I could get out of him was an embarrassed giggle, a few tears and an assurance that I'd find out soon enough.

I hadn't expected an emotional reunion with Praxagora, but nor had I expected a medium-sized bowl to be thrown at my head when Manodorus opened the door and ushered me into the house. I ducked and it hit

Manodorus just below the shoulder. I don't imagine it hurt much, but it was quite a while before he stopped sobbing. Eventually Praxagora was able to send him to the slaves' room to which she had banished Xanthias and the boys, so that she could express her opinion of me in private.

"How could you?" she wanted to know.

"How could I what?"

"You know."

"Actually, I don't."

"Xanthias and the boys."

"What have they been doing?"

"You know."

"No, I don't."

"I thought I could trust you not to do that."

"Do what?"

"You know."

After several iterations of this uninformative dialogue, I guessed whatever she objected to had been taking place in our house while I was at Euripides', and it turned out I was correct. When she had arrived back from Aegina that morning with Manodorus and he had opened the door to let her in, she had found Ararus reciting one of Lysistrata's speeches while Philip and Philetaerus were performing one of the choral dances from that play under the guidance of Xanthias. It took a long time to persuade her that it must have been Xanthias' idea and that I respected her views on future occupations for our children, which in essence amounted to 'anything but comic poetry.'

# 43

By the time the Dionysia came round, the mood of the city was far from conducive to comic festivities. The Assembly had authorised Peisander to negotiate with Alcibiades and Persia and we all knew that if he succeeded in getting them onside it would be at the price of our democracy. Cunna asked me what in Hades we thought we were doing and I couldn't really answer her so I ran through the plot of my new comedy instead.

The play was set at the second day of the Thesmophoria, an annual three-day autumn festival in honour of Demeter and her daughter Persephone who were known as the 'bringers of civilisation', which was meant to recognise the role of women in ensuring the continuity of the family home and of the city. The audience would appreciate the special relevance of the rites at a time when the continuity of our political system was under threat. Men were excluded from the festival, which was only open to married women who were all sworn to secrecy, so I didn't know much about the rites except that the women dressed and behaved as men and had to abstain from sex for three days before the festival began. I had asked Xanthias to find out what he could, but all I got from him after his investigations was a look of horror and a refusal to tell me anything but the broadest outline of each of the three days. Apparently, the first was devoted to politics and the women took over the Pnyx where the Assembly met. There they sacrificed the rotten remains of pigs and exchanged dough models of male genitalia along with plenty of obscene language. The next day was the most important and best attended, but the most mysterious of all. All I knew was that the women fasted and sang gloomy songs, fully compensated on the third day with a wild feast in honour of Persephone's return. This wasn't much to go on, so I had to make the rest of it up by parodying the male festivals I was familiar with. As the majority of my audience would be men, they wouldn't know the difference, and anyway the essence of the plot was the women's rejection of Euripides, which didn't depend on the details of the festival.

The uncertainty of the times meant that it was probably the least political play I ever wrote, with only a few references to tyranny and the Persians. I put a lot of time into complex and sophisticated music for the choruses, but the words of their songs were bland and inoffensive – largely hymns to my favourite goddess, Artemis. The main joke was transvestism, always good for a laugh but a long way from the pointed satire that I felt was my greatest strength and my way of pointing the city in the right direction. *The Thesmophoriazusae* was a deliberate contrast to *Lysistrata* in the way it treated women. A lot of people had observed, some with enthusiasm, some with disdain, that the women in that play were presented as highly competent and clever. Here I reverted to the old stereotypes of drink and sex, conveniently ignoring the fact that the festival at which it was set was said to be all about continence and abstinence. In *Lysistrata* the chorus made powerful statements about the contribution of women to Athens; in *The Thesmophoriazusae* they only commented on their domestic roles and much of the imagery was about homosexuality. It was one of my tighter plots though and made major demands on the actors. The lead character, representing Euripides' father-in-law, required the full range of acting skills, so I was glad to get Bronchus for that role, and a newcomer named Thespides was ideal for playing all the female roles. The part of Euripides himself was a comic stylisation, melodramatic, badly dressed and full of flashy ideas and complex thoughts. Anyone could have played him and though Clepsis wasn't much of an actor he managed to carry it off without trouble.

Early in the play, Euripides explains what is going to happen: "The women at the festival are going to kill me for insulting them." Their fury was caused by his portrayals of the female sex as mad, murderous, and sexually depraved, and they planned to use the festival of the Thesmophoria as an opportunity to devise a suitable revenge. A terrified Euripides, accompanied by his kinsman (never named within the play but eminently recognisable as his father-in-law Mnesilochus) and talking obscurely about the origins of the universe, seeks out his fellow tragedian, the dainty Agathon, in the hope of persuading him to disguise himself as a woman so as to spy for him and to be his advocate at the festival. Agathon's slave appears, singing pompously about Agathon's skill and, with tragic exclamations from his own plays, Euripides explains what he wants. He finds Agathon is already dressed as a woman (represented by a white mask), whereupon Mnesilochus quizzes him about all his feminine accessories and body parts and keeps threatening to bugger him. Agathon explains that he always likes to present as a woman so as to understand how women think and out of deference to cross-dressing Ionian poets, but mainly because he rather enjoys it. He tells Euripides that much as he'd like to help out, he doesn't dare go to the festival, as the women would be so jealous of his lovely feminine looks that they might kill him from pure envy. Mnesilochus agrees to go instead, so Euripides shaves him, burns the hairs off his bum, dresses him in women's clothes and a wig borrowed from Agathon, and sends him off to the festival.

I had thought of naming the heroine Praxagora, fulfilling the promise I'd made of putting her in a play, but Euripides had asked me not to on the rather flimsy grounds that he would prefer to be attacked by someone with a completely made-up name and not by someone who could be a real Athenian wife. I called her Critylla, which sounds like a name, but I don't believe it was one that had been used before or since except by me in *Lysistrata*. She kicks off the action at the women's festival with a prayer that the gods curse anyone who deals with Euripides or the Persians (another bold dig at Alcibiades), or is guilty of various sexual deceits which she describes in detail. First on the agenda for the day is how to deal with Euripides. The first woman to speak lists the vices Euripides attributes to women and tells how he has made their husbands so suspicious of potential lovers that they keep the women and their household possessions locked up. A widowed seller of religious garlands then complains that she cannot support her five children because Euripides' plays promote atheism, so no one wants to buy her wares.

Mnesilochus in his female disguise claims that the behaviour of women is in fact far worse than Euripides has represented it. (S)he describes a sexual escapade with a boyfriend three days after she was married to someone else, in a tryst involving a laurel tree and a statue of Apollo, and talks about affairs with slaves and male grooms and various tricks for deceiving husbands. The chorus is horrified and threaten to burn her pubic hair off. A fight is about to break out when a female messenger is seen approaching. It turns out to be the well-known effeminate ambassador Cleisthenes, claiming to be the representative of Athenian women. He has come with the alarming news that a man disguised as a woman is spying upon them on behalf of Euripides. Mnesilochus goes for a pee (refusing Cleisthenes' offer of assistance) and on his return struggles to answer any of the women's questions. They strip him; he tries to hide his phallus between his legs, but they see it from the back and chase it from one side to the other. Cleisthenes goes off to tell the authorities and the chorus sings about how they are searching for more men in disguise to teach them to respect the gods. They find no one.

At this point the serious parody starts, as Mnesilochus appears to grab a baby from one of the women as a hostage and threatens to kill it unless the women release him, just as Telephus' grandfather had threatened to kill Telephus in Euripides' play of that name. Undeterred, the women make preparations to set Mnesilochus on fire and he unwraps the baby to reveal that it is in fact a wine flask. He stabs it and the women determinedly catch the wine in a pan. Mnesilochus needs to contact Euripides to help him escape the furious women; he wants to send a message scratched on oar blades as Palamedes did in another Euripides play but as there are no oars around, he has to make do with votive tablets.

Now it is time for the chorus to comment on the action. They sing the praises of women and argue that if they are as bad as Euripides says, why do men guard them and ogle them? They compare individual men and women (mainly fictitious) and find the women are better; women don't steal public funds, waste their inheritance or, when in battle, throw away their – parasols. Women who bear brave sons should be honoured, they say, and those who bear cowards should be treated with contempt.

Mnesilochus still hasn't found Euripides, so he tries another Euripides plot to get his attention, parodying Helen calling for Menelaus, the husband she deserted for Paris. Euripides appears as Menelaus and rows with Critylla before he and Mnesilochus recognise each other. Critylla blocks their escape, but Euripides manages to get away and Mnesilochus is seized for execution by an official archer-policeman. His request to change out of his drag costume is refused and the chorus sings a pious hymn with no mention of men. Mnesilochus, now tied firmly to a plank, sings a long lament based on Euripides' Andromeda's appeal for rescue to the flying

Perseus. After a bit of byplay in which Euripides, disguised as the goddess Echo, confuses and infuriates Mnesilochus and the archer, Perseus appears on the stage crane, with winged feet and carrying the Gorgon's head, as in the myth. He begs the archer to let him release the 'maiden' to which the archer only observes how ugly 'she' is. Realising he needs another strategy to beat the archer, Euripides exits and the chorus invoke the goddesses Athena, Demeter and Kore.

When Euripides returns it is as a brothel keeper with a stage-naked dancing girl and a boy piper. He promises never to badmouth women if they will release Mnesilochus. The dancing girl prick-teases the archer who offers a drachma for sex with her – an absurdly high price for a common dancing girl. While negotiations are under way, Euripides and Mnesilochus sneak off and the chorus sends the archer in the wrong direction to pursue them. So, it all ends happily.

# 44

The play came second – a little disappointing but probably fair, as it didn't have any serious messages to offer. A few days after the festival I went to the tavern as usual to hear what the regulars had made of it. I had originally made those visits expecting to bask in general congratulations; when I discovered I was more likely to receive criticism I was inclined to stop going but Pherecrates told me I should go all the same, partly because I might learn from the feedback but more to stop me getting big-headed. This time though, the discussion was just starting, and was promising to be rather more favourable than usual, when Lysander's cousin Hipparchus burst in with news that the oligarchs had seized power and we were now to be governed by a council.

"They've gone and done it," he said, staring crazily at us all in turn. "It's been decided."

After a few more uninformative remarks we managed to get him to tell us that the Assembly had just voted to accept Alcibiades' terms, as recommended by all but one of our generals at Samos. Apparently General-in-Chief Peisander had just returned from there and persuaded the Assembly that the alternative would be to allow Persia to side with Sparta again, and in our present battered condition, we'd be wiped out.

"So we've given up our democracy just because it suits Alcibiades?" I asked.

"Not only ours. Peisander has been installing oligarchies in all the remaining allied cities he passed on his way back here."

"Surely some people would have tried to prevent a deal with Alcibiades like that."

"His friends have helped him there. His main opponent Androcles died mysteriously the other day and some others haven't been seen for days."

"So what is the deal?"

A couple more men had entered the tavern, looking as distraught as our first informer. "We don't know yet," one of them explained. "The original suggestion was for a government consisting of five thousand citizens with enough money to help rebuild the state's treasury in the absence of so much allied tribute, but all they've done so far is set up a panel of ten to make a detailed proposal about how it would work. Personally I don't think we'll get to five thousand. The first people chosen won't be keen to dilute their authority."

Whoever said that turned out to be right. Under Peisander's guidance the first panel proposed another panel, of five this time. Each selected some others up to a total of four hundred, as an interim step to a government of five thousand. Antiphon was Peisander's main supporter and his proposal was backed by Theogenes and Archeptolemus with Theramenes manoeuvering in the background. I thought of calling it 'The Revolution of People Who Think They Are the Father of Cunna's Daughter,' but I didn't want to give away her secret. Anyway, it ended with four hundred people who had decided they wanted to be in charge taking over the council chamber, carrying daggers and backed by a gang of one hundred and twenty aggressive youths. After the formalities of prayers and sacrifices they proceeded to exile or execute any opponents they could identify.

The army at Samos didn't think much of this and decided they were fighting as a democracy, even though Athens wasn't one any longer, a concept that didn't make much sense even then. They claimed the city had revolted from the army! And who should add to the chaos but the ever reliable Alcibiades? He turned up in Samos just as the army was about to sail to Athens to try to restore the democracy and persuaded them to hold back and negotiate for the four hundred to make way for the originally intended five thousand, a compromise most people found reasonable, though Lysander and I didn't. In the meanwhile he was careful to take credit for the fact that Persia was doing little or nothing to help the Spartans.

With the army and Alcibiades now working together to change the government, the leaders of the four hundred got nervous enough to send messengers proposing peace to Sparta but they were turned down. They were fighting among themselves, as well as with anyone who stood in the way of their holding power. I heard afterwards that Theramenes had pleaded successfully for the execution of his fellow oligarch

Archeptolemus, so the competition to be the father of Cunna's daughter Ariadne was reduced by one. It was a shame it wasn't the other way round. Cunna had told me she really liked Archeptolemus and no one really liked Theramenes.

My dear old theatre of Dionysus was full when the leaders of the four hundred called an Assembly to ratify these proposals, but the meeting had hardly got under way when a soldier from the fortifications at the harbour rushed in to announce the Spartan fleet was at the island of Salamis, only about twenty miles away. Everyone grabbed whatever arms they could find quickly and rushed down to the Peiraeus to fight them off. It was lucky the four hundred had decided to fortify the harbour and some of the walls, so when the Spartans turned up thinking it would be easy to capture the city, they were surprised to find it so well-defended and sailed on past, rounding Cape Sounion and heading for Euboea. Even so, the oligarchs were far from safe as the soldiers in Athens shared the views of their colleagues in Samos. One of the leaders was killed and another taken prisoner and the city was in a state of total confusion and panic. They had no option but to start turning four hundred into five thousand very fast, identifying who would be included and establishing a system so that each of the five thousand would get a turn in the four hundred, which was where the real power would remain.

Sparta had backed off their plan of attacking the city, but by going to Euboea they posed a major threat to our supply chain for wood and grain, so we attacked them by sea. We lost again and Euboea revolted as the man in the tavern had predicted a few months before. We were now totally exposed. Pretty much all the troops and ships we had left were on or around Samos, on the other side of the Aegean, and if we called them back to fight at home it would give Sparta and Persia total control of that part of the world. I still don't know why the Spartans didn't just move in then and finish us off. Someone called them the most helpful enemy Athens could have had. Their allies weren't much better; Corinth, Syracuse and a few smaller states seemed in no hurry to provide men or ships and they still weren't getting any help from Persia.

Our stroke of luck in avoiding being completely massacred seemed to mark the turning point in our fortunes – at least for a while. The Assembly agreed that anyone who could afford hoplite armour could be part of the five thousand (the numbers just about worked out), and that office holders would be unpaid. Of course, my inheritance made me a member of the five thousand, but I didn't pay much attention, knowing I could make a bigger impact as a comic poet. In fact the new system turned out to be a pretty good way of managing things while it lasted. And then our navy beat the Spartans and the Syracusans at Cyzicus near the Dardanelles and recaptured quite a lot of the cities and territories we had lost. Soon afterwards our democracy was restored – at least for a few years – and I heard that my welshing banker had been murdered as soon as he got back to Samos. Good news all round!

It may have been this absence of the existential terror for the future of our city that had formed the background to my best work, or it may have been that comic poets only have so much stored in their well of inspiration and mine was exhausted, but either way, it was a while before I produced anything I could be really proud of again. Over the next three years my submissions were knocked back twice, once for the Lenaea and once for the Dionysia. The plays that did get up were so trite I didn't dare face the commentary in the tavern afterwards. There was *Triphales*, a mythological burlesque telling the story of a man with three penises, perhaps suitable for a low budget comedy but Philonides, frustrated at his own lack of success as a poet, decided to make it a massive production with lots of expensive props and special effects and the plot just couldn't carry that. Then I did a second *Thesmophoriazusae*, setting it on the third day of the festival this time with the wild feast, but without the Euripidean satire that made the original so funny it didn't amount to much, and it was also unplaced. The only thing I felt proud of was the patter song listing women's clothing and accessories set to the most complex metre I'd tried to that point:

*Razor, mirror, scissors, wax, soap*
*Wigs, ribbons, head-bands, hair-grips,*
*Rouge, white face powder*
*Perfume, pumice stone, bra, hairnet*
*Veil, hair-dye, necklaces, mascara*
*Soft gown, hellebore, barrette*
*Slip, shawl, nightie, robe, gown*
*Striped jacket, curling iron*

*Earring, gemstone, hoops, choker, pins*
*Bracelet, brooches, wrist-band, beads, anklets*
*Signets, rings, chains, plasters*
*Bobble-hats, breast bands, dildoes, jewels*
*Garlands and a lot more...*

Bronchus managed that all in one breath and chucked in a couple of gratuitous curses as well without too much damage to the rhythm. Otherwise it wasn't great, but we thought it deserved at least second or third, especially as Strattis' pathetic *Myrmidons* actually won.

These days, I find it hard to look back on my other effort of that period, *Old Age*, without tearing up. The chorus of old men behaving badly had much more sexual life in them than I can muster today. When they ask the hero if he fancies "Ripe girls or fresh ones, firm as salted olives," or when the leading girl celebrates the rejuvenation of the chorus leader with the words "There's nothing like a good piece of meat," I can only feel my inadequacy and try to come to terms with the fact that I can no longer pretend it is temporary.

But my writing career did have another lease of life. There was more good stuff to add to my portfolio before I stopped writing, starting with *Wealth*, which was so good that a revised version won the Dionysia twenty years later.

# 45

*Wealth* was just the sort of escapist nonsense that Athens needed during the depressing times towards the end of the war. Such political leaders as we had were really nonentities and didn't make much of an impact for very long. Alcibiades of course was still influential but unpredictable except as likely to avenge any comic poet who mocked him if he got the chance. Democracy was back but who knew how long it would last and most citizens just wanted to keep their heads down and stay safe with their families, as I did. I spent more time with Praxagora and the boys during that interlude between oligarchies than before or afterwards.

The plot was based on the notion that the god Wealth is blind and rewards the least deserving. A bit of a commonplace I know, but better than the idea a lot of rich people like to promote that wealth is a reward for excellence. You only have to look at some of them to know that's not true. To that extent you might say it was a statement in favour of democracy, but it was a pretty trite one and I didn't try to emphasise the political message. The humour was also pretty bland and the moral tone was simplistic, but I more than made up for it with some of the best choral music I had ever produced with a lot of experimental rhythms alternating trochees (tum-ti) with anapaests (ti-ti-tum). It is one of life's cruel ironies that the updated version I produced last year won the Dionysia, even though I had had to scrap most of the choral pieces in line with current fashion. The original production came second at the Lenaea to Strattis' tragic parody *Philoctetes*, even though the best bit of tragic parody at the festival was the opening scene of my play.

An Old Man and his slave are returning from a visit to the oracle at Delphi where the master has been to consult Apollo to see if he should bring up his son as a crook so as to avoid the poverty his father has suffered from. The oracle had told him to follow the first man he meets and persuade him to come home with him. The slave bemoans in tragic verse how he is always the one who suffers from his master's follies and now they are following a blind man, when what the oracle really meant was that his son should grow up to be a… wanker. After a comic exchange of questions and answers they learn that the blind man is the god Wealth. As a boy he had wanted to visit only the just and was blinded by Zeus as a punishment.

Old Man promises that if Wealth stays with him, he'll arrange to restore his sight and make him more powerful than Zeus because after all the only reason people pray to Zeus is for wealth. Everything is down to wealth: purchased sex (though the better class of young boys take gifts, not money), the Persian court, the fleet, mercenaries, embezzlers… No one can get enough of it. He invites Wealth into his house and sends his slave to summon farmers to share the coming riches. The farmers don't quite understand why they have been summoned and exchange insults with the slave in a parody of scenes from Homer's *Odyssey*. Eventually they promise Old Man their support.

At this point a neighbour arrives and when he learns Old Man is about to become rich, he assumes it is through criminal activity and asks for some money so he can bribe politicians to let Old Man off. Old Man promises to share his wealth with everyone but explains that there will be no wealth to share until they restore the god's sight. After a vain appeal to the audience ("Is there a doctor in the house? Is there one who won't demand payment in advance?"), they set off for the temple of Asclepius, god of healing.

A furious ugly old woman appears and condemns the plan for looking to kick her out of the country. She turns out to be Poverty; the neighbour wants to run away, Old Man to stay and fight. Poverty says she can show it is wrong to make good people rich. In a brief but rather clever Contest, the old man explains that if Wealth had his sight, the good would become rich, so everyone would become good, whereas now plenty of scoundrels are rich and plenty of good people are poor. Poverty replies that without her nobody would work or till the fields, there would be no slaves, as no one would risk being a slave trafficker if he was already rich, and no luxury goods, as there'd be no one to make them, and without them there is no point being wealthy. Old Man replies by drawing a picture of extreme poverty, discomfort and hunger. Poverty points out that she is not the same as Beggary; she represents the hard-working poor, just getting by but with nothing to spare and in better condition than the flabby slobs produced by

Wealth. The poor also have a higher morality, as you can tell from politicians who become corrupt as soon as they have made a little money. She explains that she is shunned because no one likes to be made to do the right thing and that Zeus is also poor, which is why he crowns Olympic victors with olive leaves instead of gold. Old Man refuses to be persuaded and chases her away. He sets off for Asclepius' temple with Wealth and his slave.

The slave returns to tell the chorus that Wealth's sight has been restored. While they celebrate, Old Man's wife appears and the slave describes the visit to the shrine. In accordance with standard procedure for the worship of Asclepius, first they wash Wealth in the sea, then take him to the god's precinct, burn cakes and first offerings and put him to bed, making up bunks for themselves. A blind thief is there, named Lysicrates after the corrupt politician who used to fund plays for Bloody Eupolis – about the only political comment I saw fit to include in the play – along with a whole lot of sick people. The steward of the temple puts out the lamps, but the slave can't sleep, having his eye on an old lady's bowl of porridge which he attempts to seize while the steward is doing the rounds of the altars. She tries to stop him, but he hisses like a snake and she draws back, farting in terror. As Asclepius approaches in the expected manner, the slave farts too, upsetting Asclepius' daughter, though the god himself doesn't seem to mind. Squinting through the holes in his cloak, the slave sees the god doing his rounds and then grinding a poultice for Lysicrates, which turns out to be a painful punishment for obstructing Assemblies. Asclepius and the healing goddess Panacea turn their attention to Wealth. Two serpents emerge to lick his eyes and suddenly he can see and the gods and serpents vanish. Everyone rejoices that Wealth can see and that Lysicrates is blinder than ever!

There follow some Farcical Scenes, including Wealth apologising for his past misjudgements, a Good Man and his child who come to thank Wealth for restoring their fortune after the father had spent his inheritance helping his friends who never repaid him, and a professional informer who is insulted, stripped naked and chased off the stage. A wrinkled old woman wearing too much make-up comes to complain about her toy-boy who now has no need of her money and just insults her.

In the final scene, the god Hermes enters in his wide-brimmed hat and tells Old Man's slave the gods are furious that no one is sacrificing to them now that everyone gets to be wealthy without their intervention. He feels especially deprived himself and lists the goodies he is missing and asks to join the old man's household, suggesting various absurd roles, such as door hinge protector, guardian of sports, chief wheeler-dealer and saviour of crooks. Old Man rejects them all but takes him in anyway. A priest turns up, complaining he is starving as he no longer gets invited to sacrificial dinners. Old Man tells him not to worry as they have decided to put Wealth back into Athens' sadly depleted treasury. He asks the priest to lead the procession and the chorus sings them out.

It was the last day of the Lenaea festival and after the judging I had laid on a big feast for the cast. There was a slight feeling of disappointment that we had only come second but Rhombus had won the acting prize for his portrayal of the old man, which required someone of his commanding stage presence, so we were all surprised when he didn't show up for the celebrations. Callistratus, whom I had engaged as leader of the chorus, not needing him to provide the finances any more, went backstage to look for him and returned with the sad news that as soon as he had taken his final bow and left the stage, he had collapsed. He had been carried home but died on the way. It was an awful shock to us all, but at least his last action had been doing what he loved and was so good at.

We couldn't carry on celebrating after that. I didn't feel like going straight home and Praxagora wouldn't have been expecting me anyway. I thought of going to the tavern, but I wasn't in the mood to listen to criticism, so I decided to pay Cunna a visit. I hadn't been seeing much of her recently, being busy with my writing and teaching the boys Homer and music, not trusting their schoolmaster to do those subjects as well as I could. I felt her gentle sympathy and kindness would be the best way to round off an evening that had started so promisingly but ended in tragedy.

When I got to Aspasia's the house was silent and dark. I let myself in through the heavy curtain over the front door and groped my way to a couch. Finding one, I sat on something angular and bony which gave voice. "Get off! Go and find your own couch," it said. After a bit more groping I found another place to sit. Silence reigned for a while, broken only by occasional dissatisfied grunts from the other occupied couch. When I could stand it no longer, I asked if the angular, bony person knew what was going on. "Buggered if I know," was the reply. "Salabaccho was expecting me and now she's nowhere to be seen. And this place is as dark as the inside of a mule's anus. If she thinks she can treat me like this after all the expensive presents I've given her, well I don't know…" He didn't clarify exactly what he didn't know, but that didn't matter because I'd recognised the voice and we started a rather different conversation that I quickly came to regret.

"Haven't we met at Hormus' pub?" I asked.

"Yes, probably," he replied. "I go there quite a lot. When I'm not here," he added in a salacious tone. If it hadn't been so dark, he would probably have nudged me. In any case I strongly suspect he winked.

"So do I," I told him. "My name is Aristophanes." That turned out to be a big mistake.

"That's funny. I've just been sitting through your play about Wealth. It was crap, by the way, even by your standards."

"I'm sorry you didn't enjoy it."

"Enjoy it! I'd rather have my balls chewed off by the Lernaean Hydra."

"What didn't you like about it?"

"Well, the fact that it was produced at all for a start."

"Can you be a little more specific?"

"Where do I begin? OK, take the goddess Poverty – though I hope I never have to. The idea that if everyone was rich no one would work or buy and sell slaves is rubbish. Lots of rich people work. People are naturally keen to get richer and richer and the more they have the more they want. It's called greed, if you didn't know."

"Yes, but it was a comedy."

"And then when the misery of the poor is pointed out, she has to back off and say only a little bit of poverty is good. That's true, by the way, and most of the audience would have agreed with you, but then you make her lose the argument. How pointless is that?"

"All right, but what about the main message about the relationship between virtue and wealth?"

"Oh yes, that was where the whole thing really fell apart. The old woman and her toy-boy were both bad. Realistically, she would have been shamed and cast on the streets and he would have had the usual punishment for toy-boys of having his pubic hair plucked out. But you let her keep her

240

money and reputation and you let him become rich. And then the sycophant defends himself successfully, even though he doesn't really have any sort of a case. Shall I go on?"

"Actually, I'd rather you didn't."

I reached inside my tunic for the *Fuck off, I'm a comic poet* notice, then realised he wouldn't be able to see it anyway. We sat in silence and darkness for what seemed an age until Aspasia appeared with a torch. "I thought I heard voices," she said. "Why are you sitting here in the dark? Didn't you see the notice?" She pointed to a large sign propped up just inside the door, which we might well have seen if someone had thought of leaving a lamp on. It explained that the ladies of the house were taking a well-deserved break in the countryside and would be back in three days' time.

My critic, realising he wasn't going to get what he came for, left immediately and I exchanged a few pleasantries with Aspasia before following him. I was glad I stayed as she told me she had heard great things about *Wealth*. She had obviously been speaking to a more intelligent critic than I had.

# 46

I didn't have a play of my own at the Dionysia that year, at least not in my own name, but Euripides had said I could write a satyr play for him, suggesting that it would be a step towards being a tragedian which continued to be my ambition. It wasn't a big step in that direction of course. Satyr plays are written by tragic poets, it's true, but they don't really have much to do with real tragedy, being a light-hearted interlude between the tragic trilogy and the comedy, designed to give the audience a bit of a break from thinking too much during a long day at the theatre.

The play I wrote was called *The Cyclops* and it was set at Mount Etna in Sicily. It was a spoof of the famous passage in the *Odyssey* where Odysseus escapes from the one-eyed giant Cyclops' cave by blinding him and then clinging on to the belly of a sheep. In my version the satyr and his sons (the chorus) are slaves to the Cyclops when Odysseus and his men turn up asking where they can buy something to eat and learn that they are likely to be eaten themselves if the Cyclops catches them. After some banter in which the dipsomaniac satyr offers to swap the Cyclops' food for the wine Odysseus happens to be carrying, the Cyclops turns up and asks what is going on. The satyr claims that Odysseus and his men have beaten him and are taking the Cyclops' goods and have threatened violence. The Cyclops decides to eat them, despite Odysseus' comic attempts to persuade him not to. After a choral interlude, Odysseus enters from the Cyclops' cave to announce that the monster has eaten some of his men and that he has been giving him wine and he intends to blind him and save everyone, including the satyrs. A drunken Cyclops appears, wanting more of Odysseus' wine so that he can share it with his brothers. By now he is sufficiently drunk to find the satyr attractive and they head back into the cave for sex. Odysseus follows them, asking the chorus to help him burn the Cyclops' eye out, just as Odysseus did in Homer's story. The chorus won't offer any help but agree to act as a cheer squad. The Cyclops appears, now blinded, and the chorus give him false directions while Odysseus and his men escape. The chorus decide to join Odysseus and, in an appropriate finale for the festival, commit themselves to be slaves of Dionysus.

Satyr plays don't usually attract much attention, but I must admit I was rather hoping some people would notice that this one was a bit wittier than Euripides' usual output and comment accordingly. Alas in the event his tragedy *Orestes* caused such a furore I didn't think anyone was really watching my satyr play at all. The Orestes story was a familiar one based on the usual tragic dilemma – you know the sort: A murders B for some compelling reason, usually imposed on them by a god, which means C has to kill A in revenge, which upsets D who is now morally obliged to put an end to C, which E doesn't like very much and so on until some divine being appears and tells the next ones in line there's been quite enough killing and they can stop being so silly. In this case it was the story of the family of Agamemnon, who had led the Greek forces at Troy, which had been told about fifty years earlier by Aeschylus in a trilogy that was so famous it had to be learned by heart in most schools alongside Homer. In Aeschylus' version, Agamemnon was his way to Troy to reclaim his brother's wife, Helen, when he was becalmed at the Boeotian port of Aulis. The gods refused to send him favourable winds unless he sacrificed his daughter Iphigenia, which he duly did, but when he got home his wife Clytemnestra was of course obliged to kill him to avenge their daughter. (She had another motive, having shacked up with an undistinguished fellow named Aegisthus during Agamemnon's absence, who claimed to have helped Clytemnestra in order to avenge his own father who had been tricked by Agamemnon's father into eating a couple of his own sons, but this wasn't really relevant to the central tragic dilemma.) The murder of Agamemnon of course meant that his children, Orestes and Electra, had to avenge their father by killing Aegisthus and their mother Clytemnestra, which they do with some help from cousin Pylades. That doesn't go down well with the Furies, three goddesses who were the champions of justice, and they pursue Orestes, who gets out of the problem with the help of the goddess Athene. She takes him to Athens to be tried by twelve citizens, thus instituting the practice of jury trials (not necessarily a good thing in my view). He gets off, thanks to Athene's casting vote, she calms the Furies down by renaming them 'The Gracious Ladies', and the whole sorry chain of events is finally over.

A good story, and a popular one with Athenian audiences, that had been told in various ways with modest success by various tragedians since Aeschylus' masterpiece. It was not good enough for Euripides though. In his version, courts of law already exist and it is the people of Argos who condemn Orestes, Electra and Pylades, the Furies being reduced to a figment of a crazed Orestes' imagination. Euripides inserted a couple of new subplots, one involving the attempted murder of Menelaus' wife Helen, who had been recaptured from her paramour Paris after the ten-year Trojan War and was therefore pretty unpopular with the Greeks, and another being an attempt by Orestes and co. to kidnap Menelaus' daughter Hermione, I can't remember why. Rather than acknowledging divine intervention as the basis for settlement, Helen's stepfather announces that the best way of dealing with tragic dilemmas is simply to exile all the people concerned. The god that does appear at the end (Euripides could never resist gods appearing on cranes at the end of his plays) is Apollo and his main role is to foretell the future rather than settle the present.

A few people were so shocked by this corruption of the myth that they walked out during the performance. Angry muttering from many of those who stayed drowned out some of Apollo's words and the hubbub continued during my satyr play, which was hardly watched by anyone at all. Euripides himself felt obliged to leave the theatre without staying to speak to the cast and I wondered how he was going to restore his reputation. A few days later I found out when I got an urgent message from him to meet in the pub.

When I arrived, he was sitting in his preferred dark corner with a large bundle of papyri in front of him. "I just wanted to say goodbye and to give you these," he began.

"Goodbye!" I exclaimed. "Where are you going? Why? How long for?"

"I'll start by answering your second question. I'm being prosecuted for blasphemy."

"Blasphemy?"

"Yes. A large gang of citizens, encouraged no doubt by some of my playwright competitors, have taken strong exception to my *Orestes*. They didn't like the way I portrayed Orestes and Electra as mad, and the events as the result of human folly rather than divine intervention. I don't regret it for a moment because I always wanted my plays to be realistic, but it seems people prefer myth and miracles to human reality. I could defend myself and my case would be unarguably right but that doesn't mean I'd win. Most likely I'd be exiled, so I thought I might as well pre-empt that by taking myself off."

"Where are you going?"

"Macedonia, I think. King Archelaus has been inviting me pretty much every month for the last few years and now seems a good time to accept."

"But Macedonia is freezing cold in winter. Are you sure about that?"

"As the guest of the king, I expect I'd be looked after pretty well and housed somewhere in the royal apartments. In any case, it's better to leave of my own volition and go somewhere I know I'll be appreciated than to be exiled in disgrace, with who knows what conditions."

"When will you come back?"

"I'll leave that in the hands of the gods," he said with an ironic smile. "Anyway, in case I'm away for a long time, I'd like you to take these papers and give them to my nephew Euripides Junior. They are three plays I've been working on. He fancies himself as a playwright so he can finish them and present them in his own name. I'd have given them to him myself but he's serving with the navy in the Aegean." He thrust the bundle towards me. "Now, if you'll excuse me, I'll just go and visit Myrrhine, maybe for the last time. She knows she mustn't talk to me. I have no idea what will be available in Macedonia, or whether it will suit my tastes."

He rose and had started heading for the back of the pub, when I grabbed his cloak and pulled him back. "But what about me?" I asked. "You know I am relying on you to make me a successful tragic poet. You've helped me so much already, but I know I'm not there yet."

"Try Sophocles," was the answer. "Don't bother with the rest. They're rubbish. Especially that goat's curd Agathon." Those were the last words I heard him say, as he headed off into the darkness, and I didn't find them particularly promising.

I hesitated for a long time, knowing what a curmudgeon Sophocles had become, but eventually decided there was nothing to lose except my pride and knocked on his door, only to be told by a slave to come back another day. This happened three or four times until one day the door was opened by the great man himself. I had been expecting to be turned away with a curse or at best a grumpy "What do you want?", but to my great surprise he seemed delighted to see me, ushering me into his living room and groping my bottom on the way. He was nearly ninety years old now but his insatiable appetite for sex with boys and men didn't seem to have diminished. A legend had it that following an encounter with an attractive young lad he had appeared at a festival wearing the boy's cloak after a mix-up in the darkness behind the gymnasium. As a result it was sometimes hard to remember that as well as being a famous tragic poet, he was effectively a one-man history lesson, having played a role in pretty much every major event since the Second Persian Invasion when he was the youth chosen to lead the hymn of thanksgiving for our victory. He had been a friend of some of our legendary statesmen like Cimon, Ion and Lysias' father Cephalus. He had had his portrait painted by the famous artist Polygnotus. His public offices included being a Treasurer, a general alongside Pericles and, just recently, one of the commissioners tasked with putting things right after the Sicily fiasco. A few years ago, he was selected to shelter the image of the god Asclepius while his shrine was being built, for which he was awarded the title The Great Receiver. It was about sixty years since his first win at the Dionysia with his play *Ajax* and fifty since, on the death of Aeschylus, he had been acknowledged as our top tragedian. (Euripides might have disputed that, but of course he was no longer in a position to.) In addition to his plays, he wrote a hymn for Asclepius and poems for the famous writers Archilochus and Herodotus. Foreign rulers invited him to attend their courts, although unlike Aeschylus who had died in Sicily, or Euripides who had just gone off to Macedon, he never accepted these invitations.

I was still thinking of all this and wondering if I dared ask him for anything, even grudging advice, when he said, "How good of you to come and visit. I know we haven't seen much of each other since that delicious encounter after your first play, but I've been following your career with great interest and admiration. By the way, satisfy my curiosity. You did write that *Cyclops* play for Euripides, didn't you?"

"As a matter of fact, I did. How do you know?"

"I could pick your style anywhere. The language, the fantasy, the surprise turnarounds… Euripides could never have done that."

Was he jealous of Euripides? I didn't bother to think too much about that. The great man seemed to be praising me.

"Your tragic parodies are excellent. You capture the tragic tone brilliantly and you have a real flair for showing both sides of an argument. You express the central ideas in plain language, which makes it so much more effective than the bombast of writers like Aeschylus. I'm only just beginning to do that myself, though of course I can't include scatological or sexual jokes in a tragedy."

I managed to stammer a thank you before he went on. "The names you give your characters are very clever. I especially liked Cleon-yay and Cleon-Boo. And then you seem to be able to make the most absurd fantasies seem inevitable. Somehow you manage to get the audience in on the plot and feel engaged. And your slapstick scenes are not only hilarious in themselves, but they make a great set-up for serious soliloquies. You've made our fellow citizens see sense on a whole range of things without them being conscious of it."

I was almost dumbstruck at this high praise. After a long pause during which he sat nodding and smiling at me, I plucked up the courage to ask the question I had really come for. "Er, if you don't think… or maybe you do… perhaps I'm wrong… um, now that you've seen more of my work and seem to like it…"

"Oh, you're not still thinking about writing tragedies, are you? That's a very different casserole of figs. Admittedly you have shown you can generate a certain amount of pathos but not for very long; you quickly offset it with something amusing. For tragedy you have to sustain it for the whole show; you can't just mix it in with slapstick and vulgarity. You also have to develop characters in depth and with consistency; in comedy you can use stereotypes and consistency can be sacrificed for the sake of a joke. And tragedy has to be realistic. Even if we are talking about gods and mythical heroes, there has to be some grounding in the realities of life and emotions that people can relate to. You can't just escape into the kind of world your hero would like it to be. And the pathos has to carry through to the end; even if a god on the crane has put an end to a disastrous sequence of events, the audience must be left heart-broken, not revelling in a happy ending. I'm not saying you couldn't do that, but the fact that you are a good comic poet and can write a fine satyr play doesn't really suggest you could."

It wasn't the response I'd hoped for, but it probably was the one I should have expected. It was with a heavy heart that a few days later I looked at the bundle of papers Euripides had left with me to pass on to his nephew. First there was a fairly complete play called *Alcmaeon in Corinth* in which the mad Alcmaeon leaves his son and daughter to be raised by King Creon of Corinth. Creon's wife becomes jealous of the daughter and sells her into slavery. She is bought by the unknowing Alcmaeon who returns to Corinth with her, where (surprise, surprise), he is reunited with his son as well. Not all that interesting I thought, but passable. Then there was a less complete version of the beginning of the Agamemnon-Orestes story called *Iphigenia at Aulis,* which in my view was unredeemed dog shit, and I secretly wished Euripides Nephew the best of luck trying to make that interesting. Finally, there were some notes towards a tragedy about the coming of the god Dionysus to Thebes and the resulting disaster that fell on the royal family. To make this the third play in a trilogy it needed writing almost from scratch. Which gave me an idea.

# 47

I wasn't able to give much more thought to writing a tragedy in Euripides' name for a while because I still had a few comedies lined up in my own. And Praxagora, far from recovering from her injuries as everyone expected, seemed to be getting weaker and weaker. The accident seemed to have done permanent damage to her lungs as well as her hip and she was breathing with increasing difficulty. The sicker she got the more she worried about the boys and whether they were at risk of being called up to serve in the navy. In normal times, three years compulsory military service started at the age of eighteen, but the troops would be supplemented as necessary in times of war. After losing so many in the first phase of the war, and even more in our disastrous foray into Sicily, the city could now call up any male citizen under the age of fifty. Ararus was a strapping fifteen-year-old and Philip was fourteen but his promiscuous hairiness meant he could have passed for any age. It was unlikely they'd be called up so young, but that didn't stop Praxagora worrying about it.

In fact things had been going rather well for us. After the four hundred had been got rid of, we won a remarkable string of victories, and eventually recovered large chunks of our empire. An unfortunate result was that the Persian king Darius decided we were doing too well and started offering serious support to the Spartans as well as attacking us with his own forces and ships under the command of his son, Cyrus the Younger, whom he put in charge of his possessions on the other side of the Aegean. Cyrus was popular with his contemporaries, not least for his extraordinary skills at horsemanship, but was also known for his headstrong temper, neither of which qualities made him an enemy one would choose to be up against. He linked up with the Spartan general Lysander, each no doubt promising to help the other achieve absolute power in their respective domains. Lysander wasn't even a member of the Spartan royalty but that didn't stop him wanting to be king. He was a skilful naval strategist and diplomat, but more relevant to his ambitions, he was also a vicious, corrupt murderer who based his career on bribery and violence.

Most of our early successes were due, I'm sorry to say, to Alcibiades. He came back to Athens and, always keen to be in the public eye, somehow contrived to be chosen to lead the Eleusinian procession to kick off our most important secret religious rites. Precisely on what basis he was even allowed to attend, let alone start the proceedings, I was unable to tell and, after what had happened to Eupolis, not keen to question, though it might have been his attempt to dispel the stories about how he had mocked the secret ceremony with his friends in their homes. The mysteries were only supposed to be open to priests, novice priests and people who somehow had learned the secrets, generally by being in one of the first two categories, although generous sponsorship was probably another option. I had avoided Alcibiades from the time his ship had docked at the Peiraeus, but I couldn't resist watching the procession as it set off from the pottery district in the hope of seeing him uncomfortably out of his depth. He wasn't.

I don't know whether the Assembly was as put out as I was at seeing the awful man take such an inappropriate role, or whether there were particular plots against him (vindictive plots against individuals were the main feature of our democracy during these regrettable years), but at any rate he was not re-elected general and, in a fit of pique, decided to exile himself. I'm glad to say that was the last we saw of him.

The fact that the war wasn't going too badly and there didn't seem to be an immediate need for youth call-up only partly settled Praxagora's anxiety about the boys. She was still determined to find them careers, even though it seemed clear none of the three would ever have to work for an income. I explained this to her. "They could just spend their time being useful citizens, you know, voting in the Assembly, volunteering for responsible positions in the Pandionis tribe or in whatever suburb they end up living in." I thought about other options and quickly added, "Or listening to philosophers," in the forlorn hope that would clinch the argument.

"Yes, but what if the money runs out?"

"I don't think it will, unless they start throwing it around like Callias or Alcibiades. And I hope we've brought them up too well for that."

"Yes, but why run the risk? And why expose them to the temptation? Why not have them do something useful?"

This daily conversation seemed to run in perpetual circles, the only difference being that Praxagora was clearly becoming weaker all the time. Eventually we got around to some serious options.

"Look," I suggested. "We know how hard it is to make a decent return on your effort from making things anyone can make like crockery and drinking vessels and metal tools and so on. Given they don't need to spend their lives trying to do that sort of thing, they should focus on something they could be admired for. Some special artistic skill, say, like sculpture or wall painting or music."

"What do you suggest?"

"Well, you know how good Ararus is with words. He can memorise anything, even really long speeches in prose, and can talk for a full minute without taking a breath."

"Yes, I've been meaning to speak to you about that. He's very loud and I'm sure holding his breath like that can't be doing him any good."

"He could be a great actor."

"Why do you always want to get them involved in theatre? He could be a famous orator or teacher of rhetoric."

"Would that be better?"

"Well obviously it would. It would be secure and not depend on winning selection and then on the view of a bunch of idiots on the jury. And it wouldn't involve twice yearly crises as a festival approaches and nothing seems to be ready."

I was going to remind her that Philip was always inventing new rhythms and dances, which suggested he could be an outstanding playwright, but it didn't seem a promising line to take. I ended the conversation as I always did with a promise I'd look into it. She gave a half smile, but her eyes were vacant.

I must admit that till that point, my domestic affairs had never interfered too much with my plays. When the boys were at home, Praxagora and the slaves had entertained them out of earshot of the dining room where I did most of my writing, and if that failed, I would go and sit by myself in an empty theatre or temple or a quiet corner of the Arcade and think up new plot twists and jokes that I could write down when I got home. Unlike Cunna, Praxagora had never shown a great deal of interest in my work, but once she had come to accept it – and when she was in a good mood – she often came up with witty suggestions and made sure I incorporated them, which I was generally pleased to do. Now she was quiet and unhappy and her health was visibly failing daily, and we only discussed her anxieties; my pretence at sharing them slowly metamorphosed into genuine empathy which made it hard to get into the spirit of comic invention.

I had two plays lined up for the Lenaea that year and it didn't help that both of them had 'women' in the title. *The Phoenician Women*, produced in the name of my old friend Philonides but financed by me, came third. It was a straightforward spoof of Euripides' play of the same name and it should have been a great opportunity to test my ability to imitate the old boy for the whole of one play, albeit without the tragic ending, but it was as much as I could do in my distracted state to string together a few Euripides-like soliloquies and a chorus or two without aiming for anything more ambitious.

*The Lemnian Women*, which came second at the same Lenaea, and deserved to win, not only parodied Euripides but Sophocles and Aeschylus as well. It was a simple retelling of an old myth that was especially conducive to humour because it centered around offensive smells. Aphrodite, goddess of love, cursed the women of Lemnos with an evil smell for having neglected her shrines, so the men gave them a wide berth and took up with the female slaves they had taken in raids. The women of the island decided upon revenge and, one night, killed all their male relatives. A woman called Hypsipyle saved her father Swift by hiding him.

Who should turn up soon after the massacre, but Jason and the Argonauts on their way to Colchis! They stayed on Lemnos for two years and had lots of sex with the island's women, who must have stopped being so smelly. Jason gave Hypsipyle twins and swore eternal fidelity but quickly sailed away and left her as true heroes are wont to do. The other women though were still angry with her for having spared her father, so she had to flee for her life. She and her sons were taken by pirates and sold to the king of Nemea and she was put in charge of the king's son. A bunch of Argive soldiers on their way to attack Thebes asked Hypsipyle to find them water. She put the king's son down on the ground where he was promptly killed by a snake. The king was pretty cross, but luckily (in my version at least) the Argive leader turned out to be a good sort and stopped him doing anything nasty to her. In addition to the parodies, I had borrowed a pun from Euripides and turned it into a good bit of slapstick with Hypsipyle's father Swift proving to be a very slow runner when she tries to hide him.

I was on my way home from the final rehearsal, worrying about Praxagora and starting to try to imagine life without her, when I bumped into Plato, who, it seems, had been looking for me.

## 48

"Do you believe in truth?" This was the first question he asked me after dragging me over to a shaded spot in the Arcade. On the face of it, it was an easy one – you might say truth is pretty much defined as what you really can believe – but this was Plato and I suspected there might be a trick.

"Well, it depends on the circumstances," I improvised.

"You mean who you hear it from?"

"Perhaps that." I still suspected a trick.

"Because I think friends like us should always tell each other the truth."

I breathed a sigh of relief. I could relate to that. "Of course," I said. "Friends like us." He patted my thigh. I wished he wouldn't. If his eyes hadn't bulged so much, he might have been quite attractive, but I still wished he wouldn't.

"Because I've just been to your house – it was the first place I went after seeing my mother and my what's it called, half-brother Antiphon. And I wanted you to know what happened."

"Go on. I hope you were made to feel welcome."

"Er, yes, exactly. Well, when I arrived there was no one in the front room so I guessed you might be having a nap and went through to your bedroom. There was an old lady in your bed, much older than Praxagora. At first she had her back to me and a night cap on, so I thought it was you. I was just climbing into the bed to show how pleased I was to see you after all this time when she groaned and rolled over. Not to my taste at all, so I jumped out again at once. Who was she by the way? And what happened to Praxagora? She was rather beautiful as I recall."

"Er, thank you," was all I could bring myself to say.

"Anyway, enough of that. You know how anyone who is beautiful is so because they participate in the ideal form of Beauty?"

"Of course. Everyone knows that. Ha, ha!" I vaguely remembered Socrates being reputed to have said something on those lines while I was preparing the revision of *The Clouds,* but I confess I hadn't looked into it very closely.

"Well, I'll tell you who participates in the ideal form of Beauty all the way up to a Titan's armpit."

I hated that expression, especially from one with such a melodious voice, but asked whom he meant anyway.

"Your slave, that's who. Not the hairy one but the long thin one with the high-pitched voice. He is simply gorgeous and we had a lovely afternoon. The hairy one wanted to join in of course but he reminded me of a Thracian merchant I met in Tarentum who was a bit rough with me. We were stuck in southern Italy for a while during the war in Sicily and I wouldn't recommend it to anyone. Once the war was over my uncle took me to Syracuse and I've spent the last few years in the household of Dionysius the general. He's ambitious and will probably have taken over the government by the time we next hear. Anyway, it won't do you any harm if he does. He wanted to understand how Athens is governed and I told him to read your plays – not *The Clouds* of course, but the ones about peace and the jury system. And not those ones about strong women that I heard you put on after I left on my travels, women in power! That's just ridiculous. Socrates would hate that."

It was good to see Plato of course. We had become quite close in the four or five years before his uncle had taken him off on a five-year learning tour of Southern Italy and Sicily; he had forgiven me for attacking Socrates and I had forgiven him for letting me down before Agathon's symposium. Our mutual understanding that sex was not a necessary part of our relationship despite the age gap had endured, though I was a bit worried about what he must have been expecting when he called at my house. His ability to talk for hours on anything that crossed his mind had been strong before and he seemed to have lost none of it while he was away. Every time he paused for breath the image of him climbing into bed with a very unwell Praxagora struck me hard and I knew I should get back to see how she was, but when he resumed in his lovely tones, I couldn't help but listen.

"I'm not here for very long," he continued. "We were going to Asia next, but what with all that funny business going on there, I think we'll spend some time in Egypt first. I'll tell the Pharaoh and the king of Persia about your work. I wouldn't be surprised if they invite you to visit their courts. You'd enjoy that."

A long and beautifully poetic description of what he expected to see in Egypt and Persia and how much I'd enjoy it was just getting underway and, against my better judgement, I was listening spellbound when he suddenly said, "I must go and collect Antiphon. I said I'd introduce him to Socrates, as long as he promised to take notes. I plan to write up a lot of Socrates' discussions one day but I'm not very good at listening and taking notes at the same time. Of course, you must come with us."

That was my opportunity and I didn't let it slip. "I wish I could," I lied, "but there are some troubles at home."

"I thought so. You should get rid of that old woman you know. Bring back Praxagora."

"I'll try," I said with feeling, and, promising I'd give serious thought to his parting request to buy Manodorus from me, I left.

As I walked back to my house, jumbled images of Plato's visit to it came rapidly and unbidden. Suppose that had been Praxagora's last experience on earth. What a horrid thought! Could her shade ever rest peacefully after that? Would she be reliving it over and over in a kind of Sisyphean torment? Or, still more horrid to think of, did she find the episode exciting and would its premature termination make her torture more like Tantalus'? I was a sweaty gibbering mess when I got home but was relieved to find her still alive; in fact she seemed a little perkier than when I'd left for the theatre that morning.

The 'funny business' on the other side of the Aegean that Plato had referred to had been going quite well, so the likelihood our boys would be called up had almost vanished. After our fleet had been blockaded in Mytilene, the city's desperate need to build up our navy led the Assembly to decide to offer citizenship to all volunteer rowers. The recruiters were overwhelmed with applications from slaves, not all known of or expected by their masters. Manodorus tried to apply for all the wrong reasons, but I persuaded him it would be terribly uncomfortable and the men wouldn't be his type anyway. The naval strategy seemed to be working for a while with what appeared to be a great victory over the Spartans near the island of Lesbos, seventy sinkings to twenty-five, but as the reports from survivors filtered through, it became clear that it hadn't been so great after all. A lot of our rowers from the twenty-five ships lost had drowned; few slaves ever learned to swim and there was a strong feeling among the more sensitive citizens that the recruitment strategy was a rotten trick to play on well-meaning slaves. The eight captains were successfully prosecuted by the awful Theramenes and his side-kick Thrasybulus for failing to rescue enough of them, but sentiment changed quite quickly after that and the Assembly passed a law against either of those two nasties being a general ever again.

Even after that victory, things could still easily go wrong at any moment and many of us thought Cleophon was an idiot for opposing Sparta's offer of peace. They had Persia on their side with huge riches to spend, while the closure of our local silver mines meant we were rapidly running out of cash. Alcibiades, who could be relied upon to do something surprising – and it looked as if only something surprising could save us – was not coming back from his exile, and was no doubt finding new ways to outrage any nation he found himself among. In fact, things were so bad that when the lottery system threw up the name of Socrates to be a member of the emergency council, no one laughed. Of course, he moaned about the system but accepted the post anyway. To give him his due, he had made a long speech against the execution of the generals Theramenes was prosecuting, but no one really understood what he was on about and they died anyway. One of them was a son of Pericles. What would he have thought?

I had put forward a couple of proposals for the next years' plays, which I had been excited about, but I didn't give them much attention at that sad time. I felt Praxagora was slipping away and, though I might not have been a great husband, she was a pretty good wife all things considered, and I felt obliged to spend a lot of time with her. In fact, it was a wonderful time, sitting on the end of our bed and chatting in a way we had so seldom managed to do in almost twenty years of marriage. I soon decided I wouldn't choose to be anywhere else.

Of course the boys were still the main topic at first. She took me through each of their special qualities again. Ararus was a natural leader and a confident speaker on any subject, especially those he knew nothing about. She thought he could teach rhetoric like Protagoras. Philip had a great sense of rhythm and she thought he might be a serious poet – not a playwright of course, but perhaps a composer of dithyrambs or lyric poetry, a sort of male version of Sappho of Lesbos. Philetaerus was more of a problem: he was just a nice guy and we struggled to think of any careers that could be based on being a nice guy. "Politician," she would say and we'd both roar with laughter as if it was the funniest thing we'd ever heard.

"Informer," I'd reply and we'd crack up again.

"Ambassador!"

"Treasurer!"

"Tax collector!"

"Mines inspector!" We rehearsed the same litany day after day and I don't think either of us got tired of it.

At other times she talked about growing up in Aegina and some of the funny people her parents had been friends with. She was amused when I told her which of them had been victims of my father's extortion racket. But most of all we talked about my plays now, as we seldom had before. She had read them all, though she hadn't seen them all at the festivals. She told me which ones she liked, how she thought my style had been developing (mostly for the better) and she offered some suggestions which were far more perceptive and rather more kindly expressed than the ones I was used to getting from my critics in the pub. She laughed a lot when we discussed Criticus and we took it in turns to think of what he might have said about each of my plays. Once she actually guessed what he *had* said. She reminded me I had never carried out my promise to name her in a play. I explained truthfully that I had given it a lot of thought but hadn't found the right part. I promised I would – a promise I kept with my last truly original comedy a dozen or more years later. She gave me a lot of ideas for the two new plays coming up. I rather wished they hadn't both been about the underworld, but she didn't mind. In fact, she said she thought it was rather funny.

I wasn't with her when she died, but I don't think it mattered. The boys had come in by turns to kiss her and sit with her for an hour or so every day for what seemed like months but probably wasn't, even when she could only smile and touch their heads. That day, she was weaker than ever and had fallen into a peaceful sleep. I popped out to ask the boys to come and say goodbye to Mummy, but by the time I had rounded them up and come back to the bedroom she was gone. The four of us started to cry in ascending order of age and it became a general wail in a wide range of tones when Xanthias and Manodorus realised that the long-feared event had actually happened and joined in. A woman relative is supposed to wash and anoint the body but Praxagora had no women relatives in Athens, so Manodorus carried out the task. When he had finished, he laid a wreath on her breast and Ararus stepped up to seal her lips with an obol as a payment to Charon the ferryman for taking her across the River Styx to Hades. I have an idea the obol didn't stay there for long, but it didn't worry me because, at her own request, she was going to be cremated anyway and Charon wouldn't have had a job.

She and I were the same age; forty was young for a citizen woman to die but close to average for men, even without war. I began to wonder if I had much longer myself, but then I heard Sophocles had died a couple of days after her and he was ninety-one! He had been demonstrating his fitness by reciting a long speech from *Antigone* without taking a breath; he didn't quite make it but apparently, he did better than most ninety-one-year-olds would have. Some people say he would have got to the end except that some mischief-maker threw a grape into his open mouth which finished him off, but I hope that's not true. When I wasn't thinking sad thoughts about Praxagora I felt sad about him too, especially as now I would never get him to admit he was wrong about my poetic potential.

Her last words to me had been, "Don't forget what we agreed about the boys." I had often wondered why last words were deemed to be so important. Even if you imagine there is some sort of afterlife, it would be a pretty rotten one if you had to spend it worrying about whether people were carrying out your dying instructions. I trusted that if Praxagora was still aware of anything now it would be something more interesting than her sons' careers. Even so, last words do have a bit of a compulsion about them and I felt I shouldn't break a promise even if she would never know. To start with I thought I should concentrate on finding them suitable occupations rather than working at my plays for the next festival, but of course I wasn't sure where to begin, so I mooned around uselessly for a while. The boys missed their mother terribly and they always would, I knew. But they were boys and it wasn't long before I could see they were desperate to get back to their friends and their school and their games. Ten days after the cremation we were back to our normal lives though regularly conscious of a big hole in them, which often led to tears, mine included.

A normal life for me of course was producing my next plays. At the Dionysia, which took place shortly after Praxagora died, I had entered *The Singer*, a novel plot in which the hero and his fellow performers select three poets, one tragic, one comic, and one dithyrambic, to travel to the underworld to meet their famous predecessors and rescue the goddess of Poetry. On the way to Hades an overweight character called Plum gets squashed in the crane and cries out, "Help, I'm becoming a prune," – a joke Strattis copied in his next play – and it turns out that the main qualification for joining the expedition is being thin. And of course that was how they described their prospects of success. When they had finally arrived down below, they were drenched in wine and vomit by a hideous prostitute called Nais and escaped just before she started to empty her bowels on them. I made Nais talk in a clever parody of the effeminate Agathon.

It was all a bit of fun and a nice relief from the grief which came back to me in waves for several months. My sorrow was aggravated by news of the death of Euripides in Macedonia. They said he had been killed by a boar. I expect it was just the frostbite I had warned him about, but the boar story was more impressive and strangely more tragic. I would miss his fun ways and awkward habits and I'd get no more coaching from him, but I was now completely free to make what I could of his story about Dionysus coming to Thebes. It also meant I could use him instead of Sophocles in my entry for the upcoming Lenaea, which was going to be as good a practice run for writing a real tragedy of my own as you could get in the slot reserved for comedy.

# 49

Much as I wanted to concentrate on *The Frogs* for the Lenaea, I had a few distractions in addition to thinking too much about Praxagora. Lysander told me I needed to get a female slave to help bring up the boys, but remembering the problems I had with both Nerita and Human Artemis, I argued that it was quite unnecessary as Manodorus was every bit as good a nanny as any female slave would have been. Lysander hadn't met him, so I took him back to my house for a jug of wine and he agreed.

More worryingly Sparta had recaptured Aegina and redistributed some land, including my farm and those of most of my tenants. I would still probably receive rents from the city properties, Sparta not looking to populate more cities with her own people and allies, but losing the farms would make a serious dent in my income. I asked Lysander to help me do the sums. It turned out we (actually Lysander with the money of both of us) had taken some big bets on several transport ships at the height of the naval battles in the East and somehow all but one had got through and at a much higher return than normal because of the war risk. We had more than made up the two talents our welshing banker had cost me and with the money Praxagora and I hadn't been able to spend out of our large income, along with regular payments now coming in for restagings of my back catalogue at country festivals and abroad, I was still embarrassingly well off and there was still no need for the boys to earn anything themselves. Lysander couldn't understand why I was worried about their futures, even when I told him Praxagora's last words, but he did promise to introduce the boys to a couple of sculptors he knew, observing that that was a very respectable line, and (he winked) one that hardly any slaves practised.

I resolved to follow that up after the Lenaea and it was helpful that I no longer needed to worry about my promise to Praxagora so much and could really concentrate on what became the best thing I had done for years. The dramatic last half of *The Frogs* was a competition in the underworld between Aeschylus and Euripides, so you can see why I thought it was a good opportunity for extended practice in writing tragedy. I have to admit the plot owed a bit to Eupolis' posthumous and best comedy *Suburbs*, but so what? Anyway, let me take you back to the beginning.

The audience was in a pretty good mood after seeing the brilliant posthumous production of *Oedipus at Colonus*, staged by Sophocles' grandson, also called Sophocles, who went on to become a successful playwright too. He seemed a nice young man and I would like to have worked with him, but the war had put a lot of financial strain on our richest citizens, so the funding duties were split between tragedy and comedy, and he didn't need my help to produce his grandfather's plays. One effect of the cutbacks was that many comic playwrights reduced the size of their choruses from twenty-four to twelve. Philonides was nominally my producer again, but as I had been funding my own plays for a while, I was allowed to stick with twenty-four. I also bucked the money-saving trend of simplifying the masks. Good masks are essential to a good comedy.

The audience had had their Sophocles so now I was going to give them the other two great tragic dramatists of our era. If Euripides hadn't died so conveniently it would have been harder. There is a much greater gulf between the styles of Aeschylus and Euripides than between either of them and Sophocles. Sophocles was more silver-tongued, though not as sickeningly honeyed as Agathon, but that wasn't an easy contrast to make in witty speeches. There were no female parts suitable to be named after Praxagora, but there was a great part from right at the beginning for an uncouth slave, so I called him Xanthias and even gave him the line "Bugger me, you arsehole," as a tribute to our first meeting. His master is the god Dionysus (more good practice for my 'Euripides' tragedy) and his plan is to bring Euripides back from the dead (a nice allegory of my own plan). Dionysus is faithful to his comic stereotype as an effeminate, incompetent, loud-mouthed buffoon who is only really interested in food. Remember, the gods don't mind being mocked at festival times. I didn't make fun of Pluto God of the Underworld when he appeared later, in case it affected Praxagora's comfort in some way I couldn't quite grasp.

Dionysus and Xanthias start the play by arguing about whether a slave on a donkey can properly be said to be carrying anything and then debate what makes for a suitable opening for a comedy before breaking all their own rules. Dionysus dresses up like his half-brother Heracles, who is familiar with the underworld after retrieving the hell hound Cerberus, and goes to ask his advice, only to be met with hilarity at his ill-suited costume. When Dionysus asks which way is the quickest to get to Hades, Heracles tells him that he can hang himself, drink poison, or jump off a tower. Dionysus opts for the slower journey across a lake, which Heracles himself had taken. Charon the ferryman will take him across for two obols (the price was normally one obol, two being the cost of a theatre ticket). Meanwhile Xanthias asks a passing corpse to take the bags with him but the fee the corpse wants is too high.

Charon arrives in a boat with a punt pole, and offers to ferry Dionysus across the lake. Xanthias, being a slave who did not fight in the naval battle, is not allowed in the boat, and has to walk around the lake, while Dionysus' inept attempts at rowing Charon's boat make for excellent slapstick. They are observed by a chorus of frogs (the only appearance of the creatures the play is named for!) whose otherwise beautiful song includes the refrain *Brekekekèx-koàx-koáx*, which sounds like frogs croaking, but if you say it fast enough, at least in the way I trained the chorus, it sounds more like someone breaking wind. Dionysus eventually reaches the other side of the lake where he meets up with Xanthias who has walked round. More slapstick follows as they cower from imaginary beasts and then the chorus reappears, having shed their frog costumes, as Dionysian initiates in an imitation of the Eleusinian Mysteries. Two lots of costumes for the chorus, a moving boat and a donkey made it a pretty expensive production, but it all seemed to work beautifully. Alcibiades was still in exile and I was pretty confident he was not coming back, so I had the chorus leader wear an Alcibiades mask in the procession to the Eleusinian Mysteries and get lost several times en route. The chorus' Address included a few satirical jokes about politicians and attacked some of my least favourite people including Cleisthenes and Callias and that idiot Cleophon who was refusing to make peace, and his sidekick the ghastly bathhouse keeper Cleigenes. I described the horrible Cleisthenes and his nasty sexual habits as 'plucking his anus in a graveyard.' I called Callias 'cuntson' and said he had bravely put on a lion skin to fight against a fanny. Platon had written a whole play about Cleophon which came third. A lot of leading politicians had died but Athens was never short of worthy targets.

When Dionysus and Xanthias finally arrive at Pluto's door, the disguise leads Pluto's slave to think Dionysus is really the Heracles who stole their dog Cerberus. Terrified, Dionysus swaps clothes with Xanthias, a move he quickly comes to regret when a maid of the underworld goddess Persephone invites Xanthias, now in the Heracles costume, to a feast. They change clothes again and the chorus praises their willingness to do so frequently – "a pair of overshoes just like Theramenes the politician. They can go on either foot" – but no sooner is he back in his Heracles garb than Dionysus is attacked by a couple of innkeepers whose bills Heracles hadn't paid and whose mattresses he stole. It is now Xanthias' turn to be Heracles and Pluto's slave arrests him for dog-stealing. He offers his slave (Dionysus now) to be tortured in the usual way to see if his denial is true. The clever ploy fails; they are both beaten and taken to Pluto and Persephone for identification.

There followed another of my innovations in the form of a second Address which made a plea for the re-enfranchisement of everyone who had been disenfranchised when the oligarchy was overthrown. They had been misled by the rogue Phrynichus who was quite rightly assassinated after the oligarchs' revolution. I said they should be treated no worse than the slave rowers who were (rightly) given citizenship after Arginusae. The chorus then compared our political leaders to the current state of Athenian coinage: the city ignores the true stuff and chooses the bad bits. After a bit of badinage between Xanthias and another slave we prepare for the great Contest, which takes up the last half of the play. Euripides is challenging Aeschylus for the title of Best Tragic Poet. (Euripides was played by Bronchus who also represented Xanthias, so a few quick mask changes were needed from here on). Sophocles has declined to compete and Dionysus is to be the judge. As they take their places, Euripides wrestles Aeschylus for the seat of honour. They insult each other's verse, with periodic interruptions from Dionysus who tries to calm them down. Aeschylus says the contest is unequal as his own poetry has survived his death and it is not clear that Euripides' will (in a strange way this was the challenge I was setting myself!). They open proceedings with ritual prayers, Aeschylus to Demeter goddess of agriculture while the heretic Euripides addresses the Sky, Smart People and Keen Nostrils. Aeschylus speaks in old-style Homeric hexameters, Euripides in more modern rhythms.

Euripides starts by criticising Aeschylus's openings which typically involved mysterious characters standing alone on the stage listening to long, miserable songs from the chorus. When they eventually speak they suddenly come out with huge unfamiliar words whereas he, Euripides, always explained the plot from the very beginning, used common words, and gave lines to slaves and women. (Aeschylus did too, of course – Clytemnestra and Electra for a start. But somehow they weren't the sort of women you meet in the street or having lunch with your wife, like Euripides' were). Euripides went on to claim that he had taught the audience how to talk, how to react quickly, and how to know when to suspect others, all by using everyday scenes without fantasy or bombast; "my supporters are clever, not bearded thugs."

Aeschylus asks him what qualities are to be most admired in a poet. When Euripides says, "Skill and good advice," Aeschylus starts talking like a prim censor. He observes that while he had written about martial heroes, Euripides inherited a noble race and turned them into shirkers and criminals. Early writers like Orpheus, Musaeus, Herodotus and Homer also taught valuable lessons about noble behaviour, whereas Euripides put whores on stage and used language which just encouraged gossips and lying politicians. Putting his heroes in rags has encouraged people to play poor to avoid their public duties. Dionysus rudely interrupts to observe that having his wives leave him served Euripides right. The chorus sings a song of encouragement to them both, noting that the audience is pretty sophisticated and can handle a literary competition.

They then attack each other's opening scenes, Euripides making fun of the start of *The Oresteia*, and Aeschylus returning the compliment by picking holes in Euripides' opening to *Oedipus*. Aeschylus torments Euripides by getting him to recite his opening speeches and then adding to each line "and lost his little flask of oil." Euripides counters by arguing how monotonous Aeschylus' choral songs were, parodying them and ending each verse with, "Ow, what a blow, won't you come to the rescue?", followed by the clack-clack-clack of castanets (Bronchus was great at that sound).

During this performance, Dionysus has somehow come into his own. He now rules the stage, adjudicating the contestants' squabbles fairly, breaking up their prolonged rants, and showing a deep understanding of

Greek tragedy. For the final stage of the Contest, they decide to weigh their writings. Euripides goes with mentions of weighty subjects like the ship *Argo,* the goddess Persuasion, and a mace. Aeschylus responds with a huge river, Death, and two crashed chariots with their dead charioteers. Aeschylus' objects are heavier, so he wins this round but, despite Pluto's urging, Dionysus is still unable to decide whom he will revive.

He finally decides to take the poet who gives the best advice about how to save the city, starting with what to do about the exiled Alcibiades. Euripides condemns him while Aeschylus says a city that rears a lion cub should take great care of it. Asked for further advice for the city, Aeschylus says Athens should adopt Pericles' strategy and invade Sparta and spend more money on ships, while Euripides suggests the fat Cleocritus should fly on musician Cinesias' wings and spray vinegar in the eyes of naval opponents. He then says they should change political leaders for more trustworthy ones. Aeschylus disagrees, saying that a city that elects bad leaders is past saving anyway. Dionysus decides to go with his spirit and selects Aeschylus. (Of course, he didn't really win the contest – I prefer Euripides myself – but you can't really go wrong with a festival audience if you back the old against the new). Euripides feels betrayed and Dionysus mocks him with a stinging parody of his own type of intellectualising: "Who knows if life really be death…"

Pluto takes Dionysus and Aeschylus indoors to celebrate and the chorus sing Aeschylus' praise and condemn those who chatter with Socrates, and ignore the craft of tragedy. The rest of the cast return and Pluto says goodbye to Aeschylus, asking him to take various items for suicide back to Athens with him to give to certain politicians and tell them he is waiting eagerly for them to hurry up and die. Before being escorted away with a choral hymn, Aeschylus asks that his chair be kept for Sophocles and not given to the lying rogue Euripides.

I hadn't had a win for three or four years at this point, but was confident this was the play that would get me back on top and I was right. Phrynichus was second with *The Muses* and, as I mentioned earlier, Platon's *Cleophon* came third. I don't remember all the losers but was quite happy that Philon's *Buskins* was one of them. It wasn't really a play, more a kind of embarrassing dance. *The Frogs* was such a hit that within a couple of months Dionysus and Xanthias being beaten by Pluto's slave was the most popular scene on decorated vases. I was given the special prize of an olive branch for distinguished service to the profession, and, most unusual of all, I was asked to stage it again at the next year's Lenaea. Not everyone was happy though; some angry women who were fans of Euripides sent me hate messages and threatened to have me ostracised. An idle threat as there had been no ostracisms for nearly ten years, and women couldn't start a proceeding or vote on it anyway. Yet I still felt glad to know Euripides had stirred such loyalty among his fans.

# 50

As soon as the celebrations for *The Frogs* were over, I could concentrate on my tragedy. This meant agreeing with Euripides Nephew who would do what in the run-up to the Dionysia. When I had handed him the bundle of papers I had kept back the notes his uncle had made on *The Bacchae*, telling him I had lent the script to Sophocles Junior who was learning the craft and would benefit from a close study of something not written by his grandfather. The young Euripides was pleased at the thought, so, despite the fact that scarcely a word of the text had been written, was quite happy when I told him it was complete and couldn't be improved on. I suggested he leave it to me to manage and rehearse the production while he concentrated on the other two plays: *Alcmaeon of Corinth*, which was pretty much complete, and *Iphigenia at Aulis* which needed a lot of work. Once or twice he asked how rehearsals for *The Bacchae* were going and if he could see the script now, but I always came up with a plausible reason, generally to do with there not being enough copies of the text and the lead actors needing to learn their lines. By the time we got to final rehearsals, the script was complete, so I gave him a copy and invited him along. He didn't suspect a thing.

In between intense writing spells I made an effort to do something about my promise to Praxagora. I tracked down Lysander and asked him to introduce me to the sculptors he had spoken of. He said he would take the two eldest boys in turn and to different sculptors, Ararus first as the oldest.

There are two ways of making sculptures: one involves bronze casting, which is hot, dangerous and labour intensive. The artist makes a clay model and then puts another layer of clay on it. When this layer has taken the shape of the model it is taken off, reassembled and lined with wax between the two moulds and heated to an unimaginably high temperature to let all the wax burn out through vents in the outer material. Then molten metal is poured into the gap left by the wax and when that has cooled, you get rid of all the clay and there is your sculpture. Ingeniously enough, this modern system means the original clay model can be used again and again for replicas of the same sculpture. The other way of making statues is chipping away at a block of stone. The first method involves an initial bit of creative work by the artist and then lots of manual labour; the second only involves the artist or his apprentices. Lysander told me it didn't matter which the boys chose because a talented artist could succeed in either. His friend Myronias, son of the famous sculptor Myron of Eleutherae, was about to start the process of making a series of new pieces of bronze work for the Erechtheion and would be happy for Ararus to join him and observe the process for the payment of a small apprenticeship fee.

Ararus obviously enjoyed his apprenticeship while it lasted. Each evening he came back with a satisfied grin on his face. When I asked him to tell me about it he always said that he felt it suited his talents well, but wouldn't go into detail. This was promising and I was just thinking how pleased Praxagora would be if somehow she knew, when Lysander came round with an embarrassed look on his face and told me he had promised Myronias he'd stop Ararus coming to the workshop any more.

"But he's loving it!" I exclaimed.

"I'm sure he is."

"He says it suits his talents well."

"I'm afraid it does."

"Well, what's wrong with that?"

"It's the wrong type of talent for sculpture. Myronias was teaching him to give instructions to the slaves during the casting process, but Ararus felt it was an opportunity to show off his prodigious memory and acting talent. Instead of telling them what to do next, he would come up with what he thought was an apposite quotation from the classics. When they were taking the mould out of the layer of clay he would quote from Euripides' *Medea* "I'd sooner go to war three times than give birth once," and when they were taking the full mould from the furnace it was Sophocles' *Electra* and "Not from Hades' black and universal lake can you lift it."

"Quite clever," I said proudly.

"Yes, but he didn't seem to be learning much and he was starting to repeat himself, so everyone was getting a bit bored of listening to him. Myronias would probably have given him a bit longer to show he could learn about the bronze process if it wasn't for a rather unfortunate choice of a line from Aeschylus' *Agamemnon*. Just as a slave was starting to make vents for the heated wax to escape, Ararus took it into his head to shout "Ow, you've got me right in the guts!" The slave was so nervous that he might have drilled the holes too far that he stopped before he'd got through to where the wax was. When it was heated, the wax expanded but couldn't escape and eventually the whole mould blew up and destroyed the original model Myronias had spent weeks shaping. It was the biggest in the series and supposed to be the centrepiece. So he thanks you for trusting your son to him as an apprentice but says he can't afford to keep him on."

"Suppose I doubled the apprenticeship payment."

"It's not a matter of money. No artist likes to see his work destroyed, especially commissioned work that has to be redone from the start. You need to find something else for Ararus – have you thought of making him an actor?"

I groaned. "What about Philip? Can you still find him an apprenticeship?"

"Yes, I can, though I'm a bit nervous now. Praxiteles is expecting me to bring Philip round to learn his type of sculpture. He carves marble and doesn't have a team of slaves except to fetch and carry new blocks of stone and finished pieces, so there is no danger of the Ararus problem repeating."

This sounded pretty good. Philip's affinities were all about rhythm and movement and he wouldn't be shouting inappropriate lines of poetry. It wouldn't even matter if he did, because there would be no one looking to him for instruction. I couldn't see how that could go wrong but of course it did. This time it wasn't Lysander who came to see me but Praxiteles himself. His father, also Praxiteles, had worked with the great Pheidias, and he was to have a son, also Praxiteles, who later became a sculptor too. But it wasn't his family and their lack of imagination in naming children that Praxiteles wanted to talk about. In fact he was so angry he could hardly talk at all. When he finally did, he explained that he could put up with Philip prancing around the place like a sacrificial cow in the peak of the fly season, but he had not been expecting him to start trying to contribute to an almost complete work as soon as he was left alone in the studio. He told me he had almost finished a totally novel and revolutionary piece that would set a new trend in marble sculpture. He had managed to get hold of a very expensive block of Parian marble that was sufficiently large that he could depict two characters on the same base. He had decided to show Eurydice following Orpheus and his lyre out of Hades; Orpheus was about to turn round and spoil the whole thing by looking back and Eurydice was stretching out her hands towards him in fear and desperation.

All that remained to finish this work was to separate the two smallest fingers on Eurydice's outstretched left hand when the person who had commissioned it showed up for a look. He was delighted with it and said that he'd pay double the initial agreement for the finished piece. Unfortunately, while Praxiteles was showing the customer out and promising him he'd finish the hand and have the piece delivered to him next day, Philip had taken it on himself to finish the piece off. Philip's skills were to do with movement and rhythm rather than delicate manipulation of cutting tools and the inevitable happened. Eurydice lost her fingers and Praxiteles had lost an unusually large and expensive block of marble and several months' work.

I tried to persuade him that it needn't be a write-off and even suggested a few solutions like sticking it all back together with flour or putting a loaf of bread on the end of Eurydice's arm to disguise the damage, but he wasn't impressed. He wanted to focus on the fact that he had lost six months' income and how hard and costly it would be to find a similar piece of marble. I did feel sorry for him and gave him rather more money than I'd expected to pay for all three of my sons' apprenticeships.

Of course I had failed Praxagora but, wherever she might be watching from, she couldn't say I hadn't tried. I decided I'd done enough for the time being and would concentrate on my part of the posthumous Euripides trilogy for the Dionysia. When I had finally finished the script of *The Bacchae* I gave a copy to Euripides Nephew but he didn't take much notice, being more concerned with his own efforts to stage *Alcmaeon at Corinth* and to complete and present *Iphigenia at Aulis*. *The Bacchae* was to be last of the trilogy on the day and he pretty much left me to get on with it.

*Alcmaeon at Corinth* wasn't one of Euripides' best, but it wasn't his worst either. That honour was saved for later in the evening and his nephew's edition of *Iphigenia at Aulis*. Alcmaeon had led the famous group of heroes known as Sons of the Seven in the destruction of Thebes, and, under instruction from his father, and for reasons I could never quite make out, killed his own mother. This sent him mad, if he wasn't already. The play began with the god Apollo explaining that although Alcmaeon's wife did not have any children with him, Apollo, she had had two children by her husband while he was mad. (Don't ask me why she might have had children with Apollo as well. He was probably just showing off.) One of the offspring was a boy called Amphilochus, and the other a girl, Tisiphone. Alcmaeon left them to be raised by the king of Corinth whose queen became jealous of Tisiphone and sold her into slavery. Alcmaeon unknowingly purchased Tisiphone as a slave, and returned to Corinth with her, where he was reunited with Amphilochus, who pointed out that the slave was in fact his sister. The plot depended largely on the shock of recognition when Alcmaeon recognises his daughter, but even that didn't make for a very thrilling story. The whole thing was redeemed, if only just, by some great lines that made me nostalgic and a bit weepy for my old chum.

The story of *Iphigenia at Aulis* was a prequel to Aeschylus' brilliant *Oresteia* trilogy and put in train the whole chain of events which led to Clytemnestra killing her husband Agamemnon so that her children were obliged to kill her and so on until the Furies, in return for being renamed The Gracious Ladies, decided enough was enough. The play opens with a frantic Agamemnon pacing up and down outside the Boeotian port of Aulis. He has been elected leader of the Greek force to attack Troy, but they can't get there for lack of a favourable wind. His prophet tells him that the wind will only change if he sacrifices his daughter Iphigenia. He has already sent for the girl and her mother Clytemnestra to come to Aulis so he can marry her off to his number one warrior Achilles. He has second thoughts about her coming to Aulis, given what the prophet had said, and sends off another message to tell her and Clytemnestra to stay at home, but his brother Menelaus, who is keen to get going in pursuit of his wife Helen and thinks sacrificing Iphigenia is not such a bad idea, intercepts the message. When Iphigenia and Clytemnestra arrive, Agamemnon and Menelaus have both changed their mind. Menelaus says, "Don't kill your daughter."

Agamemnon says, "Don't tell Clytemnestra, but I will."

There follows some dark comedy. Clytemnestra offers to help Agamemnon prepare for a ceremony which she thinks is for Iphigenia's wedding but is actually for her sacrifice, and then Achilles, who doesn't seem to have been told about the plans for his marriage, comes to announce that his men are complaining about inactivity and ends up in a confused conversation in which Clytemnestra gets the idea he is flirting with her. An old man shows up and tells them both what is really going on and Achilles agrees to protect the mother and the daughter, for whom he now feels some responsibility as her promised bridegroom. Clytemnestra goes off to plead with Agamemnon but neither her arguments nor Iphigenia's wailing have any impact and Achilles is starting to lose his nerve, having been threatened by the rest of the Greek army who just want to get on.

The next person to change their mind is Iphigenia who suddenly decides it would be best if she was sacrificed. Achilles promises to stand by in case she changes her mind again. She doesn't, but sings a hymn and sets off to her death. The play ends with a messenger saying that just as Iphigenia was about to be sacrificed, she disappeared and her place on the altar was taken by a deer.

The play had some good bits and I'm pretty sure they were written by old Euripides. The catalogue of Greek ships on their way to Troy was as good as Homer's and the black humour and misunderstandings could only have come from the mind of my old friend. It had some terrible bits too that I attributed to the nephew. A choral song about the marriage of Achilles' parents and what he was going to do at Troy was as pointless and platitudinous as anything I've seen on stage, though nearly matched by another chorus commenting on the disagreement between Agamemnon and Menelaus. Agamemnon's lengthy exposition of Achilles' family tree must have put a lot of the audience to sleep. There were two particular things that could not possibly have come from Euripides senior. In the first place, it presented a much more positive view of the Trojan War than he had ever expressed. People later suggested his enthusiasm for Greeks against barbarians might have been kindled by his stay in Macedonia, but if they had known what I did about the composition they would have recognised that those passages were the work of another hand. And of course the ending with a dying deer replacing Iphigenia was too silly for words and could not have been written by a sensible fellow like Euripides. In any case he always liked to end his plays with a god on the crane. I wrote an alternative ending on those lines involving Artemis and gave it to Euripides Nephew in case the play was going to be presented again at some country festival. I don't know if it ever was.

The audience's reception was naturally quite cool, not to say confused, which wasn't promising for *The Bacchae*. It was lucky I had decided to open the production with a real attention grabber.

# 51

*Boom! Boom! Boooommmm!* The sound of gongs and the flashes of lightning from fires behind cleverly manipulated blankets were calculated to grab the audience's attention and they did. Gradually the flashes give way to smoke, out of which thunders the deep voice of the god Dionysus, accompanied by a heavy drumbeat: "I, son of Zeus, have come to this land…" He explains that he has returned to Greece from Asia and is at the tomb of his mother Semele, daughter of Cadmus, king of Thebes. Zeus fell for Semele and seduced her, but afterwards his wife Hera insisted Zeus appear to the woman as he does to the gods, with the foreseeable result that Semele was burnt up by lightning. Zeus saved his son by her in a cavity in his thigh to be reborn in Asia. Now Semele's sisters fail to recognise Dionysus. They claim that Semele was impregnated by a local lad and that her father Cadmus made up the story about Zeus to save her reputation. Cadmus has just abdicated in favour of his grandson Pentheus and Dionysus has taken on mortal form so as to lead his band of crazed women (maenads) against him if necessary to get some respect. He calls on the chorus of women who have followed him from Lydia to make a noise while he goes to join the maenads at Mount Cithaeron. The beautiful hymn the chorus sings about Dionysus' birth was the only substantial part of the play Euripides had written and I only added a few lines to it.

Now the scene is set, I'll give you a quick summary of the plot, which is all about the disasters that befall the Thebans as a punishment for them being slow to recognise Dionysus. I had used a slightly similar plot in my second play, *The Babylonians*, though as this was for a tragedy, I had to stress the importance of religious observance to make the story work properly and not ridicule the god and his cult as much as I had in the comedy. Most of the audience would have been in two minds about the reality of our gods but tragedy traditionally assumes a tone of extreme piety.

First, we find the old blind prophet Teiresias and the almost-as-old former king Cadmus off to join in the Bacchic rites of Dionysus up in the mountains. The new king Pentheus enters, furious that all the women have disappeared and, not believing that the stranger they are following is Dionysus, suspects they are just off having a good time. Teiresias notes that whether they are having sex depends on the morality of the individual woman, a fine distinction one never has to draw in comedy. Pentheus refuses to join the old men. He orders his bodyguard to arrest whatever women they can find and hunt down the stranger who is causing all the trouble. All this is interspersed with comments from the chorus, mostly pointless and platitudinous, but, unlike in comedy, all relating to the plot. Not finding anything very challenging in presenting the standard lines for a tragic chorus commenting on the action, I experimented by making many of their lines rhyme. In fact, in one choral verse of sixteen lines, only four of the last words don't rhyme with the last word of at least one of the others! I wonder if that will ever catch on.

A servant arrives with Dionysus, whom he has captured without resistance, but he says the chains fell off the women they had caught and put in prison, so they have escaped. Pentheus comments on Dionysus's beauty and questions him about his origins, starting the first of two Contests, which were something I was very comfortable with of course. The god cleverly avoids giving a straight answer. Pentheus starts cutting off Dionysus's hair and takes his wand. In a comic exchange, Dionysus says that's OK because Dionysus will rescue him. Pentheus says Dionysus won't because he is nowhere to be found and re-arrests him as if to prove it.

The drama increases as the palace burns down – wonderful special effects with flames and blankets again. I'd experimented with something similar in *The Clouds,* but this was much more realistic. Dionysus tells how he had escaped by creating various illusions to confuse Pentheus; he made Pentheus tie a bull's legs together, thinking they were Dionysus' hands, and then became a cloud of smoke that Pentheus stabbed fruitlessly at. To increase the dramatic effect here I used trochaic tetrameters catalectic (tum-ti-tum-ti-tum-ti-tum). The light, bouncy rhythm underlines the absurdity of the event and contrasts powerfully with the building tension.

Pentheus now turns up and orders the city gates to be locked, but just then a messenger arrives from Mount Cithaeron to report on the maenads.

He tells how he found the women sleeping in groups, chaste and sober. Their leader is Pentheus's mother Agave. She wakes them and they let their hair down, cradle and cuddle snakes, and make wine, water, milk and honey spring out of the earth. Then they suddenly grow wilder; they start to tear apart cattle with their bare hands and invade and destroy villages, seizing children. They have fire in their hair and balance children on their shoulders with no support. No weapons can harm them and so, the messenger-herdsman concludes, Pentheus should join them.

Despite warnings from Dionysus, Pentheus has decided he wants to see what these women are up to and we have the second Contest. Dionysus helps Pentheus disguise himself as a woman but tries unsuccessfully to persuade him to leave the women alone. Pentheus is hallucinating again and thinks Dionysus is a bull, but off he goes to the mountain.

We find out what happens there from another messenger. It was unusual, but I thought rather clever, that the two best speeches in the whole play were given by messengers. We used different actors with quite different tones of voice: the Pentheus actor with a light and slightly querulous tone played the first messenger whose speech started with a bit of poetry I was especially proud of: "*Our grazing herds were climbing the hills, our blazing sun was warming the earth, the crazy women were sober and chaste...*" The actor playing Dionysus with his deep booming voice played the second one and he describes how, when they arrive at a spot near the maenads, Pentheus can't see the women, so Dionysus bends a tall tree, sets Pentheus in the top branches and eases it gently back to the vertical before calling on the maenads to punish Pentheus. They try pelting him with stones and branches but can't get at him, so they uproot the tree instead. Agave, not recognising her son Pentheus, pulls his arm off and the other women tear the rest of him apart. Agave puts his head on the end of her sacred wand and sets off back to Thebes. You'll have noticed we are rather a long way from comedy's Farcical Scenes now.

When Agave gets back to Thebes, she tells the chorus she is carrying the head of a mountain lion. She is proud of her kill, invites everyone to feast on it with her, and goes to show off her prize to Cadmus and Pentheus. After a good, blood-curdling chorus I was quite proud of, Cadmus turns up with the other bits of Pentheus and makes Agave stare at her prize until she recognises her son's face. Cadmus explains that Dionysus has sent her mad because she didn't worship him and shows her the other remains of her son before starting a long, miserable lament for himself, his city and his family. The play ends with the typical Euripides finish: Dionysus appears, now as a god on the machine, and prophesies a miserable future for everyone concerned. Cadmus and his wife will become snakes and lead a barbarian army against Greece. Agave heads off into exile with a lot of wailing. The chorus ends the play with the same words Euripides used to close *Alcestis*, *Andromache* and *Helen* and very like those in his *Medea*.

Of course, in my first effort at tragedy I wanted to play to my strengths and this plot gave me ample scope. It was about as gruesome as you could want and didn't depend on examining people's inner feelings; everything they felt, however deluded, was made very explicit in their actions, just as it is in comedy. I could intensify the tragedy by using my comic technique in reverse. Just as I could make comedy funnier by couching it in tragic verse, so I could make tragedy more shocking by interspersing it with comic scenes. The decrepit pair of Teiresias and Cadmus, dressed in goatskins and carrying sacred wands as they hobble off hand-in-hand to the mountains, raised a big laugh, even from an audience that knew the tragedy waiting for them. Some of the dialogue could have come from one of my comedies – misunderstandings like Dionysus avoiding Pentheus' questions, or Pentheus telling Dionysus that Dionysus can't come to his rescue because he is nowhere to be found. And I structured the scenes carefully to bring out the comedy-tragedy contrast even more. A solemn chorus about how the gods can upset anything at any time ("*Envy the man who is happy today.*") is immediately followed by the scene where Dionysus helps Pentheus get dressed as a woman to spy on the maenads. That was pure slapstick and the audience appreciated it as such. Some of them were probably reminded of Euripides' father-in-law as I had portrayed him in my *Thesmophoriazusae*. The implication that Pentheus just might have been a voyeur kept the tone light until we got to the horrible irony of Pentheus' pleasure at being told he will be brought back to Thebes in his mother's arms: "It's what I deserve!" he exclaims.

I particularly enjoyed the opportunity to treat women differently from their comic stereotypes, because I could use those stereotypes to make their change in behaviour more shocking. The women originally portrayed as drunken sluts become as grotesquely bloodthirsty as any humans possibly can. To start with all the talk is about their love of drink and sex – they are even said to sneak off to have sex while pretending to be conducting rites, just as some of the women had in my *Lysistrata* – then they become sober, suckle snakes, and finally go wild, uprooting a tall tree and tearing first cattle and then Pentheus limb from limb. I dwelt on Agave carrying Pentheus' head back to the city believing it's the head of a lion, and on her asking for Pentheus to come and help nail it to the wall, and then trying to stick it back on to the fragments of the rest of his body. I even hinted that she might actually have recognised her son from time to time during her mania. I've always enjoyed the grotesque.

The judges enjoyed it too – or maybe they just felt they had to take the opportunity to give Euripides one more first prize. Euripides' Nephew was delighted, even when people said they thought *The Bacchae* was the best play in the trilogy. He was happy to accept the compliment for his uncle and told everyone that was the one play of the trilogy that Euripides had completed and that I had done quite an acceptable job as producer-director. I didn't mind what he said, but I wished I could have told Sophocles that I'd written it.

A few days after the festival, I bumped into Pherecrates near the temple of Asclepius. "Congratulations," he said.

"For *The Frogs*? I thought I'd seen you since then."

"You have. No, I meant for *The Bacchae*."

I was a bit startled as I hadn't yet told anyone it was my script, so I thought I'd test Pherecrates out.

"But that was by Euripides."

He came as close to smiling as I could ever remember him doing. "Oh, come on! I know your style too well – and Euripides' for that matter. In fact I've often thought they had much in common and you certainly managed to make it so the other night. But there were some things that could only have come from you."

"For example?"

"Come back to my place and we'll talk about it there."

On the way to Pherecrates' house I kept asking him how he had guessed. He wouldn't say, but I couldn't help speculating. Was it the rhymes in the choruses? Was it the slapstick dressing-up scene? Was it the early passages about the women? When we arrived and he had poured me a goblet of wine, apologising that his slave Heracles was busy, he came quickly to the point. "As I said, you did a very good job of making it Euripides-like. The first chorus, for example, I wouldn't have known."

"Actually that was the one bit that was by Euripides."

"But you used a lot of slang terms like 'mate' and 'scummy behaviour' and 'set-up.' Using the vernacular in tragedy is all very well – in fact Euripides was very good at it – but there is a fine line between common speech and vulgarity and you crossed it a few times."

"Anything else?"

"Yes. The comedy. It wasn't the first tragedy to use humour to point up the tragedy that follows, but this humour was clearly yours. Euripides would never have thought of Dionysus pouring out himself as a libation, for instance. Or seen the comic potential in the dressing-up scene. And Pentheus accusing Teiresias of being a money-grubbing quack could have come straight from any of your works, but not Euripides'. But most of all it was the sheer physicality of the play. In tragedy you do get dramatic physical action but it's generally off stage, and only one or two events in any given play. In *The Bacchae*, from about a third of the way through, it was all physical and much of it was actually represented rather than reported. You made it really grotesque."

"OK. You're obviously right. Do you think anyone else will have noticed?"

"Not many people study poetic style as closely as I have, so they'd probably only have noticed if they were looking for it. And unless you gave them some reason to, they won't have been."

"So how do you think I should break the news?"

"Why would you do that?"

"Well, it's a first, isn't it? No comic poet has ever written a successful tragedy before, and you must admit it was successful. It got a terrific reaction and you're the only person I've met who suspected it wasn't by Euripides."

"Yes?"

"So I'd like to get some credit when the time is right."

"To take credit from Euripides for the best play in the last trilogy to be produced in his name? I don't think that's very kind. And I'm not sure how you'd do it. You can't prove you didn't have a full script from Euripides all

280

along, even if you do produce a version or two in your own handwriting. Besides nobody wants to be persuaded it wasn't Euripides' work and they'd be inclined to reject the evidence even if you or I drew it to their attention. At best, if some people end up believing you, many won't and you'll be remembered by them as the person who tried to steal the credit from Euripides soon after he died. You have every reason to be satisfied with what you have done, but I'm afraid the only other person likely to appreciate it is me."

This was pretty disappointing. I'd achieved my long-term ambition but no one would know about it. I had hoped for rather more acclamation than the comments Pherecrates had made and the opportunity to feel pleased with myself. As I said goodbye and a rather rueful thank you, the excited squeals of Pherecrates' niece-turned-wife explained why Heracles wasn't available for wine-serving duties and made me think of Cunna. At least I could tell her.

# LETTING GO

# 52

If you'd asked me a few years earlier what I'd do for company and comfort if Praxagora died, I would have said I'd be spending a lot more time with Cunna, but strangely enough, that wasn't what happened at first. In between unpredictable attacks of grief and worrying about the boys' future I had thrown myself into my writing and, on the few occasions when I had thought about visiting Cunna, I decided against it for fear I might suddenly let her see how much Praxagora had meant to me. Now I felt I could put it off no longer. With Euripides gone, Plato overseas, Pherecrates showing no excitement at my tragedy skills and Lysander really only good for a laugh, I desperately needed some adult company to share my personal triumph. I just hoped she would forgive me for neglecting her for well over a year.

When I got to Aspasia's the house was silent and dark as it had been once before. This time I asked if there was anyone there, not wanting to sit on someone and find he was a vicious critic as had happened that time. There was no answer and I was about to go home when a torch illuminated the room and Ariadne walked in. She was in her twenties now and as beautiful as her mother had been when I first met her. "Oh, hello, Aristophanes dear," she greeted me. "We haven't seen you for ages. Are you waiting for Mummy?" I told her I was. "Well, she won't see you today. She's with Aspasia."

"Perhaps I can see her when she's finished with Aspasia?"

"No, I don't think so. You see, Aspasia's dying. She has no family left so Mummy wants to be with her to the end. And Mummy's going to be in charge of the house and I expect there are all sorts of questions she'll be wanting to ask Aspasia while there is still time. Why don't you come back in a few days? It'll be over by then and it will be lovely to see you." She gave me a smile that showed her mother had trained her well.

As I made my way home through the marketplace it struck me how much more crowded the city had become. Our grain supply had been threatened by the Spartans near the Dardanelles and our fleet had gone to try to keep the shipping lanes open only to be roundly defeated, losing one hundred and sixty-eight of our one hundred and eighty ships with almost four thousand men taken prisoner. Admiral Conon had fled to Cyprus, knowing what trouble he'd be in if he came home. The Spartans promised to execute any Athenians they found on that side of the Aegean so thousands of them turned up in Athens within a couple of months. With many of our farms not having recovered from the regular Spartan invasions of the countryside, food was beginning to run out.

A lot of people blamed Alcibiades for the naval loss because he had left such an incompetent fool in charge as Conon, and that meant he was even less likely to come back to Athens than before. There was some irony in his public career coming to an end over a battle he wasn't even present at, but in the event it didn't matter as the Spartans persuaded the Persians to murder him. Apparently, some Persians set fire to his house and he extinguished the blaze with his nightgown, grabbed a sword and rushed outside to challenge whoever did it only to be killed with arrows. I don't know what took them so long.

A few days after my futile visit to Cunna, news went round that Aspasia had died. The funeral was private but the street outside her house was full of mourners. No one was ashamed of having frequented Aspasia's; in fact some people were there in the street who I could swear had never been inside the house in their lives but wanted it to be thought that they had. I caught a glimpse of Cunna when the door opened to admit a priest and the bearers of the coffin who were to take it to the cemetery in the pottery district to be burned, and I wondered if I should be there consoling and supporting her. But of course, I figured, she was probably handling everything perfectly well, and if she'd felt she needed me, she would have sent me a message. I had it confirmed by some of the bystanders that Aspasia had left the house as a going concern to Cunna – all perfectly illegal of course, as a woman can't operate a business without a man nominally in charge, but no one was likely to complain.

I started wondering whether Cunna and I should marry. She had been single since before she came to Athens and now that she owned the house she'd probably retire from active duty. Friends of the resident ladies would look after her now without her having to do more than chat about philosophy and stuff. I thought perhaps I ought to remarry, if only to get some help with launching the boys into the world, but I wasn't sure about it. Athens was as full of widows as usual with more new ones every day, but the nicer ones were quickly snapped up by uncles and cousins, especially if their household was well off. I didn't have any nieces or cousins and I didn't feel like starting to date random widows in the hope one might replace Praxagora. And I wasn't so sure I wanted to be married. For female company, there was always Cunna, I hoped, or, failing her, one of her ladies, and Xanthias and Manodorus seemed to be managing the boys quite well.

I was still unsure what would be for the best when I went to see Cunna, having allowed a decent interval after the departure of Aspasia. I was wondering how to broach the subject when she pre-empted me. "If you are thinking we should get married, my love, let's not. I'd like us to spend as much time together as our other duties permit but I think our relationship works very well just as it is, and if we were together all the time, I don't expect it would." I knew her well enough to be sure she wasn't really hoping I'd disagree as some women might have been, so I didn't. She quickly changed the subject and talked about what a wonderful person Aspasia was and how much she had learned from her, not only about the craft of escorts in general, but about philosophy, mathematics, rhetoric, music and all the other bases for high-brow conversation that had helped her succeed in her line of business. She told me Aspasia had left the business to her, but of course she needed a husband to give her the legal standing to manage it and it wasn't going to be me. She wanted someone who would not expect much sex and would leave her to get on with running the house. There weren't a lot of single men of around her age to choose from. Most of the people who thought they were Ariadne's father were married and she didn't want to marry the bachelor Theogenes because that would stop the other putative fathers giving the girl all the gifts she had become used to. Eventually, we decided she should marry one of the Fatties, who were all single and uninterested in women. Not being confident in the practicality or good sense of any of them, I promised to keep an eye on things for her. A few weeks later, Aspasia's house was the venue for Cunna's wedding to the obese but kind Teleas. He didn't even bother to move in with her.

After my efforts at the last couple of festivals, I thought I'd earned some time off, so I didn't put in a proposal for the next year. I was surprised when the king archon sent for me, crowned me with an olive wreath, and told me he had decided I should put on *The Frogs* again at the next Lenaea. This was an extraordinary honour that hardly ever happened to living playwrights and I was told afterwards that it was because of my plea to have the oligarch sympathisers re-enfranchised, which had been enacted soon after the first performance. I didn't have to do much to present the play again, as the archon assigned me the original cast who only needed a couple of rehearsals to be back to their best. A little later I had cause to regret the effectiveness of my proposal, as the same people, now re-enfranchised, played a big part in the next bout of oligarchy, the one imposed by the Spartans.

Yes, that's what happened; the Spartans imposed it. Famine and disease were getting an increasing grip on the city and soon after *The Frogs'* second performance, we finally succumbed to the inevitable and surrendered. The Long Walls between the city and the harbour were pulled down and a Spartan garrison was installed to keep an eye on the group of thirty old oligarchs they had put in charge. Corinth and Thebes demanded the complete destruction of Athens and that all its citizens should be enslaved, but the Spartans refused to destroy a city that had served Greece well in the Persian Wars, and announced that Athens was to have the same friends and enemies as Sparta. This meant losing all our overseas allies and their tribute going to Sparta, and handing over all but twelve of our ships. Sparta's allies weren't impressed, as they got nothing out of Sparta's victory.

It was Theramenes who negotiated the surrender, but by now he was seriously unpopular for all his political twisting and turning, and for his part in the execution of Archeptolemus and his prosecution of the generals who failed to save enough people after the sea battle, so he didn't last long. He was denounced to the oligarchic Assembly and then, when that body appeared reluctant to punish him, his enemies struck his name from the roster of citizens and executed him without trial.

The Spartans told us the Thirty were just going to 'codify the ancient laws', but they turned out to be even more oligarchic than the Four Hundred. They executed anyone who advocated too noisily for a return to democracy, including the philosopher Polemarchus who was made to drink hemlock; his brother Lysias somehow got away with just having their shield factory confiscated. They ordered a small group to fetch the old general Leon of Salamis for execution; Socrates was one of the group and refused to go but the fatal mission went ahead anyway. A few rebellious people went to occupy the fort of Phyle, about ten miles from the city near the border with Boeotia, and the Thebans, fed up with being ignored by Sparta, gave them some support and enabled them to defy the troops sent by the Thirty for months. By now the Thirty were only hanging onto power thanks to the support of the Spartan garrison. I was sad to see Critias playing a leadership role. He had been a good poet and tragedian and in his youth his democratic instincts had led him to organise a rising of serfs in Thessaly. In his tragedy *Sisyphus* he had said, "The gods were invented by a ruler to help him keep order." It seemed that, for him, the Spartans had now taken the place of the gods.

The Spartans and the oligarchs couldn't keep order for very long. One day at the beginning of winter democrats suddenly seized the Piraeus, which was easier to do with the Long Walls destroyed. There were only about a thousand of them to start with and the oligarchs with their supporters and the Spartan garrison numbered about three times as many, but a lot of citizens rallied in support, which enabled them to hold out for almost a year. In the end the Spartans got serious and sent General Lysander with more troops. He put paid to the resistance and wanted to have all the leading democrats executed but his King Pausanias wouldn't let him. Quite the contrary, in fact; Pausanias insisted democracy be restored and nominated Thrasybulus to see to it, which he did. Finally, the exercise of codifying the laws and distinguishing them from executive decrees got under way, with special panels of citizens drawn from the annual jury pool.

After that, the city was pretty much left to its own devices such as they were, Sparta suddenly becoming very busy on the other side of the Aegean. The Persian king Darius had died and Artaxerxes succeeded him, but another son, Cyrus, had other ideas. While his father was gasping his last, Cyrus secured the loyalty of the Spartans by giving General Lysander the revenues from all of the Persian-controlled cities of Asia Minor. The Spartans helped Cyrus take on Artaxerxes with the help of a lot of mercenaries from all over Greece who didn't know what to do with themselves now the Peloponnesian War was over. They lost and Cyrus was killed, but now Sparta was seriously unpopular with the whole Persian Empire. It no longer looked as if the Spartans were the only people for whom the war hadn't been an economic disaster. In fact people began to say it was actually the Persians who had won the war.

# 53

I expect you're thinking that last bit was rather glum, but I'm sorry, that's how it is when your side loses a war that has been going on for nearly thirty years. While politicians wrangled and tried to get each other executed, the rest of us just sank into a deep depression. The pubs were quiet, the temples had few worshippers, jury trials carried little interest as offences and arguments were dealt with by the oligarchs, and later by votes in the Assembly, while we waited for the legal code to be finalised. Not even in the marketplace did one hear the usual shouts and laughter; people did their shopping quickly and went home, there being less to buy than usual anyway. For the first time I could remember, the theatres weren't full.

The only people who didn't seem much affected were the boys. Philetaerus was away for a couple of years with Plato who had offered to mentor him, perhaps disappointed that I hadn't sent him Manodorus. I knew what Plato had in mind but didn't see the harm, and it was a great opportunity for the young boy to see Egypt and the East in relative safety. Ararus and Philip were quite happy writing and performing their own comedies. Ararus took all the speaking parts while Philip seemed content to be the chorus as long as he was allowed to invent new dances to the accompaniment of Manodorus on the flute. I often came home to find a performance underway and several of their old friends from school laughing and offering critical suggestions. I knew Praxagora would have discouraged them, but I felt I had done my best to get them alternative careers. At least she'd be glad they were unlikely to be called up to fight now, the war having ended just when all three of her sons had reached the age for military service.

I had started seeing Cunna again quite regularly during those years. Business was quiet for her too and two of her girls had been seeing so few friends they had gone off to find husbands. "How's Ariadne doing?" I asked.

"Well, she's limited to new friends, of course."

"Of course?"

"Yes. Most of the old ones think they're her father."

"I see. A kind of reverse Oedipus. Well, I'm glad to hear they are cautious about that."

"Not all of them are. Polymides thought a bit of incest was right up his street and was stupid enough to tell her so. He won't be coming back."

"What about Ariphrades? His preferred activity couldn't have got you pregnant."

"He doesn't come any more. Lost the taste for it, I suppose." She laughed and we both got the giggles. When we paused, she pointed out that I wasn't Ariadne's father either, but she didn't want me sleeping with her, because it just wouldn't seem right. I laughed a bit more in order to suggest that the idea had never crossed my mind.

In fact we laughed a lot together, Cunna and I, during those years immediately after the war, rather more than people did at comedies at the time. The festivals continued and I kept writing new plays, but it was hard to come up with anything good. Even when it was safe to criticise politicians it didn't seem the right thing to do after all the fighting and executions. Reform of the state was off the agenda too; it had been reformed relentlessly in every direction in just the last few years. Domestic comedy was implausible when so few households had anything to laugh at. We were stuck with the burlesques of old myths and legends and it was hard to make them funny or even interesting without topical references.

I can't remember much about my next few productions after the second showing of *The Frogs*. One was called *The Storks* and told how Zeus' wife Hera grew jealous of his affection for Queen Gerena, 'flawless in beauty,' and turned her into a long-necked stork and instructed her to fly away. Gerena did not want to leave her newborn baby, fathered by Zeus, so she picked up the infant, wrapped him in a blanket, and carried him off in her beak. I quite enjoyed having a bird chorus again and made the storks and babies an allegory of plagiarists carrying off the scripts of deserving playwrights, but it would have been more satisfying if Eupolis had been around as my target. *The Storks* was beaten into third place. Cephisidorus won, though I wasn't the only person who had hoped the prize would go to

Pherecrates' *Chiron*, especially as the dear old man had died just a few days before the Dionysia.

Another one was *The Telemessians*. It was about ancient wars between tribes on the fringe of the Persian Empire and had something to do with an oracle, but frankly I remember little else of the plot. I took the opportunity to give Ararus and Philip a bit of coaching, and had Ararus draft the Address and Philip choreograph the chorus' entry song and then sat down with them and explained how I would have done it. For some reason they didn't seem too impressed. When I told Cunna about it she said I should be less directive. I'd made an impact with my original works and they should have the opportunity to do the same. Maybe they'd come up with a new and innovative approach to comedy too. I took Cunna's advice, but not for a few years.

In the meanwhile people kept dying. First Callistratus, then Thucydides and Agathon. I would miss Callistratus and his eyebrows and over the next few months I thought a lot about the adventures we had shared. Though I had never liked the last two, when you added their deaths to Sophocles, Euripides and Pherecrates it seemed our whole literary establishment was coming to an end and I was the only well-known writer left. Recognising the responsibility, I spent most of my time sitting at home, racking my brains for a more interesting plot than I'd come up with since *The Frogs*, and listening to the boys doing their thing with the help of Manodorus' flute.

One day Xanthias suddenly appeared by my desk with a large bag of money. "Yes, Xanthias," I said. "Can't you see I'm busy?" He would have been on firm ground to argue the point but didn't.

"I have something important to discuss," he told me in his now impeccable Greek-for-home-consumption-only. "I want to buy my freedom."

Of course this came as a bit of a shock. It was quite normal for some slaves to buy their freedom but not for domestic slaves like him. The ones who did had accumulated savings by being sent out to work at some trade like leatherwork or banking, and earning money. They would give some of their earnings to their owner, more if they were living in his house and being fed and clothed by him, less if they lived independently, and save the rest till they had enough to enable their owner to buy another slave. The price would depend on how much the owner thought it would cost to replace them, plus a bit if he particularly liked them. But to the best of my knowledge, although we'd looked after him better than many slaves were looked after, Xanthias had never earned anything. Nevertheless, the money bag seemed pretty full and when I took out the coins I was amazed.

"How did you get all this?" I asked. Xanthias reverted to his tongue-tied mode and the only answer I got was a wink and a sort of leer.

"In any case it's far too much. And I don't want to let you go."

"It's for Manodorus too."

"What? That's impossible. I can't lose both my slaves at once."

He leered again and reverted to comprehensible speech: "Don't worry. I have new slaves for you. But Manodorus and I are tired of being slaves and we just want to spend the rest of our lives together." He went on to explain how their relationship had developed ever since Manodorus replaced Human Artemis and that they had their eye on a little farmhouse down at the eastern end of Attica near the old battle site of Marathon. They would grow chickens or goats or something and talk about the good times they had had with our family.

I found it hard to object. They had been hard-working and loyal and had helped hold things together when Praxagora died. If they wanted a peaceful retirement, I felt they'd earned it. "So where are my new slaves?" I asked.

Behind the forest, Xanthias' grin widened. "Slaves come in!" he cried. "Ah, now, Aristophanes, this is Ismenias, and this is his wife Nerita."

# 54

"He blames you, you know."

"No, he doesn't."

"He does. He said so. 'It was thanks to Aristophanes,' he said."

"No, he didn't."

"I was there. I heard him."

Conversations with Lysander often started like this. I didn't want to give him the pleasure of knowing I had no idea what he was talking about and I was confident it would all become clear before long, which it did.

"Socrates said it was all because of that play you wrote making fun of him and his strange gods and false logic."

"But that was over twenty years ago."

"And your other plays too."

"But I've hardly mentioned him since then. I just joked about his personal hygiene in *The Birds* and his long, pointless chattering in *The Frogs*. Fair comment in both cases, and anyway lots of other poets have said things like that about him."

"Well Socrates hasn't forgotten *The Clouds* and he said that was why he was being tried for corrupting the city's young men. Now he's in jail waiting for someone to bring him hemlock and blaming you."

"Who prosecuted him?"

"Meletus of course; he prosecutes anyone he can. And Anytus gave evidence against him."

I could well believe that. Anytus had always hated Socrates. Initially it was because he was jealous of his relationship with Alcibiades, but more recently because the philosopher had persuaded his son to devote his life to searching for truth, while Anytus wanted him to take over the family tanning business. Poor old Anytus had turned to drink and spent his days muttering about how awful Socrates was.

"I would have thought he'd have got off. He has a lot of support among young aristocrats."

"Did have, you mean. A lot of them are dead or discredited. And he didn't help himself. After he'd been found guilty by two hundred and eighty votes to about two hundred and twenty, Meletus proposed the death sentence and it was up to Socrates to propose a less drastic punishment for himself. He suggested a trivial fine which the jury voted against. If he'd proposed to banish himself, he'd have probably got away with it. Even then he could have escaped after his friend Criton bribed the jailer, but he refused to try. He said, 'I'll stand at my post, as I always did in the army.' Another friend lamented that he didn't deserve to die and all Socrates said was, 'Would you rather I did deserve it?' He was his own worst enemy."

A few days afterwards I ran into Plato. By a sad coincidence he'd arrived back just in time for Socrates' trial. Philetaerus had come back some time earlier, full of extraordinary stories about Egypt and the East which not even Herodotus would have believed, and I wanted to get Plato's views on how he had conducted himself and, more importantly, if he had any suggestions for a career for him.

Our conversation didn't get very far, Plato breaking off to sob between sentences and often during them, and quite unable to talk about anything other than Socrates. He told me he was thinking of devoting the rest of his life to writing up Socrates' ideas and conversations.

"I hope you won't write up his speech at his trial," I said.

"What speech? He didn't make a speech at his trial." Plato's eyes bulged through the tears. He looked like a submerged frog.

"Oh yes, he did. And apparently, he blamed the whole thing on me."

"Who told you that?"

"Lysander."

"Ha! Ha! He's a tease, isn't he?" Plato started to laugh and it turned into a sob followed by hiccups. "It's so sad he didn't make a speech in his own defence. He's a very convincing speaker and he would probably have been acquitted."

"Why didn't he then?"

"I think he just wanted to show life wasn't very important and he didn't mind what happened to him. That's probably why he drank the hemlock as soon as the sun started setting when he was entitled to wait until it was totally dark."

"What a strange bloke he was! Anyway, I'm glad he didn't make a speech blaming it all on me."

"You've given me an idea. I've a pretty good idea what he would have said. I might write it up."

"Well, don't mention me, will you?"

"I wonder if Socrates would have. I'll have to think about it. Anyway, let's not quarrel now. We haven't seen each other for ages and I won't be here for long. There's no reason for me to stay in Athens now, so I'm going to Sicily again. Dionysius sends me an invitation at least once a month. You should come with me one day. He loves your plays – except *The Clouds* of course. I'll write often, as usual. And give my love to Philetaerus and that long thin slave of yours."

He was gone before I could tell him Manodorus was no longer with me and how Xanthias had startled me by replacing the two of them with slaves with the same names as the ones who had terrorised my adolescence, which I am sure he did deliberately. In fact I was no more certain that Ismenias and Nerita were the real names of my new slaves than I had been about the names of Xanthias and Artemis when I bought them. Nor had I learned anything that would help me decide a future for Philetaerus. Plato's promise that he'd write to me wasn't much consolation as I could never understand much of what he had to say. I was making my way home disconsolately, trying not to think bad things about Plato, when he forced himself on my attention again, this time without even being present.

As soon as I opened the front door pretty little Nerita put her fingers to her lips and indicated that there was something important happening in the boys' room. I was wondering if that explained the strong smell of burning that was wafting from that direction, when the boys came running out followed by Ismenias who grabbed my favourite rug, and shouting at the boys to go and fetch water, disappeared back into the room, from which large clouds of smoke had started to emerge. The rescue effort was largely successful, although Philip had to sleep on the floor for a few days while my neighbour, a part-time carpenter, made him a new couch. The walls of the room bore the traces of the fire ever after and it took months and a lot of bundles of herbs for the smell to go away.

When things had calmed down, I asked the boys what they had been doing. "We were playing Plato's Cave," they told me. On further enquiry it turned out that Philetaerus had told them about how on his trip Plato had kept talking about how human perceptions were doubly removed from reality and we were all like a group of people sitting in a cave with a fire behind them and looking at the shadows cast on the wall by objects or people or whatever in front of the fire. They had an idea it might be a good basis for a play at a small country festival and wanted to see if the idea worked in daylight, but Philip's realistic imitation of a man stumbling around in the dark had overturned the brazier.

I must admit I found the idea of turning some of Plato's weird ideas into plays quite appealing, given the lack of material coming from the city's politics at the time. Nor was there much of interest going on overseas. No one cared when Sparta conquered Elis, except possibly the Elians, and the Spartan general Lysander's self-seeking proposal that the position of king in Sparta should be elective was too silly, even for a comedy. The only thing that might have made an amusing scene or two was King Archelaus I of Macedon being killed by his royal page and lover, but that was during a Macedonian boar hunt which reminded me of the rumours about how Euripides had died and I didn't want to relive that particular grief. Similar considerations eventually put me off making Plato's philosophy a comic theme. Even if Lysander had made up the bit about Socrates blaming me at his trial, there might be a few people who thought *The Clouds* did have something to do with his execution and I didn't want to stir that up.

Lacking any other ideas, I went without an entry in the city festivals for three years in a row and had to content myself with directing re-runs of some of my most popular hits at rural festivals. The boys always came with me, "To help with the production" as they explained it, but actually to stage little plays of their own before the main festival began. Their creations were quite unusual for comic drama, tending to feature a lot of slaves and undistinguished citizens going about their normal business with very little that was ridiculous or fantastic. There were very few choral songs and those few had little or nothing to do with the plot. At Philip's insistence, the chorus did get to do a lot of dancing and I must confess the dances were interesting and original even though they were of a type that seemed out of place in comedy and could have just formed their own type of entertainment, without being part of any drama. Over time, the boys' productions became quite well known and started to draw fairly big paying audiences in the lead up to the main parts of rural festivals, but I couldn't help feeling they should be more ambitious and start writing material that was more in line with comic conventions and give them a better chance of being selected by the archons for the city festivals. After all, Philip was already the same age as I was when I had my first win at the Dionysia and Ararus was almost two years older. But of course, they took no notice of my advice.

# 55

"Let'th go, boyth! We owe Thicily a darn good thwashing after what they did to uth latht time."

I spilled my wine in horror. The long hair, the affected lisp and rhotacism, the aristocratic turn of phrase, the arrogant war-mongering – Alcibiades was alive after all! I looked round the pub and, sure enough, there at the bar was a beautiful looking, long-haired youth, holding forth to anyone who'd listen, and winking suggestively at anyone who wouldn't, in just the way Alcibiades always had. I had to pinch myself before remembering that youthful good looks don't last forever and Alcibiades had started to lose his before his last appearance in Athens and his extraordinary involvement in the Eleusinian Mysteries.

"Dionythiuth had a perfectly good peath tweaty with Carthage and he bwoke it and killed a whole bunch of Carthaginianth all over the wetht coatht. You jutht can't twust Thicilianth." Everyone in the pub cracked up at the idea of Alcibiades accusing someone else of treachery. Ever since his death at the hands of those fine-spirited Persians had been confirmed, a number of Alcibiades impersonators had sprung up and scratched a modest living by passing the cap round in pubs where they amused the drinkers. This one seemed better than the average and the latest news from the west gave him the perfect theme.

"And they dethtroyed Motya tho the poor old Carthaginianth had to build a new city called Lilybalalalabum." His imitation of Alcibiades struggling to pronounce Lilybaeum was greeted with more hilarity. "And when Himilco came and bethieged Thyracuse, Dionythiuth beat him tho badly he killed himthelf ath thoon ath he got home again to Carthage. That wath a wotten thing to do, tho let'th wevenge him."

I had gone to the pub to celebrate coming third at the Lenaea with *The Storm Cook*. I didn't actually think a third place at the Lenaea merited much celebrating but the lack of inspiration I was suffering during those years when political comedy was out-of-bounds meant it had been a while since I had produced anything at all, so I thought I'd see what the pub crowd thought of it. I never found out as the Alcibiades impersonator commanded all the attention. At least I was spared Criticus' views.

*The Storm Cook* didn't really deserve to do better than third and I began to fear that it showed I was beginning to lose my grip. The play, fittingly enough given current events, was set in Sicily and featured the famous cook Sicon represented as the God of the Winds. It was largely a parody of Euripides' *Aeolus* which dramatized the ill-fated, incestuous relationship of the siblings Canace and Macareus. Their father was the eponymous Aeolus, Master of the Winds and king of some islands off Etruria, and when his son Macareus got his daughter Canace pregnant, he somehow convinced himself that the best way to overcome the disgrace was to get all his six daughters to marry his six sons and he matched them up by drawing lots. That proved to be a rather dumb idea as Macareus drew one of Canace's sisters instead of Canace herself.

Euripides had managed to make the tale into a tragedy, although not a very successful one as the story was much too funny. I livened it up by introducing good old Heracles the Glutton again but ever since Praxagora had died I hadn't felt able to use the drunken sex-maniac stereotypes of women and had to content myself with their addiction to shopping. In one scene I had the sisters outdoing their brothers in cussing and swearing, which made for good comedy, but not a patch on some of my earlier work.

The chatter of the Alcibiades impersonator about Sicily and Dionysius made me think I should write to Plato, which I did the next day. We hadn't parted on the best of terms and, if he really was going to write the defence speech Socrates didn't actually make, I didn't want him to assign me the blame for his execution. So I expressed great concern for his safety in all the trouble with the Carthaginians, sent my best wishes to Dionysius who was hosting him again, told him Philetaerus couldn't stop talking about what a wonderful time he'd had on his trip, which wasn't true, and that he had taught his brothers all about the cave, which was. He wrote back, passing on an invitation from Dionysius to come to Sicily, which I ignored, and going on about his latest ideas about ideal forms, which I couldn't understand. He'd started putting them into the dramatic form of dialogues featuring his hero Socrates, which didn't make them much more interesting and certainly wouldn't have got him selected for a festival in either the tragedy or comedy competitions.

I was now visiting Cunna more regularly than ever as the boys had better things to do than hang around with their old man, and with Praxagora and so many friends dead, Plato away and it only being possible to take so much of Lysander, I was getting a bit lonely. Unlike Aspasia, she thought she could best maintain her dignity by pretending to be celibate, so we only made love when the girls in the house were all out, which didn't happen often. I didn't mind too much as she was ten years older than me and it had started to show, but I valued her friendship and advice. I thought she might help me get my writing career back on track.

As it turned out, when I asked her for inspiration, she wasn't as encouraging as she usually was. In fact she seemed puzzled that I was still keen to keep writing. "You've achieved more than any other comic poet and I doubt if anyone will ever match you in the future," she told me. "And you still haven't worked out how your sons are going to occupy themselves. I know Praxagora didn't want them to be comic poets but that was mainly to do with her fear they'd have to make a living for themselves and that's irrelevant now you've done so well through your own efforts and the way you invested your father's ill-gotten gains."

That was probably true, I reflected, remembering how Praxagora's opposition to a writing career for our sons had begun to diminish in the last few months of her life.

"You keep telling me how keen they are on drama and how their new interpretations are getting quite a following at rural festivals. Why not work with them and try and help them get established in the mainstream?"

This wasn't what I wanted to hear at all. I came up with a range of objections about how unsuitable their innovations were for city festivals, but my real concern was that I felt I had more great works in me if I could only find some new themes, and I didn't want to retire yet. Cunna wasn't persuaded and in the end, I agreed that I'd work with Ararus and Philip on a play for the Lenaea and see how that went.

"What about Philetaerus?" Cunna asked.

"Well, he does like acting, but mainly female parts and I'm not sure that's what I want him to do."

"If he's good at it, then you should encourage him. There's no disgrace in being a good female impersonator. I believe some of the best actors specialise in that."

"OK, I'll see if I can help them get selected for the Lenaea next year. But I am not going to stop writing myself. Please, please, please give some thought to what I could write about."

I decided I might as well start the boys off with *The Danaids*, as the play was already written and the outline had been good enough to get selected by the archon, though the original was probably not good enough to win. I hadn't given it much thought since I had had to abandon the performance at the last minute when Xanthias found out that Eupolis had plagiarised large chunks of it. You'll remember the story: it was about how Danaus fled with his fifty daughters to Argos to avoid having them marry the fifty sons of the King of Arabia, but the King of Arabia followed them and persuaded the Argives that the fifty marriages should go ahead. In the tragic *Danaids* of Euripides and *The Suppliants* of Aeschylus, this results in forty-nine of the Arabian husbands being murdered by their wives on their wedding night under instruction from Danaus, and the one who was left alive for promising not to have sex with his new wife, murdering Danaus to avenge his brothers. In my version, rather than murdering their husbands, the fifty daughters had a wild night of sex with them before cutting off forty-nine cocks.

I had some trouble finding a copy of the script as it had been over twenty years since I had put it away, but when I did, I gave it to the boys and told them they could make a few changes to bring it up to date if necessary, although I didn't think it needed much revision to be suitable for the Lenaea. They didn't seem to take much notice of that and when they took me through it a couple of weeks later it was quite a different play in many ways. First, they had cut out all the choruses and replaced them with some notes about dances without words that Philip had devised. I insisted on at least keeping one song, not only because I was quite proud of it, but because of its significance for me as the one Xanthias had picked up on in Eupolis' stolen version:

*I'm going to Argos, so follow me quick,*
*I can't bear a minute away from your prick.*

*I've a palace of pleasure to circle your head –*
*Enough to get started – and then off to bed.*
*Follow me there and then put out the light,*
*We'll see who is master on our wedding night.*

Other than that, I had to admit a couple of their innovations were quite funny. They had decided that the ship on which Danaus sailed to Argos was the first ship ever, which made for some good slapstick involving the crane and buckets of water, and, while my version had ended with the ladies triumphantly waving their husbands' private parts around in a joyful chorus, they had extended the Celebration at the end to show them indulging their nymphomania by becoming the leading escorts in Argos.

It didn't win the Lenaea, but I hadn't expected my original version to win either, and we were all pleased to come second. One of Philip's dances received a standing ovation and Philetaerus was runner-up in the actors' competition for his performance as leader of the women's chorus. It was the beginning of a series of family collaborations and we celebrated happily and long at the after-show banquet and in the pub for several days afterwards.

# 56

Plato let me down badly. I should never have given him the idea of inventing a speech Socrates might have made in his own defence but didn't; far less should I have told him Lysander had made out that Socrates blamed me. When another letter arrived from Sicily, I was puzzled by how thick the roll of papyrus seemed to be – almost as big as one of the eight rolls Thucydides had used for his boring book. My first thought was that it was going to be one of his new dialogues and he'd probably expect me to read it, which wasn't something I could look forward to, but when I saw the title *Socrates' Defence*, I rather wished it had been.

Of course it was with some trepidation that I unrolled the papyrus. It's funny how your own name jumps out at you, especially when you are hoping it won't. Sure enough, there, right near the beginning, Plato had Socrates referring to "the comedy of Aristophanes in which a certain Socrates swung around on the crane, claiming that he was treading on air and talking a lot of rubbish about things I don't know anything about." I quickly unrolled the rest of the document, afraid there'd be a lot more about me, and was very relieved to find there wasn't. Even so, it was bad enough and I just had to hope this was the only copy that had arrived in Athens, in which case there was a chance I could intercept any that came later and change or destroy them.

When I had got to the end of unrolling Plato's document a small fragment of papyrus dropped out which was a personal message. After sending his warmest love to Philetaerus and asking if I had any idea where Manodorus had gone, as he was hoping to see him on his next visit on his way to Africa, he told me there wasn't much going on in Sicily after the defeat of the Carthaginians under Himilco, so Dionysius had gone on a trip to the west coast. Plato had decided not to go with him and to use the time in writing more about Socrates. His next project, the letter said, was to write up all the speeches at Anytus' symposium and could I help him by sending the text of my own and as much as I could remember about what the others had to say. He told me not to worry about Socrates as he could make that up himself. I wrote back to say I couldn't help him as I didn't have a text of my speech because I'd been expecting he (Plato) would write it for me, and I didn't make it anyway because by the time I arrived at Anytus' house everyone had settled down to having sex with each other and the flute girls. Whether there had been any speeches before I got there, I had no idea. I couldn't resist adding rather bitterly that the absence of speeches didn't seem to stop Plato reporting them.

There might not have been much going on in Sicily to our west but there was a lot happening in the East. Sparta under King Agesilaus had invaded Persia to free the Greek states on that side of the Aegean and won a famous victory at Sardis over the Persians under Tissaphernes. They called a truce to allow time to negotiate a lasting peace, but negotiations broke down and while Tissaphernes was gathering his troops together in the south-western part of Asia Minor, Agesilaus managed to capture a huge amount of treasure further north and inland. Not long afterwards, Tissaphernes was executed by Emperor Cyrus at the instigation of his fond mother who thought Tissaphernes had been treating her son with inadequate respect.

Fighting with the Spartans led Persia back to supporting Athens, which encouraged us to assemble a large fleet with several of our allies. Conon, a fine admiral who had been sidelined after being badly beaten in the last naval battle of our war with Sparta, was put in charge and quickly captured the Spartan base on Rhodes. A Persian governor called Pharnabazus then managed to stir up trouble in Western Greece and he sent a delegation to Athens, Thebes, Corinth and Argos to encourage anti-Spartan sentiment, which they did quite successfully.

Lysander had told me all this and my head was spinning trying to remember who was who, which side they were on and why. My only real concern was whether the boys would get called up if we returned to a full-scale war footing. His was to tell me that he was right about Socrates' defence speech after all.

"But he didn't make a defence speech," I insisted.

"Oh yes, he did," he replied. "Copies are all over Athens. I've got a couple here. Would you like one?"

I didn't have long to get used to the idea that everyone would now think I had killed Socrates before the action in Asia Minor shifted to our side of the Aegean and Lysander's explanations of the confusing activities of our two traditional enemies, Persia and Sparta, took on a new importance. Persian funds had helped us rebuild our much-depleted treasury together with the Long Walls and we had taken advantage of the sudden influx of cash to start resurrecting some parts of our old empire, placing new settlements on a few islands and offering support to rebellions in distant and irrelevant places like Egypt and Cyprus. The Persians now gave Boeotia money to attack Sparta on some flimsy pretext to do with a border incursion. Naturally we joined in, along with Corinth and Argos which prompted Agesilaus to start the long march from Asia over the Hellespont and back to Sparta by land. Before he arrived the Spartans sent two separate armies to attack Haliartus in Boeotia. The Spartan general Lysander's troops arrived first but he got a bit overconfident and advanced too far and too early and was killed in an otherwise indecisive battle. When the other army under King Pausanias arrived the next day, it was too late for them to do much except reclaim the corpses of Lysander and his men and head back to Sparta where Pausanias was put on trial for being late to the battle. They say he would have been executed if he hadn't fled the city.

Things were getting serious now and my fears were realised when all three of my sons were told to equip themselves with a full set of hoplite armour and be ready to march to Corinth or join the naval action in the East. At first I thought armour would be a problem as Lysias' shield factory where I had bought my little shield had been closed down by the Spartans at the end of the big war and a few years of peace meant that all the part-time metalworkers had turned their hand to other products and would have forgotten how to make the rest of the equipment like breastplates, helmets, shin guards and so on. But Ismenias pointed out that there would be a lot of second-hand stuff around, being sold by widows of our war dead.

I still had my old armour and the child's shield, which was ideal for Philetaerus, though I did buy him a rather newer breastplate as mine was getting a bit rusty. Philip wasn't a problem as he could carry a man's shield with ease – two of them at a pinch – and we just had to find the largest pieces available for the rest of his equipment; there were plenty to choose from in the second-hand stalls in the market. Ararus is just a little taller than me and Philetaerus so we found him some small-medium items of armour, but a few attempts to carry the standard shield showed he wouldn't have lasted long in a pitched battle. We were just beginning to despair and wondering if we could find someone with a lathe and a large number of slaves to make a shield especially for him when Philip gave a whoop and pointed excitedly to a shield lying on the ground behind the last stall. It was a size I'd never seen before, half-way between the men's standard one and the children's and certainly wasn't something Lysias' factory would ever have made. To my puzzled enquiry the stallholder explained that it had belonged to a woman called Cynisca who had just won the chariot race at the Olympic Games, the first woman ever to do so, and, one would imagine, the last. Of course the rules meant she had had to engage a man to do the driving, but as the sponsor she took part in the opening ceremony and the winners' parade, which required her to carry a shield and she had had this one made to her specifications. The stallholder wasn't expecting anyone to buy it and was about to throw it away when we came along. He let us have it very cheaply, though I'd have paid a lot more to ensure Ararus would have something that would protect him.

All the boys were now kitted out and ready to go. Philip was sent off first with the land army to Corinth where we were gathering a large force and the other two joined the fleet that sailed to Rhodes. I felt that it would have been better for the fleet to have Philip give time to the rowers in the way I used to do, but, on the other hand, I felt the fleet would be safer for the smaller pair, so I didn't challenge the deployment.

The war on land didn't go very well. The troops we had sent to Corinth were soundly thrashed at a place called Nemea and I lived in a state of great anxiety until the list of those killed or missing arrived and I found that Philip was all right. He returned to Athens soon after the battle, having been injured in both legs, which curtailed his dancing, but he could still choreograph and beat time with his huge hands.

Things went rather better at sea. Conon, with the help of the Persians, had a massive victory over the Spartans near Rhodes and followed it up by sailing along the coast of Asia Minor and getting rid of all the Spartan governors, only a couple of whom were able to hold out against our fleet. Persia now controlled the Aegean with our help, but Agesilaus had got back to western Greece and our army was badly defeated again, this time at

Coronea. I was very relieved that Philip was back in Athens with the reputation of an injured war hero and that the fleet had returned from the East to defend Attica, though, when I went down to the Peiraeus to greet them, Philetaerus was not there. I had begun to assume the worst when Ararus, who arrived on a later ship, told me he had taken the opportunity to catch up with some of the friends he had made in Egypt on his tour with Plato. That was seven years ago and he hasn't been back to Athens since, though he does send me regular letters and pictures of strange birds, snakes and stick figures.

Ararus was now the only one exposed to what boring old Thucydides would have called the vicissitudes of war and it was a great relief when Corinth descended into civil strife. The oligarchs lost out and went off to Sparta who had supported them, and our troops came home, not having much to do there. It was just as well they did as Sparta came back to Corinth with the oligarchs and captured the port, which would only lead to more trouble. In any event I had two of my sons back home, one rather injured but still capable, and a third clearly having what he considered a good time in Egypt. Their absence hadn't been a bad thing as far as I was concerned. Although I was getting used to working with them on their own plays, we hadn't had much success together and I took advantage of their absence to have a final go at submitting an original play of my own in the old style and I think it was one of my best.

# 57

I must admit I got the idea for the plot from Cunna. On what turned out to be the last of my regular monthly visits she seemed to be in a sort of after-sex daze, which surprised me as she had been virtually celibate for a few years now. She explained that one of her house's regular visitors called Smoios had the same enthusiasm for the taste of piggy as old Ariphrades had had, but as none of her girls was that keen and she didn't want to lose a valuable 'friend', she had allowed him to indulge himself with her. It had been a long time since Ariphrades used to visit and she was surprised how much she enjoyed it. "I expect he just didn't want to look at my old face," she joked. That was unlikely to be true as she was still beautiful though well over sixty now, and I assured her I always liked looking at her face even though we hardly ever made love nowadays.

We went on to talk about the state of the world. She was invariably well informed thanks to the large number of politically active visitors who would chat to her while waiting for their chosen girl to become free. The city was still in a pretty miserable state and hadn't really recovered from the loss to Sparta ten years earlier. With the help of Thebes and Corinth we just about held our own in the battles against Sparta that were still taking place sporadically but the glory that was Athens had vanished and we had become an impoverished people. The poor were in favour of as much fighting as possible because it offered them paid employment, while the rich knew that they would end up paying for it through more confiscations and forced contributions. There was a view that this conflict between rich and poor could best be managed by strengthening the democracy, so pay for being in the first six thousand to get to the Assembly had been raised twice but that didn't seem to do much good.

Cunna blamed men. "You lot have been in charge while the city has lurched from disaster to disaster – losing wars, alienating our allies so we have no empire left, emptying the treasury, lurching in and out of oligarchy… You really haven't got much right, have you? Don't you think it's time to let women have a go at running things?"

I snorted indignantly but while I struggled to think up a strong case for continued male government, an idea occurred to me. "Actually, that might make for a good comedy," I suggested.

"A comedy!" Cunna was horrified. "I'm being serious. Men have failed. Women couldn't do worse and might do a lot better."

I apologised. "Yes, I understand. I didn't mean the idea is ridiculous, although I don't see how it could ever come about. For a start, men would have to vote for it and I don't think that is very likely. But it would be a great escapist fantasy like some of my best comedies – *The Acharnians* with Dicaeopolis' private peace or *The Birds'* Cloud-cuckoo-land." I went on to explain that for the idea to be made into a good comedy, the women wouldn't have to be ridiculous; in fact a lot of the fun would be in showing how they could make great decisions that would never have occurred to men. Cunna came round and by the time I left that night, the essential elements of the plot of *The Assemblywomen* had taken shape in my head and so had the name of the female lead. It was an ideal opportunity to pay a fitting and much overdue tribute to Praxagora.

The play opens with Praxagora emerging from a house into the street before dawn. She has the standard women's white mask but is wearing a false beard and men's clothing and heavy shoes that made walking awkward. A walking stick and a lit lantern that she carries shows she is going to the Assembly, where you had to be early to get paid. She addresses her lantern in tragic style, praising the vital role it plays in a woman's life – "You are always there watching when we have sex. You light up the dimples on our inner thighs while you burn off our pubes." – and complains that the women who had promised to meet her have not shown up. Eventually the chorus of Athenian women enter one by one, all dressed in the same way as Praxagora. Two of them make their own excuses – one had been having sex, and the other one's husband wouldn't go to sleep so that she could sneak out – and comment wittily on the arrival of their colleagues.

They settle into their seats in the Assembly and explain how, in addition to the false beards and walking sticks, some have improved their disguises by developing tans and stopping shaving their armpits. One woman has brought a basket full of yarn in order to get some work done before the Assembly starts and Praxagora rebukes her for risking their cover. She then gives them a pep-talk, pointing out that the best male orators are those who have been sexually penetrated the most, so women should be very good indeed. A couple of women volunteer to make speeches. The first, under the impression she is at a symposium, demands a drink. When her mistake is pointed out she observes that people who attend the Assembly must be drunk in order to make the decisions they do. The second wants to ban water jugs from taverns but foolishly invokes the Two Goddesses, which only a woman would do. She tries again but opens her address with the word 'Ladies.' Despairing of her colleagues, Praxagora takes over. She has learned the art of rhetoric while living with her husband on the Pnyx, where the Assembly is held. She lists a number of recent idiotic decisions of the Assembly and proposes that "we men" turn control of the government over to women because "after all, we employ them as stewards and treasurers in our own households." She explains that women are superior, being harder workers, who are devoted to tradition and do not bother with silly innovations. What is more, they have the ability to drive their husbands mad and they enjoy neat wine and lots of sex. As mothers, they will better protect the soldiers and feed them extra rations; as accomplished cheats, they will secure more funds for the city without being cheated themselves.

The women discuss how they plan to handle any opposition and practise raising their hands to vote without raising their legs. They set off to arrive at the Assembly by dawn in order to be among the first six thousand which entitles them to three obols and a complimentary meal. Praxagora and the two women exit and the chorus sing of their determination to act as men before they too exit with beards over their white masks and their husbands' cloaks over their heads.

When the women have all left the stage, Praxagora's elderly husband Blepyrus emerges from their house wearing his wife's nightgown and slippers. He had had a desperate need to relieve himself but hadn't been able to find his own clothes in the dark. As he squats in the street, his neighbour arrives and both men realize that their wives and clothing are missing from their homes. The neighbour leaves and another man turns up on his way home from the Assembly to find Blepyrus is now constipated. The newcomer complains that he didn't get to the Assembly in time to be paid, because it was full of "pasty-faced cobblers." He describes some of the topics the Assembly discussed, including the problem of squinting and a proposal that tailors should make cloaks free for the poor. He quotes 'a good-looking young man' (Praxagora) giving the reasons why governance of the city should be entrusted to women. They are better at keeping secrets, they are more reliable at returning borrowed items without cheating, they don't sue or inform on people and they never try to overthrow the democracy. Blepyrus has to admit (s)he has a point. When her motion is carried, the benefit to old men of being able to sleep in and not rush to the Assembly is offset by the rider that they will have to have sex with their wives every morning if they want any breakfast.

Now the chorus comes back, still in disguise and on their way home from the Assembly. They encourage each other not to draw attention to themselves until they get home and change back into their normal dress. Blepyrus finds Praxagora returning his cloak and accuses her of sneaking off with one or more lovers. She points out that she is not wearing perfume and wouldn't dream of having sex without it. She explains that she was only helping a friend in labour and had to wear his cloak for warmth and his boots and stick so the cloak wouldn't be stolen. She feigns surprise when Blepyrus tells her the Assembly's decision, but encouraged by the chorus, she lists the reasons the decision was wise. She worries about whether the audience is ready for some serious policy suggestions before coming up with some rather extreme ones, largely drawn from ideas I had got from some of Plato's crazier letters, including outlawing all private wealth and requiring equal pay for everyone. All basic needs will be met from a common fund, managed by women. Walls will be knocked down to make the city one household. The law courts will be used for common dining, the food provided by the state and served and cooked by women. People will draw lots from the ballot-boxes to learn which dining room they have been assigned to and everyone will go home drunk. Bad behaviour will result in a reduced bread ration. Slaves will work the fields and the women will supply new clothes when they are needed. There will be no more lawsuits, since there can be no debt. There will be no theft because everyone can get whatever they want. There will be no gambling because there will be no money to wager. Everyone can have sex with anyone they like for free, provided they first sleep with an ugly member of the opposite sex, so young

313

girls will be offered freely by ugly women who want first go. Prostitutes will be put out of business to give other women an opportunity and slave girls will be banned from sleeping with free men. To Blepyrus' concern that after having sex with an ugly woman he wouldn't have the energy for the one he wanted in the first place, Praxagora tells him that has been his problem for a while. (The audience found that funnier than I did.) The fact that no one will be able to tell which children are theirs means parental responsibilities will be shared by the whole community. Young men will refrain from attacking old ones in case it is their father.

Blepyrus is proud of Praxagora and her ideas and they go off together, and the chorus performs a song and dance routine which has nothing to do with the plot as is the way nowadays. I would have preferred the old-style Address, but no one was doing them anymore and I had made my political points in Praxagora's last speech.

After that interlude, Blepyrus' neighbour and his slaves lay out all his household objects that are about to be contributed to the common fund and he addresses them with respect and affection. A selfish man comes by and calls the neighbour a fool for following the new laws just because he has been told to. He plans on waiting to see if everyone else gives up their property before he does it himself. The gods are takers, not givers, he observes and anyway there might always be an earthquake or something to put a stop to the whole idea. He regrets his actions when a herald announces a lavish feast for everyone. The selfish man is not invited because he has failed to donate his own possessions.

After another irrelevant song by the chorus, we find a young girl waiting at a window for her boyfriend. An old woman arrives looking for a date and they argue about whether old or young women are best at sex. As the boyfriend still hasn't arrived, the young girl sends her maid to fetch a dildo and they exchange more insults. When the young man finally arrives, both women go indoors to see which of them he'll choose to visit. The boy is pretty clear in his preference for the young one and they sing of their lust for each other, interrupted by the old woman who insists on her right to have sex with the young man first and leads him in a Dance of the Whores based on the Adonia festival. After further quarrelling, the old woman leaves to be replaced by an older and uglier one who tries to drag the young man away but ends up in a tug of war with a third old woman who is uglier still. Eventually they join forces and drag him off to share him.

A maid turns up, extremely drunk and singing the praises of the new laws – and of Thasian wine. At Praxagora's request she is looking for Blepyrus to bring him to the communal dinner. She finds him already on his way with a young girl on each arm. They invite the audience, the judges and everyone to join their revels and the chorus leader tells the judges that if they are intelligent, they should think of the intelligent parts of the play and if they have a sense of humour, the jokes. The final celebratory song of the chorus includes a Choke of the sort that had only previously been assigned to lead actors and they describe the menu in one breath: "greasysaltedsaltfishsharkfishcatfishsmellyskullfishflatfishbraisedbeetless parrowsinoildrippinghoneyringdoveschookcocksbakedswallowsfinelycoo kedmarinatedrabbitmarrowcheesetoppedvinegarsylphium."

# 58

It would have been nice to have had a final winner but coming second at the Dionysia was quite gratifying and my old friend Rhombus' son, who had played Blepyrus and the first old woman, won the acting prize. I thought I might revive my former habit and see what they were saying in the pub, but when I got there I didn't recognise anyone and the conversation was entirely about the wars that were still going on, which I hadn't been paying any attention to. With Philip too injured to be called up and Philetaerus living the high life in Egypt, my only interest in that subject was whether Ararus would be sent off to fight the Spartans somewhere.

"Conon's dead, you know," someone observed with a wry grimace.

"Killed by the Spartans, I suppose," another replied.

"Not exactly. The Spartans had been trying to turn the Persians against us by telling them Conon and the fleet were using Persian resources to rebuild our old empire. Conon set off at the head of a legation to persuade the Persians not to believe that, but it backfired and he was arrested. He managed to escape but died in Cyprus on his way back here."

"Suspicious, if you ask me. I'll bet it was the Spartans."

"Who knows? Could have been the Spartans, could have been the Persians, could have been his own men, could have been something he ate, could have been a jealous woman – or a jealous man for that matter."

I joined the conversation. "Does that mean we'll be sending more troops to the East?"

"It looked that way for a bit when Persia started to finance the Spartan navy instead of ours. But after the failure of the all-Greek peace conference at Sparta they'll be back on our side of the sea."

That sounded bad. "What peace conference? What failure?" I asked, panic rising in my voice.

"Don't you comic poets know anything about what's going on?"

I was pleased to be still recognised but did think that was a bit unfair because we comic poets specialise in making jokes about what's going on. I had to admit though, I had been so focussed on working up a different political structure for Athens I hadn't thought much about foreign wars. "Tell me," I said.

"The ambassadors came back with suggested peace terms this morning. They were so bad the Assembly sentenced the lot of them to exile." I thought that was another stupid decision by men that I could have used in *The Assemblywomen* if it had happened a few weeks earlier, but it wouldn't affect the likelihood of the war needing more troops, which was what I was worried about.

"Does that mean we'll be raising an army to fight in the west then?" I asked.

"I doubt it. Sparta will have their hands full with Persia again and the Assembly has just decided to provide reinforcements to support Evagoras of Salamis who is aiming to get control of Cyprus. They'll probably come from the remains of Conon's fleet, rather than from here."

The news was good, but I couldn't help feeling a little disappointed no one had commented on my play. On my way out, a funny little man with a long white beard grabbed me. "Aristophanes?" he said.

"Yes," I admitted, wondering who this fellow was and why he had been sitting alone, not taking part in the conversation.

"I loved the play."

This was promising.

"You are back to your best again. I especially admired the way in which your humour was subservient to the important political message."

"Oh, yes?"

"Obviously the inversion of the male dominant society was hardly an inversion at all but rather an affirmation of that very society. It revealed the Athenian perceptual framework which divides women's subjective experience between stereotypes and confines their freedom to express this subjectivity with the same validity as men."

"Oh, yes?"

Of course, by now I had recognised Criticus and was kicking myself for not having brought my *Fuck off, I'm a comic poet* sign. As I freed myself from his grasp and headed out of the pub, his parting shot was "Have you ever met Plato? You should talk to him. Some of his ideas are quite similar to yours."

That exchange didn't annoy me as much as it would have previously, but it did confirm that I was past caring enough to go on pouring my heart and soul into coming up with new plots. I decided that my theatrical efforts would now be confined to working with Ararus and Philip, supporting and advising them at rural festivals, where their works were more popular than ever, and helping their plays get selected for the city.

I went to one of the festivals, quite a long way from Athens, where the boys were putting on a play. (I still thought of them as boys, even though they were both over thirty now). It was a special festival to celebrate the bravery of some of the locals who had been part of a force composed almost entirely of light troops and javelin throwers that had achieved a decisive victory against the Spartans, the first time light infantry had defeated heavily-armed hoplites. Between the time of that battle and the start of the festival, there arose another success for the locals to celebrate. Thrasybulus who also hailed from that part of Attica and was highly regarded for his part in overthrowing the oligarchy a dozen years earlier, had captured Byzantium, started collecting tolls from ships passing through the Hellespont, and was gathering tribute again from many of the islands that used to be part of our empire.

The boys' play was about a farmer trying to increase crop yields in all sorts of improbable ways involving frogs, magnifying glasses and broken pottery. It was a sort of agricultural domestic comedy with the humour relying on a combination of slapstick and arguments between the farmer and his slaves, who were physically endangered by some of his wilder ideas. I had helped with rehearsals and the slapstick, but the dialogue was all Ararus' and the music, Philip's. After giving the cast some last-minute instructions I took my place on one of the front benches where a sizeable crowd was waiting for the play to start. From behind me came the unmistakeable sound of a lovers' quarrel.

"You promised you'd never see him again," said a woman's voice.

"He just turned up. I pretended I was out at first, but he must have heard me breathing behind the door." The reply was deep and guttural.

"I want you to tell him you want nothing to do with him. Anyway, he's not your type." Long pause and a stifled sob. "Is he? Oh, please tell me he isn't!"

By now the voices were clearly recognisable. I turned round and, sure enough, a couple of rows behind me were my old slaves. Both seemed delighted to see me; Manodorus blew me a kiss while Xanthias stretched across the row between us to squeeze my shoulder and grunt that I must come back to their place afterwards.

Their home was a dear little cottage with chickens running around a small yard just as they had planned. Ararus and Philip came along for a drink after the cast banquet and the whole evening was like a school reunion. I had forgotten how close the boys and the slaves had been – or how much I had neglected them when I was in mid-career and writing and presenting at least one and often two plays a year. Xanthias and Manodorus couldn't refrain from sniping at each other like an old married couple, but they were clearly happy together and I could just imagine them sitting on the porch in the warm summer evenings with a jug of wine, thinking about the old days and not conversing much because they didn't need to.

Ararus, always looking for domestic themes for new plays, tried to get them to tell us about the home life of the local military hero Thrasybulus but unfortunately news had just come through that he had been killed in a raid in a town where his financial exactions had made him highly unpopular. The response to Ararus' enquiry was a tragic groan from Xanthias and a burst of sobbing from Manodorus. Nevertheless, knowing Xanthias was always well informed about everything, and still worried that Ararus might be called up again, I couldn't help asking if we were likely to be attacked by Sparta. We had heard they had made a new alliance with Persia and I had just had word from Plato in Syracuse that they had made another one with Dionysius, which seemed to set them up perfectly for an invasion of Attica.

"Don't worry," Xanthias assured me. "You can't start a war if there is no one to fight you."

I couldn't make much sense of this, as not having any opposition would seem to be ideal for an invasion, but a few days later we heard that the Spartans had marched against Argos but, finding no Argive army challenged them, they just did a bit of damage to the countryside and went home again. If that was all they would do in Attica, Ararus was quite safe, so we worked together on another presentation of *Wealth*, which I had first staged twenty years earlier at the Lenaea where it had come second. It had now been accepted for the Dionysia.

We didn't make many changes to the original, mainly getting rid of all the original choral songs and adding one new dance by Philip, and of course updating the references to politicians, but it seemed to be enough and this time it won. I was happy to let Ararus take the credit as this would give him a better chance of being selected by the archons at future city festivals. To give him a proper induction to the life of a comic poet I took him along to the pub, hoping, for the first time ever, that Criticus would be there.

# 59

It wasn't Criticus who made the first comment. "Still haven't sorted it out, have you, Aristophanes?" said an oldish man whom I vaguely remembered as having been rude about my original version when we met at Aspasia's.

"What do you mean?" I asked.

"You haven't fixed any of the problems I pointed out to you at the first production and you've had twenty years to try to come up with something that makes more sense. I still don't know what conclusion you want the audience to draw. Do you have to be good to be rich or not? Half the time you seem to be saying you do but then the old woman and her toy boy contradict all that. Both are bad but he becomes rich and she keeps her money. Why didn't he get his pubic hairs plucked out as he would have in the real world? And then you let the sycophant get away with a very feeble defence of his behaviour when he should have been exposed as a dishonest charlatan and had all his possessions confiscated."

I remembered these were pretty much the points he had insulted me with before, but I thought I might as well let Ararus have the full experience. "Anything else you'd like to point out?"

"Yes, as a matter of fact. Another point I made all those years ago. The argument poverty is good because if everyone was rich no one would work and the slave trade would disappear is pathetic. And having the goddess Poverty back off when her attention is drawn to how miserable the poor can be is truly feeble."

"Well, we won. At least the judges must have liked it."

"Bloody useless judges if you ask me. It was tedious, unsophisticated and clumsy. The humour was bland, the morality simplistic, the language banal and there was nothing topical of the sort good comic poets do so well. And you might as well not have had a chorus they had so little to do." He stormed off and I wasn't sorry to see him go. I had been looking to give Ararus an introduction into what comic poets have to put up with but the old man's comments might have put him off for life, just when he was showing some real talent of his own. I didn't think I could face any more criticism after that and signalled to Ararus that it was time to go when Criticus grabbed my arm.

"Hey, that was great, Aristophanes," he said through his long white beard. "I loved the realistic opening and the tragic tones that made the plot somehow appear logical. The action was beautifully concentrated."

"Thank you, Criticus," I said. "This is my son Ararus who did most of the rewrite. Ararus, this is Criticus. You'll find he's a very intelligent and perceptive person who shows great insight into what makes for good drama."

I don't know whether Ararus felt inspired by Criticus' comments, but he certainly set to work with enthusiasm on *Cocalus*. In fact he probably wrote more of it than I did, as well as managing all the rehearsals and leading the chorus himself, but as I'd told him I was planning to retire from composition after the Dionysia, he insisted I take the credit. When we won, I tried to make sure everyone knew he was the person really responsible, as recognition is always important to a playwright who wants to get selected for future festivals.

Exactly how *Cocalus* came to win is a bit of a mystery. It was very much in the new style of comedy with a clever plot around confused identities and a pretty disturbing rape scene, but it just wasn't the kind of comedy I enjoyed writing. There was very little fantasy or triumph and the chorus was almost non-existent. I was so frustrated I started writing another version with a more traditional format, a bigger role for the chorus and lots of good advice from them for the city, and considered submitting it for the next Lenaea but after a while I realised that not only would it not do Ararus any good, but it was so out of line with modern taste it would almost certainly not get selected anyway.

The story was based on the myth of Daedalus. After his son Icarus perished by flying too close to the sun, he had made his way to the kingdom of Cocalus in Sicily, pursued by a furious King Minos of Crete. You remember the story: Poseidon had given Minos a bull to sacrifice, but Minos decided to keep it for himself. As punishment Poseidon made Minos' wife Pasiphae fall in love with the creature, but she couldn't think of a safe way of having sex with it. The magician Daedalus came to the rescue and

322

built a hollow, wooden cow covered in real cow hide for Pasiphae to hide in and the success of the operation resulted in the birth of the Minotaur, a creature with the body of a man and the face of a bull. Minos wanted to punish Daedalus and knew he was hiding somewhere so he came up with a plan to flush him out. Knowing Daedalus would always be up for any complex challenge, he announced rich rewards for anyone who could string a thread through a conch shell. Cocalus saw an opportunity for fame and glory for his tiny kingdom if someone from his palace could solve the problem and turned to his guest Daedalus. Daedalus pierced a hole in the tip of the conch shell, smeared it with honey, and tied a thread around an ant, which, attracted by the honey, wound its way through the spirals of the empty shell taking the thread with it.

It was with great pride that Cocalus announced that his guest had solved the puzzle, but of course that led Minos to realise that Daedalus must be in Sicily, so he sailed there after him. Cocalus promised to hand Daedalus over to Minos but decided instead to get Daedalus to fix the plumbing before Minos' nightly bath and Minos boiled to death. In Ararus' version Minos was gang-raped by Cocalus' three daughters before getting into the bath. In mine, he had bought Pasiphae with him and she had fallen in love with the ant, posing another challenge for Daedalus in how to arrange for her to have sex with it.

I had resolved that would be my last play and I am going to stick to that. Ararus is rewriting my *Storm Cook* and 'modernising' it by cutting out the chorus altogether and inventing a whole lot of sexual intrigues between Aeolus' six daughters and six sons, which frankly I find a bit distasteful. One bout of incest seems quite enough for any comedy. I would also have preferred it if he had set Aeolus' kingdom of the winds somewhere other than Sicily. That island seems to haunt me. It has made me uneasy ever since the death of Eupolis, which I still feel guilty about, but a lot of my later plays were set there, however much I looked for plots at home or in other parts of Greece. And I have just heard Plato is returning from there with plans to set up a School for Philosophical Enquiry, which sounds a pretty dumb idea to me. On the other hand, he does know a lot about how to get slaves to write up prose works and have them distributed, so I think I'll give him this story of my life and ask him to deal with it for me. I just hope he doesn't insist on having sex with me in return for the favour.

# 60

I was too exhausted to get up for a while but Plato (remember he was fifteen or so years younger than me) said he had better get going. As he was cleaning himself up, he said, "Remember to examine yourself." He promised to come back to collect this story after I had put the finishing touches to it.

I couldn't summon the strength to get up, so I lay there for hours, thinking about my life. I said at the beginning of my story that I wanted to use it to explain why I did the things I did but reading it over again I'm not sure I've done that very well. Rather it seems that everything I did, I did because it appeared to be the obvious thing to do. Perhaps that's how we all work unless the gods intervene, just doing what comes next. Or perhaps it's because I can't now ascribe alternative options to my past choices. Euripides would say our nature (and Plato would say our souls) can rise above our instincts but I don't think mine ever did. In my early work at least, I showed up some of the worst aspects of our wonderful city like informers, sophists and professional litigants, which I hope made the democracy more cautious about whom it trusted, but I didn't have an agenda or a better alternative. In fact much of what I recommended backfired. Cleon was re-elected just after I tore him apart; the oligarchs I got re-enfranchised remained oligarchs and were soon in control again; I shared the blame for the execution of Socrates. I had wanted to help put a few things right as well as make people laugh. I don't know if I did. Would things have turned out differently if not for me? Would the wars have gone on for longer? Or would our defeat have been quicker and more humiliating? Would Cleon and Hyperbolus and the rest have behaved worse? Would sophistry have got a firmer grip on the city? And what about eastern religions? Would Alcibiades have been even less loyal? Would Eupolis still be alive?

Had I been a good husband to Praxagora? Not really, but others might have been worse. A good father to my children? I hope so, even though their lives aren't following the course I would have planned for them. A good friend? Actually, I never made many friends, just Lysander and Pherecrates and Euripides and Plato – and Cunna whom I miss more than any of them.

A good playwright? Yes, of course I was. The best.

# DIRECTORY OF NAMES

Compiled by the editor.

Some modern scholars offer alternative biographies of some of these characters. The ones below reflect the considered knowledge and judgment of Aristophanes, who was of course in a good position to know. Individuals for whom this autobiography is the only source are identified in italics.

> **Aristophanes**: 446-386 BCE. Comic playwright. Wrote over 40 plays of which 11 survive entire; fragments of many others have been preserved. At least six competition wins and four second places. Went bald in his 20s. Father Philippus lived in Aegina from 431. Mother Zenodora was probably not from Attica. Sons Ararus, Philip and Philetaerus (or Nicostratus).

**Achilles**: A Greek warrior-hero of the Trojan War (approx. 1100 BCE). The principal character of Homer's *Iliad.*

**Aeschylus**: 525-456? BCE Tragic playwright, considered to be the father of Greek tragedy. Wrote 70-90 plays of which seven survive. Fought against Persia at Marathon (490), Salamis (480) and Plataea (479). Said to have been killed when an eagle dropped a tortoise on his head but it was probably a tile falling from a roof.

**Agamemnon**: King of Mycenae and leader of the Greek forces at the siege of Troy. Brother of Helen's husband, Menelaus.

**Agathon**: 446-401? BCE Tragic poet. Very beautiful appearance. Delicate, artificial verse. Choruses became musical interludes unconnected to the plot. Accepted invitation to court of Macedon (407 BCE), possibly with Euripides? None of his plays survive.

**Agesilaus II**: The king of Sparta between around 400 and 360 BCE.

**Ajax**: A Greek warrior-hero of the Trojan War. From Salamis.

**Alcibiades**: 450-404 BCE. Named after his Spartan great-great-grandfather. Father Cleinias had Spartan connections. Mother Deinomache was a cousin of Pericles, who brought him up when his father died. Wife Hipparete, daughter of wealthy Hipponicus, tried to divorce him for using prostitutes. Very good looking. Fought at Potidaea (432) and at Delium

(424). After Peace of Nicias (421) advocated aggressive foreign policy. Accused of impiety (415), before leading the expedition against Sicily (414). Defected to Sparta. Intrigued with Persia on behalf of Sparta, then on behalf of Athens. Murdered by Persians.

**Ameipsias**: Comic poet.

**Amphitryon**: Father of Heracles.

**Anaxagoras**: 500-428 BCE. Philosopher born in Asia Minor who was influential in bringing the practice of philosophy to Athens. Described the world as a mixture of imperishable ingredients, where material variation was not caused by the presence of one ingredient but by the frequency of its appearance relative to other ingredients.

**Anaximander**: 610-546 BCE. All round scientist. Plotted the movements of the planets, invented the sun dial, and drew a map of the known world. Attributed existence to the 'indefinite', leading to abstract approaches to cosmogony.

**Anaximenes**: c. 586-526 BCE. Philosopher from Miletus and follower of Anaximander. Believed everything was composed of air in more or less thick vaporous states.

**Androcles**: A leading politician who was responsible for the exile of Alcibiades and opposed to oligarchy.

**Antimachus**: Drama producer attacked for meanness in *The Clouds*.

**Antiphon**: A politician and the first of the ten most famous Athenian orators. Step-brother of Plato.

**Anytus**: Powerful, upper-class politician. Wealthy tannery owner. In love with Socrates. As a general he lost Pylos to the Spartans and was charged with treason, but was acquitted after bribing the jury. Played a major role in the overthrow of the Thirty Tyrants (403 BCE). Prosecuted Socrates (399), perhaps as a disappointed lover.

**Aphrodite**: Goddess of love.

**Apollo**: God of music, poetry, prophecy, youth and healing.

**Apollodorus**: Contemporary actor.

*Ararus: The stillborn brother of Aristophanes; otherwise unattested.*

**Ararus (2)**: Aristophanes' eldest son. Comic poet. Helped produce Aristophanes' *Wealth* in 388.

**Archelaus**: King of Macedonia 413-399 BCE.

**Archeptolemus**: Son of Hippodamus. A politician opposed to Cleon. Oligarch, influential in the oligarchic revolution of 411 BCE.

*Archinous: An actor specialising in slapstick; otherwise unattested.*

*Ariadne: Here the daughter of Cunna.* In mythology, the name of the daughter of King Minos of Crete and Pasiphae.

**Ariphrades**: Comic poet, known for his enthusiasm for cunnilingus. His brother Arignotus was a lyre-player and reputed to be a long-term virgin. Another brother was an actor.

**Aristodemus**: An impoverished socialite dwarf, in love with Socrates. Referred to as 'gape-arsed' by Aristophanes, who says the arsehole was named after him (*The Banqueters*, fragment).

**Aristomenes**: Comic poet. Winner of Lenaea (438 BCE?) and Dionysia 394. Exiled for impiety after the mutilation of the Herms (415).

**Ariston**: Father of Plato. First husband of Perictione.

**Aristophanes (2)**: Red-figure vase painter of the Attic style. Painted bowls made by the potter Erginos. To bring his figures to life he developed the technique of drawing separating lines.

**Artaxerxes II**: (445-358 BCE). King of Persia. Son of Darius 2. Elder brother of Cyrus the Younger.

**Artemis**: Goddess. Daughter of Zeus and sister of Apollo. Goddess of hunting, wild nature, and chastity. Patron of girls, young women and wild animals. Protectress during childbirth.

**(Human) Artemis:** *The female slave of Aristophanes; otherwise unattested.*

**Asclepius**: God of medicine.

**Aspasia**: 470-428? BCE Born in Miletus. Lover and partner of the statesman Pericles with whom she had a son, Pericles the Younger. Married Lysicles when Pericles died and had another son with him, but Lysicles was killed in battle a few months later. Her house became an intellectual centre, frequented by many philosophers including Socrates. Ancient sources suggest (probably incorrectly) that she influenced him and helped write Pericles' funeral oration.

**Asopodorus**: A noisy citizen of short stature.

**Athene**: Goddess of wisdom, handicraft, and warfare; patron of Athens.

**Brasidas**: Spartan general during the first decade of the Peloponnesian War. Highly regarded on both sides. Killed at Amphipolis (422 BCE), fighting the Athenian troops under Cleon.

**Bronchus**: *A deep-voiced comic actor; otherwise unattested.*

**Callias**: Son of Hipponicus. Diplomat, general and politician. One of the richest men in Athens before squandering his inheritance on sycophants and loose women. His wealth came from his great-grandfather (also named Callias) who at the battle of Marathon confronted a Persian who thought he was a king because of his long hair and prostrated himself and showed him a lot of gold buried in a well. Grandfather Callias took the gold and killed the Persian.

**Callicles**: Political philosopher and advocate of Realpolitik.

**Callistratus**: Producer or co-producer of several of Aristophanes' plays. Wrote a drinking song to honour the tyrannicides.

**Carcinus**: Tragedian. Lived for a long time at the court of Dionysius II of Syracuse. Three sons, all of whom became playwrights, one of whom (also Carcinus) received a prize for only one out of his 160 plays.

**Cephalus**: Invited to Athens by Pericles from Sicily in order to establish a shield factory. Sons Lysias, Polemarchus and Euthydemus.

**Cerberus**: A multi-headed dog that guards the gates of Hades.

**Chaerephon**: 470 – 403? BCE. Socialite. Friend and admirer of Socrates.

**Charmides**: Wealthy orphan, brought up by his cousin Critias. Uncle of Plato and follower of Socrates. Property confiscated for impiety (415 BCE). Appointed as one of ten to govern the Peiraeus (404). Killed in battle (403).

**Charon**: The ferryman who took the dead across the River Styx to Hades.

**Choerine**: Unfaithful second wife of Euripides.

**Cimon**: 510-450 BCE. Athenian statesman and general. Son of Miltiades. Victor over the Persians at the battle of Marathon (490) and displayed great courage at Salamis (480).

**Cinesias**: Dithyrambic poet, known for innovation.

**Cleigenes**: Keeper of a public bath and laundry. Supporter of Cleophon.

**Cleinias**: Father of Alcibiades. Spartan connections.

**Cleisthenes**: Prominent Athenian ambassador during the Peloponnesian War. Well known for being effeminate.

**Cleocritus**: Athenian citizen who had a major role in religious ceremonies. His mother was said to resemble an ostrich for reasons that are unclear.

**Cleon**: ?- 422 BCE. Demagogue. Wealthy but not an aristocrat. Inherited a large tannery in the suburb of Cydathenaion. Irritating speaking style in the Assembly: shouty, coarse delivery, extravagant gestures, confused audience with enigmatic phrases and oracles. Suspected of extensive corruption. Allied with aristocrats against Pericles on "stay in town" strategy (431). Had Pericles temporarily removed from office for corruption (429). Won a motion to kill all adult males in Mytilene (427). Blocked peace deal (425). Doubled allies' tribute. Brought captured Spartans from Pylos to Athens from Sphacteria and got the credit when it should have gone to Demosthenes. Sent to recapture Amphipolis but defeated by Brasidas and killed (422).

**Cleonymus**: General. Associate of Cleon and leader of the extreme democrats. Probably a member of the council (426/5). Laid down more stringent rules for the collection of tribute from Athens' allies. Dropped his shield in the retreat from Delium (424).

**Cleophon**: Athenian politician and demagogue. A staunch democrat.

*Clepsis: An actor; otherwise unattested.*

*Clione: Slave girl and concubine of Aristophanes' father; otherwise unattested.*

*Clitagora: Name of a Spartan lyric poetess. Here the name of an Athenian prostitute.*

**Clytemnestra**: Wife of Agamemnon, mother of Iphigenia, Orestes and Electra.

**Conon**: (443?-389 BCE). Athenian admiral at Aegospotami (406). Helped partially rebuild Athens' empire after the Peloponnesian War.

**Cratinus**: (519?-422 BCE). Comic poet. Wrote at least 20 plays for nine wins. First victory was at the Dionysia (454). Also won at the Lenaea. Last play was *The Wine Bottle* (423). Died in 422 when very old. Weaknesses: drink and small boys.

**Cratylus**: An extreme proponent of Heraclitean philosophy ("you can't step into the same river twice"), going further, and saying that it cannot even be done once. Influenced the young Plato.

**Critias**: 460 – 403 BCE. Uncle of Plato. Friend of Socrates. A leading and violent member of the Thirty Tyrants who ran Athens in 404. Wrote tragedies, elegies and prose works, none of which survive.

*Criticus: Would-be comic poet and self-appointed drama critic; otherwise unattested.*

**Crito**: Wealthy friend of Socrates, reported to have bribed Socrates' jailer to release him.

**Croesus**: The last king of Lydia in Asia Minor (545-547 BCE), renowned for his wealth.

**Cunna**: A well-known escort.

**Cynisca**: The first (only?) woman to win the Olympic chariot race (almost certainly as trainer, not charioteer).

**Cyrus the Younger**: Son of Darius II. Persian Prince, general and governor of Lydia and Ionia.

**Darius**: Darius II, King of Persia. Illegitimate son of Artaxerxes I. Originally named Ochus.

**Demeter**: Goddess of agriculture and the harvest.

**Democritus**: 460 – 370? BCE Born in Abdera, Thrace. Developed atomic theory and is considered the father of modern science. Largely ignored in Athens, but taught Protagoras and was hated by Plato.

**Demos**: Son of Pyrilampes. Step-brother of Plato.

**Demosthenes**: General. Son of a wealthy father. Led the failed Athenian invasion of Aetolia (426 BCE). Afraid to return to Athens. Back in favour after a successful campaign a few months later. Conquered Pylos (425) but could not take the island of Sphacteria. Defeated at Delium and Sicyon (424). Signed the Peace of Nicias (421). Led evacuation of Epidaurus (417). Sent to support Sicilian expedition (413). Defeated and executed. The famous fourth century orator was probably from the same family and inherited a knife and a luxury furniture factory.

**Demostratus**: An Athenian politician. Demagogue.

**Diagoras**: Atheist philosopher and poet from the island of Melos. Probably an atheist.

**Diodotus**: Son of Eucrates. Led the opposition to the slaughter of Mytileneans (427 BCE).

**Diogenes**: Fifth century BCE philosopher from Apollonia. Following Anaximenes, he held that the entire universe is a substance he called 'air' which is infinite, alive, eternal, living, indivisible, intelligent and continuously moving. All natural things throughout the universe are this one substance under various modes.

**Dionysius**: A Sicilian general who later became tyrant of Syracuse.

**Dionysus**: God of the grape-harvest, winemaking, fertility, orchards and fruit, vegetation, insanity, ritual madness.

**Eryximachus**: Born 448 BCE. Son of Acumenus. A prominent doctor.

**Evagoras**: King of Salamis in Cyprus (411-374 BCE).

**Eucrates**: General and minor populist politician. Lazy and deceitful. Father of Diodotus.

**Eupolis**: 446-413? BCE. Comic poet. Exact contemporary of Aristophanes. First play 429, age 17. 19 plays; four wins at the Dionysia and three at the Lenaea. Known for his elegant style of writing. His *Maricas* was the first comedy to feature market women. Drowned by Alcibiades in Sicily: "You drenched me in the theatre, now I'll drench you in the sea", although other traditions suggest he was killed at sea in the battle of Cynossema.

**Euripides**: 485 – 406 BCE. Father Mnesarchus; mother Cleito became a herb seller when widowed. Family were hereditary priests of Apollo Zosterius. As a boy Euripides was a dancer and torch bearer in rites. A bit of a loner, he became a recluse on Salamis. Two bad marriages; both wives, Melito and Choerine, were unfaithful. Euripides found one of them in bed with the actor, Cephisophon. He couldn't persuade her to give him up, so he handed her over to him. Didn't really like the chorus and his lyrics were often unconnected to the plot, an approach copied by Agathon. Made frequent use of the stage machine. Interested in violent passions, the tension between the rational and irrational and the human cost of war. Represented mythical heroes as ordinary people, reacting naturally to challenging circumstances. Sympathetic to underrepresented members of society, especially women.

**Euripides' nephew**: Nephew of the great playwright and a much less successful playwright himself.

**Eurydice**: Mythological wife of Orpheus.

**Eurymedon**: An Athenian general. Active in the early years of the war and then in the Sicilian campaign.

**Glaucetes**: A fat citizen.

**Gorgias:** ? – 375 BCE? Sicilian-born philosopher who practised in various cities and charged for public exhibitions of his skill. He liked to impress audiences with unprepared replies to questions from the audience. Considered by some to be a nihilist.

**Gylippus**: A Spartan general. Expelled from Sparta for accepting bribes from Athens in 446 BCE, but reinstated.

**Heracles**: Demi-god, famous for his strength and his twelve labours. Often portrayed in comedy as fat and greedy. *Here the name of Pherecrates' slave.*

**Hegemon**: Comic poet from Thasos, nicknamed "bean soup".

**Hephaestus**: God of fire. Blacksmith. Husband of Aphrodite.

**Hera**: Queen of the gods. Wife of Zeus.

**Hermes**: God of trade, wealth, luck, fertility, animal husbandry, sleep, language, thieves, and travel. *Here the name adopted as stage name by a regular chorus leader.*

**Hermippus**: Comic poet. 40 plays. One eye. Won one Dionysia and four Lenaeas. Main theme was myth. Also wrote iambic poems and parodies. Charged Aspasia with impiety and with pimping free women. Accused Phrynichus of plagiarism.

**Herodotus**: 484-425 BCE. Born in Halicarnassus. The "father of History", though he included many myths and legends in his "factual" account which featured a detailed history of the Persian invasions of Greece (490 and 480-79).

**Hesiod**: Didactic poet active around 750-650 BCE.

**Hestia**: Virgin goddess of the hearth and of the proper conduct of the family, the home, and the state.

**Himilco**: A Carthaginian general.

**Hipparete**: Wife of Alcibiades.

**Hipparchus**: *Cousin of Lysander; otherwise unattested.*

**Hippias**: Sophist. Claimed to be an authority on everything. Preached and practised self-sufficiency.

**Hippocrates**: 459-424 BCE. General. Defeated and killed at Delium.

**Hippon**: Philosopher, probably from Samos, who held that water and fire were the primary elements, with fire originating from water and then developing itself by generating the universe, and that there is an appropriate level of moisture in all living things. Disease is caused when the moisture is out of balance. The soul is the product of mind and water.

**Homer**: The name given to the compiler of 7 oral epics of which only *The Iliad* and *The Odyssey* survive.

**Hormus**: *The owner of Aristophanes' local tavern; otherwise unattested.*

**Hyperbolus**: Son of Antiphanes, a wealthy lamp-seller who was rumoured to have been a slave. The leading demagogue after Cleon died. Aggressive foreign policy. Member of the Council. Proposed an ostracism (415-6 BCE, Alcibiades?) but was ostracised himself, possibly the last ostracism effected. Murdered in Samos (412).

**Ion**: Legendary illegitimate son of Apollo (or possibly a young servant in Apollo's temple).

*Ismenias: The name of two slaves of Aristophanes; otherwise unattested.*

**Laches**: A general, sent to Sicily with a fleet of 20 ships in order to support Athenian allies against Syracuse (427 BCE). Fellow general Charoeades was killed by the Syracusans in battle (426) and Laches took over the supreme command of the fleet. Replaced despite some successes (425). On his return to Athens, he was prosecuted by Cleon, but acquitted. Successfully moved an armistice with Sparta (423) and was involved in negotiating the Peace of Nicias (421). When the peace broke down, he was reappointed general and killed in the Athenian defeat at the Battle of Mantinea (418).

**Lamachus**: Fiery, crazy-brave general. So poor that during the campaigns in which he served as a general he would charge the state money for his clothes. His poverty and obscure family background prevented him from receiving the recognition many thought he deserved.

**Leon**: A general from Salamis. Keen democrat. Executed by the Thirty Tyrants at the direction of Sparta (404 BCE).

**Leucon**: A comic poet.

**Lycon**: Minor politician. One of the accusers of Socrates.

**Lycurgus**: Ambassador.

*Lysander: Friend of Aristophanes; otherwise unattested.*

**Lysander**: A Spartan general.

**Lysias**: Son of Cephalus; shield manufacturer with brother Polemarchus. Became a famous orator.

**Lysicles**: General, war hawk and leading democrat. Lived with Aspasia after Pericles's death (429 BCE) and had a son with her. Killed in battle (428).

**Lysicrates**: A wealthy, corrupt politician who sponsored a number of plays.

**Lysimache**: Long-serving priestess of Athene Nike.

**Magnes**: Comic poet. 11 wins, including Dionysia in both 472 and 471 BCE. Noted for his animal choruses and visual jokes. Still going in the 430s but left behind by the comedy of personal invective.

*Manodorus: Slave of Aristophanes; otherwise unattested.*

**Megara**: Wife of Heracles. Also the name of a rural district of Attica.

**Meidias**: An Athenian citizen.

**Melanthius**: A minor tragic poet.

**Meletus**: Chief prosecutor of Socrates.

**Melito**: Unfaithful first wife of Euripides.

**Menelaus**: King of Mycenaean Sparta (C12 BCE). Son of Atreus and Aerope. While he was away attending the funeral of his maternal grandfather in Crete, Paris ran off to Troy with his wife Helen, starting the Trojan War in which Menelaus was a central figure and led the Spartan contingent of the Greek army under his elder brother Agamemnon.

**Menippus**: An Athenian citizen.

**Micon**: Painter and sculptor.

**Mnesilochus**: An elderly relative of Euripides.

**Morychus**: A fat citizen.

**Musaeus**: An early poet and legendary polymath, philosopher and prophet.

**Myron**: A famous sculptor from Eleutherae in northern Attica.

*Myronias: His son, also a sculptor; otherwise unattested.*

*Myrrhine: A prostitute who works at Aristophanes' local tavern; otherwise unattested.*

*Nerita: The name of two slaves of Aristophanes; otherwise unattested.*

**Nicias**: c. 470 – 413 BCE. Politician and general. Member of the Athenian aristocracy who inherited a large fortune from his father, which was very profitably invested in slaves for lease at the silver mines around Mt. Laurium. Following the death of Pericles in 429, he became the principal rival of Cleon and the democrats in the struggle for the political leadership of the Athenian state. Moderate in his political views and opposed to the aggression and imperialism of the extreme democrats. Wanted peace with Sparta as soon as it could be obtained on acceptable terms. Achieved in 421 (the Peace of Nicias). Objected to Alcibiades' warmongering policies but was appointed to lead the expedition to Sicily (415). Unsuccessful and assassinated there.

**Opountius**: Athenian resident, originally from Locris. Otherwise unknown.

**Orpheus**: A mythological musician, poet and prophet.

**Pausanias**: A king of Sparta.

**Peisander**: Politician involved in prosecutions following the mutilation of the herms and then in establishing the oligarchy of the four hundred (411 BCE).

*Peisias: Slave dealer; otherwise unattested.*

**Peisistratus**: Tyrant of Athens in the mid-sixth century BCE. Unified Attica and laid the basis for the city's future glory.

**Pellene**: A prostitute.

**Pericles**: 495 - 429 BCE. Father Xanthippus (ostracised in 485; returned to be the victorious commander at Mycale in 480); mother Agariste from the aristocratic Alcmaeonid family, niece of the famous reformer Cleisthenes, dreamed she would give birth to a lion. Produced Aeschylus' *Persians* (472). Popular policies: reduced property qualifications for archons, introduced pay for jurors, and another payment so that the poor could watch plays (450s-440s). Introduced a citizenship law requiring that citizens have two Athenian parents (451). Elected general 15 times. Instituted a trade embargo (Megarian Decree, 433) which was a major cause of the Peloponnesian War. Married (or just lived with) Aspasia. One son:

**Pericles the Younger**. Charged with indecency twice: once for having sex with the wife of his friend and subordinate Menippus and then for using his friend Pyrilampes to entice women to come to admire the peacocks he had acquired on an embassy to Persia. Executed for desertion at Arginusae (406 BCE).

**Perictione**: Aristocratic mother of Plato, by her first husband Ariston. Second husband was Pyrilampes.

**Persephone**: Goddess of the underworld. *Here the widowed niece of Pherecrates, whom he marries.*

**Phanus**: Demagogue, closely associated with Cleon. Responsible for official documentation.

**Phaedias**: A very famous sculptor.

**Phaedrus**: Son of Pythocles. Aristocratic friend of Socrates.

**Pharnabazus II**: Persian soldier and statesman. Governor of Phrygia.

**Pherecrates**: Comic poet. 17 plays. First win 438 BCE. Two or three later successes. Introduced new themes and plots, mainly domestic and social scenes with very few personal jokes. First comedies to feature real women (escorts). Invented 'Pherecratean' metre. Had been an actor.

**Philetaerus**: Third son of Aristophanes. Thought by some to have been called Nicostratus.

**Philip**: Father of Aristophanes. Owned property on the island of Aegina, where he lived from 431.

**Philip (2)**: Second son of Aristophanes.

**Philocrates**: Bird retailer.

**Philon**: A comic poet.

**Philonides**: A comic poet who produced several of Aristophanes' plays.

**Phrynichus**: A comic poet. A supporter of the oligarchs who was assassinated when the first oligarchy was overthrown (411 BCE).

**Pittalus**: A well-known Athenian doctor.

**Plato**: 429? - 348 BCE. Best known for being a writer of Socrates' dialogues, the theory of ideal forms (Platonism) and 'platonic sex'. Real name was probably Aristocles. His father Ariston was descended from Codrus, king of Athens and from Melanthus, king of Messenia. His mother Perictione was related to Solon the great law giver. Brothers Adeimantus and Glaucon, sister Potone, half-brother Demos. His father died when he was young and his mother married her uncle Pyrilampes, many times ambassador to the Persian court and a friend of Pericles. A legend had it that bees settled on the infant Plato's lips while he was sleeping, foretokening his sweetness of style. Travelled in Italy, Sicily, Egypt and Cyrene. Went to Sicily to tutor the son of the tyrant Dionysius (388). Founded the Academy in Athens (387).

**Platon**: Innovative comic poet, younger than Aristophanes.

**Polemarchus**: Philosopher son of Cephalus, brother of Lysias and Euthydemus.

**Polygnotus**: Famous painter born in Thasos c.500 BCE, and admitted to Athenian citizenship.

*Polymides: Unpleasant 'friend' of Cunna; otherwise unattested.*

**Poseidon**: God of the sea and of horses.

*Praxagora: Aristophanes' wife (of whom nothing is known from other sources).*

**Praxiteles**: A famous sculptor.

*Praxiteles (2): His son, also a sculptor; otherwise unattested.*

**Priam**: King of Troy at the time of the Trojan War. Wife Hecuba. Fifty sons including Paris and Hector.

**Prodicus**: An early sophist from the island of Ceos who taught linguistics and ethics. Friend of Socrates.

**Protagoras:** 490 - 420 BCE. A sophistical philosopher and rhetorical theorist from Thrace who became well known in Athens. Friend of Pericles and Socrates.

**Pyrilampes**: An ambassador. Second husband of Perictione. Step-father of Plato.

***Rhombus***: *Deep-voiced actor; otherwise unattested.*

**Salabaccho**: An escort.

**Sicon**: A famous Sicilian cook and author of the first known cookbook.

**Simon**: A shoemaker whose shop was patronised by Socrates for conversation – and possibly because young boys, not allowed in the main market place, used to congregate there. Wrote the first Socratic dialogues (before Plato). Pericles once offered to provide for him if Simon would come and live with him, but he refused on the grounds that he did not wish to surrender his independence.

**Smoios**: Dirty old man, especially fond of cunnilingus.

**Socrates**: 470? - 399 BCE. Son of a stonemason (he probably trained as one) and a midwife. Married first Myrto, then the much younger shrew Xanthippe with whom he had three sons, Lamprocles, Sophroniscus, and Menexenus. Fat, pug-nosed, scruffy, often barefoot. Had some awful friends including Alcibiades and the oligarchs Charmides and Critias. Took a dialectical approach to philosophical enquiry, documented by Simon, Xenophon and Plato. Essential position: "I know nothing." Outspokenly in favour of 'mentoring' of young boys by older men. Served as a hoplite in battles at Potidaea (432), Delium (424) and Amphipolis (422). In love with Alcibiades, whose life he saved at Potidaea. Member of the Council (406). Argued unsuccessfully against the death penalty for generals who deserted drowning soldiers at Arginusae (406). Pericles the Younger was among those executed. Refused the orders of the Thirty Tyrants to bring Leon back from Salamis for execution (403). Found guilty of corrupting the minds of the youth of Athens and of impiety contrary to a law of the 430s against failing to acknowledge the gods (399). Made to take hemlock. Did not defend himself and refused an opportunity to escape.

**Solon**: c630 - 560 BCE. Athenian statesman, lawmaker and poet. Passed laws to stem the decline of Athens economically, politically and morally. Often said by later generations to have laid the foundations for Athenian democracy.

**Sophocles**: 496 - 406 BCE. Tragic poet. Father Sophilus a well-off armour manufacturer. 123 plays. 24 first prizes at Dionysia and Lenaea (an all-time record. Aeschylus had 13 and Euripides just four.). As a boy he was chosen for his beauty and voice to lead the paean after Salamis (480). His voice didn't last and he gave up chorus work. Innovative: introduced a third actor and scene painting and increased the tragic chorus from 12 performers to 15. Elected general and quelled the Samian revolt (440). General again in 425. Councillor for dealing with the Sicily crisis (413). Never accepted invitations from foreign rulers (contrast Aeschylus – Sicily and Euripides – Macedonia). Sued as senile by his sons, Iophon and Agathon, and proved he wasn't by reciting his last play *Oedipus at Colonus*, at the age of about 90. His grandson, coincidentally named Sophocles, became a tragedian.

**Sophocles (2)**: Grandson of the famous playwright and a playwright himself.

*Sosias: A slave; otherwise unattested.*


**Spintharus**: An Athenian citizen, originally from Phrygia.

**Sporgilus**: A slave and barber.

**Strattis**: A comic poet.

**Syracosius**: A minor politician.

**Teleas**: A fat citizen.

**Theogenes**: A politician. Appointed with Cleon to investigate the stalemate at Pylos (425 BCE). One of the Thirty Tyrants (404 BCE).

**Theorus**: A minor politician and ambassador to Thrace. Friend of Cleon and naturally much disliked by Aristophanes.

**Theramenes**: A prominent statesman and supporter of oligarchy (411 and 404 BCE), though he advocated moderation on both occasions and was killed for it in the second. Almost certainly responsible for the execution of admirals after Arginusae.

*Thespides:* The name of an early tragic poet. *Here an actor.*

*Thorus: An actor; otherwise unattested.*

**Thrasybulus**: An Athenian general and leader of the democrats and the sailors at Samos (411 BCE).

**Thrasymachus**: Sophist from Chalcedon on the Bosphorus who argued that might is right.

**Thucydides**: 460 - 405? BCE. Son of Olorus. Family was from Thrace in north-eastern Greece, where he owned gold mines. Failed to reach Amphipolis in time to prevent its capture by the Spartans and was exiled (424). Over the next 20 years, he worked on his history of the Peloponnesian War. A realist with a very diligent approach to history. Interested in the concept of justice. Big fan of Pericles.

**Tissaphernes**: Persian soldier and statesman. Governor of Lydia and Ionia.

*Xanthias: Aristophanes' slave. A common name for slaves, often used by Aristophanes and other comic poets. In* Frogs, *a slave called Xanthias says "Bugger me, you arsehole."*

**Xanthippe**: Socrates' much younger wife and mother of their three sons, Lamprocles, Sophroniscus and Menexenus. Often depicted as a jealous, nagging shrew.

**Zeus**: King of the gods. Father of all gods and humans.